MW00331989

Also by the Same Author

Journey Continued
Towards the Mountain
Ah, but Your Land Is Beautiful
Cry, the Beloved Country
Too Late the Phalarope
South Africa in Transition
Tales from a Troubled Land
Sponono (a play)
South African Tragedy
For You Departed
Apartheid and the Archbishop
Knocking on the Door

SAVE
THE BELOVED
COUNTRY

ALAN PATON
(1903–1988)

SAVE
THE BELOVED
COUNTRY

Alan Paton

CHARLES SCRIBNER'S SONS

New York

Edited by Hans Strydom and David Jones
Historical research by Dr. George Claassen

Copyright © 1987 by Alan Paton

First American Edition, 1989

Charles Scribner's Sons
Macmillan Publishing Company
866 Third Avenue, New York, NY 10022
Collier Macmillan Canada, Inc.

Library of Congress Cataloging-in-Publication Data
Paton, Alan.
Save the beloved country/Alan Paton.—1st American ed.
    p.   cm.
Reprint. Originally published: Melville, Republic of South Africa:
H. Strydom Publishers. 1987.
ISBN 0-684-19127-X
1. South Africa—Politics and government.   2. South Africa—Social
Conditions.   3. Apartheid—South Africa.   I. Title.
[DT779.952.P38   1989]   89-6290   CIP
305.8'00968—dc20

968

Macmillan books are available at special discounts for bulk purchases
for sales promotions, premiums, fund-raising, or educational use.
For details, contact:

Special Sales Director
Macmillan Publishing Company
866 Third Avenue
New York, NY 10022

10 9 8 7 6 5 4 3 2 1

Printed in the United States of America

I dedicate this book to Helen Suzman.

I dedicate this book to Helga Sussan.

CONTENTS

PREFACE

I NOTE THAT the Editors' blurb says of me that I only ever had one thought in mind – South Africa. This isn't quite true, but it's true enough. It is also true of most of the people I know well, and of the people I respect most.

I have come to the conclusion that the best people in the world are those who regard service to their country and their society as the chief purpose of their lives, apart from their private and personal duties and obligations.

That is the reason why I dedicate this anthology to Helen Suzman, who has served her country and her society with courage and tenacity, and of course with great distinction, and I choose her as a representative of all those who have tried to do the same.

I must admit that most of my writing in the last 20 and more years has been about South Africa. Does this tend to make one's writing boring and monotonous? That is a danger, of course, but it is not necessary to succumb to it. For our country is a microcosm of the world.

Here you can witness the age-long struggle between good and evil and you can take part in it.

Here you can see how history corrupts men and women, and you can see men and women struggling to free themselves from its corruption.

Here you can see riches and poverty, compassion and cruelty, respect and contempt for the Rule of Law, living side by side.

Here the people of three continents came together, bringing their languages and their customs and their cultures.

South Africa is what they call a "young country"; it does not have the libraries and the galleries and the noble buildings of the older countries of the world, but it is as rich a country to grow up in as any on the earth. Its written history is short, and it is a story of conquest and rebellion and struggle and oppression as fascinating as any. Therefore, the writer in South Africa has only himself or herself to blame if the writing is monotonous.

The Editors' choice is very catholic, and it certainly does justice to my articles written since 1965. They dealt with leading figures in our history, both White and Black, including four of our Prime Ministers, Smuts, Verwoerd, Vorster and PW Botha, and four of our Black leaders, Luthuli, Sobukwe, Mandela and Buthelezi.

The Government's treatment of Luthuli can only be described as scandalous, but he received world recognition when he was given the Nobel Peace Prize in 1961.

Sobukwe was sent to Robben Island for three years for incitement, but Parliament gave the Minister of Justice, Mr BJ Vorster, the power to detain him for a further six years, and in 1969 he returned to Kimberley under ban, and died under ban in 1974, having also been treated scandalously.

Mandela has been in prison since 1964, when he was given a life sentence for sabotage; the Government will commit a grave error if it allows him to die in prison.

Buthelezi is still alive and active and is Chief Minister of KwaZulu and National President of Inkatha.

The Government forced the first three of these to spend their lives and gifts in protest; I hope that they will use the life and gifts of Buthelezi before it is too late.

Of the four Prime Ministers mentioned above, it was Smuts who was the Olympian. My favourite story of Smuts was of the time when he visited the scene of the fighting on the Rand during the miners' strike of 1922. He left his car and went forward on foot, but was confronted by a miner with drawn bayonet. Smuts brushed him aside saying: "Kêrel, ek het nou nie tyd daarvoor nie."

Yet it was Verwoerd who had the greatest effect on our modern history. He, like Smuts, had a first-class intellect, but was driven almost entirely by his passion for the supremacy and survival of an Afrikanerdom into which, strangely enough, he had not been born. He was the supreme architect of Apartheid, later called Separate Development, whereby the Black races of our country would be given their own homelands where they could preserve their own languages and customs and cultures.

Verwoerd believed that one day the world would come to South Africa to admire and envy our racial arrangements, whereas, in fact, they are now falling to pieces about our ears. I have often been asked if I did not think he was an evil man, but have contented myself with the judgment that he was capable of an extraordinary degree of self-deception. This was aggravated by the fact that he was incapable of seeing Black men as his fellow-creatures.

The great problem which confronts White South Africans and their country today is whether they will be able to undo the damage of the Verwoerdian doctrines and gain, to some extent at least, the trust and confidence of Black South Africa in the goodness of their intentions.

This collection of articles does not answer that question, but it prepares us for the task of considering it knowledgeably and intelligently. I hope it reaches many people.

Alan Paton
September 26, 1987

"Kêrel, ek het nou nie tyd daarvoor nie." – "Chap, I do not have the time right now."

SAVE

THE BELOVED

COUNTRY

Why Did You Die, My Brothers?

Makwela, Ikgopoleng, and you two
    Sibekos,
what were you fighting for?
Makwela, was it for your house in
    Springs
and your security of tenure?
Or did you fight for me and my
    possessions
and this big room where I write to
    you,
a room as big as many houses?

Sibeko of Standerton, what did you
    die for?
Was it for the schooling of your
    children?
Were you so hungry for their
    learning
or were you fighting for the rich
    grand schools of my own
    children?

Sibeko of Bloemfontein, was it for
    those green pastures
of your own Free State country
that you poured out your young
    man's blood?
Was it for the sanctity of family life
and the infinitude of documents?
Or were you fighting to protect me
and my accustomed way of life?

Ikgopoleng of Lichtenburg,
was it South Africa you fought for?
Which of our nations did you die
    for?
Or did you die for my parliament
and its thousand immutable laws?
Did you forgive us all our trespasses
in that moment of dying?

I was not at your gravesides,
    brothers,
I was afraid to go there.
But I read the threnodial speeches
how you in life so unremembered
in death became immortal.

Away with your threnodial speeches,
    says the Lord.
Away with your solemn assemblies.
When you lift up your hands in
    prayer
I will hide my eyes from you.
Cease to do evil and learn to do
    right,
pursue justice and champion the
    oppressed.

I saw a new heaven and a new
    earth
for the first heaven and earth had
    passed away
and there was an end to death
and to mourning and crying and
    pain
for the old order had passed away.

Is that what you died for, my
    brothers?
Or is it true what they say
that you were led into ambush?

Alan Paton

DISINVESTMENT

I will not, by any written or spoken word, give
it any support whatsoever.

My Nightmare

I READ THAT DR VILLA-VICENCIO, *who has in the past often thought I
was right, thinks now that I am wrong in passing moral judgment on
those who advocate disinvestment. He thinks I take a simplistic view of
the whole issue. To be simplistic is bad enough, but to fall off one's pedestal
makes it worse. One is hurt, not only in one's body, but also in one's pride.
There is only one sensible thing to do in these circumstances, and that is
to go to bed. So I went to bed, to sleep, perchance to dream . . .*

They came to see me, these Americans, full of righteousness.
They flattered me too.

They told me my name was well known in America, almost as
well known as Gary Player and Chris Barnard, and now of course
Zola Budd and Bishop Tutu.

They told me the Americans had great respect for my moral
judgments and that if I came out for disinvestment it would be a
certain winner.

They asked me to become the President of the World Disinvestment Campaign. They also told me that if anyone was put out

3

of a job, it wouldn't be me. I told them I had certain moral doubts, but they explained that I was being simplistic.

After much moral wrestling I accepted the argument. No-one can be more convincing than an American.

Also I must admit that I have some moral weaknesses – one is vanity and the other is money.

When it was announced, with a great blowing of trumpets, that I had become President of the World Disinvestment Campaign, my life changed overnight.

Mr Archimedes, who hadn't spoken to me for years, came up to Botha's Hill to tell me that I was now the hero of Africa. Professor F sent me a telegram saying that I had at last atoned for praising the Israelis for rescuing their hostages from the clutches of Idi Amin.

Mr R who had venerated me when he was young and ceased to venerate me when I said that PW was astute, telephoned me to say that he now venerated me again. Chief B rang up in a fury and said that I had destroyed a friendship of nearly 40 years and that he would never speak to me again.

Cables of congratulations poured in from America, Canada, Britain, Sweden and other countries. Alas, I lost most of my capitalist friends, but one must pay a price for taking a stand.

I travelled all over the world. I was welcomed on campuses which would have shouted me down a year before. It was nice to come in out of the cold.

Then came the great day. Representatives of America, Canada, Britain, France, West Germany, Holland and Scandinavian countries met in London and declared for total disinvestment (except perhaps for a strategic mineral or two). Mrs Archimedes came up to tell me I was the hero of the whole Black world.

Disinvestment began to bite. Port Elizabeth and East London became dead cities. Even in a quiet place like Botha's Hill there were daily Black queues for food and jobs.

I must confess I didn't like passing them. Many of the people of the Valley of a Thousand Hills were my friends, but some grew very cold to me.

It was a great shock to me to hear over the radio that a mob had burned the buildings of the Valley Foundation and the Church of the Paraclete to the ground.

I telephoned the Rev John Ndlovu and told him that he had

my prayers. He said to me, we don't want your prayers, we want jobs.

Mr Archimedes, who knows I often go the Church of the Paraclete, came up to console with me. He told me one must pay a price for making a stand.

There is unrest in the valley, in Botha's Hill and Hillcrest and Kloof and Westville. I find that I spend more and more time in my study. I pull down the blinds. I find that I feel better when the blinds are down.

But Julia comes to tell me that there are Black women wanting to see me. She brings their leader into my study, a tall woman for these parts, a tall woman carrying a child and dressed in black.

She looks like a sculpture of the Sorrow of the World. She gives me the child and I see that it is dead.

> — *Why do you give this to me?*
> — Because it is yours.
> — *How can it be mine? I have never seen you before.*
> — You took its life, therefore it is yours.

She goes out of the study and calls to me. She points to the waiting women.

> — They will bring you their children too.

When the police have taken away the body of the child I come to a decision. I get into my car, my new bullet-proof car, and I drive to Pinetown and I buy something I have never bought before. It is a gun.

I go home and go into my study with the drawn blinds. There, surrounded by all the hundreds of books and papers that I wrote for the World Disinvestment Campaign, I shoot myself to death.

How could I do such a thing? How could I bring such a noble life to such an ignoble end? How could I commit such a deadly sin? I am filled with an agony of remorse. The burden of it is intolerable. I wish only to die.

But . . . what am I talking about? Am I not dead already? No, I am not! The whole thing is an unspeakable dream. I am full of joy to realise that I never had anything to do with any campaign for disinvestment.

I ring up the Rev John Ndlovu, of the Church of the Paraclete. Why did you not ring before, he asks, I began to fear that you were dead.

I hereby solemnly declare that I will never, by any word or act of mine, give any support to any campaign that will put men out of jobs — not even if they promised me that it would bring Chernenko down. Or Reagan. Or PW Botha.

I rush to the post office and send a telegram to Dr Villa-Vicencio: three cheers for simplisticity.

Dr Villa-Vicencio is Head of the Department of Religious Studies at the University of Cape Town.

~~~~~~~~~~~~~~~

An Act of Immorality

THERE IS ONLY one firm statement that I can make on disinvestment – I will have nothing to do with it. I will not, by any written or spoken word, give it any support whatsoever.

There are obviously two sides to this question. On the one side are South African industrialists, capitalists – very big money and very small money – the overwhelming majority of White South Africans, and a substantial majority of Black South Africans. On the other side are some highly educated and sophisticated Blacks, a small minority of White South Africans, and a considerable number of righteous and self-righteous people of the West, who entertain the opinion that the weakening of the South African economy will bring freedom and happiness to the suffering and oppressed people of our country.

I find myself uncompromisingly on the side of the industrialist capitalist, big money (almost entirely White), small money (almost entirely Black), the overwhelming majority of Whites and the considerable majority of Blacks. I belong, therefore, to a very mixed constituency.

I am not very interested in money, though I would not like to be without it. I am not writing this article for money. I am writing it for a simple – and to some perhaps a naive – reason. I am writing it because I think I ought to. I would much rather be writing something else.

For whom, then, is it being written? Primarily for the righteous people of the West. Not for the self-righteous, because I do not think I have the ability to persuade such people that they are

6

wrong or misguided. I am writing for those in the West who are concerned to see a more just order in South Africa, and who are concerned to know what they can do about it. I am writing for any person who has ulterior aims of his own or her own, or who is trying to further some personal cause, or who is trying to win the support of Black American voters.

Why am I totally opposed to disinvestment? It is primarily for a moral reason. It is my firm belief that those who will pay most grievously for disinvestment will be the Black workers of South Africa. I take very seriously the teachings of the Gospels, in particular the parables about giving drink to the thirsty and food to the hungry. It seems to me that Jesus attached supreme – indeed sacred – significance to such actions. Therefore, I will not help to cause any such suffering to any Black person.

I am told that this is a simplistic understanding of the teachings of the Gospels. Let it be so. That is the way I choose to understand them.

I am also told that I am ignoring the views of those Black South Africans who support disinvestment. Most of these Black South Africans will not be the ones to suffer hunger and thirst. Many of them are sophisticated, highly educated, safely placed. I also know sophisticated and highly educated Black men and women who will have nothing to do with disinvestment. I choose to associate myself with them.

I am told that, although I believe my views to be moral, they are, in fact, immoral because I will not take the side of those Black people who want disinvestment. This is a new interpretation of morality to me, that I ought to adopt certain views because some influential Black people hold them.

I do not hold these views because they are acceptable – or not acceptable – to either Black people or White people. I do not consider that the welfare of Black people or the welfare of White people are the supreme considerations. The supreme consideration to me is the welfare of my country and therefore the welfare of all its people.

There is an often-heard declaration: "We do not mind suffering. We are used to suffering." But this again is often the declaration of those who will suffer least.

To put it briefly, my conscience would not allow me to support disinvestment. For I must ask myself – and my readers who are concerned to do what is right – how long must the suffering it would cause go on before the desired end is achieved? A month? Two months? A year? Five or 10 years perhaps?

No-one can confidently answer that question, though one can say at once that disinvestment will take time to bite deep. South Africa's business community will muster every resource to save the economy from destruction. That it has its own interests to consider is, of course, to be taken for granted.

That is the kind of economic world in which we live, the kind that is to be found throughout the West. It is supposed to have some kind of correlation with freedom and with the encouragement of initiative, and with the Rule of Law.

The alternative to it is the world of the centralised economy, which not only controls enterprise, but ends up by controlling literature, the arts, the Press, the rights of free assembly and free expression and almost everything else. Both of these worlds have their credits and their debits. I choose the world of the free economy.

I have no doubt that some supporters of disinvestment hope that it will not only cause such severe damage to the economy, but will also increase endemic unrest to such an extent that armed revolution will take place and that the present Government will be overthrown by force of arms.

In the first place, let me say that the Black people of South Africa, even if they so desired, could not, unaided, wage a successful revolution.

Yet who is likely to come to their aid? In the present state of West-East relations – and that means, to a large extent, USA-USSR relations – it is hard to see any answer to this question. Of course it could happen, but only as a result of the greatest political miracle of our century, that a joint USA-USSR task force said to the South African Government: "Abolish apartheid immediately, and grant a universal franchise to all your peoples, or we will enter and utterly destroy your military power."

Suppose that a deep-biting investment campaign were followed by more far-reaching sanctions and suppose South Africa were completely isolated from the world. Suppose that the West succeeded in thus creating an economic and political vacuum in the south of the continent. I have no doubt that the USSR would embark on another African adventure. The West should be warned that its isolation campaign could have disastrous consequences for itself.

In 1934 the White Parliament of South Africa passed one of the most enlightened laws of those times, the Children's Act. The Act was a recognition that punishment was not the proper treatment for delinquent children. Punishment failed totally to treat the cause of deliquency. Punishment could change behaviour, but it was not a true reformatory instrument. And lastly, punishment could in some cases change behaviour for the worse.

It was because I held these beliefs strongly that our Minister of Education Mr JH Hofmeyr, made me the Principal of Diepkloof Reformatory in 1935. It was then the largest institution for delinquent boys in the whole of Africa. What I believed then, I believe now.

Punishment is no proper treatment for erring children, nor is it the proper treatment for erring countries. Those who think they can make us good by punishment are deceiving themselves. The United States seems to be at last giving up the idea of punishing the USSR into goodness. Why then do they think it would work with South Africa?

This is perhaps a moral argument, but it has a pragmatic side to it. The (Afrikaner) National Party would not respond to punitive measures. When the time eventually comes that it realises that its days of supremacy are drawing to a close, when at last it decides that it has to behave differently, when it decides – to put it unequivocally – that it has to behave in a more civilised manner, in a manner more acceptable to the nations of the West, that is not the time to use punitive measures.

I hold the belief – which is thought by some (or many) to be naive – that the (Afrikaner) National Party has at last decided for moral and pragmatic reasons to do better. Now is the time, therefore, for the nations of the West to bring the greatest moral and pragmatic pressure to bear on us. That excludes sanctions such as disinvestment. Re-education and punishment do not go together.

I would not write this if I did not believe that the Afrikaner Nationalist is ready to behave better. He is emerging from a morass and he cannot be expected to come out white and shining. He cannot be expected to become an angel tomorrow. He is, in fact, attempting to return to the West.

When the Voortrekkers moved north in the 1830s they were trekking away from the West. They wanted to have nothing more to do with it, especially with its ideas of equality of all people

9

before the law. Now, after 150 years, they (the majority of them) wish to return. It would be a supreme irony to punish them as they return.

The Afrikaner Nationalist often proclaims that he is a man of Africa. He did some queer things for a man of Africa. He forbade racially mixed marriages and he embarked on the foolish task of separating himself from the other men of Africa. He made it a criminal offence for certain men of Africa to love or marry certain women of Africa and broke many hearts and lives in doing so. This "man of Africa" notion is a poetic myth and it should not be accorded undue respect.

What the Afrikaner Nationalist must now do is to return to the Rule of Law and to set about the dismantling of apartheid. The nations of the West, and in particular the United States, must not underestimate their moral power to influence us in this direction.

Nor should the people of the United States be self-righteous. They should thank God every day for their Constitution, their Bill of Rights and their Supreme Court. In 1954, in the famous case of Brown v Board of Education, Topeka, the Supreme Court ordered the White people of America to do better and the court declared that separate could not be equal.

At Little Rock, Arkansas, Governor Faubus used his State militia to keep a handful of Black children out of a "White" school. But President Eisenhower federalised the militia and ordered them to ensure that the Black children got in. We in South Africa can only marvel at such things.

Americans must remember that we have no such Constitution, no such Bill of Rights. We are proud of our Supreme Court, but it does not have these august powers. Many of us have been fighting for years for a more just order, but what we have failed to do in many years, the United States Supreme Court can do in a few minutes. And now you want to punish us, too.

I have a last word to say to those fanatical divestors who think they can bring the South African Government "to its knees". They will not succeed. The Afrikaner Nationalists may at times behave like fools, but they do not behave like cowards.

But still more importantly, if the self-righteous bring our Government "to its knees", they will have to bring the whole country to its knees, for if the Afrikaner Nationalists are ever brought to their knees, it will have to be by the gun. And if they are brought to their knees, agriculture, industry, railways, ports, will all be brought to their knees. We will become one of the begging nations of the world, and the West, having broken us, will have to feed us. Russia will give us guns; America will have to give us food.

I do not argue with Black, or indeed White, South Africans who advocate disinvestment. One cannot argue with passion.

Just as I am coming to the end of this article I receive my copy of the South African Anglican newspaper, *Seek*. It contains an "Open Statement on South Africa" by the Presiding Bishop of the Episcopal Church in America, the Right Reverend John M Allin. I am going to quote some of his words.

After expressing the grief of the Church over recent events in South Africa, Bishop Allin said:

"Real reform must go forward in South Africa. The years of oppression must be redeemed. South Africa must be healed and become a land of hope and justice for all her sons and daughters.

"As Christians, we cannot condone or participate in actions that will bring any nation into full-scale civil war. We cannot abandon our fellow human beings by walking away from them or condemning them to international isolation . . .

"We must continue to help our Government realise that the best and most effective engagement in South Africa is unofficial and personal, reflected in constant contact, in commerce, in intellectual and cultural exchange.

"It is the creative engagement of constant argument. We expect our Government to argue actively, forcefully and publicly for the value of the ideals and principles upon which our nation was founded."

I cannot close with wiser words than those. As I read them I am inevitably reminded of the woman to whom Jesus said: "Neither do I condemn you; go and sin no more." Legend says of her that she became a holy woman.

Well, I can't promise that. But there is one thing that I can promise. If the nations of the West condemn us, they will only hinder the process of our emancipation from the bondage of our history. But if they stay with us, rebuke us, judge us and encourage us, the chances are that we shall do better.

Leadership – *May 1985*

JH Hofmeyr (1894–1948) is regarded as one of the first true White liberals of South Africa. A classical academic, Hofmeyr served as Deputy Prime Minister under General JC Smuts during the Second World War. Shortly before the fall of the United Party in 1948, his liberalism became an embarrassment to the party.

JC SMUTS

A man who lost his Olympian self-confidence
only twice in his life.

He Could Have Moved Faster

SMUTS HAD A GREAT MIND, but it failed to grasp the two great facts
of his own life and times. He never understood the nature and
the strength of Afrikaner Nationalism. He never foresaw the end
of the colonial age. In fact, he did not realise it was ending until
the close of the Second World War, say about 1946.

It was, of course, Afrikaner nationalism that finally overwhelmed him. As far as I know he lost his Olympian self-confidence only twice in his life. The first time was at the end of the
Anglo-Boer War, when he fell prey to melancholy, something
hitherto unknown to him. The second was when he was defeated
by Malan in 1948. His son, in his biography of his father, tells
how deep and dark was the depression into which he fell.

Why did he not understand nationalism? Partly because he had
entered a wider world where he was fêted, lionised, almost venerated. He was a Field-Marshal of the British Army. He became
the Chancellor of Cambridge University. One should note that it
was essentially a British world, the world of the British Empire
and Commonwealth, the British Navy. In 1945 the British era
came to an end. In the new world, of America and Russia, of the

new India, of an awakening Africa, Smuts was no longer the colossus.

One should also say that Smuts was not temperamentally attracted by nationalism. His holistic philosophy would have prevented it. He had a vision – far from being realised – of the unity of mankind. It is a strange thing that this hard, pragmatic, practical man also dreamed impossible dreams.

It is said that Smuts failed to give a lead to White South Africa in the matter of race politics. Could he have moved faster? The answer is Yes, but not much. He wrote to Hofmeyr in 1946 about the hostile world in which White South Africa now moved. He was distressed by the impatience of the members of the Native Representative Council, ZK Matthews, Mosaka, Selope Thema. But he wrote to Hofmeyr that he did not see what could be done to satisfy their aspirations while the White electorate was so intransigent.

I would conclude by saying that Smuts was a tough man, but White South Africa was tougher.

SATV – January 22, 1976

General JC Smuts (1870–1950), one of the heroes of the Anglo-Boer War, served two terms as South African Prime Minister, first as leader of the South African Party (1919–1924) and 15 years later as Premier of the United Party Government (1939–1948).

Dr DF Malan (1874–1959) was Prime Minister of South Africa from 1948 to 1954, when he retired from politics. A former minister in the Dutch Reformed Church and first editor of the Cape Nationalist newspaper, *Die Burger*, Malan coined the phrase apartheid in 1948.

Professor ZK Matthews, then Cape leader of the African National Congress, was the initiator of the Congress of the People that took place in June 1955 and during which the Freedom Charter – still the basic document of the ANC – was compiled.

HF VERWOERD

The fervour of his loyalty to a narrow creed
prevented him from attaining greatness.

The Man Who Began the Chaos

OF ALL OUR EIGHT Prime Ministers the two who most powerfully
dominated their parties and their Cabinets, and who most fascinated students of behaviour, were General Smuts and Dr HF
Verwoerd.

Smuts has had his fair share of biographies, the most notable
of which is Hancock's *Smuts*. Verwoerd has not been so fortunate.
The most ambitious attempt is that of GD Scholtz, which is
hagiographic, undistinguished and undramatic.

Mr Henry Kenney nowhere claims, to my knowledge, that his
Architect of Apartheid is a biography. He himself calls it "an appraisal", and I should like to say at once that it deserves high
marks as such. It is both an appraisal and a history. It is a history
of Verwoerd's political life, but says almost nothing about his
private and personal life. I shall later suggest that there is a good
reason for this.

The small boy Hendrik was two years old when his parents
emigrated from Holland to South Africa in 1903. His parents,
and later the boy himself, identified themselves with the struggle,
the sufferings, the history, the language of the Afrikaner. The

family went to Bulawayo, where Hendrik went to Milton Boys' High, and there the young boy took an intense dislike to the British, to God Save the King and to the White Rhodesian culture. He became, in fact, a fervent convert to Afrikanerdom and was to make the maintenance and future and survival of Afrikanerdom the grand pursuit of his life.

Verwoerd was highly intelligent and had a brilliant academic career. In 1936 he became editor of the newspaper *Die Transvaler*. His supreme purpose was not the purveying of news; it was the rousing of Afrikanerdom to a realisation of its high destiny. That he played his part in this arousal cannot be doubted. His reward was to be taken into Malan's Cabinet in 1950 as Minister of Native Affairs. He was to set White South Africa on a course towards a goal that could never be reached. But that was not to be realised by his party until years after his death.

What was this goal? It was nothing less than to make secure – for ever, presumably – the future of Afrikanerdom. To do this the whole society must be reconstructed and the damage done by Smuts's years of laissez faire must be repaired.

The separate "nations" must preserve their own identities and cherish their own languages and cultures. This was originally to be done under the benevolent rule of Afrikanerdom; it was later that Verwoerd introduced his party to the ideal of political independence for the other "nations".

Verwoerd was the senior architect of this grand edifice, but he needed a policeman to guard the site and to take steps against those who made trouble for the builders, who stole the bricks and suborned the works. In 1961, when he had been Prime Minister for three years, he appointed BJ Vorster as his policeman. So was accelerated the drastic erosion of the Rule of Law. Mr Kenney writes: "As Minister of Justice, BJ Vorster was the ideal choice for undertaking a campaign of mass repression."

I find Mr Kenney's record of those times faultless. He has his dislikes and prejudices, but he follows CP Scott's dictum that comment is free while facts are sacred. Mr Kenney is a loner. He dislikes the radicals, the neo-Marxists and the nationalists; he can afford to be kinder to the liberals, who are impractical and gullible. Interestingly enough, this gives a certain amount of authority to his interpretation of our history.

Why did Verwoerd's goal prove to be unreachable? Mr Kenney gives one important reason: Verwoerd was an economic illiterate.

In other words he had no conception of the limitations of ideology or of rigid systematism (I apologise for the word).

He tried to force one of the most complex of human societies, with a most complex history of conquest, great migrations, the discovery of fabulous wealth, the confinement of a Black majority to small pieces of land so that they could never become agriculturists, and finally the growth of White industrial cities that are now two-thirds Black – he tried to force this complex society into a master mould conceived in his own mind.

And when the society and its people proved recalcitrant, he cherished the foolish notion – this highly intelligent man – that the powers of the State and the law and the police could bring them to heel.

How could such an intelligent man cherish such a notion? The answer is that Verwoerd was ruled by his passions. He gave the public impression that he was ruled by an intellect of genius. He was even able to give this impression to some of his political opponents, much to their dismay, which they confided only in secret.

We are all creatures of reason and passion and many of us try to make them run together in double harness. In public Verwoerd made it appear as though he had succeeded. But, in fact, they ran in tandem and passion led the way. It was his passion for the maintenance and survival of Afrikanerdom.

All other considerations were subordinate.

His Nationalism had much in common with Communism; values such as the independence of the judiciary, the Rule of Law, the freedom of the Press, the autonomy of Church or University, all of these were subordinate values.

Mr Kenney thinks that the definitive work on Verwoerd still lies in the future. I doubt it.

I certainly find no lack of definition in Mr Kenney's own book. I doubt also if a true biography will ever be written.

It is significant that Mr Kenney does not give more than a few pages to the private life. We know that Verwoerd was a good husband and a good father, that he liked fishing and working with his hands, that overseas visitors found him charming. We are told that he trusted only those who accepted what he said without question.

Some found him cold, impersonal and aloof. Ben Schoeman at first detested him, then grew to appreciate him, a version that does not agree with the most recent one. Fred Barnard and Annetjie Boshoff thought him almost perfect. It all adds up to very little.

For better or for worse, Verwoerd will be known only for his public life, his politics, his speeches, his grandiose plans, his ideological arrogance. One thing is certain, no true nationalist will write a readable biography, for like the independence of the judiciary and the freedom of the Press, biographical truth is a subordinate value.

Was Verwoerd a great man? In the eyes of the Afrikaner Nationalism of the Sixties, yes. Otherwise no. Cassius found in himself, not in his stars, the fault that limited him. But of Verwoerd the opposite was true. He could have been great under different stars, but his adopted society had a definition of greatness that is not accepted anywhere else. It was the very fervour of his loyalty to a narrow creed that prevented him from attaining greatness.

Cape Argus – October 21, 1980

Dr. HF Verwoerd (1901–1966) became South Africa's sixth Prime Minister in 1958. Generally regarded as the architect of the homelands policy.

BJ Vorster's (1915–1983) election as Prime Minister in 1966 introduced the first gradual steps in the amelioration of apartheid legislation. He retired in 1978 and became State President, but resigned in June 1979 after the Erasmus Commission into the Information Scandal found he knew about irregularities in the financial affairs of the Department of Information.

Fred Barnard was the private secretary of Dr HF Verwoerd.

Annetjie Boshoff is the daughter of Dr HF Verwoerd and married Prof Carel Boshoff, a well-known Pretoria theologian who is the chairman of a conservative movement, the Afrikaner Volkswag (Afrikaner People's Guard).

BJ VORSTER

A man who missed the chance to be a great statesman.

An Appeal to BJ

WHAT IS MR VORSTER going to do with his vast majority? This is in my view the most important political question of the year. One cannot answer it fully, because the future in Portugal, Angola and Mozambique, not to mention South West Africa and Rhodesia, is obscure. Therefore, to some extent one must speculate.

The recent Portuguese events have made inevitable a considerable escalation of pressure. We may be entering an era of dangerous guerrilla warfare on our borders. The intensity of African feeling against us is very great.

And what is more, 26 years of apartheid legislation has increased the intensity. White South Africa is seen as an oppressor. And this is not surprising. The removal of the Coloured vote, the Group Areas Act, the cruel resettlements, the life imprisonment of Nelson Mandela and others while Robey Leibbrandt was let free, and many other acts, do not commend us to the rest of the world, least of all Black Africa.

It is true that rulers do not yield to pressure until they have to. If they leave it too late, then they will be destroyed, as Dr Caetano was destroyed. I think Mr Vorster knows this.

I think too that Mr Vorster understands clearly he can resist outside pressure only if he lessens inside pressure. He does not want a massive Black fifth column inside his own country. He realises that hostile outside pressures plus hostile inside pressure mean the end of Afrikanerdom.

Therefore, he must reduce the intensity of hostile inside pressure. The granting of independence to the homelands is not enough. He, and indeed all our political parties, must face the problems of "White" South Africa, with its four million Whites, its two million Coloured people, its 750,000 Indian people and its at least six million Blacks. It is time he acknowledged that the theory that these six million Blacks really belong to the homelands is fantasy.

He must give earnest attention to the problem of the disparity between White and Black wealth. I think he knows this. He must give attention to the poverty-stricken state of Black education, and to the fact that Black parents pay and White parents do not. I think he knows this too.

He can make Matanzima and Buthelezi into kings or emperors and it will achieve precisely nothing.

He knows he must go forward. But if he goes forward too far, he will lose his conservatives. If he goes forward too slowly, he will lose his verligtes. If he keeps them together, I see no hope for us at all. He must decide what fraction of his party he is prepared to lose. And he will naturally try to lose as few as he can.

The idea that we shall go on having White elections for another 25 years must be yielded. There is no time left for the Progs to build up from seven to 20 in 1979 and from 20 to 40 in 1984 – Orwell's year.

There is no time for Mr Gerdener to build up from none to four and from four to 12. The Progs and the Democrats and the UP can never become governments. There may be one more conventional election, and the Nats will win it again. Then they will have to choose whether to die fighting or to march forward into the new world.

And if they march forward, it must be with the Bassons and the Egins and the Gerdeners. And they will be marching, not to Pretoria, but to Umtata and Nongoma and Robben Island, not to fight but to plan the future.

If they march backwards to the wall, that will be the end. And it will be the end of me, and my children, and my children's children.

So on Mr Vorster lies a burden that is heavy to be borne. People like myself have long believed that the only hope for an evolutionary solution lies with the Afrikaner and the Black man. The Indians, the Coloured people, the English-speaking, we are not the leading actors in this drama.

Mr Vorster, I don't like your politics. Least of all do I like your apparent belief that you can rule by banning, by the police and by the gun. Whether you believe this or not I am not sure, but you certainly say it.

Our future is in your hands. If you do not have the courage to give a new lead to your party, then I foresee not merely the end of any kind of White tenure but a period of violence and grief that will make the earlier history of South Africa look quite uneventful.

Therefore, although I don't like your politics, I look to you to shoulder your immense responsibilities to us all.

Sunday Tribune – *July 14, 1974*

Nelson Mandela (1918–), former Deputy National President of the African National Congress, was sentenced to life imprisonment during the Rivonia Treason Trial in 1964 and has since become the spiritual leader of the ANC.

Robey Leibbrandt was a champion South African boxer and Nazi fanatic who was sentenced to death for plotting to assassinate General Smuts and overthrow his Government. The sentence was later commuted to life imprisonment, but he was released less than a month after the Nationalist Government came to power in 1948.

Dr Marcello Caetano (1906–) became Portuguese Prime Minister in 1968. His Government was toppled in a coup d'etat on April 24, 1974, which led to Portugal's withdrawal from its African colonies the following year.

Kaiser Matanzima (1915–) was the first Prime Minister of Transkei when it gained independence in 1976. He became President in 1979 and rejected the South African Government's new Constitution in 1983, calling for a national convention of all South Africans.

Gatsha Mangosuthu Buthelezi (1928–), heir to the chieftainship of the Buthelezi tribe, was elected Chief Minister of KwaZulu in 1976. Regarded as a moderate because of his opposition to disinvestment and violence, Buthelezi is also President of Inkatha, a large political-cultural movement mainly among Zulus.

Dr Theo Gerdener served as a minister of the Cabinet of Prime Minister BJ Vorster in the early Seventies, but later established the Democratic Party which failed to win any seats in Parliament during the General Election of 1974.

Jacob Du P (Japie) Basson (1918–) has at different times represented the United and National parties in Parliament. He was suspended from the NP caucus in 1959 because of his opposition to a clause in the Bantu Self-Government Bill, preventing White MPs from representing Blacks in Parliament, but after serving as UP MP for Bezuidenhout, rejoined the National Party.

Colin Eglin (1925–) represented the United Party in Parliament from 1958 and was one of the founder members of the Progressive Party the following year. He led the Progressive Federal Party twice, first from 1971–1981 and again from 1986.

Consider These Five Points

I REMEMBER IN MAY, 1948, the shock for many of us when the era of what could be called Smuts-English-speaking supremacy came to its end. Now 26 years later, the era of Nationalist Afrikaner supremacy is coming to its end too.

If we don't grasp the fact – if the Afrikaner Nationalists don't grasp it – our future, more so the White future than the Black, will be one of desolation. No-one will escape.

From one point of view one can feel sympathy for the Nationalist. He suffered – even if not so much as he sometimes likes to think – for 100 years under British supremacy. I myself date the birth of Afrikaner Nationalism from 1806 when the British finally annexed the Cape.

His republics were never really free. Then in 1948 he suddenly became the lord of all and has been so for 26 years. But there won't be many more.

From another point of view one can feel no sympathy at all. He rode roughshod over us all. All of us suffered under him, the English-speaking less than the others. He claimed to be maintaining the traditional way of life, but in fact he changed it radically. Customs had to be made into laws. And many of the laws were pitiless.

Although the days of Afrikaner supremacy are drawing to an end, the days of the ultimate Afrikaner responsibility are only beginning. And for better or for worse it is Mr Vorster who must bear the brunt.

Is he going to put his country first or his party? The question is as simple as that. If he puts his party first, that will be the end of the party. If he puts Afrikanerdom first, that will be the end of Afrikanerdom. And of course, the end of lots of others too.

The question that many of us are asking is whether he knows the magnitude of the crises into which we are now entering. And whether he knows that the crisis cannot be faced successfully by any one political party, however great its apparent strength.

It has become almost a South African cliché to say that you can't fight enemies abroad if you have enemies at home. But it's true.

Seven hundred million rands for the borders won't satisfy aspirations – and just aspirations – here at home.

We have been saying – for at least most of my life – that it's dangerous to hold down the lid on the boiling pot. But it's also dangerous to take it off. There's only one way to lessen the danger, and that's to damp down the fire.

And how does one do that?

1. By narrowing the wage and salary gap, the aim being, at the very least, equal pay for equal work.
2. By making Black education, first free, and when possible, compulsory.
3. By giving Black labour not only a legal but also an efficient means for presenting its just demands, in other words, trade unions.
4. By removing those humiliations which are destructive of human dignity.
5. By a more equitable sharing of political power, whatever the political structure of society may be.

There's a great deal of talk at the moment about the defence of the country. I shall choose only one comment. Chief Gatsha Buthelezi said in effect, of course we'll defend the country if you give us a country to defend.

Mr Prime Minister, that's your task, to give us a country to defend. And that is not the same as maintaining the unity of the National Party.

If you were to announce tomorrow that you are going to devote yourself, not to controlling everybody and everything, but to trying to realise the five goals set out above, you would receive from every party and every creed and every colour a volume of support that would astonish you. We don't want our problems solved by outsiders any more than you do.

Can you do it? Will you do it? I don't know, but I hope and pray that you can and will.

And if you can't and you won't, then you'd better hurry up and spend another R700 million on that collapsing house. It might last you out your lifetime, but I doubt it.

Sunday Tribune – *September 1, 1974*

A Man of Lost Chances

WHEN CHIEF BUTHELEZI heard that Mr Vorster was retiring, he said that "history" would judge the retiring Prime Minister, Mr Vorster, as a man who missed the chance to be a great statesman.

This severe but measured judgment I regard to be the plain and simple truth. When Caetano fell from power in April 1974, our southern world was changed for ever. And, what is more, Mr Vorster knew it.

That was the year when his Foreign Minister, Mr Pik Botha, made the momentous statement in New York that we would now move away from racial discrimination, and he was shortly afterwards supported by his Prime Minister, who announced that considerable changes would be seen in six months. If I remember rightly, he went further and said that these changes would surprise the nations of the world.

Well, nothing of the kind has happened. One must, therefore, ask the question, why? I can find two answers. The first is that Mr Vorster, when the time came to make the change, found himself psychologically impotent to move away from the Afrikaner Nationalist ideology, which is based upon the dogma that every race group has not only a separate identity, but also a separate destiny and self-fulfilment. It is, in fact, only the promise of self-fulfilment that offers any justification for the laws which preserve separate identity at the cost of considerable suffering, most of which has to be borne by the African, Coloured and Indian people of South Africa.

I do not find it strange that this psychological impotence afflicts the Afrikaner Nationalist. The draconian racial and security laws of the last 30 years were made for one purpose, and one only, and that was to ensure the security and survival of Afrikanerdom. Therefore, one cannot change anything until one has accepted some change in the fundamental dogma itself. Nothing that has been said by Mr Vorster, Dr Connie Mulder and Mr PW Botha has indicated any willingness to amend the dogma. On the contrary, much has been said, particularly by Dr Mulder, to indicate that the dogma is still sacrosanct. It is noticeable that by and large Mr Pik Botha avoids the subject.

There is an apocryphal story told of a flight made by the Foreign Minister from New York to Johannesburg. He found himself sitting next to a prominent Johannesburg businessman, and together they enjoyed the generous hospitality of South African Airways. They were soon plain Pik and John. John said to Pik: "Pik, tell me something, why doesn't the PM get rid of his Right wing?" And Pik said with great earnestness: "John, you don't understand, the PM is the Right wing."

The story is doubtless untrue, but it has a truth of its own. I believe that in 1974 the Prime Minister at last acknowledged the need to amend the dogma, but he couldn't do it. His heart, his passions, his history, over-ruled his head and his will, something very common among Afrikaner Nationalists.

The second reason why nothing happened was because the Prime Minister encountered overt and covert opposition to his proposals for change. Mr Vorster is not a man to fear this, but this was an opposition of a special kind. It could have broken the National Party. Nothing could have appalled Mr Vorster more than the prospect of change that could only be brought about by the aid of the opposition parties, particularly the PFP. It had been done once before, by General Hertzog in 1934, and from that day the leadership of Afrikanerdom began to pass inevitably into the hands of Dr. Malan.

Quite apart from these two difficulties, Mr Vorster had a very simplistic view of social and economic change. Economic forces could be controlled by the bulldozer, and in extreme cases by the gun. He was a policeman, not a statesman.

His force of character – which was considerable – showed itself most dramatically when he was at the microphone promising the maintenance of law and order. It was a tale of sound and fury, but for many of us it signified nothing – or rather it signified a fatal misconception of the scope and limitations of government.

It is true that Mr Vorster missed the chance to become a great statesman. But one should in fairness remember that if he had tried he might have proved a great failure, broken by the forces of Afrikaner Nationalism, the same which defeated General Hertzog and General Smuts before him. That would for him have been the ultimate tragedy.

He was certainly a powerful ruler, but he was also the creature of the National Party, and of the dogmas of Afrikaner Nationalism, which have so far been impervious to reason. He knew that they should be amended, but he couldn't do it. The great question that confronts the new Prime Minister, and the national Party, and Afrikanerdom, and every other one of us, is whether the dogmas can be amended.

If they cannot be, then all hopes of an evolutionary solution will be in vain. In famous words, the future will be too ghastly to contemplate.

Sunday Times – *October 1, 1978*

Adv RF (Pik) Botha (1932–) became South Africa's Foreign Minister in 1977 and a year later his support was chiefly responsible for the election of PW Botha as Prime Minister. He is regarded as one of the leading enlightened members in the National Party.

Dr Connie Mulder (1925–) was defeated in the race for Prime Minister by PW Botha in 1978. He resigned shortly afterwards as a Cabinet Minister and member of the National Party because of his involvement in the Information Scandal. In 1987 he was re-elected to Parliament under the banner of the Conservative Party.

PW Botha (1916–) became Prime Minister in 1978 and through a successful referendum in 1983, changed the Constitution to include Coloureds and Indians in separate chambers of Parliament. He then became South Africa's first executive State President. His scrapping of many apartheid laws led to a split in the ruling National Party in 1982.

General JBM Hertzog (1866–1942) was Prime Minister of South Africa for 15 years, the longest unbroken reign in the country's history (1924–1939). He was also the founder of the National Party in 1914.

PW BOTHA

He has come to realise that the Afrikaner cannot rule by the gun.

Give Us the Lead Now

IN 1974 PRESIDENT CAETANO of Portugal fell from power. Angola achieved its independence in 1975 and so did Mozambique. Two great buffers between the White-ruled Republic of South Africa and the Black-ruled continent were removed. In 1980 Zimbabwe-Rhodesia elected Mr Robert Mugabe by a great majority to lead the country to independence. The date for the independence of Namibia-South West Africa is not yet certain but it is near.

All these events have an unmistakeable message for White South Africa.

She must face at last the question that she has been evading for the greater part of this century. How does she prepare herself to give to Black South Africans a share in the responsibility of government?

At the moment she rules the greater part of the country by right of conquest. But conquest has been undone in one African country after another. It goes without saying that it must be undone here.

For many White South Africans the victory of Mr Mugabe is bitter news. They would rather have had Bishop Abel Muzorewa.

It is now surely clear that the Bishop never had the stature and the skill to rule such a divided country. If he had been elected the country would have been plunged back into civil war. Whatever irregularities may have taken place in the elections, Mr Mugabe's victory is beyond dispute.

Why did Mr Mugabe win?

It is widely thought that the people believed he was more likely to bring peace than any other leader, and that could well be a cardinal reason. But he promised more than peace. He promised social reforms which would improve the quality of life for the ordinary people.

It seems indisputable that Mr Mugabe will have to institute far-reaching land reforms. In Rhodesia the White twentieth of the population owns half of the land.

Responsible leaders of White agriculture have already approached Mr Mugabe in an attempt to convince him that nationalisation of the land could lead to the collapse of food production, and that the amount of land owned by Black farmers could be considerably increased without resorting to nationalisation.

It is understandable that most White Rhodesians were shattered by the magnitude of Mr Mugabe's victory. They were surrounded and excluded by jubilant Blacks celebrating the advent of liberation. They had been misled by falsely optimistic predictions. Now they had to face real majority rule, with a Prime Minister who had been a guerrilla leader, whose troops had committed atrocities (by no means their monopoly) and who himself had made chilling pronouncements about land, the capitalist system and the virtues of Marxism.

White people were still more confused by the claims that Mr Mugabe was simultaneously a devoted Marxist and a devout Catholic.

Can Mr Mugabe be trusted?

That means can he be trusted to maintain the high standard of industry and agriculture, and can he be trusted to see that White Rhodesians are themselves given some kind of hope and security, the kind of hope and security that must nevertheless be compatible with those social reforms that are both imperative and inevitable?

There are signs – even though there are no proofs – that Mr Mugabe has no doctrinaire Marxist solution for the new country. He has spoken of a broad-based government and no true Marxist does that. He has spoken of the necessity to forgive and forget the grim past. He has asked General Walls to stay and help him. And he has maintained correct relations with the Governor.

The future is unpredictable, but whose future is not in the present state of the world?

Can we learn from the lessons of Zimbabwe-Rhodesia? We can indeed.

White South Africa should realise anew that its ignorance of Black thinking and Black aspirations are abysmal, that the Black attitude to the urban terrorist is almost totally different from its own, that the Land Act of 1913 that forbade Black purchase of "White" land is remembered by Black people to this day and that Black confidence and Black impatience increase continually.

White Rhodesia turned Mr Nkomo from a moderate to a guerrilla fighter. White South Africa has up till now been travelling that same road.

South Africa can no longer afford the unedifying spectacle of Dr Treurnicht challenging (never directly) the Prime Minister and the Prime Minister rebuking (never directly) his colleague. This is the kind of vacillation that cost Rhodesia dear.

It is time for the Prime Minister to send Dr Treurnicht packing and to give the country that clear lead that Mr Ian Smith failed to give to our neighbour.

Sunday Tribune – *March 9, 1980*

General Peter Walls was Commander-in-Chief of the Rhodesian Armed Forces in the last stages of the Rhodesian bush war, which lasted from 1972–1979.

Joshua Nkomo (1917–) became leader of the Zimbabwe African People's Union (Zapu) at its establishment in 1961. After spending years in gaol, he co-led the Patriotic Front to victory in the Rhodesian War and was appointed to the first Zimbabwean Cabinet after independence in 1980 under the leadership of Robert Mugabe.

Dr Ap Treurnicht was Deputy Minister for Bantu Administration and Education.

Ian Smith (1919–) led the Rhodesian Front Party to a Unilateral Declarations of Independence in 1965 and ruled the country as Prime Minister until handing over the reins to Bishop Abel Muzorewa in 1979.

PW's Afrikaner Prison

WHAT IS THE MEANING of the word "nation" and of the word "national"? It was at least 100 years ago that the Afrikaner Nationalist identified his nationhood with South Africa.

Yet he did not identify his nation with the other nations that occupied the same country.

Have we any other nations beside the Afrikaner nation? We certainly have at least one and that is the Zulu nation.

The Xhosas also must be regarded as a nation, though they are divided between two States, Transkei and Ciskei.

After that we encounter some difficulties. Are the Venda people a nation?

Can the Ndebele be called a nation when some speak Sotho and some speak Ndebele?

The question yet to be asked is whether they have anything that can be called a "common interest".

But before we do that we must note that the English-speaking people of South Africa do not regard themselves as a nation.

The Afrikaner philosophies of volkseie, national identity, tried very hard to persuade the English to develop a sense of national identity.

But they did not because they felt that being part of the great British Commonwealth was good enough for anybody.

Nor after South Africa left the Commonwealth did the English go searching for an identity, perhaps because they didn't care or because they were too lazy, or perhaps for some like myself because they thought the whole idea was vulgar.

South African Indians are not a nation and never will be.

They are caught between White power and Black power and they occupy — most of them quietly and circumspectly, and perhaps a little apprehensively — a kind of middle ground.

There is one further complication – Hindus and Muslims cannot be said to be enamoured of one another.

The Coloured people are not a nation and never will be.

They have certainly been brought closer together by the Group Areas Act and the Population Registration Act, and above all, by the removal of their franchise.

They lived for centuries in relative peace with White South Africans, but the extent of their alienation is now very great.

Well, that is our list of nations, and a real hotchpotch we are.

How could we all share in a common national purpose?

There is one factor above all others that makes the achievement of a South African nationalism a matter of the utmost difficulty.

It is not primarily political; it is economic.

One cannot expect people who earn 2,3,4 units per annum to make any kind of common cause with people who earn only one unit.

The opposite is equally true. The two ways of life, the two standards of living, the deepest aspirations, have little in common.

Some very intelligent South Africans are deeply pessimistic about the closing of the economic gulf.

Others regard with hope the undoubted improvement in Black (real) income over the years.

The gulf will close and the greatest barrier to a united nationalism will gradually disappear.

At the other extreme are those who demand an equalisation of income tomorrow and who pour scorn and anger, not only on the possibility of an evolutionary process, but on those Blacks who benefit by it and who therefore "blunt the edge of the revolution".

These are the radical socialists, the neo-Marxists, who still believe that Marxism does not lead to Leninism and Stalinism, who believe that the USSR – or perhaps China – is the only just society in the world.

These radicals pride themselves in the mental liberation they enjoy inside their ideological straitjackets.

One cannot argue with them because they reason and think only in fixed categories.

But let us return to our elusive subject, the "national interest". Are we in South Africa moving any nearer to a South African nationalism?

Is the Afrikaner Nationalist beginning to realise that the old time-honoured saying 'een volk, een kerk, een taal' (one people, one church, one language) is no slogan for the future?

It may be a fine slogan for an underdog, but for an overdog with some very vigorous underdogs to rule over, it's no slogan at all.

The question is this – is Mr PW Botha moving nearer to a South African Nationalism?

So now I reply, very carefully. Yes, Mr Botha is moving nearer to a South African Nationalism.

Yes, his first aim is to give the Afrikaner security, but it is not his only aim.

Yes, he was born a Nat but it would be presumptuous for me to say that he will die a Nat.

No, he is not a swindler. Mr Botha is an Afrikaner who was born in the prison of Afrikaner Nationalism, but he does not want himself or his people to die in prison.

He has come to realise that Afrikaner Nationalism by itself will not save the Afrikaner.

He has come to realise that in the end the Afrikaner cannot rule by the gun, but in the meantime he feels the need for plenty of guns (nearly R3-thousand-million worth of them in fact).

He talks endlessly about the total onslaught, but he will not face the fact that nobody did more to make it possible than himself and his party.

When he says he wants a future for every child, White, Black, or Brown, I believe he means it.

When he shakes the hand of a little Indian girl at a school opening, I do not believe he is being a hypocrite.

Somewhere inside the Nationalist armourplate, a South African is trying to get out.

When Dr Aggett dies in prison in circumstances that can only be described as being in the highest degree questionable, Mr Botha does not come out firmly and say that he condemns any ill-treatment of detainees.

In fact, he says almost nothing. He heads a Government that gives to its police powers denied to judges.

He sends young men to prison for long terms because it is against their religion to lift a gun.

Each of these things in my view cancels out his smiling at a little Indian girl.

Will PW's new "national" dispensation work?

I think the answer is No.

Should I hope that if it doesn't work PW will try to find something that will work better?

The answer is Yes.

Why are there no Black people in the new "national dispensation"?

The official answer is that Black people have their own "national interests in their own lands".

The true answer is that the National Party is afraid of the Black man; or to put it more gently, it is afraid of the numerical superiority of the Black man.

This fear is by no means confined to the National Party.

The trouble with these Black men is that when they've been defeated they won't lie down.

It is significant that when the Black man wants to frighten the White man, he talks of the "unitary state".

Will the National Party – in the foreseeable future – agree to a unitary state? The answer is No.

What about a federation? Or a confederation? PW doesn't like either of these ideas, so he has opted for a constellation, which will presumably be bound together by a "constellational interest".

There will be no centralised power, even of the most innocuous kind.

But it is power that is at the very heart of our problems.

Even if PW gets his constellation, which is doubtful, it will be financed and kept going by its richest member, the Republic of South Africa.

Are the Afrikaner Nationalists too frightened to contemplate federation or confederation, from which for the first time a "national interest" would emerge?

At the moment, yes. I don't know about the future.

They obviously don't like the ideas of the Buthelezi Commission.

On the other hand the radicals think that federalism is an immoral concept and that White people take refuge in it because they want to deny Blacks the ultimate justice.

I myself, seeing no immediate likelihood of the unitary State, and having no desire to live in a unitary State brought about by revolution, am attracted to federation or confederation.

I find nothing immoral in doing so. I find nothing immoral in the Canadian and Australian constitutions.

I sometimes wonder why the Progressive Federal Party says so little about these matters.

If I do have a nationalism, it is a South African Nationalism.

I am not in general attracted by nationalism.

But a South African Nationalism would not be characterised by the arrogance and aggressiveness and exclusivity of so many nationalisms, for one simple reason – it could come into being only because of a realisation that we South Africans share a common humanity and a common land.

Here I felt compelled to sound a solemn note – if we never realise this South African Nationalism, if we never learn to accept one another because of a common humanity and because of the love of our common land, then we are going to kill one another.

We are going to invite the total onslaught of which we hear so much.

I must remind you of the grotesque and almost unbelievable truth that the pursuit of this nationalism was made a criminal offence in 1968.

In that year Mr PW Botha and his party made it a criminal offence to pursue such a nationalism.

They did this by passing the Prohibition of Political Interference Act.

The whole President's Council should have gone to prison under this Act, and PW should have gone with them as prime instigator.

But in this country Prime Ministers don't go to prison.

The Rev Allan Hendrickse should now be charged for deciding to support the President's Council, but he won't go to prison either.

Circumstances alter cases. What was totally offensive to PW and his party in 1968 has become in great measure acceptable.

It is for this mercy that we give thanks, that what was offensive and criminal 15 years ago is now desirable and legal.

But it is only a small mercy, because PW Botha and his party evade the greatest of all the problems, the participation of African people in government, real government.

And as long as he evades it, his hopes for a just and peaceful future for our country, which I believe to be sincere and honest, will come to nothing.

I cannot give a bright and cheerful view of the future. You can't undo conquest with the same ease as you made it.

You can't climb out of a morass with a clean and shining countenance.

Will we ever find a "national interest"?

The material components are there in abundance – the railways, the ports, the airways, the roads, the cities, the posts and telegraphs, the rich farms and vineyards.

Indeed the list is impressive but the great majority of the people of South Africa regard them as "White."

If these "White" assets were destroyed by revolution, we would become a starving nation, but that argument carries no weight with revolutionaries.

Our daunting and seemingly impossible task is to create a true "national interest" and we shan't do that until we create, or until we are in the process of creating, a new South African Nationalism.

Leadership SA – *April 1983*
Condensed by the Sunday Times – *April 24, 1983*

Dr Neil Aggett (1952–1982) was acting Transvaal regional secretary of the African Food and Canning Workers' Union (AFCWU) when he was detained by the Security Police on November 27, 1981. On February 5, 1982, he was found dead in his cell, the first White to die in detention since the introduction of the General Law Amendment Act, which introduced detention without trial for up to 90 days (later extended to 180). Nobody was held responsible for his death.

The Buthelezi Commission, named after the Chief Minister of KwaZulu, Gatsha Mangosuthu Buthelezi, supported the principle of power sharing between Black leaders of KwaZulu and the White provincial government of Natal when it brought out its report in 1982.

The President's Council was established in 1979 as an advisory body consisting of Whites, Coloureds and Indians. The exclusion of Blacks led to widespread opposition, especially from the Progressive Federal Party. It consists of different committees which study problem areas in South African society.

The Rev Allan Hendrickse (1927–) became leader of the Coloured Labour Party in 1978 and led the LP to an overwhelming victory in the election of 1984 for the first Coloured House of Representatives. His participation in the new tricameral parliamentary system was unpopular among his own people. He received a post in the first Cabinet of State President PW Botha, but resigned in 1987 after repeated clashes with Botha over the Group Areas Act.

Will PW Lead Us Forward?

I HAVE LIVED UNDER ALL eight of our Prime Ministers. I have observed them all closely, except the first, Louis Botha, who died when I was 16. I was foolhardy enough to say at a lunch in November that PW was the most astute of them all. One paper reported me as saying he was the best of them all. I did not say that. But I do not mind saying that he is the best politician of them all.

A better politician than Smuts? I have no doubt. Smuts failed to understand the strength and the implacability of the Afrikaner Nationalism of his day.

Smuts and Verwoerd were the most gifted. Both had a streak of arrogance, which I suppose is to be expected. They both enjoyed (naturally) the extreme deference they received from others. Smuts had the extraordinary political weakness I have mentioned above. Verwoerd also had an extraordinary weakness: he thought he knew everything. He thought he had the solution (apparently final) of all the complex problems of South Africa. His solution has proved unworkable.

Who was the best Prime Minister of them all? I think it is an impossible question and has no answer. Our first seven Prime Ministers lived in a world that has passed away, the world of White supremacy. Which of them knew that it was passing away? Only one, I think. Smuts had occasional and fitful glimpses of it, but they came to nothing. Vorster's trip to see Kaunda at the Victoria Falls was an almost meaningless adventure.

Our eighth Prime Minister is in a situation different from those of his predecessors. The future is sniffing and snarling at the door of the Afrikaner fortress more ominously than ever before. Does PW know this? I think he does. Does he know it well enough? I don't know. All I know is that he has the chance of becoming the most important Prime Minister in our history to date. But the difficulties in the way of his becoming so are nothing less than immense.

I want to say something about these difficulties, but first I want to ask: Why did he embark on the task of drawing up a new constitution? It is said that he did so because the Westminster constitution had failed. The truth is that we never had a Westminster constitution, because in 1910 our Union of South Africa constitution entrenched the Colour bar.

What is more, it was Westminster that allowed us to do so. Schreiner, Rubusana, Abdurahman and Jabavu went to London to urge Westminster not to do it. Nobody listened. Westminster did more than that: it gave us the constitutional power to destroy the Cape franchise.

PW had other reasons than Westminster. He was under pressure from Afrikaner pragmatists who knew that the Colour bar could no longer be maintained in its existing form. He was also under pressure from the Afrikaner conscience, which having been quiescent and acquiescent for so long, was becoming more and more troubled by the cruelties and injustices of the Colour bar. He, and his military advisers, know that the battle for Afrikaner survival could not be won on the Border if there was unrest at home.

And lastly, he, like all other Afrikaners except the most isolationist, wanted to be part of the democratic West. In the years 1939 to 1945, the Afrikaner Nationalists proclaimed loudly that the affairs of the West were no concern of theirs, but those were the last of their extreme anti-British years. PW knows that if we are finally given up by the West, it will be the end of Afrikanerdom.

Which of these four factors was the strongest? PW is not a man who is pushed forward by others. All four factors operated within himself as well. I think the first was the strongest – the pragmatical realisation that the Colour bar was becoming more and more difficult, morally, militarily and economically to maintain.

Will PW lead us forward into a better future? I don't know; nobody knows. Will he try? I have no doubt. That the new dispensation is a big hoax is for me impossible to believe. Quite a high percentage of those who call it a hoax are, consciously or unconsciously, anti-Afrikaner.

It is possible to take two radically opposing views of the dispensation. One is to regard it as the first relaxation of the rigid Colour bar. The other is to regard it as an invitation to Indian and Coloured people to join White South Africa in the laager. If the second view proves correct, there will be no ultimate solution except that of cataclysm.

What is the fundamental flaw in the dispensation and, therefore, the fundamental flaw in PW's reasoning about the future? I am not referring to the obvious flaw that Africans are excluded. I am referring to the ostensible reasons for which they are excluded. These reasons are not logical; they are deeply emotional.

It was Verwoerd in 1959 who gave the Afrikaner Nationalists a way of escape from the harsh realities of apartheid. He called it separate development and he invented the happy homelands, which had all the potentialities for a full, independent and satisfying existence. It is this self-deception that rules Nationalist politics even till today.

PW will not lead us into a better future until he realises that the happy homelands are a myth. This is an immensely difficult thing for an Afrikaner Nationalist to do. The happy homelands are his security.

When I look at PW's noble brow and his clear eyes and his strong chin, I think he ought to know that the happy homelands are a myth. But then I realise that he is (or was) a devout Afrikaner Nationalist and that his mind therefore cannot work quite like mine.

Take Gerrit Viljoen, Pik Botha, Magnus Malan and PW himself – they are all intelligent and they all believe (or they will all say they believe) in the happy homelands. They just will not face the truth that the homelands never will be viable States, that the overwhelming percentage of the country's wealth is in "White" South Africa and that the progress made by the homelands since 1959 has been pitiful.

Verwoerd made the remarkable prophecy that by 1976 (or 1978) the homelands would have proved so successful that Black migration would be reversed and that Blacks would begin to migrate from the White cities to the Black territories. It didn't happen and it shows no sign of happening.

Do I see any chance that PW will rethink the whole matter of the homelands? If there is no such rethinking, the new dispensation must inevitably fail.

There is a small indication of a rethinking. It has always been noteworthy to me – in my long years of watching Prime Ministers – that the Afrikaner Nationalists have shied away from any discussion of a federal or confederal plan for South Africa. They have taken refuge in the vague word "constellation". The reason is obvious. A federal or confederal South Africa would need some kind of central Government, however weak it might be, and African people would have to be represented in such a Government.

Now, in the spring number of *Leadership SA*, our Prime Minister actually used the words "confederation of States". He also said that he had been "propagating" a broader concept than what is generally understood by a "constellation of States". I am surprised that these remarks have not received greater publicity.

These are our prospects for our immediate future. They're not good, but they could be worse. And lastly, PW, if you are really keen on keeping the favour of the West, you'll have to do something about repairing the damage done to the Rule of Law by your predecessors. I regretfully place on record that you were a

38

consenting party. You shouldn't have been. Now is the time to make amends.

The Star — *December 30, 1983*

William P Schreiner (1857–1919), one of the leaders of the Afrikaner Bond in the Cape Province, became Prime Minister of the Cape Colony in 1898. He led a delegation to London in 1909 to protest against the limited political rights given to non-Whites by the South Africa Act. After 1910, he became a senator in the first Union Parliament and was South African High Commissioner in London from 1914–1919.

The Rev Dr Walter B Rubasana (1858–1936) was the first Black member of the Cape Provincial Council, representing Tembuland from 1910–1914. He accompanied the Schreiner delegation.

Abdullah Abdurahman (1872–1940), a Coloured member of the Cape Provincial Council, was elected President of the African Political Organisation in 1905. He accompanied the Schreiner delegation.

John Tengo Jabavu (1859–1921), one of South Africa's first Black journalists and statesmen, was one of the founders of the South African Native College, which later became the University of Fort Hare. He accompanied the Schreiner delegation.

Dr Gerrit Viljoen was Minister of National Education.

General Magnus Malan was Minister of Defence.

✕✕✕✕✕✕✕✕✕✕✕

Why PW Drew Back

WHY DO WE THINK IT important to assess the value of Mr Botha's contribution to the future of South Africa? In the first place because he is the first Nationalist Prime Minister who has had much appeal for non-Nationalists. In the second place because he is the first Prime Minister to have given hope to those South Africans who think that social, political and economic change is essential and inevitable. We felt he held the key to our future.

He aroused these hopes in 1979. He did an extraordinarily brave thing. He visited Soweto and was welcomed by the people of that great sprawling city, the creation of White South Africa, the growing Black child of which the White parent is so afraid. He chose the Nationalist town of Upington to say that his aim was to build a country where every child, White, Black, and Brown, would have a future. He thus gave hope to many South Africans who had almost given up hoping. I was one of these. I had never heard a Nationalist Prime Minister speak like that before.

Mr Botha's actions in 1979 divided my friends into two. There were those who, like myself, were given hope. There were others who thought that the whole thing was a sham, a move to quieten the clamour for sanctions, even worse, an attempt to deceive the outside world.

One of these friends wrote to me remonstrating with me for using my influence as a writer (she thought it was quite considerable) to give people a dangerous sense of euphoria. I had written that I thought the Prime Minister a convert to verligtheid, a convert to enlightenment, and that I believed he had realised that South Africa was in a state of crisis that threatened not only the peace of the whole country, but the existence of Afrikanerdom itself. She asked me to face the possibility that I was helping the Prime Minister to shut White South Africans off from the realities of the situation. I replied that I was waiting till June.

She was not my only critic. Others thought that I was too naive, too trusting, too gullible, that I did not realise that a Nat is a Nat is a Nat, that I did not realise that the Prime Minister was putting on a big, spurious, dishonest act.

I don't believe that the Prime Minister was putting on a dishonest act. I believe that something quite different happened. I believe that he drew back from the shocking possibility – dreaded by all his predecessors – that he might break the National Party, the defender of the faith of all true Afrikaners, their only security in a dangerous world that would destroy them without mercy.

It has been estimated by some that Mr Botha would have lost say 30 to 40 Right-wing MPs and would still have retained a substantial majority in the House. But other observers have suggested that his loss would have been greater and that he might have lost command of Afrikanerdom. He would not have been able to lead his people on the only course that he felt would be safe. Therefore, he drew back from the brink.

Thus it was that the session which had promised so much achieved almost nothing, and that is the judgment I must pass at the end of June. But I do not believe that this happened because Mr Botha is a deceiver. It happened because in the last resort he is an Afrikaner Nationalist. He puts his party before the country. He does not do this because he is a rogue, but because he suffers from the same psychological impotence that paralysed his predecessor though I believe in a lesser degree. There is another reason: he thinks the party and the country are one and the same thing.

Therefore the hopes that were aroused in me have come to nothing. Mr Botha has failed all those of us, of whatever race or colour, who saw in him a hope for the future. The most bitterly disappointed are those Black leaders who do not want to achieve the freedom of their people by blood, violence and destruction. All these people, I should say without exception, believe that Mr Botha should have got rid of Dr Treurnicht this session, especially after Dr Treurnicht had championed the Colour bar in Craven Week. The Prime Minister did say forthrightly that the Coloured people were not lepers, but he still kept Dr Treurnicht.

I am one of many who believe that if the Prime Minister wants to perform his duty to Afrikanerdom, he must get rid of Dr Treurnicht. The trouble is again psychological. He cannot yet accept that the breaking of the National Party is essential for the salvation of Afrikanerdom.

This psychological difficulty can hardly be exaggerated. The Prime Minister has grown up believing the party to be the only defender against a hostile world. He has in fact given the best part of his life to the party. How then can he break it?

The talk is that Mr Botha will hold an early election in November. Let us suppose that the PFP increases its representation, that the HNP makes a gain here and there, and that Mr Botha secures a substantial majority.

Do we then have to go through this all again? Will Mr Botha still hesitate to grasp the nettle? Will he have made it clear during the campaign that the National Party is committed to a steady removal of all discrimination, to the repeal or drastic revision of laws like the Group Areas Act, to a sustained progress towards equalisation of education, to the abolition of the Mixed Marriages Act and to the upholding of the freedom of Church, Press and University? If he does not do that, the election will achieve nothing. We shall stand exactly where we stood before. I would not expect him to announce the restoration of the rule of law, or the abolition of detention without trial or access. His mind on these matters has up till now appeared completely closed.

Did Mr Botha calculate carefully that he could afford another year of uncertainty? It was a dangerous calculation because the rate of racial polarisation is increasing. Time will tell, and soon, whether his calculation was justified.

The people who thought I was gullible will think I am still gullible. So let me state my opinion that if Mr Botha continues to believe that he can save South Africa from destruction, and at the same time save the National Party intact, many of us will revert to the hopelessness of 1978.

I have two grave fears about Mr Botha. The first is that he will in the last resort put the unity of the party above all else. The second is even graver. I fear he will be tempted to use police and military power to contain economic and social forces that are totally unamenable to such containment. I thought his TV interview on June 22 was ominous. He said the State had not yet used its full might. Did he mean the Army? Is that how we are going to live? Is that the kind of security he is going to give to every South African child?

I ask myself a difficult question. Is it psychologically possible for an Afrikaner Nationalist, or any extreme nationalist for that matter, to desire for other people the same security, the same liberty, the same opportunity, that he desires for his own? I think the answer is NO. The answer troubles me, because I believe that no political leader who regards himself as first and foremost an Afrikaner will ever lead this country to safety.

Am I asking too much of you and your party, Mr Botha? If I am, then you and I will go down together.

The Craven Rugby Week was instituted in 1964 when provincial teams at secondary school level for the first time competed against one another. It was named after the President of the South African Rugby Board, Dr Danie Craven.
PFP – Progressive Federal Party
HNP – Hestigte Nasionale Party (Re-established National Party)

The Liberal Recipe—So Late

SO BETWEEN THEM Allan Hendrickse and FW de Klerk have saved the country. They certainly have saved the Prime Minister's bacon. If Mr Hendrickse had withdrawn his Labour Party from the new constitutional dispensation, he would have done great damage to PW's new international reputation.

Mr Hendrickse and his party have a political clout that no "Coloured" party has had before.

The Government has referred the whole issue to a select committee and, as soon as the new Parliament meets, this will become a joint committee. (Ha! Ha! – no, sorry, I withdraw that.)

Is this real change? I have no doubt that it is. To some of us it is small change, but to the Afrikaner Nationalist it is a big change.

And it is change in the Afrikaner Nationalist that we want.

Mr PW Botha is entering a period of recurring crises. If they are all dealt with as this one has been dealt with, there is some hope for our future.

What will the next crisis be? Mixed Marriages, Immorality, Group Areas, Population Registration? I hope the last two rather than the first two.

I don't see much point in allowing mixed marriages unless one amends the last two Acts, which undoubtedly are the cornerstones of apartheid.

With great respect to brave Helen (Suzman) and my learned Judge-President, I don't think there is any point in calling at this time for a Bill of Rights, nearly every law on the statute book would be challenged in the courts.

Our judges would be worn out. Dear Vause Raw is right – there would be chaos.

The passing of a Bill of Rights would "ring the bells of Heaven the wildest peal of years". But it's a long way off. It would mean that a new age had dawned.

Do I think that people like Mr Hendrickse and Dr JN Reddy are going to participate in a giant "cosmetic" swindle? No I don't.

They are going to participate in something very imperfect, but I think they may teach Mr Botha some things that he doesn't yet know.

They may teach him that the Afrikaner fear of the African is something to be confronted, not evaded.

They may teach him that the myth of the "happy homelands" is the biggest evasion of all.

They may convey to him something of their abhorrence of the heartless programme of relocations and resettlements, which in themselves alone could destroy whatever good Mr Botha may have done abroad.

I have not touched on the gravest weakness of the new dispensation. Everyone knows what it is.

Perhaps Mr Botha's new colleagues may persuade him that it requires the most urgent reconsideration.

FW de Klerk was Minister of Home Affairs and National Education.

Wyatt Vause Raw (1921–) became leader of the New Republic Party in 1978 after representing the United Party in Parliament since 1955. He resigned as leader of the NRP in 1984.

Dr JN Reddy (1925–) served as Chairman of the Executive Committee of the South African Indian Council from 1973–80. In 1984, he established the Solidarity Party and was elected to Parliament for Glenview, becoming the leader of the Official Opposition in the House of Delegates.

Helen Suzman (1917–) is the longest serving Member of Parliament in South Africa, since 1953. She first represented the United Party, later the Progressive (1959) and then the Progressive Federal Party. Her attacks on South Africa's security legislation have won her world-wide acclaim as a campaigner for human rights.

AFRIKANER NATIONALISM AND ITS POLICIES

Afrikanerdom is trying to break out of the fortress that it built for its own protection.

I personally have forgiven Mr Botha for what he and his party did to us in 1968. What we were doing in 1968, he is trying – in his own way – to do.

Perhaps in dying, we taught him something that would take him 16 years to understand: that there is no future for South Africa unless we all – and that means all – work together in building it.

Sunday Times – *July 8, 1984*

Peter Brown Rebanned

NOT ONE OF US WHO has come here to protest against this second five-year ban on Mr Peter Brown knows the reasons why he has been banned. I myself do not know, yet I was more intimately associated with him in politics than anyone else.

He was the National Chairman of the Liberal Party and I was its National President. He never took any action that caused me any disquiet. He never concealed any action from me. He never lied. He never intrigued. Any kind of underground dealing was foreign – and is foreign – to his nature. Why then has he been banned again? is the question that we are asking. But before I try to answer it, let me say a few words about the meaning of banning.

It is the Minister who bans, and he bans persons because unrestricted they are a danger to the security of the State. Mr Peter Brown has been banned because in the view of the Minister he is a danger to the security of the State. If that means that he would, if he were freed, make plans to overthrow the Government by violence, or incite others to do so, or behave violently, then it is a nonsensical allegation. It cannot be challenged except in the way that we challenge it today. It cannot be challenged in a court of law, because banning, although it is a legalised process, is beyond legal challenge.

We have condemned before today this supra-legal process of banning and we do it again today. Another five years of a kind of imprisonment have been imposed on Mr Peter Brown. Yet his offence is unknown. He has not been charged with any offence. He has not been brought before any court and proved to be guilty. Yet a sentence of great severity has been imposed upon him.

One of the most inhuman requirements of this sentence is that he shall not attend any gathering and this has been interpreted by the courts to mean that he shall virtually abstain from social life.

One of the consequences of this is that the friends of banned persons begin to avoid them lest they cause trouble for them. It so happens that Mr Peter Brown likes people and their company, though I must admit that he likes some people and some company better than he likes others, a characteristic that he shares with most of us. Therefore, when I heard that the ban had been renewed, I experienced – as many of you did too – a feeling of grief as well as of anger.

One feels grief, not only because the whole pattern of a man's life, and his wife's life, and his children's lives, is being changed, but because the power that does it is a cruel power, seemingly inflexible, august in its majesty because it is the power of the State. Yet one feels anger also, because this power is puerile as well, in that it cannot abide opposition, it cannot abide those who criticise its policies. It reacts, not with gravity and dignity, but with a viciousness that ill befits so august an authority. The trouble is that the august power of the State is in the custody of a human Government, whose representatives are not gods, but humans. One of them has described the wives and families of African men as "appendages". Another has threatened the representatives of the South African Council of Churches that their cloth will not save them from his wrath. Another described a retired Chief Justice of the Supreme Court of South Africa as a mischief-maker.

Every free man is required to respect the lawfully constituted authority. Every free man recognises that there can be no freedom without order. But no free man gives a slavish obedience to authority, nor can he respect an order that does not respect the claims of justice. It is because Mr Peter Brown does not give a slavish obedience to authority, and because he does not respect an order that permits injustice, that he has again been silenced and restricted. We are not allowed by law to tell you what he has said, or to repeat or publish his words. But luckily we do not need to.

What we are saying here tonight are the things he would have said.

And he would say here unequivocally that he helped to found the Liberal Party because to him apartheid was a cruel and repressive policy, because separate development was to him only a new name for an old authoritarianism, because the existing order was unjust, because husbands working in our towns and cities (where their work was indispensable) were separated by law from their wives and children, because profits counted more than persons, because the working people of South Africa were denied a fair share of the wealth they helped to create.

Mr Brown sees clearly that the essence of separate development is not that it provides separate freedoms – that is the dream. In essence it is something done by people who have power to people who have none – that is the reality. (Some climb on the bandwagon so that they too can enjoy this power.)

It is not easy to criticize the lawfully constituted authority, nor to reject its policies. It is even less easy if one is law-abiding, if one has been brought up to be obedient and to have respect for authority. It may be easy for an anarchist, who does not believe in authority anyway. But it is not easy for a liberal, I mean a liberal spelt with a small "l".

And especially is it not easy, if for the first time in one's life one is kept under surveillance, and one's telephone is tapped, and one's mail is opened, and one's name is taken. One is accused (or one's party is accused, which is safer, but is really the same thing) of furthering the aims of Communism. And then perhaps there is the threat of a day of reckoning, and perhaps one can see that day coming, and one has to decide whether to stop protesting and criticizing, and to stop making common cause with those of one's fellow-countrymen who are of different race and colour from oneself, and to be good and be quiet and be nothing at all, so that the coming of the day may be staved off.

But perhaps one decides that one must not stop protesting and criticising, perhaps one decides it would be better to lie down and die than to yield one's meaning as a man, perhaps one decides that to be good and be quiet and be nothing is to betray those of one's fellow-countrymen who had made common cause, very often in the face of threats and loss and intimidation, perhaps one decides that that is what life is, not a time in which to be good and be quiet and be nothing, but a time in which to be true to the things one believes and to be true to those who also believe in them, even though it is going to change one's life, and the life of one's wife and children.

So if we grieve for Peter Brown and his wife and children, let us not grieve inordinately. There is no other way in which he could have lived his life. We may grieve for him, but would we have had him be something else? If he had been something else, then we would all have been impoverished.

There are those who ask, what good has it done? It has done a lot of good. It enables us to say, South Africa is a land of fear, but it is a land of courage also. Yet nevertheless, whatever evil, whatever good, has come of this, we are here to make our protest against this act of tyranny and inhumanity. Why cannot the Government say to a person whose ban is about to expire: "Your ban is not to be renewed, but we can impose a new one on the day we believe that your words and actions are a danger to the security of the State"? Why cannot they say that? Is there any reason, can there by any reason, for them not to say that? It at least allows some measure of freedom to the person whose ban is about to expire, to decide how he will live his life in the future. Who is the danger to racial peace, Mr Brown or Dr Ras Beyers? And which one walks free?

Let me say in conclusion that the onus for making South Africa a land of courage does not rest on Peter Brown alone. It rests on all of us, on those who know and respect him, on those of us who followed him when he was National Chairman of the Liberal Party. It rests on any one of us who loves South Africa, and wants to see her right not wrong, just not cruel, so confident in her cause that she need not deprive one of her best citizens of his freedom to try to make her cause better still.

A speech delivered in Pietermaritzburg on August 8, 1969

Dr Ras Beyers' appointment in 1966 as legal adviser of the Mineworkers' Union (the trade union for White mineworkers in South Africa) led to serious rifts in the union. His appointment was later set aside by the Supreme Court.

><><><><><><><><

Politics and Sport

IT IS FASCINATING to note that so many White South Africans who pride themselves on being realists, imagine that human activities such as politics, sport, literature, can co-exist without ever influencing one another. At long last it appears that politics and sport are inseparables, just as it is slowly dawning on some that politics and religion are also inseparables.

One thing is certain – South African sport is never going to be the same again. Those nasty demonstrators in Britain have seen to that. But it is quite absurd to believe that they brought politics into sport. We White South Africans did that long ago, and now – through our elected representatives – we have confirmed that politics and sport are going to stay together.

49

It is laughable and pathetic to see so many of our fellow-countrymen making fools of themselves over these issues. Miss Elsie Clayton, well-known for her anti-liberalism, writes to the newspaper expressing her contempt for the unsporting attitude of the demonstrators, and she does this a few days after the Government has refused to allow Mr Papwa Sewgolum to play in the South African Open golf tournament. A few days after that again, the Government refused to allow Arthur Ashe to come to South Africa to play tennis. And now comes the crowning absurdity. The police are investigating the affairs of the South African Soccer Federation, the largest soccer organisation in the country, which has no Colour bar in its constitution and whose clubs contain African, Indian and Coloured players. This investigation is being conducted by the police on behalf of the Group Areas Board, which has ordered several clubs belonging to the federation to report to the board bringing copies of their constitutions.

The federation has for a long time been the target of race fanatics who consider it offensive for Africans to play with or against Indians, or with or against Coloured people. The Johannesburg City Council smashed the federation's national soccer league when it – under pressure no doubt – closed the Natalspruit ground to all federation teams. Last year the police ordered the Klip River Football Association to expel its African and Coloured members. In Benoni, Johannesburg, and now in Durban, the police have conducted investigations.

It should be made quite clear that the police are not trying to prevent Indians, African, and Coloured footballers from playing together. They are only trying to prevent them from playing together on the same ground. It is as if the Immorality Act were not intended to prevent people of different races from sleeping together, but only to prevent them from sleeping together in the same place. And why should Afrikaners be allowed to play with or against the English, or the Hollanders, or the Jews? And why should the Zulus be allowed to play with or against the Xhosas?

It is fantastic that all this is happening on the eve of an election which is to decide whether the Government is to be given a mandate to pursue its "outward-looking" policies. The suggestion has been put forward that the Government will pursue a verkrampte policy until it has safely won the election, and thereafter will resume its verligte policy. This may well contain some truth. If it does, then it only emphasises the often baffling nature of the spasm which is convulsing Nationalist Afrikanerdom.

If the Government genuinely desires to pursue a more "outward-looking" policy in sport, then what is the point of this senseless threat to the South African Soccer Federation, news of which is certain to reach the outside world? This action, and the barring of Arthur Ashe and Papwa Sewgolum, and Minister Connie Mulder's blunder at Empangeni, where he said it was by no means decided that Maoris would be allowed to play in South Africa, have virtually put an end to South African participation in international sport.

And the blame lies fairly and squarely at our own door. One may feel sorry for the Springbok rugby players, and there is no doubt that they bore themselves with fortitude. But a great deal of the blame lies at their door also. If any of them opposed apartheid in sport, they have never come out and said so. The main blame lies with the Government, but White sportsmen throughout South Africa must bear it too.

The young man, by name Peter Hain, who spearheaded the demonstrations in Britain, is South African born. The Government can also bear the main responsibility for his actions. They treated his parents with vindictive cruelty, for no other offence than that they opposed the policies of apartheid with great courage and vigour. The Government will also bear the main responsibility if the Jacquessons join the anti-apartheid cause; they too were treated as no human beings should ever be treated.

Reality stands for abolition of all discrimination in sport on the grounds of race and colour. It believes that South Africa should be represented abroad by teams drawn from the ranks of her best players. It believes that sport in South Africa should be unrestricted. *Reality* condemns root and branch the Group Areas Act and the power which it has to interfere, not in the mere matter of location, but in every activity that occurs there.

If the White voters of South Africa wake up, we could return at once to the world of international sport. Will these events wake them up?

Alas, they will not.

Reality – *March 1970*

Verligte – enlightened
Verkrampte – conservative
Dr Connie Mulder was Minister of Plural Relations and Development.

Apartheid Is Self-Defeating

APARTHEID, WHICH HAD replaced segregation, has now in its turn been replaced by the policy and doctrine of separate development. This is something more than the remorseless separation of the races in every department of life where it was possible.

It is the theory that there are in South Africa many nations, and that they will never acquire identity or self-realisation or concord by being thrown together into the melting pot of a common society.

Especially will the less privileged groups never achieve it, for they will be exploited and forever doomed to an inferior position.

How much better if they try, and are encouraged and assisted to try, to achieve self-realisation in their own homelands, where they can have their own languages and control their own education and have their own churches and hotels and banks and above all their own Governments.

To achieve this, people must return to their own homelands and leave the desolation and heartbreak of their ghettos in the White cities.

For a time they may have to suffer deprivations, but these will eventually disappear, even as the power of the State will wither away in the perfect Communist society.

And the White people, too, will grow more generous as they grow less fearful, as the White cities grow Whiter and the Black homelands grow Blacker.

That then is the dream, the apocalyptic dream, of separate development. Have I any right to criticise it, who have an apocalyptic dream of my own?

For the common society is an apocalyptic dream, just as is the dream of separate nations, happy, equal, prosperous and living at peace with one another.

The believer in separate nations regards the believer in the common society as a sentimental idealist, and he points to India, Cyprus, Ireland, the United States of America.

Furthermore, he often regards him as actively or passively evil, as wittingly or unwittingly furthering the aims of Communism.

Communism he regards with horror, first because it is godless, second because it is equalitarian; the fact that it is totalitarian is much less important, because our rulers favour totalitarian measures when there is any threat to the security of the State, which means, as it usually means in most countries, a threat to the existing Government, and that means a threat to the policies of separate development, and that means in large measure, but not altogether, a threat to Afrikaner Nationalist supremacy.

The possibility that these homelands could ever achieve any kind of economic independence, or any kind of healthy economic relationship with White South Africa, seems to me to be remote.

The most valuable resource of these homelands is their labour, which they export to White South Africa. It is their labour that has built the reasonably strong economy of White South Africa, and it is only this reasonably strong economy that can enable White South Africa to press ahead with separate development.

Yet if she presses ahead with separate development, her aim must be the repatriation of Black labour, and this will reduce her own ability to press ahead with the programme.

In other words if you have separate development, you can't have it. This struggle between ideology and economics is continuous. It is for all the world like a tug of war, in which no-one dare win, lest all collapses. We like to talk of our traditional way of life, but it is very much ad hoc.

You may be sure that within the National Party there are grave misgivings that the programme of separate development is going too fast and too far, just as there are misgivings among the more idealistic Nationalists that it is not going far and fast enough.

Some observers say that there is a ferment inside the National Party, but we must remember that there are other observers who would regard it as nothing more than a slight simmer. Most of these would be Black.

It is true that the standard of Black living has risen during the last 20 years, but the ratio of Black income to White income does not change.

This is one of the things that concerns me most. For it is not only colour and race that separate man from man. The standard of living separates them just as much.

We do not so much fear the man who lives as we do. It is the man who lives on a scale far above us and far below us whom we fear most. This makes him more other than ever. And as long as we fear him for this otherness, we shall never live in harmony with him.

Individual man can overcome his fear of those who are so different, collective man never.

Those of us who have spent years of our lives in trying to reform a rigidly apartheid society, if we do not become totally discouraged, are continually trying to find ways of loosening this rigidity.

The creation of the Coloured Representative Council has by no means resulted in the creation of a wholly subservient body. Nor has the creation of the Transkei Territorial Authority (sic) resulted in this. It has, in fact, enabled the leaders of that authority to talk to the White Government in forthright language, the like of which has not been heard in South Africa since the banning of the two African congresses.

Now a new Zululand Territorial Authority has been created with the same results. Therefore, some of us who opposed separate development, and who founded political organisations for the purpose of opposing it, are now hoping that these new instruments of power which have been created by the supreme White Parliament will have an effectiveness far greater than that intended by their creators, and will bring about improvements in the political and economic status of Africans which would never have been brought about by that supreme Parliament acting alone.

The Star – *August 2, 1971*

※※※※※※※※※

We Must Act Quickly

ALAN: I SAY, PATON, what's all this about your seeing hope in separate development? Some people say you've gone crazy. Others say your mental powers are declining. Some say your passport went to your head. Tell me, are you now a protagonist of separate development?

PATON: No. I never was and I never shall be.

ALAN: Well what did you say then?

PATON: I said that the Government, after destroying all the opposition which they didn't like, had created new instruments of authority which they thought they would like, and my hope was that these new instruments, used skilfully, would bring results never foreseen by their creators, results of great importance to Black people.

ALAN: What sort of results?

PATON: Well, the first result, obviously, is that the Government, having destroyed all the political platforms they didn't like, then created three new platforms which they are not going to like either. Black people are telling them things which they couldn't say before without getting into big trouble.

ALAN: Do you think that's important?

PATON: It is of the greatest importance. The Government say to John Black: "Your limit is independence." And John Black says: "Good, now listen to me, I'm sick and tired of seeing people pushed around and I won't be pushed any more." This gives a boost to everyone who is tired of seeing people pushed around. Therefore it is to be highly praised and it is, whether you like it or not, a by-product of separate development.

ALAN: So you don't think the three chiefs are stooges?

PATON: I do not. I used to call Chief Matanzima a stooge, but I hope not to do it again.

His speech at the airport was full of truths that White South Africa needs to hear. It looks as though England has done one good thing for him, and that is to help him to get rid of his anti-British feelings.

ALAN: But he has very recently said that Nationalists were heirs to the British policy of segregation and are trying their best to improve it.

PATON: That's a very strange reading of history. I think he will have to think it all out afresh. Yet something more important happened to him. He saw apartheid for the first time as the outside world sees it, not as a noble scheme to "avoid clashes", but as an instrument of domination.

ALAN: What could that lead to?

PATON: It could lead to a radically different race policy in the homelands. This would affect White South Africa considerably.

ALAN: So you accept separate development?

PATON: I accept it as a fact of life. I accept that the policy is irreversible. It may not go forward as planned, but it will never go back. If, for example the United Party came to power, they might modify the policy, but they could never withdraw the powers that have been ceded to the territorial authorities, nor the public platforms they have been given.

ALAN: So you don't agree with those who regard separate development as a gigantic fraud?

PATON: The policy has strong fraudulent elements. It wasn't planned so that all men could be free. It was planned so that White domination could be maintained, world opinion pacified and Afrikaner idealism satisfied. It was the alternative to baasskap, but it contains within itself both the baasskap and the idealism. This tension runs right through the Nationalist Party and may lead to important changes.

ALAN: Do you honestly foresee the day when there will be eight or nine independent States, all economically strong, living in harmony together, in what we now call the Republic of South Africa?

PATON: Of course not. Nobody does. But I believe that the attempt to achieve such a goal may bring improvements in the conditions of Black men which they would never have achieved under a Minister of Bantu Affairs in a supreme White Government.

ALAN: What kind of improvements?

PATON: In the first place, education. The Territorial Authorities must press for free and compulsory education. They must argue that they can never administer or develop autonomous homelands unless their children are educated. They must ask for massive White South African aid. They must argue that White South Africa has free and compulsory education because Black South Africa has made it a wealthy country.

ALAN: What else?

PATON: In the second place the authorities must demand an end to the humiliations to which their nationals are subjected in White South Africa. They may be tempted to humiliate White nationals in the homelands, but they musn't yield to such temptations. However, Chief Matanzima should demand an end to the Colour bar in Umtata.

There is a third thing. Chief Buthelezi has inherited 29 fragments of the old Zululand. I don't suppose for one moment he'll get the old Zululand back. But he has a powerful case for consolidation. He has a powerful case for at least a joint control of Richards Bay.

ALAN: Do you really think they'll get these things?

PATON: Before I try to answer that, I want to mention one more essential. There can never be racial harmony in South Africa while the gap between White income and Black income is so stupendous. A White person earns six, seven, eight, nine, ten times as much as a Black one. The Territorial Authorities must exert ceaseless pressure on White South African and overseas industrialists to pay equitable wages. If they allow industrialists to enter the homelands, they must demand such wages.

You ask if they'll get these things. All I can say is that their moral case is extremely strong. And it is my belief that White South Africans are growing more vulnerable to moral demands.

ALAN: Why? Because they're getting better?

PATON: Not necessarily. You must never forget that White South Africa prides itself on being a moral and Christian nation. That is why moral arguments are so uncomfortable, especially when they are advanced by Black people.

ALAN: Do you realise that this programme you envisage would be regarded by activists, Black Power people and many students as just stalling?

PATON: Of course. But I am faced with the hard and ugly possibility that the activists, Black Power people and students are going to receive the pitiless attention of the Security Police, more so than now.

ALAN: Do you think they will be rendered powerless?

PATON: It is not absolutely certain. But they will certainly be rendered powerless unless there occurs some catastrophic event which will bring to an end the present local order of things. I am using catastrophic not to mean disastrous, but to describe an event of such magnitude that the order can never be the same again.

ALAN: What possible event?

PATON: I can think of two. The first would be the relatively sudden awakening of Black South Africans to the fact that they need no longer submit to being pushed around. The second would be a resurgence of anti-apartheid movements throughout the world.

ALAN: Why should such events happen?

PATON: They would happen – if they happen – because they had been triggered off by a preliminary catastrophic event in the world order.

ALAN: This is theoretical.

PATON: It's not theoretical at all. In fact, it has already happened, with the admission of China to the United Nations.

ALAN: Do you think that event is as important as all that?

PATON: Yes, I do. Activist movements in South Africa and anti-apartheid movements outside are disillusioned with America, Britain, France, Germany and even Russia. Now a new champion arrives on the scene.

ALAN: Have you told this to the Security Police?

PATON: You must be joking. They know it very well. What they don't know is that anti-Chinese speeches, trials of priests and terrorists and calls for Anglo-Afrikaner unity are futile.

ALAN: You sound very serious.

PATON: I am serious. As I see it, the Prime Minister is faced with a difficult choice, more difficult than any of his predecessors faced. Will he intensify security measures, or will he make some generous gesture to all those who have suffered under Nationalist race policies?

ALAN: You mean speed up the homelands?

PATON: That's only one urgency. Other urgencies are the revision of Group Areas, Race Classification, Job Reservation, Resettlement and the rest. But his greatest problem is what is the White homeland going to be like, with its 3 1/2 million Whites, 2 million Coloured people, nearly 1 million Indians and 8 1/2 million Africans? Are 3 1/2 million still going to rule a country of 15 million? You can't solve that problem by pretending that the 8 1/2 million belong somewhere else.

ALAN: You make it sound insoluble.

PATON: If your aim is to perpetuate White domination, then the problem is totally insoluble. The idea that White people acting unilaterally will solve South Africa's problems cannot be held any longer. Whatever we do, we should do it quickly. Mr Gerdener gives us till 1980. But if Mr Vorster tries to solve our problems by more detentions and more intimidations and more trials, the end of Afrikanerdom will be near.

Sunday Times – *November 7, 1971*

Change or Die

DOES A RULING GROUP change towards those it rules because of consideration of justice? The answer is, almost certainly, no. Does it change because of internal and external pressures? Possibly, yes. This second answer is not wholly encouraging. If the internal and external pressures become really dangerous, it may be too late to change. The people exerting the pressures may no longer care if you change. The time has come to destroy you.

But the answer is not wholly discouraging. A ruling group may consent to change while it can still influence the situation. It may realise that the way to survival no longer lies in resistance to change. It may see the clouds on the horizon and know what they mean.

There is a not very nice picture that comes often to my mind. A man lives in a house full of possessions. The poor and the angry and the dispossessed keep knocking at the door. Inside some members of his family urge him to open the door and others tell him that he must never open the door.

Then comes the final imperious knock and he knows at last that he must open. And when he opens, it is Death who is waiting for him.

And the man is me, my wife, our children; he is the White man; above all he is the Afrikaner.

But I am not writing to spread gloom. I am writing especially for those inside the house who are telling the man to open the door. I am writing for White students and priests and newspapermen and trade unionists, for Young Turks and the young people of the United Party and the National Party and the Progressive Party, for all those who are working for change in this implacable land.

Why on earth do they do it?

They do it because of those strange unweighable and immeasurable things like hope and faith. And I admire them for it in this faithless world where for many nothing exists that cannot be weighed and measured, a world that believes in so little.

What a strange thing, to have been away from South Africa for some months, from its threats and banning and denial of passports, and its impalacability, and then to want to get back to it again!

Some people would say: Of course, you want to get back, to your White comforts and privileges. Whatever truth there is in this it's not true enough. You want to get back because it's there that your life has meaning.

You want to get back to those stubborn things which are the very stuff of your life. You want to get back to the students and the priests and the newspapermen. They make you feel you are alive more than all the sights of Paris and London and even Copenhagen.

These young White people, the Young Turks, the young UPs and Progs and Nats, what do they want?

Well, at least it is clear what a great many of them want. They want nothing less than a new country. They have realised that White leadership and Anglo-Afrikaner solidarity and Afrikaner supremacy don't mean anything any more.

Nothing means anything at all if its architects and planners are all White.

I am no longer a party man, and I must confess my impatience with those who think that any existing political party can possibly hold the best, wisest, most practicable solution for our problems, or can possibly know the best, wisest, most practicable way towards such a solution.

Some of the computer-like arguments between party and party are exasperating. The house is burning down and the would-be saviours are arguing about what colour to choose for the buckets.

I don't expect younger White people to rush into a new party. But I do expect them to drop these useless recriminations.

Are there any things they might all agree about? I believe so and here they are. But I do not dogmatise about them.

1. The days of White domination are over.
2. The days of unilateral White political decisions are over.
3. The progress of the homelands to political independence – however much may be left to be desired – is irreversible.
4. The possibility that all or most of the homelands will eventually form a Black Federation must be recognised.
5. The possibility that the Black Federation may itself offer to federate with "White" South Africa must be recognised.
6. If it does not make this offer, or if the offer is refused, "White" South Africa will be assured.

7. The offer will not be made if "White" South Africa is not prepared to begin the dismantaling of the machinery of apartheid.
8. It is the political constitution of the future "White" South Africa that is the supreme political question facing all White people, especially young White people. When I say "young", I don't mean only students. I mean all who are young enough to know that we must change or die.

I beg to close with three questions to all White people who understand that we change or die.

Is there any future for apartheid in "White" South Africa? Is Afrikaner-English co-operation good enough, and is Afrikaner-English-Coloured-Asian co-operation not only unattainable, but downright dangerous? Is there any place for the qualified franchise in "White" South Africa, or is it only another of these unilateral gifts?

Change is in the air. It will come whether we White people like it or not. It won't — it cannot — be completely safe, completely sure, completely satisfying.

But it will be safer and surer and more satisfying if we take our share in bringing it about, in the company of all our fellow South Africans.

Sunday Tribune — *October 28, 1973*

In 1975, dissent in the United Party led to the expulsion of the Young Turks, a group of parliamentarians who were against the party's policy on Black-White relations. They established the Reform Party, which later amalgamated with the Progressive Party.

><><><><><><

My 50 Years of Afrikaans

I MIGHT BE CALLED a half-authority on Afrikaans, for while it is now 100 years old, I have spoken it for half that time. At school we learned the Dutch of Holland, and Dutch was one of the two official languages of the Union of South Africa.

But in 1925 Afrikaans became an official language and I, a 22-year-old schoolmaster, decided to learn it, partly because such competence meant a double increment in salary and partly because I had at that early age been infected by the bug of racial amity and co-operation.

I was later to be punished for having this disease, ironically by those on whose behalf I had contracted it.

To learn Afrikaans I went to Piketberg, to the home of Frikkie Burger who was my colleague at Ixopo High School. His family spoke no English.

For a week I toiled and struggled, sweating and groaning, and I thought I would give it up. Then suddenly I was on the plateau, beginning to move at great speed.

At the end of a mouth I was virtually bilingual.

Although my companions, who were the young farmers of Piketberg, were unilingual, they could swear in English as well as anybody. When I retaliated in Afrikaans with a "thunder and lightning" they were absolutely aghast; there is no other way to describe it. They beseeched me not to do it and promised not to use their own powerful English vocabulary.

By the time I left them I could read *Die Burger* with ease if not always with pleasure. This feat astonished my companions, for some of them found its Afrikaans at times incomprehensible.

Owing to my racial-amity infection, I was never able to see Afrikaans as a kitchen language, a vulgar patois, a language in which one called an entomologist a "gogga-ekspert", though regrettably there was such a word.

It was the language of my friend Frikkie Burger and if it was good enough for him and his family, it was good enough for me.

What was happening was that the Dutch language was being shorn of its pomposity and rigidity and solemnity and was being made into a supple and vigorous instrument, one of the simplest languages in the world, simple and more consistent than English and very much simpler than Zulu.

In my opinion many Afrikaners are far too sensitive about the metamorphosis of Dutch. They like to think it was brought about by some incorporeal something known as the "genius of language".

And, of course, it was, but the genius of language used many human agencies, and they must have been the Germans, the Huguenots, the Malays, the Khoikhoi, the servants and the slaves, and perhaps even those "passing soldiers and sailors". Some oversensitive Afrikaners like to think that the Malays and the Khoikhoi introduced a few new words, like piesang and donga.

But the influence of servants and slaves on the speech of the Dutch children must have been immense. One can well imagine the indignation of the mythical first parent who heard with horror the mythical first child say: "Ek is." And what does it matter anyway when you have produced one of the youngest and freshest languages in the world? And how did the Spanish produce Spanish and the French produce French?

There must have been much refined horror on the way.

It would be a fool or a philologist that would think it possible to discuss Afrikaans and not to discuss Afrikaner Nationalism.

For other people it just can't be done. My knowledge of Afrikaans, and of Afrikaans literature and Afrikaner history, increased again when I became principal of Diepkloof Reformatory in 1935. Afrikaans was the language of the reformatory and – may my sensitive friends pardon me – it was the language of the Black delinquent boy.

Although Afrikaner Nationalism outlawed the Liberal Party and inflicted grave punishments on many of my friends, I have never felt any animus against the Afrikaans language. It still remains for me one of the most vigorous and expressive languages in the world.

In 1972 Karel Schoeman published *Na Die Geliefde Land*, a novel which to me is a masterpiece. It is written in Afrikaans, but it speaks to me about my own country more powerfully than any other book has done.

It is – whatever the oversensitive critics say – the story of the death of Afrikanerdom. In Schoeman's story the language still lives on, but it is now the language of grief and desolation.

Will that be the fate of Afrikaans, of the language in which the aspirations of the Afrikaner were sung and spoken? May it be preserved from such an end.

But Afrikanerdom will have to show a wisdom and a courage greater than any yet seen in the course of its rugged history.

The Daily News – *August 8, 1975*

Na Die Geliefde Land – To the Promised Land

English-Speakers, Wake Up

IF ENGLISH-SPEAKING people don't wake up, we are going to be caught between the fires of Afrikaner and Black nationalism. Dr Jacobs of the UP says so, but I don't quite understand what this means. Must we wake up and get the hell out of here? Or must we wake up and try to put out the fires? Or must we wake up and get out of the dangerous middle ground, which means must we choose a side?

If things get bad, some English people will get out; more English than Afrikaners. This is not because Afrikaners are braver, but because their psychological and historical bonds are stronger.

Some of them say they could not live anywhere else, therefore they would rather die. This is what one calls hyperbole. Hyperbole is what one says before the event.

Must we choose a side? Some of our radical young may choose the Black side. They will be looked at askance by most of our other young.

Some of our older generation – what shall we call them? Pragmatists? – may choose the Afrikaner side.

These are the Horwoods and the Worralls. They will be looked at askance by most of the rest of their generation.

That's a fact of life. Mr Vorster says we've never been closer together. The fact is that we and the Afrikaners have lived for generations in a kind of love-hate relationship, in which the love has never been quite love, and the hate has never been quite hate.

We are now left with the third possible meaning of what Dr Jacobs said – namely, that we should wake up and try to put out the fires.

I shall assume that Dr Jacobs means that we have a constructive, a mediatory, a monitory role to play to prevent the Afrikaner elephant and the African elephant getting into a titanic fight, in which only the grass will suffer.

And we English and the Indian people, and to a lesser extent – I believe – the Coloured people, will be the grass. Our world will be a desolation for generations to come.

Some of my English friends were displeased when I once said that the two main actors of our drama – which may or may not become a tragedy – are the Afrikaner and the Black and that the rest of us are spectators. It was very hyperbole, I admit.

The roles of the English Press, of the universities, of Nusas (with its moments of aberration) of churchmen, are not the roles of spectators. They are important and they are going to continue to be important.

These bodies are not, however, representative of English-speaking South Africa.

The Right wing of Dr Jacobs's own party, the UP, cannot conceal its dislike of the English Press, or of turbulent academics and students and priests. The UP must bear a great deal of the responsibility for preventing the English from waking up. This advice to wake up comes, therefore, somewhat oddly from a UP man.

It is not only the UP that is to blame. The English people it so largely represents are equally at fault. The UP began with Afrikaner-English reconciliation in 1910 and, since that became irrelevant, it hasn't been able to find anything else.

Now shall we wake up, we the heirs of Magna Carta and Arbroath and Fairbairn and Pringle? We English-speaking people should be unanimous on certain things.

We should resist any interference with the Rule of Law. We should work for the opening of the universities, for the restoration of the freedom of speech and expression, for the elimination of poverty and the rights of all children to free and compulsory education.

Senators Horwood and Worrall should take time off from telling us how wonderful Mr Vorster is and go and ask him how he can endure to be the Prime Minister of a country that spends between R400 and R500 a year on the education of each White child and between R30 and R40 on each Black one.

And we should pursue Mr Pik Botha relentlessly and ask how he intends to discharge the obligation that he undertook when he promised the United Nations a year or more ago that we would move away from racial discrimination.

Are the English-speaking people going to succeed in their constructive, mediatory, monitory role? The answer is, no-one knows. The answer is, we can't stop trying.

One last word. There may be war. We all trust not. A few of us may refuse to fight. Most of us will do what is expected of us. Many of us will wish that we were fighting for a more just society.

But we don't want any advice about patriotism from the Nationalists. We know as much about patriotism as they do. We might be pardoned for thinking we know more.

Sunday Times – March 7, 1976

Dr Gideon F Jacobs (1922–) represented the United Party in Parliament. He is a former Director of the Graduate School for Business Administration at the University of the Witwatersrand.

Dr Owen Horwood was Minister of Finance and Mr Pik Botha was South African Ambassador to the US, combining this post with that of permanent representative at the United Nations.

Dr Denis Worrall (1935–) gave up a brilliant academic career to enter politics, but his support for a con-sociative democracy while being Chairman of the President's Council's Constitutional Committee, led to his posting to Australia and later to the UK as Ambassador. In 1987, he resigned and lost a dramatic tussle as an Independent during the General Election against the architect of the tricameral Parliament, Minister Chris Heunis, by only 39 votes.

Apartheid in Its Death Throes

DO YOU WANT TO KNOW what it is like to live under apartheid? Then you should really ask a Black person. I am White and the laws of apartheid are made by White people to preserve the privileges of White people. Therefore, the laws of apartheid weigh far more heavily on Black people than on White.

Do these laws weigh heavily on White people at all? Only in two respects. In the first place, the laws corrupt you. They corrupt you because they give a protection to four million White people that is denied to 19 million Black and "Coloured" people. But if you tell a Black man this, he could easily laugh his head off. He could say to you: "I'll change places with you any day. I'll choose any day laws that corrupt me rather than laws that push me around."

The law also weighs heavily on White people – some White people – who hate apartheid, who try to reject it in their own lives, who are every day reminded of the cruelty of the laws that they cannot change.

Your cynical Black friend will say to you: "I am very sad about your suffering, but you continue to enjoy all the protection of the

66

apartheid laws, all the days of your life." And he will be right too. If you lived a life of continuous disobedience to the apartheid laws, you would spend your life in jail.

What are the apartheid laws? They are like the sands of the sea in number. The be-all and end-all of apartheid policy is to separate the races in every conceivable place and at every conceivable time, provided such separation does not harm the economy and that means, to put it badly, the interests of Whites. Some exceptions are made, for example, in luxury hotels and on sports fields, but these can be made only with Government permission. The law will not say, for example, that Black people may not work in a White factory. But the law will say that there must be separate toilet facilities, separate change rooms, separate cafeterias, for White and Black.

Black and White are separated in residential areas, in schools and universities, in hotels and hospitals, in cinemas and theatres, on the beaches and in the national parks, on trains and buses. Certain kinds of employment are forbidden altogether to Black people. Intermarriage between Whites and Blacks is totally forbidden; sexual relations are criminal offences.

I cannot go with a Black African friend to theatre or cinema. But worse, I cannot even visit him in his home without a permit. And that would be difficult to get. The official assumption would be that something criminal or subversive was afoot. Strangely enough, it is much easier for my Black African friends to visit me. If my friend comes in the daytime, it would be assumed that he was coming to do some job about the house or garden.

One of the cruelest laws is the Population Registration Act. Every person must have a race. It therefore can happen that a person who has lived his or her whole life as White is declared to be "Coloured". Sometimes such a person commits suicide. A child is heartbroken because it has to leave a White school and go to another. Sometimes the child commits suicide too.

The most evil thing about the Population Registration Act is that if I have a grudge against a person living as White, and if I know his past history, I can inform the authorities in secret that he is in fact Coloured.

Why do we have these laws? We have them to maintain our White identity. We want to preserve our power and our whiteness. We are afraid because we constitute only 17 percent of the total population. Our basic motive is fear.

There are many White people in South Africa who will be angry with me for saying they are afraid. They are religious people and they want to believe that their laws are Christian. God made the races and therefore He wants them kept separate. He wants each race to achieve its own noble destiny. The laws may sometimes be cruel but the end is so noble that a little cruelty can be forgiven. In other words, Apartheid and Christianity are almost the same thing. We suffer from a terrible blindness that will not let us see that apartheid is not a grand and majestic racial plan.

Apartheid is an ugly thing, but you must not believe that the Black people of South Africa live lives of unrelieved unhappiness. All of us were born to this way of life, and in a sense we get used to it. But there are some – of all races – who protest against these laws. Some do it so vigorously that the authorities take grave steps against them.

Another thing. When the White men settled in South Africa, they set aside 13 percent of its area for Black homelands. One, Transkei, is now independent and the other homelands are moving towards political independence. None will ever achieve economic independence; all the wealth, the big cities, the industries are in White South Africa. This policy is called "Separate Development". To some extent it softens apartheid, because it gives Black people a place where they don't get pushed around so much. But the fact is not altered that most of the grown men have to work in White South Africa.

Yet, in one remarkable way, the whole apartheid picture is changing. On June 16, 1976, the great Black town of Soweto, satellite of White Johannesburg, erupted into death and violence. The Government likes to believe that the riots were caused by secret subversive forces, but the real causes were the discriminatory laws and the winning of independence by the Black people in Angola and Mozambique. Until these laws are removed, this bitter unrest will continue. On June 16, 1976, the Black people of Soweto and elsewhere suddenly realised their own power. South Africa will never be the same again.

On June 16, 1977, the anniversary of Soweto brought more rioting and death, but not on the scale that was feared. Has White South Africa been given a respite? And will it use it? On the answers to these questions our whole future depends. Perhaps even the peace of the world depends on it. That is why the United States is going to bring increasing pressure to bear on the Gov-

68

ernment of South Africa to make drastic social, political and economic changes. The life of apartheid is drawing to its end.

NBC TV Guide – *July 23, 1977*

xxxxxxxxxxxxx

Death in Detention

IT IS TIME TO BRING the scandal of death in detention to an end. The members of the National Party may think there's a funny side to it, but it threatens to bring death to them too, and to the Afrikanerdom they profess to defend.

The callousness of the Minister of Justice, Mr Jimmy Kruger, is beyond belief. What merit does he find in joking about death on an occasion such as this? What does it show – wit, toughness and a sturdy realism? Or does it show a stupidity also beyond belief?

What would the Nationalist reaction have been if a Black speaker had made similar remarks to a Black meeting on the occasion of the death, say, of a White Minister of State?

Their anger would have been extreme and they would have regarded such behaviour as a proof of the inate savagery of Black people.

Professor Marius Barnard has expressed the feelings of innumerable South Africans in his notable words:

"I have spent 30 years working with life and death, and no death has ever left me feeling cold or indifferent."

That is the voice of humanity speaking, not the mindless oratory that is poured out at party congresses.

If Mr Kruger is left cold by the death of a man in detention, then he is left cold. But he should not say so in public and certainly not on an occasion like this, when a great part of the nation is stunned with anger and grief.

In any case a Minister of Justice should never "be left cold" by death in detention. In the eyes of the world he is responsible for it. If I were Minister of Justice and a man died in detention, I would – however personally blameless I was – take the responsibility for it. But it is clear that the present Minister does not see things that way.

The sympathy of many of us – who are not left cold by this event – goes out to Mrs Steve Biko, her children and Mr Biko's mother. But our sympathy must go out to ourselves as well, and to our country, which assailed from without must be assailed by this bitter blow from within.

I have no doubt that the death of Mr Biko will take a place in our history alongside Soweto and Sharpeville and will be remembered when Blood River and the Anglo-Boer War have been forgotten.

It would appear that the laughing Transvaal congress has no conception of the gravity of this event. I like to think that there were some who did not join the laughter when the Minister was joking about death, not only because of its tastelessness, but also because they realised that the significance of this death was totally uncomprehended by this arrogant assembly.

The Government is making one thing more and more clear. They will treat with no militant Black leader whatsoever. They should have a respect for militancy, having had their own Strydoms and Verwoerds and Vorsters. But they do not. The destination of any militant leader is almost sure to be detention. Any Black man who thinks that he has a right equal to any White man to move about South Africa freely, and to share equally in its resources, and to share equally in its government, will end up in detention.

But there is a possibility more grave than that, the possibility that he may die there. When one examines the statistics, it does indeed seem to be a possibility. Twenty deaths in 18 months is a figure that cannot lightly be explained away. The people of the country are profoundly distrustful of the way in which the Security Police operate. And in my opinion they have every right to be.

If there is one thing that fills me with deep anxiety about the future, it is the apparent inability of our rulers to understand the consequences – for themselves as well as for us – of such an event as the death of Steve Biko in detention. If they did, they would not behave in the irresponsible fashion adopted by the Minister of Justice.

Professor Barnard also said: "But if a member of the Government insists on making a statement like this in public, then we may as well close all our information offices and cancel all publicity aimed at showing South Africa in a better light."

That is the simple truth. Mr Kruger is not just a Nationalist making jokes to the boys. He is my Minister of Justice and his behaviour fills me with shame.

The spring has come 74 times in my life. One of my greatest joys has always been to see the trees coming into new leaf and the hills changing to green. Our garden is always full of the sound of birds. But in these last two springs the joy has had undertones of grief.

Is this what one has lived 74 years for, to end up with Soweto and the death of Steve Biko? Visitors say: "Ah, but your country is beautiful." I have no doubt about that and I have no doubt in my mind that the Afrikaner Nationalists love it deeply. But they are loving it the wrong way.

Sunday Tribune – *September 8, 1977*

Jimmy Kruger (1917–1987) became notorious when, as South African Minister of Justice, Police and Prisons, he stated in 1977 that the death in detention of Steve Biko, a Black dissident leader, left him cold.

Professor Marius Barnard is a Progressive Federal Party MP. He is a former heart surgeon, the brother of Professor Christiaan Barnard.

Steve Biko (1946–1977), a leader of the South African Black Consciousness Movement, died in police custody. His death caused an international furore and in 1987 a film on his life was made by Sir Richard Attenborough.

≈≈≈≈≈≈≈≈≈≈

Scrap This Act

I DON'T KNOW WHO first made the profound observation that sex is here to stay. It seems to be incontrovertible. Sex has perpetuated, delighted and terrified human society ever since it was first invented.

With the passage of time, human legislators have come to realise their limitations in dealing with sex. Many of them came to realise that the punishment of the "offence" was often more harmful to society than the offence itself. Rulers and legislators have become more sensible, perhaps more humane. In countries like Britain,

Germany, France, and many of the states of America, a considerable measure of freedom is granted in the realm of sex.

Times Square, New York, has become a place notorious for its live shows and sexual aberrations. The new mayor means to clean it up, but he does not intend to abolish the shows and the display of aberrations. He thinks they should have a place of their own, but not in the heart of the city. Most Americans agree with him.

South Africa knows very little of this permissiveness.

The newspapers and the magazines are more daring than they used to be. Many of the advertisements for massage parlours are highly suggestive. The personal columns of some newspapers contain invitations which can only be construed as sexual. But we are still one of the strictest countries in the world in regard to the control of sex.

However, we differ from other countries in one striking respect. A sexual "offence" becomes many times more offensive when it takes place between persons of different race; or to be more accurate, when it is committed by a White person and a person not White.

The Immorality Act of 1927 forbade sexual commerce between a White person and an African. The amended Act of 1950 forbade sexual commerce between a White person and any person not White.

Has the Immorality Act had any deterrent effect whatsoever? It is almost impossible to answer such a question. There are probably some persons who are deterred by it. But in general it appears to have had almost none. The "offence" continues unabated. The number of offences reported has grown less, but that is generally supposed to be due to a change in police attitudes.

The punishments continue to be relatively light, except that in some cases the social consequences of the punishment, or even the social consequences of an acquittal, are catastrophic, even leading to suicide. These social consequences are felt almost exclusively by White offenders.

Has the Immorality Act had any beneficial social effect whatsoever? It would depend on the point of view. A harsh puritannical bigot would welcome the punishment of an offender as a right and proper act, contributing mightily to the status of our nation. If a White man commits suicide, that would leave him cold. If the wife and children are left ashamed and destitute, that is to be regretted, but it is not too high a price to pay for the maintenance of the lofty standards of the new immaculate nation. And tomorrow a similar tragedy would make it immaculate again.

For the rest of us, the Immorality Act had no beneficial social effect whatsoever. If purity can only be maintained by cruelty, then let us have a bit of dirt. Some of us may even jib a little, but ultimately a bit of dirt is better than this cruel self-righteousness which cloaks a psychological mess that doesn't bear looking into.

The Immorality Act often has another kind of tragic consequence. It cannot envisage any kind of loving relationship between a White person and a person not White. It condemns persons to enter furtive alliances or to go into exile. It is therefore in itself an immoral law.

And what about the other side of the Immorality Act? This cruel Act is also the joke of the nation. Excelsior does not mean Longfellow, it means the shame (with a snigger) of the Orange Free State. One cannot but admire the old renegade of the Western Transvaal who described the whole thing as "boeresport".

The Act ought to go, but it won't – yet. It's like many of the laws made by the National Party. It was made with a totally false idea of what one can do with political and legislative power. As an instrument of social value it has been a total failure. But it must be maintained because of the incomputable value of its witness to our morality. We'll vote for it even if we have to stagger to the polls.

Sunday Tribune – *February 12, 1978*

><><><><><><><><

30 Years of Nationalist Rule

THIRTY YEARS AGO on May 26, 1948, the National Party came narrowly to power. Today it commands nine out of every 11 seats in the House of Assembly.

From the very first it planned a new heaven and a new earth. The plan has at least two tremendous defects. The first is that it isn't going to work. The second is that it demands the sacrifice of what are called civil liberties.

In South Africa, Parliament is sovereign. Its laws cannot be struck down by the Supreme Court, except in the rare event that they conflict with the entrenched clause of the Constitution.

The Minister of Justice can, by edict alone, silence the voice, restrict the movements, control the associations of any person whomsoever, including one of his brother ministers if he wishes, though probably excluding his Prime Minister (a pretty case that would be).

It doesn't help for the Minister to assert that the Security Police are the finest body of men that ever walked the earth. He himself has now at last – after incalculable damage has been done to our reputation – acknowledged that detained people need protection. One would like to believe that he has done this out of humanity, but he has in fact done it because of the civilised world's abhorrence. Death in detention used to leave him cold, but it doesn't any more, though for the wrong reasons. It is my opinion that even if the Minister had not appointed watchdogs, the incidence of death in detention would have shown a sharp decline.

There is one other area of liberty that has suffered great erosion in the last 30 years. That is the area of communication, of writing, reporting, criticising, the world of the Press, the theatre, the book, particularly the novel. The minister can by edict destroy a newspaper or a magazine. If I remember rightly, the first Prime Minister to threaten the Press was General Hertzog in 1924. It has been threatened ever since and it will be threatened again. Each new threat means a further diminution of freedom. The freedom of the Press is not the freedom of journalists; it is the freedom of the citizen to know what is happening in the world and in his own society.

Is South Africa one of the most cruel regimes on the earth? I think the answer is, No: though a Black person might well answer, Yes. But its banning and detention laws are a disgrace to the Western world and a scandal in a Christian nation.

I cannot do better than close with an extract from *The Mentor* for February 1978. It records with "deep sadness" the death of Dr Richard Turner and it quotes from a speech by Martin Luther King.

"If a man happened to be 36 years old, as I happened to be, and some truth stands before the door of his life, some great opportunity to stand up for that which is right and that which is just and he refuses to stand up because he wants to live longer, or he is afraid his home will get bombed, or he is afraid that he will lose his job, or he is afraid that he will get shot, he may go on and live until he is 80 . . . and then the cessation of breath is merely the belated announcement of an earlier death of the spirit.

"A man dies when he refuses to stand up for that which is right. A man dies when he refuses to take a stand for that which is true. So we are going to stand up right here . . . letting the world know that we are determined to be free."

These are hard words but they are true. We have lost a lot of freedom in the last 30 years. But it's only when we don't stand up for it that we lose all.

Sunday Tribune – *May 21, 1978*

Dr Richard Turner, a former Nusas leader and lecturer in political science, was shot dead at his home in Durban in 1978. He was banned in 1973 and wrote *The Eye of the Needle*, a controversial analysis of apartheid. His murderer was never found.

∞∞∞∞∞∞∞∞

Crossroads: A Test for Survival

IT IS NATURAL AT a time like this for many anti-Nationalists to feel sympathy for the retiring Prime Minister. It is also natural to acknowledge that his successor will face problems of a magnitude never experienced by any of his predecessors.

These problems are nothing less than the future of South Africa and all its peoples. They include inescapably the future of Afrikaner Nationalism and of Afrikanerdom itself.

There are foolish people who still believe that Afrikanerdom can be preserved by the gun. But the truth is that Afrikaner Nationalism as it is now in 1978 cannot be preserved at all.

Who saw that clearly in 1974? No-one less than the Prime Minister himself. He promised us that he would surprise the world. But he didn't do anything of the kind.

Whether the task was beyond him or whether he came to believe that he had to choose between meaningful change and splitting the National Party, perhaps we shall never know. He has now bequeathed the dilemma to his successor.

Adam Small's background is not the same as mine. But I know well the anger and pain with which he writes. There is one thing I cannot understand about the Afrikaner Nationalists. Among themselves they observe the highest standards of conduct. But they seem to have little compassion for others.

It is true that they let Arthur Blaxall out of prison because of his age. They forgave the young students of the ARM because of their youth. They eased Helen Joseph's restrictions because of her health. But their race laws and their security laws have no element of mercy.

Mr Vorster was a champion of law and order, but it was in fact his law and his order. He regarded disloyalty to the State as the greatest of offences, but it has to be his State. Disloyalty to General Smuts's State was no disloyalty to him. The maintenance of law and order he put above any human consideration.

Can Afrikaner Nationalism change to survive? Or is it impotent to change? Did Dr Verwoerd bind it in changes from which it cannot escape? The test is here now, and it is at the place called Crossroads.

Is Nationalism going to tell the world that it needs Black labourers, but that it will only employ them at the cost of their family lives? Is it going to tell the world that compassion is a beautiful thing, but first and foremost the law must be upheld?

After their defeat in 1902, the Afrikaners showed extraordinary qualities of courage and resolution. You can see the same qualities in Crossroads today. But the Afrikaner was dealing with a conqueror suddenly turned humane. What Afrikaner was ever bulldozed out of his humble home when he trekked to the cities? And is he going to do it to others now?

Our new Prime Minister will assume office in a world increasingly hostile. Is he going to provoke its hostility still further by bulldozing Crossroads and subjecting its people to unpardonable police raids? Because that will be the effect of such action. For better or for worse, the eyes of the world are on his congregation of 20 000 souls striving to live decent human lives.

If there is ever to be peace in our country, if White South Africa is ever to atone for its cruelty and its arrogance, the Nationalists will have to search their hearts over the policy by which one uses a man's work and not only takes no responsibility for his wife and children, but refuses to allow them to be together.

Adam Small asks if this is perhaps a phase of wickedness working itself out – before the turn of the fever?

He says: "I do not think so, but I pray that it is." His prayer is echoed by millions of his fellow South Africans.

Mr Vorster said: "I thank my Maker for the chances and opportunity that I have had. I have had a full life and I am thankful for that."

Good and humble words, but they would be given a deeper and nobler meaning if they could be spoken by those whose homes are now threatened because these same changes and opportunities are denied them.

The Star – September 23, 1978

Adam Small (1936–) is one of South Africa's most important poets and playwrights who mainly writes in the Cape Coloured Afrikans idiom of his people.

The Rev Arthur Blaxall was sentenced to two years and four months imprisonment on charges under the Suppression of Communism Act in 1964. Already 72 at that stage, he only spent one night in gaol before the Government released him on compassionate grounds.

ARM – African Resistance Movement. An organisation of White university students and elements from the Left wing of the Liberal Party which resorted to sabotage before it was banned by the Government in 1964.

✂✂✂✂✂✂✂✂✂✂

What a Monstrosity

THOSE PEOPLE WHO ARE asking for another General Election are asking for the moon. Those who think that the National Party would lose 30 to 40 seats don't understand South Africa politics. Those who thought that the Prime Minister would emerge as a knight in shining armour just don't understand Afrikaner Nationalism.

In any event what is Afrikaner Nationalism? Judge Mostert makes a brave stand for the independence of the judiciary and talks about "the public interest", but feels that he must assert that he is an Afrikaner Nationalist. He doesn't understand Afrikaner Nationalism either, because there is no room for an independent Judiciary in a Nationalist framework. Consult the shade of Chief Justice Kotze, who was dismissed by President Kruger in 1898 for asserting the testing right of the courts.

Dr Willem de Klerk makes a brave stand for the necessity of freedom of information, and has delivered some trenchant remarkes about the necessity for probity in public life, but he also has to assure us that he is an Afrikaner Nationalist. He too doesn't understand Afrikaner Nationalism, because there is no room for an independent Press in a Nationalist framework.

A much better guide in these matters is Dr Connie Mulder. Where the safety of the country is at stake, there are no rules. That is the truth about supremacist nationalism, which Afrikaner Nationalism surely is.

Another good guide is General van den Bergh. He told the Erasmus Commission that if he wanted to do something, nobody would stop him, and that he would stop at nothing. This is the man who, before he became BOSS (Bureau of State Security), controlled the Security Police, one of whose members told an inquest court that he did not work under statute.

The lightweight companion of these two is Dr Eschel Rhoodie, but he is not a true Nationalist because he puts pleasure above the sacred value of the volk.

And that is the essence of Afrikaner Nationalism. The volk is the supreme value in the hierarchy. Every other value is subordinate, the integrity of Judiciary, of Press, the integrity of scholar or churchman, the great values of justice and liberty, even the great virtues, notably the virtue of compassion. If it serves the ideal of the security of the volk, you may bulldoze the poor and the voiceless out of their homes and possessions, you may separate a man from his wife and children, you may say to a man, I want your labour, but I don't want your family.

But the Nationalist is most often a Christian. How is he going to reconcile the bulldozing with the love of his fellow-man? There is only one way to do it. Christianity and Nationalism must be used, to make the monstrosity known as Christian-Nationalism. So is established the heresy that a man's greatest glory is to be the member of a volk. So we arrive at the specious conclusion that when we bulldoze a family out of its home, we do it not in the interests of one volk, but in the interest of all volk. No wonder that Black people often regard White people as a lot of hypocrites.

All of this has an older name of course. It is the doctrine that the end justifies the means. It is the justification of the Group Areas Act and the Population Registration Act and all the Security Acts. Mulder and Van den Bergh and Rhoodie have been caught out, but they were only carrying the fundamental doctrines a bit too far. They weren't giving Christianity its fair share in the monstrosity known as Christian-Nationalism.

I wouldn't mind if people like Judge Mostert and editor De Klerk said we are Afrikaners, and proud of it. But when they say we are Afrikaner Nationalists and proud of it they are giving the Afrikaner Nationalism a meaning that it doesn't possess. They are giving to it a meaning which the National Party has never given it, nor the Broederbond, nor the prophets Diederichs and Meyer and Cronje, nor indeed the present Prime Minister.

Is Mr P W Botha going to lead us into a new era? I find it very doubtful. He holds the heresy that a man's greatest possession is his membership of a race, a heresy I might add, which can be found nowhere in the Christian faith that he holds. No person who regards himself as first and foremost an Afrikaner is going to give any sense of security or any sense of belonging to 20 million other South Africans.

Sunday Tribune – December 17, 1978

Judge Anton Mostert was appointed as a one-man commission in 1977 to study exchange rate irregularities. During his research he stumbled across alleged irregularities in secret accounts of the Department of Information.

Dr Willem de Klerk, a former Potchefstroom University-trained theologian, was editor of Die Transvaler and Rapport, resigning from both posts after clashes with management. He coined the phrases verlig (enlightened) and verkramp (conservative) in Afrikaner politics.

General Hendrik van den Bergh (1915–) became well-known when he broke up the Rivonia conspiracy, through which the top echelon of the ANC leadership was imprisoned. He later headed the Bureau of State Security until his involvement in the Information Scandal led to his demise in 1978.

The Erasmus Commission was appointed to enquire into the activities of the Department of Information in 1978. Its report led to the fall of the Department's Minister, Dr Connie Mulder, and the resignation of Vorster in 1979.

Dr Eschel Rhoodie headed the Department of Information as Secretary. He was later gaoled for 12 years on charges of fraud, but was acquitted by the Appeal Court.

The Afrikaner Broederbond was established in 1918 to promote the interests of the Afrikaner nation. It soon became a powerful secret body manipulating the socio-political life of South Africa behind the scenes and is still regarded as the power behind the ruling National Party.

Dr Nicholaas Diederichs (1903–1978) was elected as South Africa's third State President in 1975. When he was the country's Minister of Finance, he became known throughout the world as 'Mr Gold' because of his confidence in the precious metal's future as an international currency.

Dr PJ Meyer was a former Chairman of the Broederbond, Chairman of the South African Broadcasting Corporation and Chancellor of the Rand Afrikaans University.

Professor Geoff Cronje (1907–) was head of the Department of Sociology at the University of Pretoria (1934–66) and of the Department of Dramatology (1965–72). He was one of the chief defenders of the apartheid principle on sociological grounds when it was adopted by the National Party in the Fifties.

I Erred in Good Company

IT IS QUITE TRUE that on May 17, 1980, I went to watch my first rugby game for 27 years. What's the matter with me? Have I ceased to have any principles?

Or have I become like the film tycoon Samuel Goldwyn, who after setting out his case to wealthy potential backers is said to have concluded by saying:

"Gentlemen, those are my principles and if you don't like them, I've got others."

Or worst of all, have I gone Nat?

The Liberal Party of South Africa was formed in 1953 and I was one of the foundation members.

We came together, people of all races, because we totally rejected the Colour bar.

We were a group of idealists, I admit that. We were more idealist than pragmatist.

Some of us wanted to get from A to Z and would have rejected to move from A to B.

Those were the radicals of our party. We never broke into liberals and radicals, nor did we ever break into free-enterprisers and socialists.

It was our common rejection of the Colour bar that brought some strange bedfellows together. This is the common lot of any political party.

The party never took a resolution that its members must not attend any Colour-bar game of sport.

It was a resolution that I took for myself. It was a sacrifice for me, especially as regards rugby, cricket and tennis.

But I still went to the theatre and the cinemas. I bathed on the White beaches, I borrowed books from the Colour-bar library.

Why should I choose to abstain from sport and not from the cinema? There is no logical answer to that question.

Mind you, I erred in good company. Two of my close political associates, members of the Indian Congress, were JS and HM. They were haters of the Colour bar, but lovers of cricket.

So what did they do?

They went to the cricket and sat in a segregated area. They used to smile at themselves for doing it, a bit wryly perhaps, but also tolerantly of themselves and their frailties.

I watched with great approval the attempts of Cheeky Watson and his brother to breach the Colour bar in rugby.

I listened with intense disapproval when Danie Craven said about four years ago, I think, that no Black would ever wear the Springbok colours.

I disapproved strongly of Gary Player when he went to see Dr Verwoerd to get advice on how to be an ambassador abroad.

I don't disapprove of them any more. They are converts.

I was converted a bit sooner, but I am also a convert.

I applauded the recent action of two White schoolboys, Afrikaans-speaking I would guess, who defied their headmasters and attended the Craven Week trials.

I applauded what happened in Bloemfontein when a senior citizen rebuked a young White player for playing in an open team.

The senior citizen was asked to leave. Five years ago it would have been the young one who would have had to go.

I applauded Butch Lochner, convener of the Springbok selection panel, when he predicted that a Black would get Springbok colours this year.

Most wonderful achievement of all is the Comrades Marathon, where runners of all races are cheered by spectators of all races.

Some people think I have gone ga-ga.

It is my nature, I think, and perhaps also my belief, to encourage any sign of social change, or to put it more seriously, any sign of amendment.

Therefore I decided to go and watch my first rugby for 27 years.

I decided not to wait for the total "normalisation" of our society.

81

But I had another reason, the same reason that allowed JS and HM to go to the cricket. I went there because I wanted to.

Sunday Times – *June 8, 1980*

Cheeky Watson, a provincial rugby player of the Eastern Province, attempted to break the Colour bar by joining a non-White club in Port Elizabeth before South African sport was desegregated in the mid-Seventies.
Dr Danie Craven (1910–) represented South Africa at rugby from 1931–1938 and has been President of the South African Rugby Board since 1957.

⋙⋙⋙⋙⋘⋘⋘⋘

Will the Next Jopie Be Black?

WHEN I READ IN MY paper that the play "So het dit gebeur", which is the story of Jopie Fourie, would be shown that evening on SABC-TV, I decided to watch it. It is a story that has always fascinated me, of the reaction in 1914, often violent, of so many Afrikaners to taking part in any war waged by Britain, the decision of Jopie Fourie and others to go into active rebellion, a course taken by him while he still held a commission in the Union Defence Force, and the order by General Smuts for Fourie's immediate execution.

So Fourie went to join the Valhalla of Afrikaner heroes for "rebellion" against the British. The first of these heroes were the five who were hanged at Slagter's Nek. Their execution was made all the more terrible because the gallows collapsed and the five men had to be hanged again.

According to FV Engelenburg, Prime Minister Louis Botha did not know of Smuts's decision to execute Fourie. If he had known, it is doubtful whether he would have intervened. The relationship between Botha and Smuts has had no parallel in our paliamentry history. Botha, whose education had been elementary, had the greatest respect for Smuts's intellect, and Smuts had an equal respect for the humanity and integrity of his Prime Minister.

Indeed Smuts's words at Botha's grave have in my view never been surpassed in history, and rank with the beauty and simplicity of David's lament for Jonathan. Smuts said:

"We came together with a closeness seldom vouchsafed to friends. This entitles me to call him the greatest, cleanest, sweetest soul of all the land – of all my days."

The rebellion was much more painful to Botha than to Smuts. Botha wept over the bodies of his old comrades whom he had killed on the battlefield. Smuts ordered, without visible emotion, the execution of Fourie.

I watched the film "So het dit gebeur" with absorption. The script was good and the acting was good. The sentiment was a bit overpowering, but for every Afrikaner, Fourie is portrayed as a hero, almost a saint. The officials of court and prison act correctly. There is no suggestion that some of them might be British.

The execution is carried out with propriety. The script and the direction had one considerable weakness and that was the miserable, almost snivelling, predikant who stayed with Fourie during his last hours. If I am ever condemned to death, may I be spared such a companion.

Well the film is over. I turn off the TV and sit and meditate. Nowhere has it been suggested that Fourie did anything dishonourable. He quite clearly had a right to rebel. He quite clearly disregarded altogether the teaching of Paul the Apostle that the powers that be are ordained by God and that whoever resists them is resisting the Ordinance of God. He was, however, in good company, for no less a person than Mr BJ Vorster was prepared to do the same in 1940. Let us face the truth of that somewhat cynical saying: circumstances alter cases.

The fact is the Afrikaner Nationalists – and they are by no means alone in this regard – revere the State, provided it is their State. Mr Vorster believed in law and order provided it was his law and order. Gandhi, the American rebels, the French rebels, Lenin – the list is endless.

The fact is that throughout history there have been men and women who believed that they had a right to rebel. To call Fourie a "rebel" really proves nothing. A "rebel" is always someone who rebels against you.

My thoughts then went to Robben Island and to Nelson Mandela. I do not see any difference between what Fourie did and what Mandela did. The idea that one is a patriot and the other a traitor is quite preposterous. Yet one gets a play on SABC-TV and the other grows old on Robben Island.

Will our next Jopie Fourie be a Black one? We are integrating the armed forces. What happens if we get a Black rebellion? Will the Black Jopie Fourie be regarded as a patriot or a rebel?

Have we learned anything from the events of 1914? Are we compelled to do it all over again? Does man learn anything from history? Is Mr PW Botha going to embark on a new course that will make it less and less likely that we produce a Black Jopie Fourie?

The responsibility that rests on him and his Government and on the Opposition can only be described as awesome. We have finished watching the film "So het dit gebeur". We are now going to watch the sequel "Sal dit weer gebeur?"

It promises to be painfully exciting.

The Star – *May 11, 1981*

"So het dit gebeur." – "So it happened."
"Dit sal weer gebeur." – "It will happen again."

❧❧❧❧❧❧❧❧❧❧

The Nat Weapon That Silences

THE RECENT BANNINGS of Mrs Fatima Meer and Mr Mewa Ramgobin raise again the whole question of the use by a Government of this remorseless weapon against its opponents.

Mrs Meer was silenced from 1954 to 1956 and again from 1976 to 1981.

No sooner had the second ban expired than she was banned again for five years.

In 1986 when she reaches the age of 56, she will have spent 12 years, not only in silence, but cut off from any kind of normal life, and denied many of those simple pleasures that make life more tolerable in a semi-totalitarian society.

Mr Ramgobin was silenced from November 1965 to November 1970 and again from September 1971 to September 1976.

His ban was renewed in September 1976 and expired again in September 1981. On the day of its expiry it was renewed until September 1986.

In September 1986, when he will be 53 years old, he will have spent 20 years of his life in political and social isolation.

I cite the cases of these two persons because it happens that they are well known to me. I have known them both for 30 years. Their tongues are sharper than mine, though in my palmier days my own was described as "venomous" ("venynig") by no less an authority on such matters as Dr Verwoerd.

I ask myself the difficult question, why was it necessary on the very day of the expiry of their bans to renew them?

They were given no chance to show that they had changed from baddies to goodies, nor to show that age had mellowed them, nor to show that a blinding flash of light had suddenly revealed to them the virtues of the doctrines of racial separation.

I have my own opinion as to why their bans were renewed almost automatically. But I must confess that I have no access to the thousands of dossiers, to the tapes of telephone conversations, to the secret-eye photographs of clandestine visitors. Nor do I have access to the new and fantastic machine which I could set up on my desk at Botha's Hill and which would enable me to know exactly what dark thoughts Mrs Meer is thinking in Durban and Mr Ramgobin in Verulam.

Therefore, although so ill-equipped, I venture with impudence and temerity, and with scant respect for the majesty of Dons (Department of National Security), to say exactly why their bans have been renewed.

Their bans have been renewed because of the sharpness of their tongues, because they won't go down on their knees before the State and also alas! because age has not mellowed them, at least not in the direction that would be pleasing to the Security Police.

Also they have gifts of political leadership and the Government is suspicious – and afraid too, let us face it – of any gift of political leadership that is manifested outside the Broederbond and the National Party.

Neither Mrs Meer nor Mr Ramgobin has ever made a bomb and neither is likely even to have thought of making a bomb. They are silenced for the simple reason that if they were unsilenced they could be expected to say exactly that they thought.

Neither has ever made a bomb, or ever thought of making a bomb. One could describe their lives as upright and honourable.

I find the fact that the Government silenced them both a grotesque comment on the state of our society.

They too were silenced, because they believed they had a fight, and more than that, a duty to protest against the Group Areas Act and the Population Registration Act and the Act which created separate universities, and the cruel and heartless destruction of the simple and humble communities that hardworking people had legally established in the so-called "black spots".

Our Government has always wanted to be regarded as a nation of the West. But its security laws are not paralleled in any nation of the West. Their like is only to be found in those nations which are ruled by Governments which are totalitarian or near-totalitarian in nature, whose policies and philosophies we find abhorrent and un-Christian.

Our erosion of the rule of law has placed us firmly in the company of those whom we regard as our enemies. We are nearer to Moscow than we are to London or Washington.

I think it was some two years ago that the Prime Minister promised us an inquiry into the whole matter of security legislation.

What had happened to it?

One thing is certain, we shall never be welcome in the Western community of nations so long as we continue to withhold from the courts those powers that properly belong to them, and are sacrosanct in any civilised and democratic country.

Sunday Tribune – *October 6, 1981*

Professor Fatima Meer, a sociologist at the University of Natal, was the first person to be banned under the 1976 Internal Security Act. Her banning order was extended for another five years in 1981.

Mawalal Mewa Ramgobin (1932–) became an executive member of the Natal Indian Congress in 1971 and co-treasurer of the United Democratic Front in 1983. Numerous banning orders were served on him and in 1984 he fled into the British Consulate in Durban to avoid being re-detained.

>>>>>>>>>>>>>>>>

Around a Totem Pole

MY FRIEND ASKED: "Have you heard?" I said: "No." He said: "They've split." No-one asked who had split, and no-one said who had split. We knew it wasn't Inkatha or the PFP or the Dutch

86

Reformed Church. We knew it could be only one thing, the great National Party that has ruled us for 34 years. Ruthlessly? To a large degree, yes. Justly? To a large degree, no. Compassionately? You could make a list but it wouldn't be very long.

So again the rest of South Africa downs tools and watches the Nats dancing around the totem pole. Where are they dancing to, life or perdition? There is not one person in the whole of South Africa who knows.

Is this split in the National Party an important event? Dr Van Zyl Slabbert says our politics have entered a "totally new phase" and that this event would have a profound influence on their future course. Chief Gatsha Buthelezi says it is "probably one of the most important political happenings of the past three decades". I have no doubt that both these men are right.

There is inevitably an element which will regard the split in the party as a totally irrelevant event.

They will regard the dancing round the totem pole as taking place on the fringes of our political life, while the real action is taking place among those who are not taking part in it. One understands this thinking, but it is totally unrelated to reality.

It is the kind of thinking, or rather wishing, which comes naturally to those who have for so many years reaped no reward at all for all the work they have done. I have thought that way myself.

I no longer think that way. I know that my political future lies, such as it is, for better for worse, for richer for poorer, and in sickness and in health, in the hands of the National Party of South Africa, established in 1914, broken and purified in 1934, re-united in 1939, triumphant in 1948 and torn with the dreaded broedertwis in 1982.

I have been reproached in the past for having opted out, but that is nonsense. For 13 years my friends and I were in active opposition to the National Party, until our party was outlawed in 1968.

Today, 14 years later, I am writing an article in which I express my concern for my country as actively as ever I did. Today, in 1982, the National Party rules large areas of my life, but the more important areas of my life it cannot touch at all.

But that's not quite true. It could take me into detention, deny me access to all human contact, interrogate me for countless hours. It could transport my naked and dying body in a truck from Port Elizabeth to Pretoria.

It could, in fact, commit the extreme offence that can be committed by any Government against God or any person. It could destroy my soul.

It will deny that it has ever committed any such offence. The fact is that the great majority of the people of South Africa do not believe it.

Chief Buthelezi warns us not to be too optimistic that this break will resolve the political jam altogether. He says it is difficult to predict what the Prime Minister will do. He could well move in the direction of reform, or he could be so afraid of losing more Right-wing support that he will mark time for the rest of his political career.

That is also my assessment of the dangers of the future.

A break in the National Party does not mean the emergence of a new, shining, intelligent, farseeing, civilised Government. It simply means, for the moment, the creation of two National Parties, both wedded to the idea of separate development.

Dr Nic Olivier, once a Nat, now a Prog, has warned Progs that if the Prime Minister makes another speech like the one he made at Upington in the good old days, they must not jump to the conclusion that he is now going to behave like a Prog.

He isn't. He's a Nat. He was born a Nat, and if you asked him he would say that he will die a Nat. His ideas of reform and change are therefore seen to have considerable limitations.

This is the most sombre view to be taken of the dance around the totem pole. You can see PW there, grim and unsmiling, but you can also see the pipe of peace sticking out of his pocket.

You can see Andries there too, also grim and unsmiling, but there's no pipe of peace sticking out of his pocket. In fact he hasn't got one. Being an intelligent man, he knows the word "peace" all right, but it is not part of his working vocabulary.

Can't we end on a more cheerful note? Chief Buthelezi says the Prime Minister "could well move in the direction of reform."

In view of all the circumstances, that's quite a strong statement. But I also believe it.

I believe that he WANTS to move in that direction. I believe that he has two very powerful men in his Cabinet who not only WANT to move, but they are determined that the Prime Minister is going to move too.

They are Dr Gerrit Viljoen and General Magnus Malan (don't get excited. I don't know either of them. But I can see both of

88

them dancing round the totem pole. They do not appear at this distance to be accomplished dancers, or even to be enjoying it. But I wonder who is?).

Now I must close, but if I had time, I'd tell you my biggest fear of all. My biggest fear is that there are deep, very deep, incompatibilities between the philosophy of Afrikaner Nationalism and the political philosophy of the West, to which in a strange way we still belong.

One of these deep incompatibilities is the role of the State in the life of the people it governs.

But that will have to wait for next time. Ah, I forgot. What's going to happen to the Broederbond?

Sunday Tribune – *February 28, 1982*

Inkatha, a Zulu cultural movement established in 1928, was revived and politically inspired in 1975 by Chief Buthelezi. One of its main aims is to establish a non-racial South Africa. Because it is against violence and disinvestment, it is scorned by the ANC and PAC. Inkatha claims membership of nearly a million.

Dr Frederik van Zyl Slabbert (1940–) became leader of the Progressive Federal Party in 1979 but resigned as leader of the Official Opposition in Parliament in 1986, arguing that Parliament had become irrelevant. Since then he has become active in extra-parliamentary politics, leading a mainly Afrikaner delegation of the Institute for a Democratic Alternative for South Africa (Idasa) to Dakar, Senegal, in 1987 to hold talks with the banned African National Congress.

Broedertwis – family feud

>>><<<<<<<<<<

A Verdict on the Volkswag

THE SPECTACLE OF NATIONAL Party bigshots condemning the Afrikanervolkswag for "politicising culture" is enough to bring tears to the most cynical eyes.

Dr Gerrit Viljoen said that the founding of this new movement was "an event of a political abuse of culture without precedent in Afrikaner history".

I shall mercifully assume that Dr Viljoen was too young to attend the centenary celebrations of the Great Trek in Pretoria in 1938. I shall also assume that he has forgotten that he was head of a powerful Afrikaner body whose aim was to gain control of both politics and culture.

89

I don't altogether relish the task of reminding modern Nationalist politicians of their discreditable past, especially when I believe that they are trying to be better. But they must not be too pious. I hear a rumour that our Prime Minister may be going to see the Pope, but I must say that I shan't believe it till I see it. If he does go to see the Pope, it will show that he didn't read the good old *Kerkbode* properly, especially when it was edited by the redoubtable Treurnicht, who must be one of the greatest living exponents of the "Roman danger".

Do I think that the Afrikanervolkswag is a danger to the country? I don't really think so. It might be ugly and unpleasant, but I don't think it is a danger in the sense that it might send Afrikanerdom back to the morass from which it is now emerging. I don't think we shall ever see Dr Treurnicht as our Prime Minister, nor Mr Eugene Terre'Blanche as a Minister of State. If by a chance, which I think is very remote, this gang came to power, that would be not the salvation, but the end of the Afrikaner. That would be the end of our return to the West, which even now is not all that certain. That would be the end of constructive involvement. At long last those forces which have threatened for more than 30 years to destroy Afrikanerdom and White South Africa would turn and rend us. That's what we could expect from Dr Treurnicht and Mr Terre'Blanche.

For a long time I have been distrusted by the radical Left and even by some of my former friends. This is because I have refused to recognise Mr PW Botha as a rogue. I have also refused to regard all his changes as "cosmetic". In fact, I resolved some time ago not to use the word "cosmetic" again except to ridicule it, because it is one of those words that saves one the trouble of thinking. I know very well that the Nkomati Accord was brought about by the iron hand in the velvet glove, but I would rather have to make do with the Accord than to make do without it.

Although I have poked fun at those Afrikaners who have forgotten how they used to speak and behave in the past, I do not poke fun at their present attempts to do better. And I would like to point out that one doesn't always do better solely for moral reasons.

I believe that Afrikanerdom is trying to break out of the fortress that it built for its own protection, because it realises that there is neither life nor future in a fortress. I believe that the great majority of Afrikaners (and the English too) were afraid to stand up for their moral beliefs in the days of Verwoerd, Vorster and Van den Bergh, and that they are now beginning to stand up for them. I believe that more and more Afrikaner Nationalists are beginning to believe that there is SOMETHING MORALLY WRONG in the Group Areas Act, the Population Registration Act and the Separate Amenities Act, and in detention without charge or trial or access, and in these heartless removals. I do not expect them to repeal them at once. I do not expect Mr PW Botha to turn into Van Zyl Slabbert overnight.

Mr PW Botha is soon going to travel to Europe. He is doing this for one reason that is above all others – he wants to return to the West. Let me put it more exactly – he wants to feel the security of belonging to the West. I hope with all my heart that he realises he can't return to the West unless he also returns – not all at once, I'm sure – to the moral and political values of the West.

When you come back, Mr Prime Minister, you must look very hard at the laws that you and your party have made in your discreditable past.

Sunday Tribune – *May 13, 1984*

Die Kerkbode – The official mouthpiece of the largest church in South Africa, the NG Kerk, or Dutch Reformed Church.
The Afrikanervolkswag was founded as a cultural movement for conservative Afrikaners after the split of the National Party in 1982, its members mainly supporters of the Conservative Party.
Eugene Terre'Blanche (1941–) founded the Afrikaner Weerstandsbeweging (Afrikaner Resistance Movement) in 1973. Since then it has grown strongly, its support mainly responsible for the Conservative Party becoming the Official Opposition in 1987.
The Nkomati Peace Accord was signed on March 16, 1984, between South Africa and Mozambique. Its chief clause contains a non-aggression pact.

⨯⨯⨯⨯⨯⨯⨯⨯⨯⨯⨯

The Alternatives

ALTERNATIVE FORMS OF constitution . . . This title was given to me by the Editor. Why does he suggest a title like that? Haven't we just been given a new constitution? Why, then, should we now consider alternatives?

The answer is simple. It is because of the guess, or the fear, or the conviction, that the new one isn't going to work.

In 1984 the Afrikaner Nationalists, despite strong Right-wing opposition, took what they thought was a brave and generous step forward. They received handsome support from the White English-speaking voters. But the response from Coloured and Indian South Africans was poor indeed.

This lack of support for the two new Houses is one weakness of the new dispensation. The other great weakness is that no provision is made for Black parliamentary participation.

This is because of the basic – and potentially fatal – flaw in Nationalist political thinking, the assumption that Africans will enjoy participation in the "homelands", and that the homelands have a viable future and will become satisfying places to live in.

There is also a potential weakness in the new dispensation.

Some, perhaps many, of the Coloured and Indian participants are hoping that they will change the mind of the Nationalists about Black parliamentary participation.

What will they do if they fail to change it? Will they walk out? The new Constitution makes provision for a walk-out. It empowers the White House of Assembly to govern alone. We shall be back to where we started.

Therefore, it is reasonable to discuss alternatives. What could they possibly be?

There is one alternative of which a great deal is heard, and that is a unitary State with a universal suffrage. That was the policy of the old Liberal Party of the Fifties.

It was the policy of a party with highly moral motives. I accepted the decision out of loyalty, not because I believed it possible. I am no longer a member of a party and therefore I am able to say that such a unitary State could be achieved only by revolution. And a sad unitary State it would be, of decaying cities, idle ports, broken-down railways and, worst of all, a destroyed agriculture.

The Nationalist rejection of the unitary State is – so far as we can see – final and absolute. Is the rejection of the federal State also final and absolute?

In the spring 1983 number of the journal *Leadership SA*, Mr PW Botha, then Prime Minister, replying to a question put to him, used these words: "This brings me to another idea that I have been propagating, which is a broader concept than what is generally understood by a 'constellation of States'."

This wider constellation would include a voluntary co-operation on transport, tourism, health services, veterinary services, conservation of water, utilisation of water and energy, etc. Such a constellation could have very useful talks.

Then we have what I term a "confederation of States".

A confederation of States is a more regular sort of co-operative commonwealth, if one can call it that. It is clear that Mr PW Botha, in using the word "confederation", was not envisaging the establishing of any kind of central Government.

The stress is on voluntary co-operation. One cannot honestly call this an advance in constitutional evolution.

The Progressive Federal Party also rejects the unitary State and majority government. It stands for a federation with decentralisation and separation of powers, and a Bill of Rights guarded over by a strong independent judiciary.

But constitution-making is not as easy as all that. The party proposes a "minority veto on vital levels of political decision-making", but says that this must not be seen as a "measure to preserve the privileged position of a minority at the expense of other groups in society". But many people see it as exactly that.

However, the PFP does not intend to impose its will on others. It will "when returned to power", immediately take steps to convene a national convention.

Until now the National Party has rejected the idea of a national convention.

That is because the party intends to keep control of any kind of constitutional evolution.

Some people entertain the notion that when the Government is "brought to its knees" it will call a national convention.

I do not think this is in the least likely. I do not believe that the Government will be brought to its knees in the near or middle future. And if it waits till it is brought to its knees it will be too late for any kind of convention.

Even if the PFP came to power, a national convention might prove to be a bitter occasion, nothing like the convention of 1908–1909, where the Afrikaners and the English had many common interests, not the least of these being the maintenance of White supremacy.

There is only one time for a national convention and that is now, or in the immediate future.

Therefore, this dream of sitting down together, which is my dream also, looks as though it will remain a dream.

It will be clear to my readers that, in my opinion, constitutional development, in the near and middle future, will remain in the hands of the National Party.

There is one other development that could be a part of our evolution, and that would be the acceptance of the recommendations of the Buthelezi Commission that Natal-Zululand be given a kind of semi-autonomy. I think it would work.

Race relations in Natal-Zululand are better than anywhere else in the country.

Such a move would take 5 million Blacks and nearly 1 million Indians off the Government's hands.

Is there any chance of it? Only if the National Party thinks that such a move would be in its own interests.

Our State President has just said that South Africa stands on the threshold of an exciting era of peace and prosperity for all.

Bishop Tutu has just said that President Reagan could act to bring apartheid to an end tomorrow.

Both of these statements are born of hope, and both have an extraordinary element of fantasy. The future is going to be far more complicated.

We are on a road that winds uphill all the way, and the one thing to do is to grit our teeth, gird our loins and walk it.

Will we make it? I don't know and no-one else knows either.

Sunday Star – December 30, 1984

The Ending of an Absurdity

IT SEEMS ALMOST CERTAIN that the Prevention of Political Interference Act of 1968 will be repealed this year. This Act of 17 years ago made it illegal for a person to belong, not merely to a mixed political party, but to any kind of mixed racial organisation which involved itself in political matters.

The Act was an example of the arrogant political excesses of the Verwoerd-Vorster era. Mr P W Botha in his new dispensation, however imperfect it may be, recognises the absurdity of making it a crime for South Africans of one racial group to associate with others in an attempt to plan for the future of a very complex society.

It should, however, be noted that Mr P W Botha himself created another absurdity known as "own affairs". But that is a difficulty that confronts every half-emancipated Afrikaner Nationalist. He wants things to be different, but he wants them to stay the same. He wants to be more just, but he wants to remain the boss. It just cannot be done.

Will the repeal of the Act bring about any change? Yes it will, but nothing overwhelming. It could bring about a closer link, or a fusion, of the PFP and Solidarity. It could mean the opening of the doors of Inkatha to all people. It could mean that the UDF might become a more cohesive organisation and might be able to spell out its policies and programmes more clearly.

Could the repeal of the Act bring about the launching of a new Liberal Party? I can't answer this question for anyone else but myself. My answer is No. The powerful motive behind the Liberal Party of 1953–1968 was a total rejection of the policies of apartheid and of the political philosophy of Malan, Strijdom, Verwoerd and Vorster. The powerful motive has gone. We are no longer confronted by an arrogant and relentless juggernaut, but by a shambling giant who doesn't know where he is going.

There is another reason why the Liberal Party could not be resurrected. For 17 years many young people who would have joined the party have gone to the PFP, the UDF, or to no place at all. Some have gone abroad. Some – and very brave they are – have gone to prison because they will not fight for a Colour-bar country, or for the maintenance of White supremacy. The political scene has altered beyond recall. I hear that Mr Ernie Wentzel, a leading member of the old Liberal Party, for whose opinion I have considerable regard, has said that "the time is not ripe" for a resurrection. I do not think the time will ever be ripe. I do not believe that any resurrection of any old party, or any fusion of any existing parties, or any creation of any new party, will be the salvation of our country. I believe that we need a new and bold approach to the whole question of the Constitution.

I think the New Dispensation is already obsolescent. It is too contrived, too artificial. It is too obviously an attempt to give and to keep it all. I do not see any hope for the future except in a Federal Constitution, with a Federal Government that is given the minimum of power. If the National Party is afraid of such a mighty task let it start by allowing either the unification of Natal and Zululand, or the creation of a federal link between them.

The repeal of the Political Interference Act of 1968 is a relatively small step. So would be the repeal of the Mixed Marriages Act and the racial clause of the Immorality Act (though the repeal of the first might mean a new life for some people). The real obstacles to the creation of a new South Africa are the Urban Areas Act and its pass laws, the Group Areas Act and the Population Registration Act, three giant pillars buttressed by the infamous security laws.

However, let me say that I welcome the repeal of the Act. I welcome the admission by our rulers that they have made serious mistakes in the past. I am waiting to welcome some word of apology, some act of reparation, to those people on whom they inflicted such hardship and suffering. They might as well do the job properly.

The Daily News – *June 4, 1985*

✕✕✕✕✕✕✕✕✕✕

Trying to Put Out a Fire

I WROTE JUST FOUR months ago for one of the great papers of North America that my country, South Africa, was in a mess. Well, it still is. A fortnight ago the Government declared a state of emergency in 36 of our 200-odd magisterial districts.

Does declaring a state of emergency do any lasting good? The answer is No. Does it do any temporary good? The answer is, I don't know.

The man's house is burning down and he calls in the whole extended family to fetch buckets of water. But some don't help, because they want the house to burn down. They never liked the house anyway, and it was they who set it on fire. There are others who don't bring any water, because they are afraid of those who started the fire. And lastly, there are those who are closest to the man, his loving wife and his own children, who answer his call and bring buckets of water.

It is a terrible dilemma to have your house burning down when you know that your urgent task is to make it a better house, to build on more rooms and make the whole thing like new. But you can't get on with building because you must first put out the fire. Your neighbours gather in the street and some of them curse you because you want to put out the fire. Some of your extended family try to obstruct you, and in your anger, or your fear, you knock them down. There is an outcry from the neighbours because you have knocked one of your family down. They threaten you will all kinds of punishments: they will cut off your food, they will knock holes in your buckets. But one of their threats makes your blood run cold. They threaten to cut off your water, they threaten to deny you the very thing that you need to save your house.

This parable, this story, this allegory, tells you what a mess we are in now. I could write it all in much better language, but I haven't the time to write it that way, nor have you the time to read it. This fire that we are trying to put out now has been smouldering for more than three centuries. It is the fire of conquest, the fire of the resentment of the conquered. It has broken out three times in this very century: in 1960 (Sharpeville), 1976 (Soweto) and 1985 (Uitenhage). The people of England were lucky. They were conquered in 1066 and then, with the help of time, they conquered their conquerors. That has not happened here. If there is to be any solution to our complex problems, we can certainly not depend on the help of time. But first let me answer the question: Was the declaration of emergency necessary?

I have spent most of my adult life in opposition to the Afrikaner National Party. Our present tragic situation is largely – not wholly – its own doing. But I think that the Government was forced to declare an emergency. The rule of the Black townships – if it can be called rule – was passing into the hands of radical scholars and students who had become impervious to the demands of reason, whose main purpose in life was to stone and burn and kill, whose main driving force was hatred – there is no other word – of all authority, whether White or Black. No Black councillor, no Black policeman, was safe any more. Black policemen and their families were withdrawn from many townships and given temporary accommodation in or near police stations. Buses, ambulances, offices, schools, clinics were all in danger.

97

Will the declaration of a state of emergency have any positive result? If you take into custody all those who start fires in the house, and who will not help to carry water, will you be able to put the fire out? and if you do put it out, what will you then do with those you took into custody? As I write, these are unanswerable questions. The declaration of a state of emergency is in itself a sign of defeat. Is the defeat temporary or permanent? That is also an unanswerable question.

Is a revolution imminent? Some people believe so; some want to believe so – but my answer is No. Those who want revolution are in no position to wage it. They could not wage it without outside help. And who will give that? The West? Or the USSR? Or, magic of magics, a joint USA/Russian task force, put together at Geneva later this year, no doubt?

No country in the world has a more enigmatic future before it than our own. At the moment I do not see any solution from within and I certainly don't see any solution from without. Righteous, and especially self-righteous, people from the West think they can in some way compel us to do better. I do not think for a moment that they will succeed. There is only one country in the world that will ever solve our problems – if they are soluble – and that is South Africa itself. I guess that will be true for another 10 or 20 years.

Reaction within South Africa itself to the declaration of a state of emergency has been diverse. The extreme Right (White) and the extreme Left (Black) both welcome the declaration, though for two diametrically opposite reasons. But the general – and what one would call moderate – reaction has been that such a declaration is of value only if it gives time for political and social and economic reforms, which must have two main objectives: one to give Black people a better life and the other to reduce the fear and hatred that at present play such a part in our lives.

Can it be done? Well, that's the question that I asked in the beginning. Nadezhda Mandelstam, who lived under Stalin's terror, wrote two wonderful books: First *Hope Against Hope* and then *Hope Abandoned.* We're still writing the first book here.

Sunday Times – *August 4, 1985*

Hope Deferred . . .

I HAVE BEEN THINKING A great deal over the writing of this article, and the dominant words in my mind come out of the Book of Proverbs. I remember them from my very young days, but it is unlikely that I understood them fully. The proverb is: Hope deferred makes the heart sick.

I don't think there is one person among my friends and acquaintances who does not know what these words mean.

We still hope against hope that our country will emerge from the darkness through which we are now living. That is the genius of language – to produce a phrase like "hoping against hope".

That is what most of us are doing now. Except, of course, those who have abandoned hope.

What have we White people done? Have we really created a generation of Black and Coloured children who actually hate us?

Whose idea of living is to burn, stone and kill? Who don't at this time see anything else to live for? Have we really done that?

Last week I attended the Reconciliation Initiative in Maritzburg.

I was told by a young White man from the Cape who does some kind of youth work that he had met young Coloured children who actually wanted to die.

When they were asked why they stoned and burnt and killed, one of them said: "Because we want to be killed, that's why."

This was a girl, not a boy, and she was 12 years old. It is bad enough when we consider what we have done, but it is worse when we ask ourselves if it can be undone. And if you think it cannot be undone, you fall into despair.

I myself am not inclined to despair, but I have certainly experienced moods of melancholy during these past few months.

I must relate a sad story about myself. At half past six in the morning my wife gets up to open the house and at a quarter of seven she brings me the morning paper.

On the morning of June 24 great headlines tell me that 325 people have died. Where did they die? In the Cape, or Port Elizabeth, or Soweto?

99

I force myself to read on and learn that they died when their plane crashed into the sea off Ireland. My emotion is one of relief that this tragedy happened in some other country.

What has our great fear been, a fear by no means confined to White people?

Our great fear has been that our country may become ungovernable. This word "ungovernable" has come to convey more fear than "violence" or "stoning" or "burning". What happens when the controls of society collapse?

There is no sign of collapse in the quiet village of Botha's Hill.

I go into our main street and it is full of people, the majority of whom are Black. They are going about their business, shopping and posting letters and talking and laughing.

I have lived here for 17 years, and many of the Black people call me "Mkhulu", which means "Grandfather".

Overhead every hour or so are the planes that fly regularly between Durban and Johannesburg. Everything seems peaceful and orderly, but the fear persists that it might all break down.

I have been a Prime Minister watcher for most of my life. I watch our State President very closely.

I have often stood up for him in the past, and I made some of my friends uneasy on this account. They need not have been. My brain is not softening.

All I want to see is our country emerging from the morass in which we have all been living. I believe the State President wants to see that, too.

I do not expect him fully to satisfy me, or the PFP, or the UDF, or the Black Sash, or the SA Council of Churches.

If I have learnt anything about the National Party in these past 37 years, it is that it will do things its own way.

I have never met the State President, but we have exchanged firm and courteous letters.

I am going to use this article to make some suggestions as to how the process of reform can be accelerated. If the Transvaal party congress can urge him to go faster – so I read – then I can do it, too.

Before I do this I want to comment on a report in a Paris letter that a military coup is imminent. It would be a triumph for Dr Treurnicht, a kind of Gotterdammerung. Surely our soldiers can't be as mad as that.

President Botha has said that he cannot issue a "declaration of intent" because that would prejudice consultations.

I think he is mistaken. All that is wanted from him is a declaration that his aim is the dismantling of apartheid.

He has said that he is not in favour of calling a national convention. I think he is right. It would in present circumstances be almost impossible to get a national convention.

It is time to stop looking back to the National Convention of 1908-09. It was called in quite different circumstances.

It was a convention of four White self-governing States with strong common material interests, and one other common interest – namely, the maintenance of White supremacy.

We shall have to feel our way forward to any kind of national consultation. I watch with hope the PFP's efforts in this direction.

The State President should announce that he earnestly desires the end of the state of emergency and that he will lift it the moment he is satisfied that the grave danger to life and property in the townships is decreasing.

How can he help to bring this about? It will be extremely difficult. His party made two cardinal errors in the Cape – it abolished the Coloured vote and it destroyed District Six. We are paying a heavy price for that today.

The State President should repeal the Group Areas Act. If any law has made us all strangers to one another, it is this Act.

But the State President has declared its repeal to be non-negotiable. He should not make such statements.

Nothing is non-negotiable today except the very foundation of society, the rule of law, which has suffered such damage at the hands of the National Party.

I don't think the State President is ready to repeal the Group Areas Act, but he should find it possible to set aside residential areas open to anybody who wants to live in an open neighbourhood.

The Government should release the Rivonia prisoners unconditionally. What they will then do is unpredictable.

But as long as they sit in prison much of the future is only too predictable. Will Mandela embark on a campaign of violence, or will he try to use his great influence to help bind up the nation's wounds? Here one must hope against hope.

There is one last thing that the State President could do to appease the wrath of the Western world. He could abolish detention without trial.

It was argued once that we could not afford the cost of so many courts and judges, but we nevertheless had money to appoint innumerable boards of control.

The trouble, Mr State President, is that your two predecessors, Dr Verwoerd and Mr Vorster, had more faith in policemen than in judges.

Mr State President, I wish you well in your position of great responsibility, and make these proposals to you with one thought in my mind: the good of our country.

Hope deferred makes the heart sick. Well, give us something to hope for.

Sunday Times — *September 22, 1985*

District Six, an old suburb close to the Cape Town city centre mainly inhabited by Coloureds, was demolished in the early Seventies under the Group Areas Act. The inhabitants were resettled on the Cape Flats and today the whole area is still virtually undeveloped.

The Rivonia Trial was the result of a police raid on Liliesleaf Farm, Rivonia, in July 1963, which led to the arrest of numerous members of the banned African National Congress. Eight accused, including Nelson Mandela, Walter Sisulu and Govan Mbeki, were sentenced to life imprisonment in June 1964 on charges that they wanted to overthrow the State through guerrilla struggle.

The Day of the Vow

ON DECEMBER 7, 1838, the Voortrekkers, knowing that Dingane was determined to exterminate them, or at least to drive them out of Natal, took the Vow that if God gave them the victory they would keep that day holy and regard it as a Sabbath. A second vow was taken, that they would build a church to the glory of God.

The Voortrekkers defeated Dingane on December 16 at the battle of Blood River. The Zulus lost 3,000 dead, the Boers had two men wounded, one of them their Commandant-General, Andries Pretorius. The battle was the beginning of the end of Zulu power.

Afrikaner fervour reached its peak in December 1938, the centenary of Blood River, when a quarter of a million Afrikaners gathered for the laying of the foundation stone of the Voortrekker Monument outside Pretoria.

The annual commemoration continued to be arrogant and exclusive, and reached its second peak in December 1948, the year in which the National Party came to power under Dr Malan. The Day of the Vow was now used, not primarily as a commemoration, but as an occasion to glorify the Afrikaner and his achievements and to strengthen his will to face whatever might come, even as Dr Malan said, a "second Blood River". This fervour continued under Strijdom and Verwoerd and then began to abate. Thinking Afrikaner Nationalists were beginning to question the wisdom and the morality of commemorating a victory over their Black countrymen.

Eugene Terre'Blanche, of the Afrikaner Weerbestand, looks with disfavour on any Afrikaner who begins to doubt his God-given destiny. He and 7,000 others renewed the Vow at Paarde-kraal this year. They are opposed to any programme of "reform", and therefore opposed to President P W Botha and the National Party as it now is. Terre'Blanche is aiming to become the leader of Afrikanerdom. If he were to achieve his aim, that would be the end of his people. Economic sanctions would give way to active military intervention.

Is there any fear of this? I think not. It is hard for me to believe that the Afrikaner people would choose a ranting demagogue for their leader. They have done their share of ranting in the past, but I would not describe any of their Prime Ministers as a demagogue. The Terre'Blanches probably contributed 10 to 15 percent of the 250,000 people at the Centenary celebrations. They captured the occasion, that is true, but it was a special occasion, highly emotional, and it will not recur.

Does that mean that Terre'Blanche is a person of no account? Unfortunately it does not. He and his kind – Treurnicht, Boshoff, Jaap Marais and the rest – have one powerful card to play. They may not win the game, but they can – so it would appear – paralyse their opponents. They can hold up the repeal or the emendation of the Group Areas Act. They could bring all the work of the Natal-KwaZulu Indaba to a fruitless end. They could so seriously impede the campaign for "reform" that new sanctions might be imposed.

Does that mean that the State President is afraid of the Right wing of Afrikanerdom? Does it mean that the Right wing, though opposed to "reform", will dictate its pace? I do not see what other conclusions are possible.

Sunday Tribune – December 4, 1986

Dingaan (also known as Dingane, 1795–1839) was king of the Zulu nation when Piet Retief, the Voortrekker leader, and his party were murdered by the Zulus in 1838. Dingaan was defeated by the Voortrekkers at Blood River in December 1838 and murdered the following year after he fled from his half-brother, Mpande.

⧓⧓⧓⧓⧓⧓⧓⧓⧓

The Frightened Voters

WELL, THE ELECTIONS have come and gone. Some said they were totally irrelevant, but they were not. They showed clearly the state of White South Africa. This revelation depressed many of my friends. It didn't depress me, but I am a stoic of many years' standing.

By "stoic" I don't mean a person not affected by passion or emotion. I mean rather one who accepts the fact of a situation without moaning. I concede at once that one's age has a good deal to do with this, although the virtues of courage and wisdom are also involved.

Why did White South Africans move so decidedly to the Right? Because they were frightened, of course, or to put it less bluntly, they wanted security. They decided that greater security was offered by the NP than by the PFP. There is no doubt in my mind that they were greatly influenced by the advertising campaign of the NP. These remarks apply more to English-speaking Whites than to others.

Afrikaners moved more spectacularly to the Right. They gave the CP more than half-a-million votes, while the NP received just over a million. If we accept that a sizeable fraction of these million votes came from English-speaking people, it would mean that the CP must have received more than 40 percent of the Afrikaner vote. That is a sobering conclusion.

The PFP had to pay for this move to the Right. Colin Eglin gave an interview to *Leadership* magazine just before the elections in which he spoke of the possibility of the PFP-NRP Alliance picking up another eight seats, whereas in fact the PFP-NRP total dropped by 10 seats.

He said further that "the concept of alternative government has caught on like wildfire," whereas it is the CP that has capitalised on the concept. Colin Eglin played a statesmanlike role in the elections and the results must have been hard for him to bear.

Would the results have been different if the PFP had played its cards better?

The answer is NO. White South Africans were going to move to the Right and nothing could have stopped them. The main reason was fear, of the ANC, of the UDF, of Cosatu, indeed of the future.

A second and lesser reason was the ill-advised sanctions campaign of the West. It may be possible to lead Afrikaner Nationalists, but it is impossible to coerce them. The West, and particularly the United States Congress, has made a grave error, it has undertaken a course of action the results of which it cannot foresee.

The NP dominates the White Parliament to an extraordinary degree. It holds 123 seats to the 22 of the CP and the 19 of the PFP. What is it going to do with this majority? Ambassador Koornhof told President Reagan that Pretoria placed its first priority in ending violence.

That is what many of us fear, that the Government's main instrument for the next two years (that is, to the next election) will be the police and the army. Neither the police nor the army are agents of reform; their job is to maintain the status quo.

The National Party will not look over its shoulder at the 22 seats won by the CP; it will look at the CP's half-a-million votes. Those of us who were hopeful that the Government would repeal (or greatly change) the Group Areas Act and the Population Registration Act will be disappointed.

So we shall have to be stoical.

The NP will reform at its own pace, and that will be slow. We face the almost certain possibility that the situation in 1989 will be much the same as it is in 1987.

People like myself will fervently hope that the 1989 election will not show a further growth in the CP. We will also hope that PW Botha will no longer be the leader of the NP, though whom will we get in his place?

It is now not likely to be Minister Heunis. Will it be General Magnus Malan? Or will it be Minister Gerrit Viljoen? Not likely. He knows more about the university than he does about the police or the army.

What is the future of the Independents? No-one knows. We know less about the future than at any other time in our history. The NP's present tendency is not so much to lose on the Left as on the Right.

And it would appear that the Independents are not likely to incline towards the PFP. Some cruel observer has said that it would be like marrying a corpse.

And the PFP itself? It clearly has no future as a White, privileged, professional party. Its only hope of providing an "alternative Government" is to become a non-racial party, representative of all the people of South Africa.

But it will be hard going, because such a campaign would meet with the antagonism of the UDF and Cosatu, just as the Liberal Party incurred the hostility of the congresses in the Fifties. We were accused of "dividing the people" and "blunting the revolution".

But in my view the PFP has no option. It is not very encouraging to think that they must now go through the same evolutionary process as the Liberal Party went through 30 years ago.

There is one actor in this drama I have not mentioned yet, and that is Chief Mangosuthu Buthelezi. He is still one of the most powerful figures on the political stage, fluent, extremely knowledgeable, impossible to buy (whatever some of his more foolish critics assert).

He will sit down and talk to PW Botha if another powerful figure, Nelson Mandela, is released. Our future would then depend on the relationship between the two men. If Mandela demanded, as his wife Winnie has already done, a complete handover of power, then White South Africa would have to go back to the police and the army, a melancholy thought.

Meanwhile, I hope that PW Botha and Chris Heunis will give earnest and favourable consideration to the proposals of the KwaZulu/Natal Indaba. At the present moment they offer the only hope to be seen on our dark horizon.

Is the horizon really so dark as all this? Has White South Africa jettisoned reform in favour of security? I don't think so.

Reform and security run like two contrary tides in the same sea. White South Africa – with the exception of the CP – is more and more convinced of the need for social and political change, but would rather trust the NP than the PFP to bring it about.

Therefore, the next two years will bring nothing spectacular in the social and political sphere. We shall do nothing much to please the West, who, in the mistaken belief that a ruined economy will lead by some kind of miracle to an African Utopia, will no doubt tighten the grip of sanctions.

Will the Afrikaner, having struggled so long with the Blacks and the British, now win the struggle with himself, or will he throw it all away? The answer to that question is the answer to the future of our country.

Sunday Times – *May 17, 1987*

THE TWO CULTURES

What the Nationalists expound with grim single-mindedness is accepted with resignation
by the English.

The "Unreliable" English

I ASK THE READER'S indulgence for two abbreviations used in this
article. I have used the word "English" to mean English-speaking
South Africans and I have used the word "Afrikaner" to mean all
Afrikaners except the dissenters, to whom I apologise. As Afrikaner dissent grows, it will be a usage less and less permissible.

So far as I know, there exists no study of the influence of the
English culture on the Afrikaans, nor of the influence of the
Afrikaans culture on the English. It is possible that there are
unpublished theses lying in the archives of our universities, but
it is hard to understand why no substantial study has ever been
published. In this brief article I do nothing more than offer a few
notes.

In my lifetime English political thinking has been powerfully
influenced by Afrikaner Nationalist thought. How much of this
influence is deep and permanent, and how much is a yielding to
necessity, one cannot say. It has been especially powerful in two
fields, that of race theory and practice, and that of the theory and
practice of law, the safeguarding of civil liberties, and the relationship of the individual to the State.

At one time the contrary influence was also strong, as can be seen in the lives and actions of Generals Botha, Smuts and Hertzog, but the incompatibility between British justice and South African racial policy existed even earlier than that, and indeed had come into existence more than 100 years earlier, at the time of the British occupations of the Cape. Since the coming of the Nationalists into power in 1948, the British traditions in both these fields have lost much ground and a great many English-speaking South Africans either have ceased to believe in them, or have acquiesced in their decline.

There is no overt Nationalist Party opposition to any interference with the liberty of the individual and the power of the courts. Opposition begins in the United Party, though its attitude is very far from *fiat justitia ruat caelum* and the strength of opposition increases as one moves further Left. What is more, the more radical the opposition, the more radical becomes the reaction of the Government and this development does not cause English-speaking South Africa much concern. The days are gone when one died for the rights of dissenters. In fact, the dissenter on the Left who has suffered under the hand of Government, can hardly conceal his pleasure when he hears the heartfelt cries of the dissenter on the Right, who now fears that he may have to take some of the medicine he helped to concoct.

The reasons for the strength of Afrikaner influence on English political thought are many. One is that it is more comfortable to be on the band-wagon than off it, even though one is not permitted to do more than give an occasional rat-tat-tat on the smallest drum. Another is that the race policies of Afrikaner Nationalism seem to be immutable, except for the names, and therefore one must accept them if one hopes to achieve anything at all. But I think that the most important reason is that Afrikaners and English-speaking South Africans share the same fear and that is of their Black fellow-countrymen and their Black fellow-continentals. Fear of the Coloured people has never been considerable and fear (and dislike) of the Indian people has much abated.

But the support given by the English to Afrikaner race policies and to the Nationalist concept of the State is not wholly dependable. What the Nationalists expound with such grim single-mindedness is accepted with a kind of cynicism and resignation by the English.

The number of English speakers who are real authoritarians is limited. They are all anti-Communists, that goes without saying, but in addition they are all anti-British, anti-American, anti-liberal, anti-student and certainly anti-Church when the Church becomes too critical of the State, and they constitute a high percentage of letter-writers to the Press, indicting epistles which cause the blood pressure to rise sharply in liberal and progressive arteries. Most of them espouse the cause of religion, but it must be establishment religion, confining itself to the worship of God and the things of the soul, keeping clear of politics and protest and showing a proper respect for the powers that be. These authoritarians evoke little warmth from the other members of their group and this gives rise to the Nationalist suspicion that the English would not be wholly reliable in an emergency, and that therefore they must be given no position of any real responsibility.

Why is it that while one acknowledges the power of Afrikaner political influence on the English, one still suspects that the English are not wholly reliable? The answer lies, I think, in their religion and morality. Roman Catholics and Anglicans and Methodists and Presbyterians increasingly are less puritanical; Sunday is for them a day of relaxation as well as of worship and, with exceptions, their priests and ministers take a tolerant view of mini-skirts, the moderate and pleasurable use of liquor, horse racing and the like. They counsel moderation rather than prohibition, and their ministers, especially in the country towns, have nothing like the power of the dominees. One can safely say that English religion and morality are more permissive than those of the Dutch Reformed Church.

It is this permissiveness that makes the English unreliable. Authority does not bear down so heavily on the individual. Dr Albert Hertzog is quite justified in believing, according to his lights, that only the Calvinists are reliable, although we should note that Calvinist scholars of repute maintain that Dr Hertzog's Calvinism is an aberration, notably in its espousal of apartheid and separate development. Dr Hertzog is abundantly right in distrusting the verligtes also, for they manifest in themselves the sign of English influence, a phenomenon with which we shall now deal.

There can be no doubt that a considerable number of Afrikaners envy the English their more permissive religion and morality and have been profoundly influenced by them. The mini-skirt wearers of Durban, and the long-haired boys, are often Afrikaans-speaking. So are the beauty queens and the Sunday beachgoers. I have no doubt that Mr Vorster would play golf on Sundays were it not for the rigid views of so many of his supporters. The influence of the English Press on the Afrikaans has been immense, as has also been the influence of what were once English monopolies, commerce and industry, banking and the stock exchange.

The Afrikaner world becomes day by day more like the English world. At one time the Afrikaner was in danger of becoming recognisably Anglicised; today the likelihood is just as great, but it takes place in a different way. The Afrikaner no more becomes an Englishman, yet he becomes less and less like the Afrikaner whose passing moves Dr Hertzog to a state of frenzy. We are Anglicising and Afrikanerising one another, that is the truth of it. I see little chance that either will swallow up the other. I see only an irresistible process of cross-fertilisation, which could be arrested only by Nazi methods. Luckily our authoritarian Government, though it can be callous and cruel, is not likely to exterminate dissenters.

If it is true that the influence of English permissiveness has powerfully affected the Afrikaner, is it likely also to affect Afrikaner authoritarianism? Is it likely that Afrikaner conformity will begin to decline, in politics, religion, literature and education? Is the increasing diversification in Afrikaner behaviour likely to weaken that political influence which the Afrikaner group has exerted on the English? Are Afrikaner students, for example, going to say that they are not satisfied to leave all racial contact to the Government? Are Afrikaner newspapers going to begin exposing national scandals like Limehill? Uys Krige and Leo Marquard are veteran dissenters, but Afrikanerdom continues to throw up others, Beyers Naudés and Bill de Klerks and Andre Brinks and those stout hearts who still belong to Nusas and champion it.

I have no means of conducting a reliable survey, but it seems to me that Afrikaner dissent is growing, not declining; and what is more, it is manifesting itself at a time when to dissent is more dangerous than it used to be. It is difficult to estimate the staying power of Stellenbosch dissent, and one may exaggerate its importance, but it seems to show that among young Afrikaners there are those who wish to communicate direct with their contemporaries of other races, and are not content to accept the services of official intermediaries.

Would the decline of Afrikaner authoritarianism cause also a relaxation of rigid race policies? Would a weakening of the young Afrikaner belief that father is always right, that the Party, the State, the Prime Minister, are always right, result in a serious questioning of all those Afrikaner dogmas that have determined Afrikaner conduct for so long? One cannot answer these questions with any certainty. The imponderables are too many. Let us conclude by looking at them briefly.

All over the world dogmatic belief is losing its hold on the human mind. The younger generations no longer take for granted the beliefs of the older. They want things to be proved and if they cannot be proved, they must not be believed. Dogmatic religion is adhered to by fundamentalists only, for the reason, conscious and unconscious, that they need something unquestioned and immutable to hold on to amidst the changes and chances of this mortal life.

But more and more people would rather face the changes and chances than accept the dogmas. In planning a journey to the moon there is no place for dogma and more and more human activity is of this nature. This means that there is a decay of authoritarianism in the fields of belief, custom, tradition, religion and morality.

Yet a contrary trend must also be recognised. In our own country in 1970 the mini-skirt flourishes alongside the BOSS Act and the threat to strengthen the hold of censorship. The governmental authoritarianism is by no means confined to the Communist countries. It is strong in Greece, Brazil and South Africa. It rests too on a dogma, namely that national need, national emergency, demand a measure of totalitarian authority. Those who hold this dogma are interested in power, those who oppose it are interested in freedom. Who wins? That is the question that I cannot answer.

And there is a third, and peculiarly South African factor, already alluded to, and that is the White man's fear of the Black. Would a decay in authoritarianism mean that politicians could no longer use the "swart gevaar" and the appeal to tradition as a rallying-call? Would a decay in authoritarianism be accompanied by a lessening of White fear? I have always believed that a narrowing of the Black-White income gap would lead to a lessening of racial tension, and it seems to be possible that under a declining authoritarianism the standard of Black living would begin to rise appreciably and that it would be accompanied by the growth of a stable, urban, property-owning, African middle-class, which would be conservative and non-revolutionary.

Indeed none of the changes discussed here, actual and potential, partake of the nature of revolution and they will not satisfy those who want justice tomorrow. Yet history may one day say that Afrikanerdom was saved from a final and bloody confrontation with its Black fellow-countrymen by the fact that Afrikaners had to live cheek by jowl with the permissive English, who, it appeared, had no interest other than making money. It's an odd thesis, but then previews of history are often unbelievable.

Fiat justitia ruat caelum – Let there be justice, may the heavens fall.
Dr Albert Hertzog represented the National Party in Parliament from 1948–70, but was dismissed from the Cabinet in 1969 because of his conservative views. He formed the conservative Herstigte Nasionale Party the following year. The HNP never won a seat in Parliament.
Limehill in Natal was one of the areas in which Blacks were moved on a large scale during Minister MC Botha's resettlement programmes of the Seventies. According to the plan the Government resettled many Blacks who were living in White areas, often breaking down their homes to move them to new regions.
Dr CF Beyers Naudé (1915–) resigned his post as Moderator of the Southern Transvaal Synod of the Dutch Reformed Church in 1963 and established the Christian Institute, which was banned in 1977. In the same year he was served with a banning order. He was banned again, but has since been unbanned.
"swart gevaar" – "black danger"

Afrikaners and the English

I USE THE TITLE "Afrikaners and the English" only for the sake of simplicity and brevity, because the fact is that White English-speaking South Africans have never acquired a one-word name. In my time, descriptions such as "Englican" or "Anglikaner" were proposed, but they never caught on, fortunately. So I call ourselves the English. I apologise to all those of Scottish, Irish and Welsh descent and I suppose I should apologise to the English, too. But I note in passing that the Afrikaners do not make such distinctions. They call us the English, "die Engelse".

That is the first important difference between the Afrikaners and ourselves. They have a name and we don't. Theirs was first used, so it is said, by Hendrik Bibault of the Cape as far back as 1707, when he defiantly told the messenger of the landdrost (magistrate): "Ik ben een Africaander." It means a member of the Afrikaner people, who also call themselves a nation. It is interesting to note that the South African English have never called themselves a nation. One has a name and the other has not. One is a nation and the other is not. The answer to this riddle lies in history.

The Afrikaner nation was born in the southernmost part of the continent of Africa where, on April 6, 1952, the Dutchman Jan van Riebeeck, with Dutch soldiers and Dutch burghers, arrived at the Cape to found a refreshment station for the ships of the Dutch East India Company on their long voyage from Holland to Batavia and back. The first progenitors of the Afrikaner were the Dutch, but other substantial contributors were later arrivals of Germans and French Huguenots; minor ones were the English, the Irish and especially the Scots, who in a time of dearth provided the Dutch Reformed Church with some famous predikants. The physical land, too, played a great part in the evolution of the Afrikaner and the Afrikaans language. The early trekkers moved further and further from Cape Town into a magnificent interior of mountains and plains. They moved with their ox-wagons, their manservants and maidservants, their cattle and their sheep. They were a religious people, and they not only read the Book daily but they found in the journeys of the Israelites a strong parallel to their own. The indigenous people of the country, the Khoikhoi (Hottentots) and the San (Bushmen), did not offer strong resistance to their advance. They either became servants, or retreated further into the interior.

To this land the trekkers gave a fierce and possessive love. They called a great part of it by its Khoikhoi name, the "Karoo". It is hard to imagine two parts of the world that are in greater contrast than Holland and the Karoo. Though often semi-desert, the Karoo was a land of space and freedom, of heat and rock and thorn, with oases of coolness and green. The new land not only gave new words to the language, but it gave new meanings to old words, the veld (open grassland), the kloof (ravine), the krantz (rock wall), the vlakte (plain). The trekkers had ceased to be Europeans.

It is my belief – poetic rather than scientific – that if one is to understand the northern Afrikaner, one must have some knowledge of the Karoo. It is a tough land and it produced a tough people. The ox and the thorn became part of the language and later part of the literature. The trekkers had little affinity with the people they left behind in the sheltered valleys and the fertile vineyards of the Cape. One can, of course, stress too far the differences between the Cape Dutch and those who had trekked into the interior, but differences there were. The trekkers were mastering a hard land, they lived by the Bible and the gun, their culture was of the flocks and the herds and the mountains and the sky; and many of them had come to cherish the invincible belief that it was God himself who had called them to possess this unbelievable land. The British, by waging the Anglo-Boer War of 1899, made the Cape Dutch and the people of the northern republics realise that they were one people, Afrikaners. And it was the fierce doctrines of the trekkers, bred of the life of the Karoo, that came to dominate Afrikaner thinking and in the end to rule, and rule relentlessly, all the other people of this southern land.

It is fascinating to consider the influence that the Karoo has had upon South African literature, of both the Afrikaner and the English. The first South African novel to gain fame abroad was Olive Schreiner's *The Story of an African Farm* and among its attractions were its descriptions of the Karoo countryside, unknown to the people of England. Some of the purest and most loved of all South African short stories are contained in *The Little Karoo*, written by Pauline Smith. The first volume of Guy Butler's splendid autobiography is entitled *Karoo Morning*. The Karoo provided much of the inspiration for CJ Langenhoven's *Die Stem van Suid-Afrika*, the poem which in 1957 was declared by Parliament to be the national anthem. Its first stanza runs:

Uit die blou van onse hemel,
uit die diepte van ons see,
Oor ons ewige gebergtes waar
die kranse antwoord gee,
Deur ons vergelate vlaktes
met die kreun van ossewa,
Reis die stem van ons
geliefde, van ons land,
Suid-Afrika

which can be translated roughly as:

> Out of the blue of our heaven,
> the depth of our sea,
> Over our eternal mountains
> where the krantzes give reply,
> From our remotest plains
> with the groaning of the wagons
> Rises the voice of our
> beloved, of our land,
> South Africa.

Before pursuing further the question of the historical evolution of the Afrikaner, one should stress more strongly the influence of the evolving language. In one way the Afrikaner made the language, in another the language made the Afrikaner. The fact that he had a language unique to himself did a great deal to strengthen his sense of identity, and eventually to develop his pride in being an Afrikaner, a new nation on the face of the earth. Dutch was the language of the first settlers, who were brought to the Cape by the Dutch East India Company in 1652. But gradually there developed a new language, later to be called Afrikaans. The striking difference between Dutch and Afrikaans lies in the extreme simplicity of the latter, the dropping of inflections, the omission of gender. The Dutch *de* and *het* gave place to a universal *die*. One of the most striking changes was from "I am, you are, he is, we are . . ." to "I is, you is, he is, we is . . ."

And how did these changes come about? Some Afrikaners are unduly sensitive on this point. The fact is that Dutch was spoken by hundreds of servants and slaves, and that hundreds of Dutch children spent hundreds of hours with servants and slaves. The linguistic changes that came about through the use of this "kitchen Dutch" were resisted by the Church, the older generations, the purists. But in the end the children beat them all. Some of these changes were being resisted as late as the beginning of the present century. (This is illustrated to perfection by the classic story of the Afrikaans *ek* and the Dutch *ik*. The old Cape statesman JH Hofmeyr, while not opposed to Afrikaans, thought that the use of *ek* was straying too far from the Dutch. He was voicing his objections to a group that included the young JH Hofmeyr, his cousin's son, the child prodigy of the Cape Province. Perhaps he thought that with the small genius on his side, the battle would be won. So the old JH said to the young JH: "What do you say, *ik* or *ek?*" And the boy replied firmly: "*Ek se ik.*") The Germans and the French, the English and the Scots and the Irish, bequeathed their surnames to the Afrikaner when they were themselves absorbed into the new nation and their children, too, began to speak the evolving language of the Dutch children.

So the Afrikaner nation was launched on its journey. But it was still to experience two tremendous encounters. The first was with the Black tribesmen of the eastern frontier; both Afrikaner and tribesman were cattle owners and they each required land. So began the series of conflicts which now are called the Frontier Wars. This time the Black rivals did not melt away like the Khoikhoi and the San. It would be true to say that during the Frontier Wars the Black man became part of the White man's mind, just as the White man became part of his. And there they have both stayed ever since.

The second encounter was with the British, first with the Governor and his officials who took over the Cape in 1806 and later with the settlers in 1820, who, with many accessions, were to become the English-speaking people of South Africa. The historian OK Freund writes that in the first decade of British rule the Cape administration espoused the cause of employers and slave owners. But the institution of the "Black Circuit", through which farmers could be brought to court at the instance of missionaries and Koikhoi servants, did much to destroy this relationship, as did the recruitment of Khoikhoi soldiers. Many of the missionaries were British, and the farmers had little time for them; the farmers wanted labourers but the missionaries wanted souls. The most famous of all the missionaries was the Reverend John Philip, who was superintendent of London missions in the Cape from 1819 to 1851 and whose name is held in detestation by many Afrikaners up to this day for his harsh criticism of the labour practices of his time. In 1815 came the Slagter's Nek rebellion, one of the most remembered events in Afrikaner history. A White officer accompanied by Khoikhoi soldiers was sent to arrest one Frederick Bezuidenhout, who had for two years defied the summons of cruelty. Bezuidenhout fired on the soldiers and was killed, whereupon his brother and friends went into open rebellion. Six of the rebels were sentenced to death and five were hanged. The gallows collapsed and they had to be re-hanged. This distressing event was to be remembered as a symbol of British oppression.

The Afrikaner farmers of the eastern borders became more and more disillusioned with the Cape government, its inability to control the depredations of Xhosa tribesmen and its susceptibility to the missionary lobby. In 1828 the Governor promulgated Ordinance Number 50, which gave new rights to Khoikhoi, San and Coloured (mixed race) people. But the final straw was the emancipation of the slaves; not so much the actual deed, as the circumstances under which it was carried out, circumstances which made it virtually impossible for any slave owner to get his lawful compensation. Anna Steenkamp, niece of the Afrikaner leader Piet Retief, made a statement which has become historic:

> And yet it is not so much their freedom which drove us to such lengths as their being placed on equal footing with Christians, contrary to the laws of God, and the natural distinction of race and colour, so that it was intolerable for any decent Christian to bow down beneath such a yoke, wherefore we withdrew in order to preserve our doctrines in purity.

So began the great northward migration that came to be called the Great Trek.

Afrikaner antagonism toward the Cape Government did not extend to the 1820 settlers. On the whole the relations between the two were good. Men like Piet Retief commanded the respect of the settlers and they were regretful when he decided to join the Great Trek. The patriarch Jacobus Uys also joined the Trek, and the settlers gave him a farewell present of a Bible. The border was restless and Professor EA Walker, in *A History of Southern Africa*, records that Englishmen in some cases withdrew westward "since they did not know how to trek". By September of 1827 some 2,000 souls, "the flower of the frontiersmen" as Governor D'Urban called them, had crossed the Orange River and had opened a new chapter in history.

The origins of the Afrikaner and of the new 1820 settlers were very different. The Afrikaner had been made in South Africa, the settler had been made in Europe, in the most powerful country of the age. The Afrikaner had the language of the rock and the thorn, of the vlakte and the krantz, while the settler had the tongue of Shakespeare and Milton. The anthem *Die Stem van Suid-Afrika* could hardly have been more different from "God Save the King", which became "God Save the Queen" at the very time of the Great Trek. The settlers concerned themselves a great deal about the freedom of the Press, an issue which would not concern Afrikaners at all until the 1970s. To put it succinctly, the Afrikaners' fierce attachment was to South Africa; the settlers' first loyalty was to Queen and Empire. Yet there were many similarities. The Sunday-best photographs of both groups of that time were very alike. The older men look upright and patriarchal, the women modest and virtuous.

The descendants of the 1820 settlers of the Eastern Cape Province and of the 1850 settlers of Natal all became known as "die Engelse". I am descended from the second group; my maternal grandfather came to Natal as a boy to go to school, where he was known as "Kaffir James", an appellation which was intended to be descriptive and not insulting. Some time after he returned he married my grandmother, whose eldest child, my mother, was born in 1873. My mother married James Paton in 1902. He was a Scot from Glasgow and had emigrated to South Africa in the strangest times, the years of the Anglo-Boer War. He did not come to fight, but to seek a new life in what were called "the colonies". He and my mother, who had never been outside South Africa, always referred to Britain as "home".

Their four children never used that expression. My own two sons certainly did not. My grandchildren would be astonished if their parents were to refer to Britain as "home". After all, where was "home" but the place where they lived? I cannot remember having heard a born South African talk of Britain as "home" for many years. Nevertheless, when I was a boy in Pietermaritzburg in the early years of this century, British Nationalist feeling was very strong. The ships of the Royal Navy, seen in majestic procession on the cinema screen, aroused inordinate pride in us children and the sight of the Royal Family could bring lumps to the throat and tears to the eyes. British Nationalism was equally marked in the nearby city of Durban, and indeed in Natal generally, although it declined as one travelled north. It picked up again in Johannesburg and on the Reef, due to the great influx of Britishers after the rich gold deposits were discovered in 1886. It declined in the platteland (countryside), picked up again in Kimberley, was strong in East London and Port Elizabeth, disappeared in the Karoo and picked up again in the Cape Peninsula. Also, there was a strong phenomenon in the Western Province: the existence of Afrikaners who were ardent British Nationalists.

The British Nationalists of the South Africa of 1902 did not realise that the Anglo-Boer War heralded the end of British imperialism and a sharp decline in British Nationalism. The granting of responsible government to the defeated republics of the Transvaal and the Orange Free State in 1906 and 1907 was a sign of the times. But Afrikaner Nationalism was not yet greatly feared, largely due to the policy of conciliation pursued by the two Boer generals, Louis Botha and JC Smuts. Smuts was called "the handyman of the British Empire", and all things British seemed safe and secure.

The Afrikaners and the English at last came together in apparent concord in the Union of South Africa in 1910, which brought the two old colonies of the Cape Province and Natal, and the two new colonies of the Transvaal and the Orange River, into a unitary State with Louis Botha as its first Prime Minister.

But there were Afrikaners who saw no cause for celebration. They had lost their republics, had been made British subjects and now had become part of the British Empire. They regarded Botha, who was the Prime Minister, and Smuts, who held three portfolios in his Government, as traitors, and rejoiced when General JBM Hertzog, who had been dropped from the Cabinet by Botha in 1912, founded the National Party in 1914. The aim of the party was clear: to encourage the growth of Afrikaner Nationalism, to separate Afrikaans children from all others in the schools and universities, to set up separate Afrikaner cultural organisations and eventually, by means of superior Afrikaner numbers, to capture the government. The more fiery of the Nationalists lived for the day when the Union of South Africa would become a republic, and the most fiery wanted a republic free of all connection with the British Empire.

Afrikaner Nationalists were angered by the way in which the English-speaking gave their first loyalty to the Empire and to the Royal Family. They were angered by the use of the word "home", by the words "colony" and "colonists" and by the expression "going out to South Africa". They objected to the use of the term "overseas" as it was applied by the British, signifying only travel from Britain to other countries. They resented the importation of bishops by the Anglican Church; these bishops criticised the racial laws and policies of the country and, when they had done their stint, returned "home" to retire.

The First World War caused a resurgence in Afrikaner and British Nationalism alike. The "true" Afrikaners were angered when Botha and Smuts took South Africa into what was a "foreign war". Some went into rebellion, which Botha took it upon himself to crush. The story was told that one of his trusty Boer War commandants, when he received a telegram from his old General calling on his services, replied instantly: "Certainly, on which side do we fight?" Captain JJ ("Jopie") Fourie, who went into rebellion without resigning his commission, was sentenced to death, and Smuts was never forgiven for his execution. In the election of 1915 the infant National Party secured 77,000 votes to Botha's 95,000, its success filling the British Nationalists with apprehension, which was deepened in 1924 when General Hertzog, with the support of Colonel FHP Cresswell of the Labour Party, led the National Party to an electoral victory.

The following years saw a rapid growth of Afrikaner consciousness. In 1925 Afrikaans was accorded equal status with English and Dutch, and Dutch soon disappeared from the scene. In 1926 the Balfour Declaration affirmed that Britain and the Dominions were equal in status. In 1927 Hertzog gave South Africa a new flag. In 1928 the Union concluded a commercial treaty with Germany. Each of these events struck fear into the hearts of the English-speaking, but they were reassured when Hertzog united with Smuts in 1934, in the great United Party. The leadership of "true" Afrikaners, however, passed to Dr DF Malan, who led 19 "purified" Nationalists in the House of Assembly. The centenary celebration of the Great Trek, held in 1938 and characterised by wagon-treks from many parts of South Africa to Pretoria, was the occasion of a tremendous resurgence in Afrikaner patriotism, but it was the patriotism of Malan, not of Hertzog, that triumphed. Malan Nationalists came to dominate the cultural life of the Afrikaner.

The powerful Afrikaner Broederbond, which had been formed as a cultural organisation in 1918 with a membership confidential and confined to male Protestant Afrikaners, now began to exert great influence in every sphere of Afrikaner life, including the political. When the Broederbond was attached, it compared itself to the Sons of England and the Freemasons. The comparison was absurd. Hertzog, and later Smuts, regarded the Broederbond as an enemy of what might be called "South Africanism". During the Second World War Smuts declared it a political organisation and banned its members from the public service. This ban was lifted when the National Party came to power in 1948. From that time onwards the Broederbond grew more and more powerful; Broederbonders today hold almost all the prominent public posts in South Africa, including those in the Cabinet. Who rules the country? It is a pointless question, for it is impossible to separate the Broederbond from the Government.

The English have none of this nationalistic and commemorative fervour, and they never will have. There is no single historical bond that can draw them all together. To them, history means something quite different from what it means to the Afrikaner. They are, therefore, said to be supine, money-grabbing, materialistic. But they are not. They just do not have the urge – which for the Afrikaner seems to be an historical necessity – to find an identity. It is true that each group has its national monument in South Africa, one the Voortrekker Monument in Pretoria, and the other the Settlers Monument, built much more recently in Grahamstown; but the two buildings have little in common except – if I may coin a word – their monumentality.

In 1938, at any of the centenary meetings, the shouting of "vryheid" (freedom) would be taken up by the great crowds and would bring the proceedings to a temporary stop, just as at many meetings of Black people today the shouting of "amandla", the Zulu word for "power", can do the same.

The apprehension of the English was increased by the Voortrekker celebrations, but their waning British Nationalism was given a boost by the Second World War. Their heroes were Smuts and Churchill. Afrikaner Nationalists fell into disarray. The British and their allies won the war. South African British Nationalism rose from its sick-bed and inspired thousands to cheer the Royal Family on its tour of South Africa in 1947. That – in my view – was almost its last kick. On May 26, 1948, when Dr Malan and the National Party, aided by Mr NC Havenga and his Afrikaner Party, came to power, it received the *coup de grâce*. From that day, Afrikaner Nationalism entered a new, vigorous, exciting age. The Nationalists now had power. At long last reparation was to be made to the Afrikaner for what Smuts had called the "century of wrong". At long last the separation of the races, apartheid, in every possible place and at every possible time, would become the law of the land. There would be a new heaven and a new earth.

Some Afrikaners hold the view that it was the declaration of the Republic of South Africa in 1961 that put an end to South African British Nationalism. But it was already dying then. When the Liberal Party was founded in 1953, many of its members were English-speaking, but I do not remember that one of them looked to Britain and the Empire. It was South Africa that commanded our allegiance, and it was the challenges of South Africa that we wanted to meet. In 1981 the British Nationalism of the English-speaking South African exists no more. But we still do not think of ourselves as a nation. In 1953 we of the Liberal Party pledged ourselves to a South African Nationalism. We spoke English, but we were South Africans first. "True" Afrikaners found our wider patriotism intolerable. They urged us to find an identity. They had found theirs and look how happy they were! They pitied anyone who had no identity. In the end, in 1968 through the Prevention of Political Interference Act, they made our wider patriotism illegal. They outlawed the Liberal Party. They made it illegal for any person of one official race group to make common political cause with any person of another race group.

It is quite true that the English-speaking do not today have an identity. They do not appear to think it important. It is ironic that it was under an Afrikaner Prime Minister, General Smuts, that they appeared to have one, and it is a mark of his greatness that he was able to hold such diverse elements together. The White English-speaking people of South Africa have only one thing in common and that is their language. They consist of many groups. They are those who are attracted by any South African who holds the same ideals as they do. There are those whose whole life appears to be bound up in business. There are the rich, whose children go to schools for the rich. Many of them support the Progressive Federal Party and the New Republic Party, the successor to the United Party. Some support the National Party, and if they achieve prominence thereby, they are regarded as having done something rather reprehensible. And there are a great many English-speaking people who just don't want to know, and don't want their children to know either. While Smuts was alive they could leave it all to him. We are a mixed bunch, and we don't have the bonds that bind so many Afrikaners together; we never had a Karoo, we never trekked, we never developed a new language, we never were defeated in war, we never had to pick ourselves up out of the dust.

The Afrikaners had been prepared for the great day of Nationalist power by their prophets, who taught them that a man's greatest possession was not his individuality but his membership of a nation. Dr N Diederichs, later the State President, taught that the nation contained the essence of being human: "Love of nation is not in the first place love of people, territories or states, but rather love of the ever-prevailing values, on which the nation is based." For the Afrikaner, what were these values? They were the doctrines of which Anna Steenkamp had written, and they were to be preserved in purity. Those English who also believed in ever-prevailing values could not accept these doctrines, and the other English didn't go in much for doctrines anyhow. Dr PJ Meyer, once chairman of the Broederbond, taught that not only the individual, but also the nation, as part of Creation, has been called by God. He wrote: "The Afrikaner accepts his national task as a divine task, in which his individual life-task, and his personal service to God has (sic) been absorbed in a wider organic context."

So Afrikanerdom embarked on its national task of reconstructing the entire South African society, observing a rigid separation of the races but affirming its intention to guarantee that each group would maintain its own identity, preserve its own language and culture and where possible rule its own territory. This was not possible for the Coloured people, but they would be removed from the common electoral roll and be given their own independent institutions, so that they need no longer have to suffer the humiliation of being the hangers-on of the Whites. To this great end, law after law poured out of Parliament: the Mixed Marriages Act, the amended Immorality Act, the Group Areas Act, the Population Registration Act, the Bantu Education Act, the Separate Representation of Voters Act and the law which would stamp out all over-zealous opposition, the Suppression of Communism Act.

The Afrikaans commentator, WA de Klerk, wrote the following remarkable passage in his book, *The Puritans in Africa:*

Never in history have so few legislated so programmatically, thoroughly and religiously, in such a short time, for so many divergent groups, cultures and traditions, than (sic) the Nationalist Afrikaners of the second half of the 20th Century. Never has such a small minority of all those affected done so with such a high sense of purpose, vocation and idealism. Never has such a volume of criticism been so wide of the mark.

For almost all of it was directed against the 'harsh oppressive policies' of the Nationalist Government: against the 'tyranny of apartheid'. *It was ineffective because it did not understand that the manifest harshnesses, the patent injustices, were all the oblique but necessary results of a most rational, most passionate, most radical will to restructure the world according to a vision of justice, all with a view to lasting peace, progress, and prosperity.* [His italics.]

These extravagant words may appear true to an Afrikaner Nationalist, but they will not appear true to anyone else. Non-Afrikaners, including the English, find it impossible to believe that manifest harshnesses and patent injustices have anything to do with a vision of justice. I do not regard the English as morally superior to the Afrikaners, but they would feel extremely uncomfortable if their harshnesses became manifest and their injustices became patent. The present rulers of South Africa are more inflexible than we could ever be. I have never been able to understand how a religious people, for such I believe the Afrikaners to be, can at times lack all compassion. I cannot understand how a Christian minister can, as in South Africa has happened more than once, refuse to conduct a funeral service for a White member of his congregation because Black people have come to the church to pay their last respects. Nor can I understand how any Minister of State can allow his servants to bulldoze the pitiful shack of some Black family and to turn out women and small children into the pouring rain. It must be added that there are welcome signs that many Afrikaner Nationalists, too, are beginning to find such actions abhorrent.

Anna Steenkamp, writing nearly 150 years ago, had expressed what is still the driving power behind Afrikaner Nationalism; doctrines which were to have been preserved in purity, but which in the last decade have come under question from Afrikaner students, intellectuals and editors, which has never happened before. They had always been questioned by liberal Afrikaners such as Leo Marquard, one of the first vice-presidents of the Liberal Party and a South African delegate to the United Nations Educational, Scientific and Cultural Organisation; but he could be ignored – for one thing his conceptual language was English. More painful was the criticism of Dr CF Beyers Naudé, a leading minister and theologian of the great Nederduits Gereformeerde Kerk, now an outcast, silenced, a "banned person" in terms of the Internal Security Act.

The Afrikaner justifies his veneration for the State through St Paul. "You must all obey the governing authorities: Since all government comes from God, the civil authorities were appointed by God, and so anyone who resists authority is rebelling against God's decision." But circumstances alter cases. When, in the days of the Second World War, General Smuts headed the Government, many Afrikaners did not find it necessary to obey this injunction. Now that the State is *their* State, they find it necessary, not only for themselves, but for all others. But the English, though many of them can be as scared of the State as anyone else, do not regard it in the same religious light. The law is there to be obeyed, but if you think it is unjust you may, if you wish, protest against it. Many of your fellow English will regard you as an extremist and your action as "going too far, old boy", but only the most rabid would regard you as a traitor and a Communist. So also the English do not have the Afrikaners' extreme regard for law and order. They do not want to rule everything and everybody. In general they are readier to accept the injunction, "live and let live".

I do not wish to end on a note of self-congratulation. I am simply reporting what appears to be a characteristic of the majority of English-speaking people. I cannot, however, claim that it is a characteristic of theirs to cry out against injustice, though some of them do. In spite of the example of Thomas Pringle and John Fairbairn, who fought strenuously and successfully against the autocracy of the first English governors of the Cape, many of them are indifferent to the freedom of the Press, and some are hostile to it. Though some have it in great measure, they are not notably characterised by moral courage: indeed, one of the greatest examples of moral courage in White South Africa is Beyers Naudé, an Afrikaner. But his courage has not earned him the admiration of Afrikanerdom. Afrikanerdom has thrown him out.

Have the Afrikaners and the English grown closer together in the last 80 years? The answer is both yes and no. White South Africans have been living together in almost complete civil peace since the end of the Anglo-Boer War. The reason for this is not altogether a lofty one. The fact is that the respective material interests of English and Afrikaner have over the years grown more and more alike. Our external enemies, Russia, Cuba, Nigeria, the United Nations, the Third World, the anti-apartheid movements, the Dutch Government, the Swedish Government, even the Government of our erstwhile sister-dominion New Zealand, make no distinction between the Afrikaners and the English. To use the present Prime Minister Mr PW Botha's exaggerated words, together we face a "total onslaught".

Yet the "total onslaught" is also a decisive factor. Many of our young White men, when they are called up for military service, cannot help asking why there should be a total onslaught. Are not the racial policies of the National Party Government its direct cause? Why must a young man who is not a Nationalist and who is, in fact, opposed to the racial policies of the Government, why must he go to fight and perhaps lose his life in defending these policies? Is he really fighting for his country, or is he, in fact, fighting for the National Party and for the doctrines of apartheid? Many of these young men are totally unmoved by the argument that they are fighting against world Communism, against godlessness, and for human freedom. They ask whether human freedom is embodied in the Group Areas Act, the Mixed Marriages Act, the pass laws.

They are also unmoved by the argument that Russia wants our great mineral wealth and they use the answering argument that Russia would not dare to eye our mineral wealth unless we had made it possible for her to pose as the champion of the oppressed Black peoples of South Africa. Most, though by no means all, of these doubters are English-speaking, though there is no means of accurately determining the racial composition of the young men who question military service. It is not considered a fit subject for investigation. In fact, the discussion of the rights and wrongs of military service is also not considered a fit subject. Mr PW Botha has said that the honour and duty of military service "should not be made subservient to one's religious convictions". This is a very extraordinary observation to be made by a professing Christian.

The patriotic enthusiasm of most young Afrikaners is assured. They will go to fight for their country and to repel those evil forces that threaten it. Their reasoning is – in general – highly simplistic. But why do the young English go to fight? I have pondered this question long and earnestly. Some go because of simplistic zeal, but I should say not many. Some go because they feel it a duty to defend their country, just as their fathers and grandfathers did in 1939. But I have come to the conclusion that most of them go either because they cannot claim to have conscientious objections, or because they do not want to leave South Africa and go into exile. They go because that is the law and they do not have strong enough reasons to defy it.

That both Afrikaners and English have a true love of country I do not doubt. But the Afrikaner's love is in general more fierce, more emotional, more aggressive. This does not make him braver or better than anyone else. It is his history that has done it to him. I am not a believer in historical determinism and I believe that parts of one's historical heritage must sometimes be questioned and sometimes disowned. I acknowledge that my forefathers did not fight Black warriors in 1838 or British soldiers in 1881, so in my history I have no Blood River and no Majuba; and that therefore I cannot feel the same about South Africa as the zealous Afrikaner feels. I acknowledge also that I don't want to.

Can these, fairly deep, differences be reconciled? I do not know, nor do I think that it is a very important question. There are much graver ones waiting to be answered. South Africa in a sense is a parasitic society, White on Black, Black on White. Such a society cannot endure. The affluence of White South Africans has become a danger to them and the greatest danger would be if they resorted to military force to maintain it. I believe that more and more Afrikaners are awakening to this pitiless truth. The Great Plan of which WA de Klerk has written, the great edifice of which the late Prime Minister HF Verwoerd was the chief architect, undoubtedly is now falling to pieces about us. The racial separation which was to bring harmony and peace has brought instead an alienation and an estrangement between White and Black which should terrify us all. The common material interests that have brought the Afrikaners and the English together hardly exist in respect of White and Black in modern South Africa: though some progress has been made in reducing the "wage gap", the standard of living of the average White is still several times as high as the average Black standard. So long as these conditions prevail, there will be no chance whatever that White and Black will ever share a common South African loyalty.

The future of both the Afrikaners and the English is uncertain. Most of the responsibility for this uncertainty is their own. In the circumstances there is only one sensible thing for them to do and that is to devote all their energy and intelligence to the creation of a more just society. In such a society race and race identity will cease to be the determinative factors that they have been for over 300 years, the more oppressively so in our present century. Are the Afrikaners and the English psychologically able to create with Black people a just order of society? Are Black people willing to co-operate with Whites in creating such an order, or have recent events led them to believe that they can build a new society without White participation? And will their new order of society accord justice for all? These, and not quibbles over English or Afrikaner "identity", are the questions which must find answers in the present decade.

Guy Butler has written extensively on his birthplace, the Karoo. He is a former academic from Rhodes University.

>>>>>>>>>>>>>

English Nationalism in SA

IT CAN BE ARGUED that the events that followed the Great Trek, the discovery of diamonds and gold, the growth of the English-speaking minority in the Transvaal, the arrogance of Milner, the Jameson Raid and finally the Anglo-Boer War were the creators of Afrikaner Nationalism. These were certainly the political events. But there were others also. One factor was the growing pride in possessing a language of one's own, the new language Afrikaans. Another was the effect of living for generations in the South African countryside, with its mountains and plains, its solitude and its great distances, its openness, its grass and its thorn trees, its present awareness of living in a country of Black and conquered people who outnumbered them greatly.

When I was a boy in Pietermaritzburg in the early years of this country, British Nationalist feeling was strong in the city of my birth and in the nearby town of Durban, and in Natal generally, except that it declined as one travelled north. But it picked up again in Johannesburg and on the Reef, declined on the Platteland, picked up in Kimberley, was strong in the Eastern Province, declined and then picked up again in the Cape Peninsula. There was a strange phenomenon in the Western Province, that of Afrikaners who were British Nationalists, genuinely and extremely so. It may still persist in places, though I do not know of them. The sight on the cinema screen of the ships of the Royal Navy in majestic procession aroused inordinate pride and the sight of the Royal Family could bring lumps to the throat and tears to the eyes.

The British Nationalists of the South Africa of 1902 did not realise that the Anglo-Boer War heralded the end of British Imperialism and a sharp decline in British Nationalism. The granting of responsible government to the defeated republics of the Transvaal and the Orange Free State in 1906 and 1907 was a sign of the times. The coming into being of the Union of South Africa in 1910 under the leadership of two Boer generals evoked either admiration for the two generals or fear for the future of all things British. These fears appeared to be justified when General Hertzog left Botha and Smuts in 1912 and founded the Nationalist Party in 1914. But British Nationalist feeling reached a tremendous pitch when Britain declared war on Germany in 1914.

Of the depth and reality of South African British Nationalism in those years there could be no doubt. And it was reassured by the immediate decision of Botha and Smuts that if Britain was at war, the Union of South Africa was at war too.

British Nationalism in South Africa needed reassuring. In 1915 Hertzog's number of MPs advanced from 16 to 27. British Nationalism has lived in anxiety since the beginning of the century. Afrikaner Nationalism feared it even relentless, so forbidding, so exclusive, that British Nationalists feared it even when it seemed to be powerless. In the election of 1920 the Afrikaner Nationalists advanced from 27 to 44. Alarmed by this, the British Nationalists of the Unionist Party amalgamated with Smuts's South African Party. The new party gained a respectable number of new seats, but this was at the expense of the Labour Party. Hertzog went up from 44 to 45.

In fact, British Nationalism was a declining force in South African politics. This was not only because Afrikaner Nationalism was gaining strength. It was because the young English-speaking people were gradually losing their deep feeling for the British Empire, the British Navy, the British Royal House. I say "gradually" because in a time of relatively uneventful development they would move forward along the road of South Africanism, but in a time of crisis they would again become British. This was shown when Hertzog's Nationalists, with the aid of Labour, came to power in 1924.

I shall consider only three legislative Acts of this period. In 1926 the Balfour Declaration affirmed that Britain and the Dominions were equal in status and in 1934 the statute of Westminster and the South African Status Act gave legal effect to the Declaration. In 1927 the Government gave to South Africa a new flag, the same which we fly today. In 1928 the Union concluded a commercial treaty with Germany. Each of these Acts struck fear into the hearts of British Nationalists. This is the place to make the important point that it was not legislation that concerned other groups in the population that disturbed the British Nationalists. It was legislation that affected them and their own security. In 1936 the Hertzog-Smuts Coalition Government removed the 80-year-old Cape franchise from qualified Black voters and there were found only 11 MPs to oppose it, and of those 11 three were Afrikaners.

The British Nationalists received the greatest fright of all during the 1938 celebration of the centenary of the Great Trek. The depth of Afrikaner fervour, the exclusiveness of Afrikaner Nationalism, the extent of Afrikaner bitterness, filled them with foreboding. The more intelligent British Nationalists knew that they were encountering something that they had in such large measure made themselves. I think at this point I should tell you that when Hertzog's Nationalists and Smuts's South African Party fused in 1934, they commanded 117 seats in the Lower House. Dr Malan would not join the New United Party, and he led 19 purified Nationalists. Colonel Stallard led four British Nationalists, called the Dominion Party. The other British Nationalists clung to Smuts; he gave them a security that Stallard could not give. But if a General Election had been held in 1938, at the height of the Voortrekker celebrations, I have no doubt that Malan would have increased his total considerably.

Those days from 1934 to 1939 were full of drama. Stallard used Malan to frighten Smuts's British Nationalists and Malan used, not Stallard, but Hofmeyr, to frighten Hertzog's Plattelanders. Malan saw no reason to use Stallard as a bogy man, because he calculated, and rightly, that British Nationalism was dying. He reckoned that Hofmeyr's liberalism was much more dangerous.

The Voortrekker celebrations greatly strengthened the power of Afrikaner Nationalism. They strengthened British Nationalism in a negative and reactionary way. But British Nationalism received a more positive transfusion when Smuts defeated Hertzog by 13 votes and took South Africa into the war against Hitler. Smuts, I think quite coolly and calculatingly, allowed British Nationalism its head. He took Colonel Stallard, leader of the Dominion Party, into his Cabinet.

It was a power to be used against Hitler and therefore Smuts would use it. Yet he was almost completely trusted by English-speaking South Africans, largely because his admiration for Britain and Churchill and the Royal Family was so obviously genuine.

I wish to point to something very important here. Hitler's influence in South Africa was very great, and one of the extraordinary consequences of the war was to make men and women realise the need for what could be called a New Order of Society. The spectrum was complete. On the extreme Right Mr Oswald Pirow wanted a White totalitarianism and on the extreme Left the Communist wanted an end to capitalism, privilege and racial discrimination and did not shrink from the idea of Black majority rule so long as it was Communist. In the middle were a great many White people in South Africa who realised that although they were fighting a herrenvolk ideology, they themselves supported a way of life in which the herrenvolk ideology was clearly to be discerned.

The feeling of guilt for the present and the past, and of responsibility for a new order which would be more just than the old, was particularly noticeable in two widely differing organisations, the English-speaking Churches and the South African Army, especially the Army up North. In neither case was it concerned for the preservation of the British Empire. The leaders of the Army Education Corps, which opened the eyes of many White soldiers to the facts of South African life, were EG Malherbe, Alfred Hoernlé and Leo Marquard, not one of them of British descent. It will be seen that even in time of war the attention of English-speaking South Africans was increasingly being directed towards their own country. The Diocese of Johannesburg, under Bishop Geoffrey Clayton, appointed a commission to state, after study and discussion, what it believed to be the mind and will of Christ for the country in every possible department of life. On January 21, 1942, Smuts said in the Cape Town City Hall that segregation had fallen on evil days. He said: "How can it be otherwise? The whole trend both in this country and the African continent has been in the opposite direction, towards closer contacts between the various sections. Isolation has gone. The old isolations of South Africa have gone and gone for ever." A cynic might say that Smuts and John of Patmos had much in common.

If I may again return to myself, I must record that the Bishop of Johannesburg's commission took me a big step further. I had to face the issue of human equality, which in South Africa means racial equality. I cannot describe to you the difficulty of that. No less a man than JH Hofmeyr could prostrate himself humbly before the God of Justice, but was terrified of the God of Equality. Various subterfuges were adopted by White Christian South Africans. One was to assert that all men were equal in God's sight, but that to see them thus was a Divine not a human attribute. Another subterfuge was to declare that it was an obvious characteristic of God's Creation that men were not equal and that the real impiety was to declare that men were equal. After all were not some men 6'2" in height and others only 6' 1½"? Beethoven could not solve a quadratic and Newton could not compose a symphony.

White men might conceivably accept Chief Gatsha Buthelezi as an equal, but what about Buthelezi's chauffeur? As for me, I accepted that there was apart from differences of height or musical or mathematical ability, a profound sense in which all men were equal. For a Christian such an acknowledgement is ultimately ineluctable. "If I, your Lord and Master, have washed your feet, ye ought also to wash one another's feet."

In the election of 1943 Smuts pushed up his war majority from 13 votes to 64. In May 1945 Germany capitulated. On September 7 Smuts lost the safe seat of Kimberley to the Nationalist Party. In January 1947 Smuts lost the safe seat of Hottentot Holland. Later in the year one of his MPs, JB Wolmarans, crossed the floor and joined the Nationalists. A cold wind blew through the ranks of remaining British Nationalists, who had been given a last opportunity of expressing their deepest feeling during the triumphal 1947 visit to South Africa of King George VI, Queen Elizabeth and the two princesses. On May 26, 1948, Dr Malan achieved the unbelievable feat; aided by Havenga's Afrikaner Party, he defeated Smuts by five seats, although he polled 150,000 less votes. This was due to the electoral arrangement, agreed to in 1909, whereby the quota in urban constituencies could be overloaded 15 percent and in rural constituencies underloaded 15 percent.

The age of what might be called Smuts-English-speaking suprem-acy had come to an end. The age of Afrikaner Nationalist su-premacy had begun.

Heavy blows were inflicted on Smuts's United Party and on the remnants of British Nationalism. The Government immediately released Robey Leibbrandt and others who had been imprisoned for offences similar to those of Mandela and Sisulu. General Evered Poole, an English-speaking South African and Deputy Chief of the General Staff, was sent off to Berlin to an inferior post when he was due to become the Chief of Staff. A strange phenomenon was the founding and instantaneous success of the Torch Commando, an organisation of ex-soldiers Afrikaans and English-speaking, for the purpose of resisting the intention of the Government to remove Coloured voters to a separate roll; but South Africa being what it is, the Torch Commando did not admit Coloured members and excluded Coloured and African people from its Alamein Day celebration.

In the 1953 election Malan and Havenga who had now com-bined, increased their number of seats from 79 to 94, and Senator Heaton Nicholls of Natal broke away from the United Party to establish the Union Federal Party, the last bastion of British Na-tionalism. In the same year the non-racial Liberal Party was founded, seeking a new South African Nationalism. The Torch Commando, disheartened by the election results, began to fade away and some of its British Nationalists joined the Federal Party. The heart of British Nationalism beat most strongly in Natal and less strongly in Johannesburg, East London, Port Elizabeth, Gra-hamstown and Cape Town. There was loud talk in Natal about breaking away from the Union, but it came to nothing.

The truth is that Natal was part of the South African economy and money sometimes talks louder than blood. In the view of people like myself, the thought of seceding was grotesque. For one thing, we had become South Africans; for another we did not expect that the views of Natal British Nationalists on questions of race and the rule of law would be tremendously different from those of Afrikaner Nationalists.

Each of them had different nationalisms, but their racial atti-tudes were much the same. It was – and is – often said that Afrikaner racial attitudes are open and honest and that English-speaking racial attitudes are concealed and dishonest. There is truth in this, but it has never made me think that one was better than the other. In fact, increasing numbers of Afrikaners are beginning to recognise that being open and honest about racial attitudes does not necessarily make them morally good.

Let me say again that the last efforts of British Nationalism were made on its own behalf. There is a legend that British like fair play and it has its measure of truth. But the dying British Nationalism of the 1950s had no thoughts for anything but itself.

On August 3, 1960, came the culminating event. The Prime Minister, Dr Verwoerd, announced that a referendum would be held to ascertain whether or not a simple majority of the people desired a republican form of Government. By "the people" was meant of course the White people. There were great anti-republican meetings, 40,000 people in Durban and 25,000 in Pietermaritzburg.

The result of the referendum was

For a Republic – 850,000
Against a Republic – 776,000

On May 31, 1961, South Africa became a Republic. Not all the anti-republican votes were those of British Nationalists by any means. But the declaration of the Republic meant the death of British Nationalism. From the date of the Treaty of Vereeniging it had lasted not quite 60 years. It had its good points, no doubt, but like all exclusive nationalisms it put itself first. Its successor, Afrikaner Nationalism, had been no better. But its day as an aggressive and divisive force is coming to an end too. The country of the future, if it is to have any peace at all, cannot be the home of aggressive and competing nationalisms. I say to those of you who are listening to me, with all the earnestness that I can command, that there are only two possible futures – a country which has achieved or is in process of achieving a common South African Nationalism which would by its very composition be inclusive and exclusive, or a country where either the White man has gone, or goes on living here in the grief and desolation that is so superbly described in Karel Schoeman's novel *Na die geliefde land*.

I conclude by asking the question, has British Nationalism in South Africa been succeeded by what one might call an English-speaking Nationalism? My answer is No. Although I do not move in every English-speaking circle, at least I move in the circle of those who might be expected to be the leaders of such nationalism.

Yet the fact that they are English-speaking does not determine their conduct.

They may well be proud of their English and British heritage, they may be proud of the English language and its literature, yet it would seem absurd to them to let these things determine their lives, or to boast about them. The English-speaking peoples are to be found in every political party except perhaps in the Herstigte Nationale Party. The days are past when they could be expected to rise and assert themselves as a group, or make a great song about their identity. Some of them do not belong to any party, because they like myself have only one nationalism and that is the South African Nationalism that has not yet come. It lacks all competitive and aggressive elements. One must not suppose that when an English-speaking person is expressing anti-Afrikaner or anti-Black or anti-Indian sentiments, that this indicates any English-speaking Nationalism. It does indicate a kind of racialism and it should not be dignified by the name of nationalism.

It will be for others to discuss other fascinating questions, whether Afrikaner Nationalism and White arrogance have created a new Black Nationalism that transcends all tribal – or if you wish – all national differences. And there is the question as to whether the clash between Afrikaner Nationalism and Black Nationalism will be final and catastrophic. And the question of the duty of the Christian Church and the Christian himself in these demanding days.

The task of English-speaking people will not be to assert their identity as English-speaking, but to bring so far as they can the influences of reason and tolerance to bear on our situation. And the task of the English-speaking Christian will be to stand for the Christian belief that there are values that transcend the values of nationalism. That is not to say that there are no values in nationalism, but it is to affirm the Christian belief that to be a son or daughter of God is more fundamental than to be an Afrikaner or a Zulu or an Englishman.

Pro Veritate – January 1975

Lord Milner, the High Commissioner to South Africa after the Anglo-Boer War, treated the Boers with disdain and tried to implement a policy of Anglicization, which led to the founding of Christian National Educational schools by Afrikaners.

The Jameson Raid was an abortive attempt by Cecil John Rhodes, then Prime Minister of the Cape Province, to take over the Transvaal Government by supporters of Britain.

Under Dr Leander Starr Jameson, the raiders were captured by the Boers at Paardekraal, near Krugersdorp, early in 1896. It led to the resignation of Rhodes.

Professor EG Malherbe became Principal and Vice-Chancellor of Natal University College in 1945 and led it to the status of the University of Natal a few years later. He retired in 1965.

The Labour Party was established in 1969 by Coloured politicians and obtained an outright majority during elections for the Coloured Representative Council in 1975. After the Coloured elections of 1984, it became the ruling party in the House of Representatives in the new tricameral Parliament.

Herrenvolk – ideology: the idea that certain members of the human race are superior to others.

In 1902 the British forces of Lord Kitchener finally defeated the two Boer republics after hostilities which lasted nearly three years came to an end with the signing of the Treaty of Vereeniging.

<hr />

My Two Great Loves

I AM AN English-speaking South African, born in Maritzburg, Natal, in 1903. Seven years later I became a South African when the Union was formed in 1910.

Two of the first loves of my life have been my country and my language. Language is more than a matter of words, it is more importantly a matter of meanings. It therefore enshrines one's deepest values.

What are, in my opinion of course, the deepest values held by the British people and therefore enshrined in the English language? For the purpose of this article, I specifically exclude the discussion of religious values.

To me the greatest of these values is that of individual freedom. That includes the freedom of the citizen and his protection against the overwhelming power of the State.

For him this freedom from excessive and unnecessary interference by the State in his private life has been won by centuries of struggle against authoritarian power.

The most famous event in this struggle is the Magna Carta of 1215. It was followed by the famous declaration made by the nobles and commons of Scotland at Arbroath – "We fight not for honour, but for that freedom which no good man will surrender but with his life."

This was a new idea that individual men and women had freedom that no State could touch. The new idea came to later flowering in America (the present United States) and France. But its beginnings were in Britain and it was expressed in the English tongue.

Certain other values are inseparable from the basic value of freedom – the rule of law, habeus corpus and a deep respect for the courts of law and especially the judiciary. The British people, always wary of sentimentality and big words, had a phrase for it all. It was called "playing the game".

I have been asked the question: "Are these values binding on the conscience of the White English-speaking South Africans?"

I wish I could answer yes, but the facts are against me.

As far back as 1938 the Minister of the Interior in the United Party Government, Mr R Stuttaford, introduced a Bill which would prevent Transvaal Indians from buying land except in "de-fined Indian areas".

JH Hofmeyr moved an amendment for which he received only 11 votes. The majority of the English-speaking MPs were in favour of the Bill.

In the Government of 1946, Smuts, under pressure from the English-speaking Dominion Party and from the Durban City Council, froze all property transactions between Indian and other races and introduced an Asiatic Bill, which was the forerunner of the Group Areas Act of 1950.

In 1951 came the formation of the Torch Commando, with very large support from English-speaking war veterans, and with the firm intention of opposing any interference with the Coloured vote. But the commando, fighting for Coloured rights, did not want Coloured members, who finally withdrew their support of the commando.

I could continue in this strain and become tedious. The fact is that the English-speaking people did not regard their highest moral values as binding upon them. I shall testify that in the Fifties the English-speaking people were a frightened lot.

I am glad to record my opinion that they are less frightened now than they were then. For that we can largely thank the Press and we can be abundantly thankful that finally the Afrikaans Press broke out of its servile status as the hand-maiden of the National Party.

Could the English-speaking people have played a decisive po-litical role after 1948? The answer is no. The day of the Afrikaner had come. His day of reckoning is still to come.

Does the proposed constitution measure up to these values? The answer is no.

Millions of African people are excluded altogether from the only legislative process that matters.

This can only result in further alienation.

There is no sign of any recognition of the right of the individual as against the almighty State. The new presidential powers offend all the values of the democratic world.

Allow me to end on a personal note. I have never said one word in praise of the constitution. To me it represents, not a political brainwave, but an urgent and misguided effort on the part of Afrikaner Nationalism to break out of the prison that it has built for itself in the last 35 years.

They are going to find it mighty difficult.

Sunday Express – *July 31, 1983*

SHARPEVILLE

I am certain the police have received the strictest instructions to guard against panic.

The Anger Has Cooled

THE MEMORY OF SHARPEVILLE has dimmed, prosperity has returned. But beneath the peace lie tyranny and corruption in government to preserve a Colour-bar society.

Five years ago I would have reported differently. At Sharpeville
on March 21, 1960, in the Transvaal, 69 Africans were shot after
a demonstration which, while frightening to the White police because of its sheer size, was unarmed. As a result of this, Africans
marched in great numbers into Cape Town and Durban. A nation-
wide emergency was declared in which a number of my friends
and associates were imprisoned, and months later released without
charge, trial, or verdict.

The anger of the outside world was intense. Money poured out
of the country. The markets tumbled. It seemed that great
changes were imminent. It seemed as though the Nationalist Government under Dr Hendrik Verwoerd would at last have to make
concessions and to relax its inflexible policies of apartheid, racial
separation.

In 1965 my report is quite different. There has been no second
Sharpeville. I am certain that the police have received the strictest

instructions to guard against panic in mob situations. The anger of the countries of the West has cooled. The anger of the other African countries is seen to be less dangerous because of their military and economic weakness and because of their own dividedness.

Money has poured back into the country. The markets have recovered, and we have been passing through a period of unprecedented economic prosperity. It seems as though Dr Verwoerd will not need to make any concessions. He will, on the contrary, be able to proceed unchecked with his racial programme, and to act more and more drastically against his political opponents.

Whatever their polices may be, they are either said to be Communists or to be furthering, wittingly or unwittingly, the aims of Communism. A person like myself, for example, is thought by a great number of White South Africans to belong to one of these groups. It would avail nothing to tell them that I see no solution in violence and that I do not believe in totalitarian rule, because such an assertion would brand me as either a rogue or a fool.

It is doubtful whether there is a country in the world so convinced as is White South Africa of its rightness, of the beauty of its (White) girls, of the happiness of its citizens (except those, of course, who are unjustifiably dissatisfied, largely because they are exploited by agitators), of the harmony of its race relations. And one who questions these convictions is classified as not a searcher after truth, but a Communist, an agitator, a hater of the good, a creator of chaos.

Our Government's status in the eyes of the West has certainly not deteriorated since 1960. In some respects it may have improved. The restlessness of Africa, the cool and sometimes hostile attitude of some of the new countries towards America and Britain, the chaos in the Congo, the increasing influence of Russia and China in the African continent, all these things have improved our image.

The South African Foundation, established largely by businessmen, invites Western leaders, largely businessmen, to visit South Africa. Most of these visitors praise our stability, admire our industry, and either commend our racial policies or tell us that they are our own concern.

Since 1960 White South Africa, also influenced by events in Africa, has moved massively to the Right; that is to say, to the side of White supremacy, apartheid and authoritarian State powers. White immigrants from Kenya, Zambia, Rhodesia and Tanganyika have strengthened this swing. Although most of them are English-speaking, they find no difficulty in supporting the Afrikaner Nationalists, largely because they themselves seem to have developed an intense dislike of Britain and all things British.

This is also true, though to a lesser extent, of immigrants from Britain itself, who soon adapt themselves to the racial situation, and who soon realise that it is the Colour bar that protects their privileged position.

It is the boast of White South Africans that in a restless continent, their own country is a haven of prosperity, peace and order. Up to a certain point this boast is justified. Visitors who have been influenced by scare stories and exaggerated anti-apartheid propaganda, are genuinely surprised when they find that Black people are not shot or thrashed in the streets, that the racially mixed crowds in the cities move about their business with a minimum of friction, that Africans laugh and talk with great vivacity. In every city great new buildings are being erected. The road system for a country of this size and population is quite remarkable, the air services are splendid. South Africa is a modern, vigorous, highly industrialized society.

Whatever other motives there may be for the swing to the Right, one is undoubtedly the fear that this prosperity and efficiency might be destroyed if the policies of apartheid, with their underlying assumption of White supremacy, were relaxed in any way. Dr Verwoerd has said that White South Africa, in resisting any such change, would be "like granite".

It is necessary to examine further the contention that South Africa is a land of law and order. In 1960 I might have described it as a volcano, or as a pot whose lid was being riveted down on forces which would ultimately be uncontrollable.

Today it does not appear to be so. Our rulers contend that more and more non-White people are accepting the policy of separate development, and that apart from the disturbances of agitators, satisfaction reigns.

My own view is otherwise. This outward appearance of peace is due to the tremendous powers at the disposal of the Government to silence its opponents, to banish them to remote places, to confine them to restricted areas, to deny them entry to schools, colleges, factories, courts of law and other places. The Government can forbid them to attend meetings, order them to stay at home for any daily period up to 24 hours, all this without charge, trial, or verdict. Many of these opponents are dealt with under the Suppression of Communism Act, though they have never had any connection with Communism.

The great power of the Government has also been shown in other ways. The Communist Party was banned in 1950. The African National Congress and the Pan-African Congress were banned in 1960. But now one hears every few days of some new trial that is beginning, of persons who refuse to give up their political work, and continue it in secret. The penalties are severe, and it seldom happens that a person is charged on only one count. It must also be noted that one simply cannot start a new organisation, because it is also a serious offence to further aims *similar* to the aims of a banned organisation.

Others have done more than continue organisational work. They have planned and in some cases carried out sabotage. They have trained others in sabotage. They have left the country without passports and have undergone military training abroad.

Sabotage trials were the feature of 1964 and heavy sentences were imposed – from five years to life imprisonment. Many of these saboteurs were young White men and women, who, frustrated by the absoluteness of the Government's power, were angered by the use of that power to cripple legitimate political opposition. They thought – foolishly and tragically – that they could persuade by violence. Many of them were products of our universities, and one can only guess at the depth of the frustration that allowed them to believe that they could shake White supremacy by toppling over a couple of pylons.

The most tragic case of all was that of John Harris, a young White schoolmaster, who thought he could shake White supremacy by planting a bomb in the White concourse of the Johannesburg railway station. By this act he caused the death of an elderly woman and grave injuries to others. Until then his record had been one of outstanding service to the cause of non-racialism in sport. For his act of sabotage he was hanged.

The security measures adopted by the saboteurs were extremely inefficient. But it was not only that which enabled the police to uncover the entire organisation. The police were aided by a new law which empowers them to detain any person for a period of 90 days in solitary confinement, without warrant or charge, and to detain such person for subsequent periods of 90 days (until he "answers satisfactorily" the questions put to him).

Many of us fear that in some cases the questioning was carried out brutally. Two detainees committed suicide and others attempted to do so. The results were all that the police could have desired. They soon had detainees willing to give evidence for the State, willing to reveal the names of accomplices not yet discovered.

One would think that the Christian world would regard with horror this interference with the very springs of human personality. But many White South African Christians feel no such horror. Law and order have been preserved. Communists and liberals have been routed. These people believe that God, Who desires order and Who has placed magistrates in authority over us, has been well served. Why should one pity those who have betrayed their own comrades? Would they not have created chaos had they been able?

The problem of Church and Christian in a secular society is, of course, not peculiar to South Africa. Therefore, if I should criticise Church and Christian in the South African society, I must not be imaged to believe that Church and Christian are not corrupted in other societies. Nor must it be imagined that I consider myself uncorrupted.

Only a few Christians have died because they chose to obey God rather than man. "Take up your cross and follow me," is not only the hardest of all commandments. It is the one which Christians in general take least seriously.

Yet there should always be a tension between what we are and what we wish to be, and by tension I mean a fruitful and creative one. There should always be a tension – and this is a statement that would shock many White South Africans – between Church and State, and between Christian and society.

The Church in South Africa is situated in a Colour-bar society and has been profoundly affected by it. The Church is placed in a society in which, as a result of the laws of separate development, contact between races has grown less. Each racial group has its own group areas, and I, for example, being White, may not visit a friend in an African group area without a permit.

Separate development, and separate group areas, make inter-racial worship difficult. Even before the advent of the group area laws, inter-racial worship was not a general practice. Christianity is essentially a non-racial religion, but it finds itself here in a society where rulers abhor non-racialism and who legislate to destroy it.

Therefore, White South African Christians can do one of three things. They can welcome the laws and regard enforced separation as completely compatible with Christianity. Or they can through fear or apathy submit to the "authority of the magistrates". Or they can honestly try in thought and action to reject any kind of racial discrimination.

Sometimes all three kinds of Christians are found in the same congregation, and this confronts the minister with the danger that if he condemns racial discrimination, he will be accused of dividing the Church, and of "bringing politics into religion". This had happened to some, in both Afrikaans and English-speaking churches.

What I am in effect saying is that the problems of the Church and the Christian in a Colour-bar society such as exists in South Africa are immense. But I am also saying that the corruption is immense too. The tension between what we are and what we earnestly wish to be is nothing like as great as it should be. Indeed for many White Christians there is no tension at all, because society as it is, is precisely what they wish it to be. They fear change more than they fear God.

On the whole the tension between Church and State is least noticeable in the case of the Dutch Reformed churches, of which there are three, one large and two small. Half of South Africa's three million White people adhere to these churches, and the overwhelming majority of these Christians are Afrikaans-speaking. They vote for Dr Verwoerd. They believe in the politics of separate racial development. And they believe in separate racial churches, though the big Dutch Reformed Church has declared that its services are open to all.

Other churches, in so far as their White membership is concerned, are overwhelmingly English-speaking and to them adhere one million White people. They are the Methodist, Anglican, Roman Catholic, Presbyterian and Congregational churches. They have also about three million non-White adherents, while the Dutch Reformed churches have about half-a-million (according to the census of 1960) and this doubtless is relevant to the question of protest.

One must not suppose, however, that the members of the English-speaking churches are united in their opposition to the policies of apartheid and separate racial development. Most of those who are articulate in their opposition are members of the clergy. I will hazard the guess that not more than 20 percent of the White laity support such opposition.

Recently a Methodist minister in a Transvaal country town aroused anger when he entertained both Black and White Christians at tea in his house. He was later transferred to another district. Yet this year the President of the Methodist Conference in South Africa is an African, the Rev Seth Mokitimi, the first African president in the history of the Methodist Church.

This is the bewildering picture of the Church in the South African society. It is certainly not the picture of a transforming or crusading Church. Some of us look wistfully to America, where churchmen seem to us to be playing an active and creative part in the civil rights campaign.

It is a fact that those South Africans who have in the last 10 years suffered for their beliefs, and for their rejection of apartheid, have in the main been members of political groups, not churchmen. If one believes apartheid to be evil, the fact becomes melancholy.

The Lutheran – *June 2, 1965*

On March 21 1960, 69 Black demonstrators died and 180 were wounded when police at Sharpeville, near Vereeniging, opened fire into a crowd protesting against the Pass Laws.

SOWETO

I fear Afrikanerdom could be destroyed. If
so, it began on June 16, 1976.

And What Next?

MY RULERS ARE THE AFRIKANERS OR, to be more accurate, the
Afrikaner Nationalists. They decide in what areas I may live,
where my grandchildren may go to school and where they may
not, with whom I may have a sexual relationship and with whom
I may not. They decide who may and who may not live in my
house.

I am writing because I fear for the future of Afrikanerdom. I
fear it could be destroyed. And I fear that the process of destruction has actually begun. If so, it began on June 16, 1976.

These riots in Soweto and other Black towns, this burning down
of shops and clinics and schools and universities, are they going
to stop, or is this a chain-reaction that cannot stop until everything
is destroyed?

It is hatred that is at work, the hatred of a people who, for
generations, but in particular for the last 28 years, have been
treated as persons of no account, with no voice of their own affairs,
forbidden to buy land or houses in the towns and cities whose
wealth they made, and deemed to be domiciled in some remote
homeland that many of them have never seen.

And, worst of all, this hatred is being manifested for the greater part by schoolchildren, who won't go to school, who burn down their classrooms and who terrorise their own parents, who threaten their own fathers if they go in the morning to their work in the cities, who warn them not to come back at night if they value their lives.

I have my own fears, too. If Afrikanerdom is destroyed there will be no room for any White person any more.

It does not matter so much to me, but it matters a great deal to my children and my children's children. If Afrikanerdom is destroyed, that will be the end of the White tenure of South Africa. Whites will be tolerated only as engineers and menials.

But deeper even than the fear is the pain and anger that a lifetime of service to one's country may be brought to nothing by arrogant men, who have devoted all their wits – which are not inconsiderable – to their own preservation, should in the end destroy themselves – and many of us also.

In 1948 the Afrikaner Nationalist came to power and he has been there ever since. He enacted a series of racial laws the like of which the world had never seen before, and will certainly never see again.

Our rulers have always agreed that the making of these laws were their domestic concern. At first it seemed that they might get away with it.

But inexorably the anger of the outside world mounted in intensity. It reached a high point in 1960, when South African police – initially in panic, I believe – killed 69 Black people in Sharpeville. We recovered economically from that, but Sharpeville came to be commemorated year after year in many countries of the world.

This commemoration is in itself a proof of the world's anger. The number of Black people killed by rulers in Nigeria, the Sudan, Bangladesh, were a hundred, even a thousand, times as great as the number killed in Sharpeville.

But in these other instances the rulers were Black and the Black world has now forgotten the massacres.

In South Africa the rulers are White and the Black world does not forget. The roots of its anger are deep in the past, in the conquest of the world by the White sailors and soldiers of Europe, the slave trade, the arrogance of Cortes and Pizarro, the corralling and destruction of the American Indians, the partition of Africa and, in this century, the massacre at Amritsar in 1919 by General Reginald Dyer of 379 Indian demonstrators.

Two powerful weapons have not yet been used against us, the military and the economic. White South Africa could not withstand them. That is why I fear for the future.

Apartheid, the policy of race separation, introduced in 1948 with such arrogance, is no longer our domestic concern. From our perspective it seems to have become the concern of the world. It overshadows nuclear war, population explosion, the energy problem, even property and starvation, in the councils of the nations.

I don't think Dr Kissinger understands this fully. Perhaps his successor will understand it better. Our rulers fear he may understand it too well.

How does one move away from racial discrimination when one has for 28 years been constructing a new order based on it?

The Afrikaner Nationalist has a quibble that he does not discriminate, he only differentiates, but no-one understands this except himself.

In any event, how does one move away from discrimination and yet retain differentiation? I think the answer, given by reason, is that it is impossible.

The supreme irrational axiom is that you can develop separately – that you can, in fact, compel by law to develop separately – the dozen or more races, with their dozen or more languages, that inhabit one and the same piece of land.

It is the fundamental axiom of separate development and its collapse is bringing down the whole superstructure of reason in ruins about those who held it.

Why is there this fundamental irrationality in Christian-Nationalism?

It is because the belief that man's most important possession is his nationality, that nationality is the only thing that gives meaning and purpose to his life, is entirely irreconcilable with the Christian belief that man's most important possession is his humanity and that his dignity comes, not from his nation, but from the fact that he is made in the image of His Creator? You can't have it both ways.

Why did the Afrikaner try to have it both ways?

He was a creature of the earth if ever there was one and being faced on the one hand by the fierce warriors of the Xhosas and the Zulu and on the other by the empire-hungry British, he found a more earthy security in being an Afrikaner, a son of Africa, than of being merely a son of God. No man was ever more fit to hold the motto: Have faith in God, but keep your powder dry.

But the day of the gun has gone – for him at least. He dare not use the gun any more. If he were to use the gun again – and here I am not talking about police action – the anger of the world, including the West, would burst its bounds and Afrikanerdom would come to its end.

More and more Afrikaners know this. Police action during this period of rioting and burning has been restricted.

Then what weapon do you use if you can't use the gun? Here Afrikaner Nationalism is torn in two.

One part of it believes that this rioting and unrest is the work of enemy forces – Communists, liberals, radicals, Black Power – and that they can be contained by stricter and harsher laws.

The other part believes that the roots go deeper and that the unrest is the result of resentment and frustration.

But it is psychologically difficult for a devout Afrikaner to go one step further and to recognise that the resentment and frustration are caused by the laws of apartheid and separate development, which the late Dr Verwoerd, the predecessor of Mr Vorster, exalted almost to the status of a gospel.

The prime political aim of Afrikanerdom is to preserve its unity. Only by preserving its unity can it find security in a hostile world.

To question apartheid seriously is to threaten Afrikaner unity. Therefore, one does not question apartheid seriously. How then does the Afrikaner politician deal with the dangerous situation that confronts Afrikanerdom today?

I don't know the answer to this question. Afrikaner politicians have for the last 28 years been digging for their people – and mine – a grave so big and so deep that I don't know if they will ever get out of it. They know that change is imperative, but they are as afraid to make change as they are not to make it.

Thirty years ago, in *Cry, the Beloved Country,* I put these words into the mouth of the Black priest Msimangu: "I have one great fear in my heart, that one day when they turn to loving, they will find we are turned to hating." Has that day come?

New York Times Sunday Magazine
Extracts by The Star – *September 20, 1976*

Where the Responsibility Lies

PROFESSOR GC OOTHUIZEN, Professor of the Science of Religion at the University of Durban-Westville, has added his voice to those who are warning South Africans that more Sowetos are coming unless they "stop living on the fat of the land".

Professor Oosthuizen's arguments are unassailable. Many Blacks believe the White man will listen only if they burn things down. The Black churches have not condemned outright the violence of Black youth.

To ascribe everything to Communism is to sidestep the real issues. Yet it often seems to the African that only Russia, China and Cuba will ever help him.

My criticism of Professor Oosthuizen's interview – and I rely solely on the report in last week's *Sunday Tribune* – is that he sidesteps too.

He talks about the need for "deep respect in racial relationships". But nowhere does he acknowledge that much of this respect has been destroyed by the discriminatory laws.

And he certainly nowhere acknowledges that it is in particular the discriminatory laws of the past 28 years that have caused such bitter resentment, and that these laws are the work of the National Party, which is overwhelmingly the party of the Afrikaner Nationalists.

Professor Oosthuizen says people like Professor Dreyer Kruger of Grahamstown and myself tend "to overlook the role played by the English section".

This is absolutely untrue. I remember distinctly that Professor Kruger did not spare the United Party and the PRP.

After Soweto I wrote that "we, the White people of South Africa, must repent of our wickedness, of our arrogance, of our complacency, of our blindness".

I wrote that the tsotsis were "the outcasts of our affluent society". In this responsibility we all share, English and Afrikaner.

Many of us – the English – are only too willing to let the Afrikaner carry the can. There is much truth in that witty epigram that the Natal English think Prog, vote UP and thank God for the Nationalists.

But it is legitimate to distinguish between the responsibility of White South Africa and that of Afrikaner Nationalism.

It was the Afrikaner Nationalist who codified and entrenched in law all the arrogance and prejudice of White South Africa.

It was he who codified the prejudice of White Durban into the Group Areas Act.

It was he who made the Mixed Marriages Act, who strengthened the Immorality Act, who took away the Black vote, and then the Coloured vote – with what calamitous results.

It was he who created Bantu education, whose children are now burning down the schools.

The question of the sins of the past is largely irrelevant. The responsibility of the present – insofar as Whites are concerned – lies overwhelmingly with Mr Vorster and the National Party Government. This is not a racial statement. It is the plain and simple truth.

Sunday Tribune – *October 3, 1976*

Tsotsis – Black gangsters

UITENHAGE

> At the moment our country is in a hell of a
> mess.

The Mess We're In

THEY WRITE TO ME FROM the United States, they come to see me, they call me long-distance. Some of them are my friends and they are anxious about me and my family. They want to know if the country is blowing up. Why do the police kill so many Black people? Is it civil war? Is it the end? Is this the revolution?

I hope that some of them will read these words. They are not meant to disturb nor to reassure. They are meant to state the plain and simple truth as seen by one who has lived in this strange country for 82 years, who belongs to no party, who holds on ideology, who doesn't believe in Utopia, who holds firm beliefs about the rule of law and the total freedom of the citizen under the law.

At the moment our country is in a hell of a mess.

This mess is physically encountered in what are called the Black townships. The Black people who live there work in the factories, the offices, the shops, of the White towns.

Their relations with White people are often good. But they hate the laws that control their lives with a bitter hatred. Their children hate these laws more than their parents. They show their hatred by stoning and burning buses, schools, shops.

In recent months their hatred has been directed against what is called "the establishment", and against anyone who works for the establishment. In some Black townships the life of a Black policeman is in danger.

These hated laws are the laws of apartheid. But more profoundly, they are the laws of conquest, the laws made by the conqueror for the conquered. This means, in effect, the laws made by the Whites for the Blacks.

These laws control movement, work, place of residence and other matters innumerable. In part they affect White people, but only minimally. Very few White people have to enter Black areas to work; most Black people have to enter White areas to work. Black people experience an amount of police surveillance unknown to the vast majority of White people.

In 1960 (Sharpeville), in 1976 (Soweto) and now in 1985 (Uitenhage), Black people came into conflict with the police and many died.

Nineteen recently died in Uitenhage, when a small number of police confronted some thousands of Blacks who refused to halt their procession. If the Uitenhage incident had been isolated, it would not have attracted world attention, but it was only one of many. We appear to be entering a period of endemic unrest with violence. The country is in a state of deep depression.

Our State President, Mr PW Botha, has appointed an urgent Commission of Inquiry into the Uitenhage shootings, headed by an eminent judge. The President would like the sub judice rule to operate, the Speaker says it does not.

I shall content myself by saying that the training of our police in riot duties leaves a great deal to be desired, and secondly, that the selection process for police candidates is equally defective.

During the last century there was a long series of frontier wars between Afrikaner trekkers going north and African tribes coming south. The memories of those wars lie deep in the Afrikaner mind and some of our White policemen think they are still fighting them.

I shall close with one last observation: the civil control of the police, that is the control exercised by the Minister of Law and Order (formerly Justice), during the greater part of my lifetime, has also left much to be desired. It has – to a large extent, not entirely – been the control of Black people by White authority.

I now come to the heart of my subject and I will antagonise some readers, and persuade others that my mental powers are failing.

I am going to state that it is one of the great ironies of my political life that just as the Afrikaner Nationalist is at last beginning to realise that the day of conquest has gone, and that the time to undo conquest has come, and just as he is taking his first tottering steps towards the undoing, he is confronted by this violent manifestation of Black hatred of his apartheid laws.

That he will therefore give up his talks, I do not believe. That he will lose more Afrikaner Nationalists to the extreme Right is very possible. The future is hard and challenging and I cannot tell you what it will be, and no-one else can either.

I have a word to say to those Americans who think they can hasten the "day of liberation" by damaging the South African economy, as for example, by disinvestment.

Must Americans therefore leave us alone to go our own sweet way? Certainly not.

The Afrikaner Nationalist, who boasts that he is an African, is much more a man of the West. He is very sensitive to the moral judgment of the West. He is more sensitive to it now than at any other time in my 82 years. He is certainly less arrogant than he was 30 years ago. He is readier to listen to righteous judgment, but reacts negatively to self-righteous denunciation.

The economic power of America is awesome, but Americans mustn't underestimate their moral power. The one thing they mustn't do is to isolate us from the world. That would bring danger for us all.

As I put down my pen, it is announced that our Minister of Law and Order has clamped down on meetings by 29 organisations. It will achieve nothing except to strengthen opposition. I believe that the Afrikaner Nationalist Government is facing the crisis of its life. So are we all.

New York Times – *April 1985*
As reproduced in the Sunday Star – *April 7, 1985*

BUTHELEZI AND INDABA

A total or near-total rejection of the proposals would be a calamity.

A Letter to Gatsha Buthelezi

RESPECTED MINISTER, I am not the representative of any recognised body of White South African opinion and therefore I am presuming on the fact that many of these South Africans regard me as capable of expressing their views on national actions, especially those who are concerned with racial and moral questions, as indeed most of them are.

I presume, therefore, to offer to your King, your Government, your people and yourself the humble apologies of these White citizens of South Africa for the treatment which you have received at the hands of our Government and our Prime Minister in the matter of the unilateral transfer of territory controlled by your Government to the foreign State of Swaziland.

The treatment abundantly justifies the allegation often made by you, Chief Minister, that our Government seems quite unable (for racial, historical and psychological reasons, no doubt) of dealing with yourself, or your Government, or your people, as fellow

South Africans whose opinions and aspirations are of vital importance for our future.

For what it is worth, Chief Minister, I send you this apology on behalf of many White South Africans for the treatment to which you have been subjected.

I find it impossible to close this letter without any reference to the part played by Dr Piet Koornhof, the Minister of Co-operation and Development. One day he will know, if he does not know it already, that he is being used as an instrument to achieve a purpose that is unworthy of a Christian Government. What is worse, for him, is that he agrees to do it.

Sunday Tribune – *June 20, 1986*

~~~~~~~~~~~~

Indaba Without Fear

THE HISTORY OF the relations between the colonists, Natal and the Zulu nation is nothing for a White Natalian to be proud of. The founder of the Zulu kingdom, Shaka, the son of Senzangakhona and Nandi, was assassinated and succeeded by his half-brother, Dingane, in 1928. King Dingane's power began to wane after his decisive defeat by the Voortrekkers at Blood River in 1838, and in 1840 he again was defeated by his half-brother, Mpande. He fled north across the Pongola River, but was captured and put to death either by the Swazis or by members of the Nyawo tribe.

King Dingane was succeeded in 1840 by Mpande, who was first a vassal of the Boers and later, in 1843, of the British. He became very obese as a result of some bodily malfunction and could hardly move and in 1857 his son Cetshwayo took over the administration. Mpande died in 1872 and Cetshwayo became the fourth Zulu king.

King Cetshwayo was a good ruler. He was more intelligent than his father. He revitalised the army and was not a tyrant. But his fate and the fate of his kingdom were sealed. The White colonists did not like having a powerful Black neighbour and they coveted the rich Zulu lands. Cetshwayo's friend, Sir Theophilus Shepstone, turned against him and tried to persuade the British Government that there could be no stability in South Africa so long as there was an independent Zulu Kingdom. The High Commissioner, Sir Bartle Frere, shared this belief and, taking advantage of some border incidents, ordered Cetshwayo to disband his army within 30 days. The King refused and Lod Chelmsford invaded Zululand.

POPULATION OF NATAL

	millions
Zulus	5,5
Indians	1,0
Whites	0,8
Coloureds	0,2

On January 22, 1879, the British suffered the terrible defeat if Isandhlwana, not because of their inferior military skill, but because of the negligence of Chelmsford. But the end was inevitable and in July Zulu power was crushed for ever at Ulundi.

The Zulu Kingdom was also destroyed. The country was split up into 13 chiefdoms. White magistrates supplanted the chiefs as the most powerful men in Zululand. In 1897 the British Government allowed the colony of Natal to annex the Zulu country, but at first did not allow the alienation of Zulu lands. In 1905 the final disaster struck the Zulu people when the colony was allowed to alienate about two-fifths of the country. It is hardly necessary to state that the colony took all the best land. The British Government must bear a great deal of the responsibility for this unforgivable action.

In 1910 the Zulus, in common with all other Black people in South Africa, became inhabitants of the new Union of South Africa, which was created as a result of the National Convention of 1908–09. Only White South Africans were represented and the new Union constitution contained a Colour bar, which again was a gift from the British Government and which has determined our history since. From 1910 onwards the Zulus, along with other South African Blacks, suffered under racially discriminatory laws, one of the most inhumane being the Natives Land Act of 1913, which prevented any Black man from buying "White" land and virtually denied to the Zulu people the right to become farmers in the land of their birth. From 1948 onwards, the Zulus, again with all these other Black people, suffered under the apartheid legislation of the Nationalist Government. In the 1960s the Zulus were allocated a number of separate areas in Natal and Zululand, which together became KwaZulu. One of the most catastrophic effects of these laws was that they virtually made White and Black South Africans strangers to each other. Yet in 1986 they spent many days in Durban in the series of meetings known as the Kwazulu-Natal Indaba, discussing, sensibly and reasonably, how a new legislative body could be established which would rule, as a part of the Republic of South Africa, a new province comprising the regions originally known as Natal and Zululand.

How was it possible to hold such meetings after a history such as I have recapitulated above? It is a miracle. How does such a miracle come to pass?

I find this a fascinating question. I have lived on the edge of the Valley of a Thousand Hills for more than 30 years and I have been down into the valley, say, 1,500 times. In all those years I encountered only on one occasion what one might call racial hostility. One day I was returning to my home at Botha's Hill, climbing the hill that leads to the ridge above. I stopped and offered a lift to a young Black man on one side of the road and to a young Black woman on the other. She accepted at once, but the young man interposed himself between her and the car and said to her: "No, not with a White man."

Do the Zulu people possess some special quality of personality and character that makes them more friendly, more forgiving? Is it true that they accepted their defeat at Ulundi in a philosophical spirit and decided to make the best of a bad job? Is it true, as many people think, that the influence of Chief Mangosuthu Buthelezi is extremely powerful and is in favour of moderation and friendliness? It seems that these things are true, though one must in honesty remark that qualities such as moderation and friendliness have a stronger appeal for the old than for the young and for the rural than for the town dweller.

There is another reason for this apparent miracle. The White people of Natal, under the influence of fear for the future and a desire to avoid economic disaster, and also under the growing influence of sheer human decency, have come to realise that if they cannot work closely with the Zulu people, their doom is certain. This human decency was not unduly manifest in the early and fierce days of the National Party Government, say, its first 20 years, when many White people (mainly English-speaking) thought it best to keep what is called a low profile and not to say that apartheid was both cruel and impracticable. I can testify to the fact that many English-speaking people who today support the Indaba kept their distance from the Liberal Party of the Fifties and Sixties and regarded their views and principles as extreme. There is no doubt that the political climate has become far more favourable for the growth of decency and good sense.

The Indian population of Natal, except for their radical Left, would welcome the creation of a Natal/Zululand legislative assembly. The White Natalians' contempt for their Indian fellow-citizens has greatly abated in my lifetime. There are several reasons for this. One is the fact that the Natal Indians have become an English-speaking people, another is the realisation that they are believers in democracy and moderation, and the third is the growth of White tolerance. It is also reassuring for Indian people to sit down and talk with their Zulu fellow-Natalians and this helps to abate their real racial fear of the Zulu people, a fear which was intensified during the Durban riots of 1949.

The Coloured people of Natal form by far the smallest racial group and they would have little to fear – and much to gain – from taking their part in a non-racial legislative body.

So as far as one can see, the miracle has, in fact, come to pass.

What were the events which led up to the Indaba? The most important was the setting up of the Buthelezi Commission, which was established by the KwaZulu Legislative Assembly by its resolution of May 29, 1980. Its chairman was Professor GDL Schreiner, of the University of Natal, who was assisted by more than 40 commissioners, widely representative of the whole communities of Natal and KwaZulu. The commission was rightly claimed to be the first real Black initiative in constitution making and offered itself as a non-partisan middle way between White and Black aspirations. In fact, it set out to find an answer to that most difficult of South African questions, "What are White hopes and what are Black hopes and can they be hoped together?"

One can paraphrase very briefly the political recommendations of the Buthelezi Commission. They were that some single legislative body be set up to administer the area of KwaZulu-Natal, that it would not be constructed on the Westminster model in which the ruling party is inordinately powerful, and that the area

163

would remain a part of the Republic of South Africa. The reality of White fears of Black domination was honestly faced and there was discussion of the future constitution of the Republic itself, with a clear preference for some kind of federal dispensation. Two possible solutions were totally rejected. The first was the continuance of the present system of White domination and racial separation, even when it is decked out in the fine tricameral clothes designed by the indefatigable Minister Chris Heunis. The second rejected solution was that of universal suffrage in a unitary State.

The report of the Commission was presented to Chief Buthelezi on March 2, 1982. It was rejected however, by both the National Party and the New Republic Party (NRP). The NRP was the successor to the once powerful United Party. It was therefore a great setback to the supporters of the Buthelezi Commission when the most influential White politicians of Natal rejected the proposals. It seemed as though a great deal of thought and labour had come to nothing and as though White Natal had no conception of the gravity of the racial situation and of the need to give all South Africans some message of hope for the future.

Fortunately for the people of the region, and ultimately for all the people of South Africa, the KwaZulu-Natal negotiations were not brought to an end by the rejection of the Buthelezi Commission Report by the NRP. The highly respected Mr Brank Martin of the party, and a prominent member of the Natal Provincial Executive (a body now appointed by the State President after the abolition of the Natal Provincial Council in 1985), was convinced that the administration of the region could not be carried out efficiently by two separate bodies. The self-ruling homeland of KwaZulu consisted of some 50 separate pieces of land, at least half of which were mere pockets. It was the intention of the Government to "consolidate" KwaZulu, which, presumably, meant to reduce the number of pieces to about 20.

Martin is not an ideologue and he did not feel bound by the NRP's decision to reject the proposals of the Buthelezi Commission. He is a pragmatist and in the interest of good administration was willing to face even the amalgamation of KwaZulu and Natal and its rule by a single legislative body. He realised that the NRP's earlier rejection had led to an estrangement between Ulundi and Pietermaritzburg and he had no desire for this to continue. What was more, he realised that any movement for reconciliation would have the support of many of the leaders of industry and commerce in Natal, including those of the powerful sugar industry. Indeed, it was they who were responsible for the Lombard Report, which had concluded that because KwaZulu could not be consolidated, the region formed by it and Natal was an entity.

The stage was not set for a reconciliation between Pietermaritzburg and Ulundi. KwaZulu-Natal was lucky to have two men of the calibre of Buthelezi and Martin, two sensible idealists, both of whom preferred co-operation to conflict. They were prepared to work together, in the first place for a joint administrative authority, and in the second place for a joint legislative authority. So was launched what came to be known as the Indaba. "Indaba" is a Zulu word and in this context can be taken to mean a gathering at which important matters are to be discussed. Chief Buthelezi nominated Dr Oscar Dhlomo as the leader of the delegates from KwaZulu, and he acquitted himself with distinction, so also did Dr Frank Mdlalose, who represented Inkatha.

The organisers invited a wide range of organisations and persons to attend the Indaba. These included Chief Buthelezi's powerful movement, Inkatha, which claims to have more than a million members; the ruling National Party; the White Parliamentary Opposition, both from Left and Right; the members of the Coloured House of Representatives and the Indian House of Delegates; representatives of business and the sugar industry and a number of local and national experts. Labour was represented by the Trade Council of South Africa and the Black Allied Workers' Union.

The African National Congress was also invited, but its representatives could not have attended if they had wanted to, the congress having been banned in South Africa since 1960. The United Democratic Front (UDF) refused to accept the invitation. This was hardly surprising, since it is hostile to Chief Buthelezi and is ideologically committed to a unitary State with a universal suffrage. Mrs Winnie Mandela, who is strongly sympathetic to the UDF, had stated in public that the time for gatherings such as national conventions was past and that the next inevitable step was for the National Party Government to abdicate and to hand over power to the Black majority, a forthright but quite useless suggestion. For the same reasons the Natal Indian Congress did not attend. Nor did any of the trade union movements, except those mentioned above. The National Party also attended as observers but not delegates, as indeed was expected, for the party does not attend gatherings not called by itself. It was also not surprising that none of the Afrikaner conservative groups attended, because they are ideologically wedded to the Verwoerdian theories of racial separation, whereas the Buthelezi Commission, and consequently the Indaba, had already rejected the "homeland policy" of the National Party as totally unacceptable on both moral and pragmatic grounds. However, non-party Afrikaners were represented as observers in three national organisations; the Afrikaanse Handelsinstituut, the Federasie van Afrikaanse Kultuurverenigings, and the Rapportryers, and one local organisation, the Durbanse Sakekamer.

What and whom did the Indaba represent? It represented the moderate, peace-loving, conflict-hating, middle-of-the-road people of KwaZulu and Natal. These people are often called the "silent majority" and are often supposed to be starry-eyed and useless. But for the eight months of 1986 that the Indaba lasted, from April 3 to November 28, they proved themselves to be neither silent nor useless. Professor Desmond Clarence, retired Vice-Chancellor of the University of Natal, was invited by the organisers to become the chairman, and John Kane-Berman, Director of the South African Institute of Race Relations, to become the vice-chairman, and they earned the respect and the trust of the delegates. One should record that for eight months the deliberations were earnest and orderly; there were no what are called "racial incidents". I shall later record one incident of what might be called a sharp difference on racial grounds. The delegates from the Afrikaner organisations, while they could not be described as enthusiastic supporters of the Indaba and while they were to dissociate themselves from some of its findings, nevertheless acknowledged the urgent need in South Africa for such discussions. That is indeed what brought all these prominent people together. They realised that their country was in a mess and, for a variety of reasons, they wanted to find some way out of the morass.

The UDF would not have been impressed by some of these reasons. It would have seen the motives of the White people present as purely those of self-interest, a desire to save their skins, their possessions and their enterprises. They were there to save capitalism and to resist socialism. The UDF regards both the Indian and Coloured representatives in the tricameral parliament as stooges; from them would come no liberation and no triumph of the labouring masses. But the UDF would have directed their most severe criticism at Buthelezi. They call him a stooge and in their view he has betrayed the forces of liberation and has deserted the Black people in their hour of need. They think also that he is a hypocrite; that he speaks honeyed words in favour of freedom and democracy, but his henchmen in Inkatha will use violence whenever it suits them. The incompatibility of UDF and Inkatha is equalled only by that between the Nationalists and Treurnicht's Conservative Party.

Since Buthelezi was the originator of the commission and the joint-originator of the Indaba, it is relevant to consider briefly what kind of man he is. I wrote about him 13 years ago: "I should say, leaving personal relations out of account, that his loyalties are to Christ, humanity, South Africa and the Zulu people in that order. This must not be thought inconsistent with his statement that his first duty is to the Zulu people. That is his job. He is a pragmatist as well as idealist." Like all generalised statements, this one is not perfect, but I still think it comes near the truth. I shall venture another generalisation: the Indaba was a great success largely because Buthelezi is the Chief Minister of the KwaZulu Government and because the White people of Natal are not afraid of him. He speaks a language that they can understand. It is this quality that his enemies regard as hypocritical.

It is now time to consider the findings of the Indaba and I shall confine myself to its constitutional proposals, on the ground that if they are accepted, all things will fall into place. If they are rejected, then the Governments will proceed along its present course of trying to make the tricameral constitution work. The Indaba is in itself a recognition by a number of influential citizens of KwaZulu and Natal that the new constitution is unworkable and unacceptable – and is, in fact, already obsolescent. This is a fact that will not escape the notice of the Government. The constitutional proposals contain a Bill of Rights, but this requires a separate treatment.

The first provision of the constitution is for the appointment of a Governor of the Province by the State President: one of his duties will be to ensure that the legislature does not exceed its powers and attempt to legislate on matters outside its area of competence, i.e. matters which fall under the central Government. These matters include foreign affairs, defence, national intelligence, police, posts and telecommunications, mineral and energy affairs, SATS (i.e. railways and harbours), aviation and inland revenue. In other words, the province will not be an independent State (as in theory the Transkei, Bophuthatswana, Venda and the Ciskei are), but a self-governing unit forming part of the Republic of South Africa.

There will be two Houses in the legislature. There will be a first chamber of 100 members elected on the basis of universal adult suffrage, with a Prime Minister and a 10-member Cabinet. There will also be a system of proportional representation, which will mean that the minority groups – and here we are speaking of racial groups, and particularly the English-speaking and Indian people of Kwazulu-Natal – will be represented in the first chamber. The first must be regarded as one of the most important decisions of the Indaba, because it is the first acceptance of a large gathering of South Africans of the principle of universal adult suffrage. How was this possible? It was certainly not due to any noble recognition of the justice of such a franchise. It was due to the fact that the minority groups of KwaZulu and Natal are not afraid of Chief Buthelezi, Dr Dhlomo and the other distinguished Zulu delegates. One other thing is worth noting. The Indaba was not characterised by any denial of racial differences, or any denial of racial fears, or by any lofty declarations that the concept of race was unimportant, and that all the delegates were brothers and sisters together. Ever since Jan van Riebeeck landed at the Cape on April 6, 1652, the concept of race has been dominant and it became even more dominant in the following three centuries. The Indaba did not attempt to deny the importance of the concept. What it did do was to confront it openly and sensibly and to suggest ways and means of preventing it from endangering any further the lives of millions of human beings.

This was very evident from the proposals adopted for the constitution of the second chamber. This would consist of 50 members, comprised as follows:

> The African background group, 10 members;
> The Afrikaans background group, 10 members;
> The Asian background group, 10 members;
> The English background group, 10 members;
> The South African group, 10 members.

Voters may decide, whatever their own racial origins, to declare themselves to be members of the South African group. I wrote earlier that I would record one instance of a sharp difference on racial grounds. This occurred when one of the Coloured delegations objected to the fact that there was no group for Coloured people, who constitute about two percent of the population of KwaZulu-Natal. When one considers the disproportionate representation given to Afrikaners, English and Indians, this claim does not seem absurd, but although the criticism was sharp, it was exaggerated by one newspaper, and it was said to have created a crisis that threatened the whole Indaba. This was not so and the delegation's ruffled feelings were finally assuaged. This was, however, further evidence of the dominance of the concept of race.

Naturally the proposals for the constitution of the second chamber have been heavily criticised by non-racial idealists and by radicals. Although I do not claim to be a radical, and regard myself as a non-racial idealist, yet I would be prepared to accept the proposals. After the past 30 years of strife and frustration, it gave me grounds for hope that an imperfect solution should be accepted by so large and influential a gathering.

The rights of minorities are still further safeguarded by Clause 5(a)(i) of Section III, Procedures. It reads:

> In the case of legislation which affects the religious, language, cultural or other rights of the members of a Background Group or the South African Group, such legislation will require, in addition to majorities in both chambers, a majority of that group in the second chamber.

One can hardly think of greater safeguards than these.

The important question now is, what will be the attitude of the central Government (which means the National Party) to the Indaba proposals. They have already been rejected by Minister Stoffel Botha, who not long ago was Administrator of Natal and who no doubt feels that his criticism would carry considerable authority. He rejects the proposals on the ground that they do not offer enough security to minority groups and he is, of course, thinking of the Afrikaner. When the proposals were presented formally to Mr Chris Heunis, Minister of Constitutional Development, however, the Minister was more encouraging and said he would require time to consider them. Of course he will require time, because if his response is favourable, or even partly so, his Government would not like to make it public until the White General

Election of May is safely past, for fear that this would strengthen the Right-wing opposition of the Conservative Party and the Herstigte Nasionale Party.

There are several obstacles in the way of Government approval of self-governing KwaZulu-Natal. One is that the proposals do not come from the National Party. The second is that the very holding of the Indaba is not only an implicit rejection of the tricameral constitution, but is also a repudiation of the policies of racial separation, which still prevail in the political world in South Africa. A third obstacle is the Bill of Rights. How can a self-governing unit of the Republic affirm civil rights which are totally incompatible with laws of the Republic? One could give many examples of incompatibility but I shall give only one. The Bill of Rights declares that "everyone has the right to lawfully own land and occupy property anywhere in the province". How can the province guarantee such a right while the Group Areas Act expressly denies it? Will the central Government legislate that the Act will not apply to the new province?

In my view the greatest obstacle of all in the way of Government acceptance is the fact that the Indaba proposals are in a large sense revolutionary and the National Party has in the seven or eight years of "Reform Era" shown no enthusiasm for revolutionary proposals, especially when they come from a non-party source. The three Afrikaner delegations presented a minority report. In spite of the way in which the proposed new constitution protects minority rights, they found them unacceptable. They suffer also from the Afrikaner Nationalist fear of a future in which the conquered become the equal of their conquerors. In this context the resignation of Mr Wynand Malan, MP, from the country's ruling party gives great encouragement to people like the majority of the delegates to the Indaba. Mr Malan has not made the task of the party any easier, but who expects an easy road into the future?

A total or near-total rejection of the Indaba proposals by the ruling party would be a calamity. The total or near-total acceptance would give hope to many who despair of the future. If a new province of Natal should become (in spite of the constitution of the second chamber) an example of a successful non-racial Government, it might inspire the people of other parts of South Africa to set up Indabas of their own and so open the way to the creation of a Federal Republic of South Africa, which many believe to be not only the sensible constitutional solution of our most complex problems, but an alternative to the unitary State that they so fear.

The burden of responsibility that lies on the shoulders of the National Party is immense. It is the hope that the party would consider most earnestly its duty to those who work so hard and faithfully for the Indaba and for the country of which Natal-KwaZulu is only a part.

Optima – *March 1987*

Dr Oscar Dhlomo (1943–) is Secretary-General of Inkatha and one of the leading Black voices of moderation in South African politics.
Dr Frank Mdlalose (1931–) was elected National Chairman of Inkatha in 1976.

ALBERT LUTHULI

His dream was of one South Africa, a society
open to all.

The Memorial Service

ON JULY 21, 1967, Albert Luthuli was struck down and killed by
a train on a narrow railway bridge near his home. On July 23,
1972, 3,000 people gathered in the church at Groutville to attend
a memorial service and to see Mrs Nokukhanya Luthuli unveil
the memorial stone which has been erected on his grave.

It was a church service which included prayers, worship, singing, speeches, even jokes. All White and Indian people had to
obtain permits, because although the church stands on mission
land, the short road to it runs through an African reserve. These
permits enjoined them to behave themselves with dignity, and to
refrain from criticism of the Administration, the Government, or
any of its officials.

These conditions were well obeyed. No-one wanted particularly
to criticise the Government and its officials. But from first to last
there was a complete rejection, implicit and explicit, of apartheid,
separate development, race discrimination of any kind whatever,
and a complete condemnation of the injustices which are inseparable from these things. The permits were obeyed in the letter
and totally ignored in the spirit.

There was a complete absence of fear or hostility. The majority of the congregation was African, but there was a representative number of Coloured, Indian and White people. Luthuli, and the memory of Luthuli, meant something to every person present. There was naturally not the same depth of emotion as there had been five years earlier. The congregation was quieter, but their beliefs and hopes were obviously the same as ever. It is true that the powers-that-be lash out just as viciously as they did five years ago, but there was no sign whatever that this inhibited the speakers or those who applauded them.

Mrs Luthuli sat in the front row, where she had sat five years earlier, flanked by members of her family, including Dr Albertine Ngakane from London. Mrs Thulani Ngcabashe from the United States was not present, nor her husband, nor Dr Pascal Ngakane. Both sons-in-law had been refused visas to enter South Africa. As usual, Mrs. Luthuli was quiet and composed, serious for the most part, but smiling when there was a good story. Her face is that of one who has suffered and endured and never capitulated.

In 1967 the Security Police had sat conspicuously in the front of the church. In 1972 they were not immediately visible, certainly not from the platform. Their presence was not so palpably felt as it had been at the funeral. Why should that be? Were they behaving more considerately? Or were they more sure of themselves? Were they trying to behave less provocatively? Did they think that a memorial service was less dangerous than a funeral service? Not being in their confidence, I cannot answer these questions.

Several men – who quite obviously had been loyal adherents of Luthuli and therefore of the banned African National Congress, and who were dressed in a uniform of khaki shirt and long trousers, with beret, and carrying a flag of green and black – entered the church with stirring shouts of "Africa", "Mayibuye", and singing the song "We shall follow Luthuli". Since the Congress was banned, it has been illegal to display symbols, uniforms, flags, even photographs, which relate to it. Were these men breaking the law? Their uniforms and their flag were not *identical* with the uniforms and flags of the ANC, but there could hardly have been a person in the hall who did not understand that they were supposed to *resemble* the originals. These men were repeating actions taken at the funeral service in 1967, and so far as I know no action was taken then.

One speaker seemed clearly to break the law. This was Mr Sonny Leon, the leader of the Coloured Labour Party, who played portions of Luthuli's Nobel Peace Prize speech to the audience.

The meeting, under the presidency of the Rev BMB Ngidi, began with prayer, reading, and a sermon by the Rev Mr Hendrikse. The opening key speech was given by Chief Gatsha Buthelezi. I quote from his speech, because it was of the same character as all that followed. He said of Luthuli:

> He kindled a spark in men's hearts, he gave them the knowledge that God did not create second or third-class human beings, and by doing so Chief Luthuli struck fear in the hearts of all those who dehumanise and degrade other human beings for no earthly reason except that they were born with a pigmentation of skin different from their own.
>
> For daring to stand for this he suffered the modern South African version of crucifixion.

That is what I meant when I say that speakers did not waste their time on the Administration and its officials. But they condemned utterly the system that the Administration and its officials were trying to administer. Chief Buthelezi struck a grave note which was to be struck again by others. Warning against the growing drift to violence, he said that if disaster overtook South Africa, the country – and by that he must have meant White authority – would be harshly judged because what Luthuli stood for had been "ignored for the sake of political expediency".

Chief Gatsha received a warm welcome and much applause. It is true that he is the Chief Executive of the new country of KwaZulu, it is true that he is involved in a White-conceived machinery, yet he has made it crystal clear – except to those who will not hear – that he does not believe in it, but that he believes it is his duty to act thus for his people.

I shall not weary the reader by writing about all the speeches. There were 13 of them, and 13 is enough. The speakers were there by Mrs Luthuli's invitation, and she was no doubt assisted by advisers, but the choices were approved by her. There was Edgar Brookes, one time head of Adams College, Senator representing Africans, and National Chairman of the Liberal Party. Then the venerable Rev Sivetye telling the story of Luthuli's life. Then Archbishop Hurley, followed by myself. Then Paul Pretorius, the President of the National Union of South African Students, who had elected Luthuli their Honorary President although he was *persona non grata* with the Government. The speeches were interspersed with songs from choirs.

Eighty-six-year-old Selby Msimang, a veteran of the ANC, one time colleague of Luthuli, Matthews, Xuma, Mosaka, and others on the ill-fated Natives Representative Council, one time office-bearer in the outlawed Liberal Party, said of White South Africa: "She has no peace. She is in perpetual fear . . . Every White man and woman has to undergo intensive military training for an imaginary war." He was much applauded, as was Mr Simelane, a colleague of Luthuli in the ANC, banned at the time of the funeral but now free to speak. It fills one with wonder that persons who keep silent when they are banned speak the plain and simple truth when their ban expires. Then Sonny Leon, who played his tape. Then Mr Mayet, presumably to represent the Indian community; but why was the newly-resurrected Indian Congress not invited?

An unexpected speaker was Mrs Helen Suzman, who had come specially from Johannesburg. The Rev Ngidi, the presiding minister, asked the congregation to honour her, and it did so willingly.

The service was closed by Bishop Zulu, the benediction, Nkosi Sikelela, and Morena Boloka. Then we went to the graveyard to see the unveiling. This I cannot report upon, for I was unable to see anything. The crowd pressed round the stone, and how Mrs Luthuli and her daughter Mrs Goba found room to unveil it, I do not know. It was a pity that the stone had not been effectively cordoned off.

I have written that the grave and sombre note was sounded several times. Luthuli's dream was of one South Africa, a society open to all. Is the dream being made unrealisable by present events? Has White South Africa in its passion to preserve itself already destroyed itself, and by its cruel laws alienated Black South Africa for ever? And must there therefore be war to the death? Nobody knows the answer to these questions.

I wrote earlier that I must in honesty refer to the conflict between the pragmatists and the all-or-nothing diehards. One thing was noticeable. The new militant Black body, the South African Students' Organisation, was not represented. Why should they come, to stand on the same platform as Gatsha, Buthelezi who is helping the White Government "to give some kind of authenticity to their lie"? Or Sonny Leon, who uses the machinery of the

Coloured Representative Council? Or Edgar Brookes, or myself, White liberals who blunt the edge of revolution?

Will this attitude become more and more prevalent? The answer I think is Yes. Will it become predominant? The answer is I don't know. Judging by two things alone, the welcome to Buthelezi, and the applause for Helen Suzman, the congregation at Groutville still upheld Luthuli's dream of one South Africa, a society open to all.

What hope there is for relatively peaceful change, who knows? I tried to end my own address – otherwise grave – on the note of hope. I used as my theme one of Luthuli's own themes, the lifetime of knocking on a door that would not open.

> Luthuli was a Christian, and one of the best-known sayings of Jesus is, "Knock and it shall be opened unto you." Yet how, and when, not one of us knows. But of one thing we may be certain, that time is coming.

So came to an end a great day, worthy of the man whose memory we honoured. Nkosi sikelel' iAfrika.

Reality – *September 1972*

Albert Luthuli (1898–1967) became President-General of the African National Congress in 1952, but his restriction to the Lower Tugela the following year made his leadership of the movement virtually impossible. He received the Nobel Peace Prize in 1961.

Mayibuye – Give it back.

Sonny Leon was a founder member of the Coloured Labour Party in 1969 and became leader of the Coloured Representative Council in 1974, immediately refusing to approve the CRC's budget on the ground that it was racially discriminatory. The Government replaced him as chairman with Mrs Alathea Jansen.

Nkosi sikelel' iAfrika – God bless Africa.

JFH Mayet, a Transvaal executive member of the South African Indian Council in the Seventies, was appointed to the President's Council in 1980.

Morena Boloka – God save.

ROBERT SOBUKWE

Everywhere the clenched fist salute is given
and the cry, 'Amandla'.

I Could Have Wept

WE LEAVE ON FRIDAY MORNING for the funeral, Peter Brown and
I. That night we stay at Colesberg in the Cape Province, the beginning of the Great Karoo.

I would not like to live there, but I understand its spell. We
enter one great bowl after another, surrounded by strangely fash-
ioned hills.

As we enter one bowl, Brown says, "Look at that, Paton," and
as we enter the next I say, "Look at that, Brown."

Colesberg, Noupoort, Middelburg and then Graaff-Reinet,
Jewel of the Karoo, that harsh land of sky and hill and stone that
played such a part in the making of the Afrikaner.

The town is tense with expectation. The route to the
Show Ground has been shut off. Traffic cops are everywhere,
but the police are hidden away, and will remain so until the
funeral is over.

Already Black people are streaming towards the ground. White
people stand on their verandahs. What they feel, one does not
know. Nothing of this kind has been seen before in the Great
Karoo.

Everywhere the clenched-fist salute is given and the cry, "Amandla", is answered by the cry, "Ngawethu". The showground is certainly no jewel of the Karoo, an arid oval with a number of rickety stands.

We, with Monica Wilson and her son and daughter-in-law and Margaret Nash, find seats on the lowest row of one of the stands, seats which no-one wants perhaps because of the pitiless sun.

Behind us is Helen Suzman, but she does not stay there long because dignitaries arrive to take her to the covered platform in the centre of the ground.

More and more people, many of them youngsters, are leaving the stands surrounding the platform. A dignitary pleads for them to return, but they will not. This pleading goes on for 20 minutes perhaps, without result.

We in the stands do not know that the demonstrators are demanding the eviction of Chief Buthelezi. Nor do we see the unforgivable manner of his eviction.

His bodyguard has to fire shots. Will he fall? And if he falls, will he ever rise again? If he does not, the consequences for South Africa will be incomputable.

They say that he wept. I do not wonder, I could have wept also.

The demonstrators are not satisfied. Mr Sonny Leon and his colleagues leave, he looking very angry. Next leaves the Transkei delegation, led by Professor Njisane, clad in dark suits.

The religious ceremony begins, a prayer, a lesson, an anthem, an address. But it does not stay religious long.

Mr Pitje, his old fire by no means gone, lambasts the White liberals, beginning with one of the noblest of all White South Africans, WP Schreiner, who went to London in 1909 with Dube, Rubusana, Abdurahman and JT Jabavu to urge the British Government and Parliament not to incorporate the Colour bar in the Act of Union.

I am beginning to understand that the real complaint against White liberals is not their hypocrisy, or their cowardice, but their powerlessness. They were and are politically powerless, just as the great Luthuli and the great ZK Matthews and now Robert Sobukwe were all politically powerless.

I am irritated to think that Sobukwe's funeral is made the occasion to attack Schreiner and White liberals. I say to myself, paraphrasing the words of Victor Borge, that's what I am and that's what I'm gonna be.

In a way this is not Sobukwe's occasion. And certainly not Mrs Sobukwe's. It is the occasion of the demonstrators.

I cannot support the belief that this is the work of a hundred school children. It is not the children who are making those speeches, some of which were not reported because they were too inflammatory. The currents and cross-currents and undercurrents are innumerable. ANC, PAC, SASO, BPC, Black Consciousness, Black Power, they are all here.

I am told that I have insulted Black people by attaching too much importance to the demonstrators. But they ran the show. When Buthelezi was evicted I did not hear one voice raised in protest in that vast assembly. I do not deduce from this that the assembly supported them. I deduce that the assembly was afraid of them.

At one o'clock I decided to leave. I had come to a funeral and this was not a funeral. I did not want to hear any more speeches. I returned to the hotel, but at three o'clock I went to the burial ground and looked at the graves of past Sobukwes. The sun was pitiless, and I returned to the junction of the main road and the road to the cemetery. Coming up the main road was the vast procession and I stood bareheaded to pay my last respects, and to receive the jeers of the demonstrators.

They did not see an old White man, hat in hand before the cortege of a Black man whom he had known long ago. They saw only one of the hated oppressors.

Then a drop of sweetness. A Black woman in a yellow-brown robe asked for a lift to the town. She sat in front, and three of her friends, members of a choir, I think, sat behind.

She introduced all four by name and I said my name was Paton. "Alan Paton?" asked one. "I know you." Two of them had read *Cry, the Beloved Country*. They marvelled that I had come from Durban for the funeral. We parted in a great invocation of divine blessings.

Then a drop of sourness. Ten or 12 young White policemen sitting on a wall. Jeers from one or two. Did they know me? Or was I just a White man who had come to the funeral of a Black revolutionary? Or had they seen my four passengers?

I thought of returning to ask what right they had to call out to civilians. But I did not, partly because the sun was pitiless.

Then the Press, of course. The hotel was full of them. What did I think? I thought it was an ominous historical occasion, and that it put the future of Inkatha, the Triple Alliance and Chief Buthelezi himself in question.

These remarks have greatly angered the Chief. He has told a friend that if I were big enough I would withdraw them. Well I withdraw them, though I must admit that I am not quite sure how big that makes me.

There are very few people for whom I would withdraw. The Chief is one, Helen Suzman is another, WP Schreiner too, of course, but I was only six when he went to London.

If I had foreseen the consequences of my remarks I would have said that the events at Graaff-Reinet posed a grave challenge to the future of Inkatha, the alliance and the Chief, and a grave challenge to the future of our country. Well, they do.

Is this insensate mindlessness, this unrelieved hatred, going to defeat the integrity and the humanity of a Buthelezi in the struggle for the Black soul? It is a question that has to be confronted.

Gatsha Buthelezi, I have prayed for some time that you will reap the fruits of your labours and live to see the realisation of your aspirations. And I shall continue to do so.

Bishop Tutu is reported to have said at or after this funeral occasion, that at last he sees the dawn of freedom.

Well, if it comes after the manner of Graaff-Reinet, God help us all.

Sunday Tribune – *March 19, 1978*

Robert Sobukwe (1924–1978) was an early leader of the Youth League of the African National Congress, but in protest against the growing influence of White Communists within the movement broke away from the ANC to establish the Pan Africanist Congress in 1959.

Amandla – Power

Ngawethu – It is ours.

Professor Monica Wilson, a leading social anthropologist who taught at the University of Cape Town from 1952–73, became known for her research on the rituals and villages of the Nyakyusa in Central Africa.

Margaret Nash's pioneering research on the Black peoples of Southern Africa made her one of the region's most important social anthropologists.

Professor Mlahleni Njisane was Transkei Ambassador to South Africa in the mid-Seventies.

Godfrey Pitje was a lecturer in anthropology at the University of Fort Hare, where he became President of the Youth League of the African National Congress in 1949.

Bishop Desmond Tutu (1931–) was elected Secretary-General of the South African Council of Churches in 1978 and received the Nobel Peace Prize in 1984. He became head of the Anglican Church of South Africa in 1986.

BISHOP TUTU

I think your morality is confused, as was the
morality of the Church in the inquisition.

Your Philosophies Trouble Me

MY CONGRATULATIONS, Bishop Tutu. I have no doubt that the
majority of the people of South Africa congratulate you also. I
congratulate you also on the magnificence of the Nobel Prize and
I hope that you use it wisely and well and generously.

From what I read, that is your intention, and I read that your
first concern will be Black education.

I have never won a prize like that. I am afraid that my skin is
not the right colour. But if I did ever win a prize like that my first
concern would be the same as yours.

Now quite apart from the joy that has come to your family and
your friends, and to Black people in general, you are also entering
a new period in your life of increased responsibility.

Your words and actions are going to count more in the future
than they have counted in the past. You are, in fact, the first Black
man to assume a position of national responsibility since the days
of Albert Luthuli, your predecessor.

You assume this position at a time when our country is fragmented as never before. The hard fact is that we have nothing in our country that could be called a "common interest".

What are you going to do?

Are you going to help us to find a common interest, or are you going to bring some of the fragments together?

I do not envy you your responsibility. It will require a measure of wisdom and courage that has never been required and certainly has never been shown before.

I remember well when Albert Luthuli was awarded the Nobel Prize for Peace. There was similar rejoicing, but those were easier days. I was one of the guests at the farewell lunch and after the lunch we all went to the Louis Botha Airport where a vast crowd had gathered.

In those days the main hall was for "Whites Only", but no-one took any notice of that, not even the authorities, who decided not to try to control the uncontrollable.

However, the authorities were afraid that the crowd might try to follow Luthuli on to the tarmac. But who could control them? There was only one person who could, and that was Luthuli himself.

He was given a box to stand on, and he said to the crowd: "Soon I shall be going out of that gate and you must understand that nobody – absolutely nobody – must follow me." Nobody did.

There was more White and official anger against Luthuli's award than against Tutu's. Both have been described as "political awards". And, of course, they are.

Who can separate politics from peace in these days? Who can indeed separate politics from anything?

Our State President has refused to make any observation. Mr Pik Botha has said "no comment" – and that certainly is the wisest thing he has said for some considerable time.

The award of the Nobel Prize to Bishop Tutu is a clear signal to our country. It is first a signal that the outside world will not leave us alone. It is secondly a signal that the demand for the ending of apartheid and separate development will go on increasing in intensity.

Will the West finally ditch us?

Will they finally say: "We tried constructive engagement, but you yourselves wouldn't do anything"?

Will the West agree to the ultimate step of economic sanctions?

This is a momentous question, and I don't answer it with any authority except my own.

I hope with all my heart that the West won't cast us out, not only for the sake of South Africa, but for the sake of the West too.

I am not a fanatical anti-Communist, but if the West casts us out, that would be a clear signal to the Soviet Union that perhaps the time had come for a new adventure.

Then God save us all.

Bishop Tutu, I want to ask you a last question. I do not understand how your Christian conscience allows you to advocate disinvestment. I do not understand how you can put a man out of work for a high moral principle.

You and I both know well the parable of the sheep and the goats, and we know well the importance that Jesus attached to the feeding of the hungry and the giving of water to the thirsty.

Yet you could put a man out of a job and make his family go hungry so that some high moral principle could be upheld.

It would go against my own deepest principles to advocate anything that would put a man – and especially a Black man – out of a job.

Therefore I cannot understand your position.

I think your morality is confused just as was the morality of the Church in the inquisition, or the morality of Dr Verwoerd in his utopian dreams. You come near to saying that the end justifies the means, which is a thing no Christian can do.

However, I wish you luck, wisdom and courage. You'll need them all.

Our rulers have done some unforgiveable things. We had Albert Luthuli but they threw him away.

We had ZK Matthews and they threw him away. We had Robert Sobukwe – he was thrown away.

I hope they don't throw you away, too.

Sunday Times – *October 21, 1984*

NELSON MANDELA

I cannot sell my birthright, nor am I prepared
to sell the birthright of the people.

Mandela and Botha

A STRANGE THOUGHT CAME to me while I was thinking about Mandela. It has been Black men who have made the great political speeches of my life – Luthuli, Matthews, Sobukwe and Mandela. There was only one White exception and that was JH Hofmeyr, but he belonged to the pre-modern age.

All the others belong to the modern age, which for me began in 1948, when the Afrikaner Nationalists came to power.

Not one of the Nationalists ever made a great political speech – that is, of course, in my opinion – but what they did do was to create the opportunity for the great speeches of Luthuli, Matthews, Sobukwe and Mandela.

There is only one Nationalist politician who has come near to making a great political speech and that is PW Botha.

Whether he will ever succeed in making one, I don't know.

He still has a long way to go and he hasn't got a lot of time to make it.

He is 69 years of age. He is a little older than Mandela, who this year will be 67.

A short while ago, PW Botha "stunned the House" by offering Mandela his freedom, after 21 years in prison.

It was something that his two predecessors, Verwoerd and Vorster, would, and could, never have done.

Our State President undoubtedly considered the matter very carefully and consulted his closest colleagues. Then he made his offer. He would free Mandela if he renounced violence.

The whole matter was regarded as so important that Mandela was allowed to make a public statement – the first since his statement from the dock in the Rivonia Trial in 1964, at which he was sentenced to imprisonment for life.

His public statement was read by his daughter, Zindzi, at a meeting at Jabulani, Soweto. In his statement Mandela refused to accept the State President's offer.

Of this refusal, Mrs Helen Suzman said:

"It is a grim reflection on the apartheid system that a man chooses to remain in jail after more than 21 years' imprisonment rather than live a life of united freedom under that system."

It is not only a grim reflection. It is also the act of a very extraordinary man, a man of the class of Luthuli, Matthews and Sobukwe.

They would have done the same.

All these four men were by talents and character equipped to play a part in government equal to that of PW Botha. Not one of them was allowed to do so.

All of them were compelled by the National Party to lead a life devoted to resistance and protest.

One cannot say that the National Party destroyed their lives, because, in fact, it made them immortal.

In refusing the offer of freedom, Mandela demanded that the Government itself should renounce violence.

What did he mean? Does not every Government in the last resort use violence?

That may be true, but not every Government takes away from people houses and property that they had legally acquired and is prepared to use force to remove them.

Not every Government denies people the right to go to any place to seek work.

Not every Government sends to prison people who are in possession of documents published by organisations that have been banned.

One of the greatest offences of the National Party was that it gave powers to the Minister of Justice to detain and imprison men and women without any reference to the courts of law.

It is these forced removals, and this contempt of the Rule of Law, that have alienated our country more and more from the democratic countries of the world.

This alienation grows day by day.

Mandela's great statement included these words:

"I am not less life-loving than you are. But I cannot sell my birthright, nor am I prepared to sell the birthright of the people, in order to be free."

Then he asked what such a freedom was worth? And he said: "Only free men can negotiate. Prisoners cannot enter into contracts."

He ended by saying: "I will return."

Will Mandela return? Nobody knows the answer. The difficulties in the way of his return are formidable.

He asked that PW Botha should show that he is different from Malan, Strijdom and Verwoerd.

The irony of this is that PW Botha is different. But is the difference enough?

Mandela is, in fact, demanding the repeal of many of the security laws. And the end of detention without trial. And the end of the monstrous powers that our White Parliament has given to the Minister.

Mandela said categorically: "Let him say that he will dismantle apartheid."

Mandela is saying: "I can't accept this. You must offer much more than that."

I have no doubt that PW Botha understands very well what Mandela is saying.

Mandela has put PW Botha in a position where he must move faster, or stay where he is, or retreat – all of which three courses are immensely difficult.

We are living through one of the most historic periods of our 300 years. Perhaps a new era is beginning.

Either PW Botha has taken a great step of which he understands the full meaning, or he has not fully understood it.

I hope the first is true. What should he do now?

I presume to try to answer this question, but it must be clear that I have no responsibility whatsoever. I have retired from the game and now watch from the sidelines.

What should he do?

The first thing he should do is to unban Mrs Mandela unconditionally.

The second thing he should do is to arrange for special facilities at Pollsmoor, where Mandela and his "comrades" can receive any-one they wish – their families, the UDF, Helen Suzman, Van Zyl Slabbert, Buthelezi, Qoboza, Tutu, Boesak, even their friend Oliver Tambo, anyone at all – not to exchange compliments, but to deliberate on how to co-operate with the National Party in the planning of a new era.

Or to decide not to co-operate at all and to stay in prison till the "day of liberation".

They must decide whether to ask for anything, or to ask for something less.

They will need almost divine wisdom, for which 21 years in prison may or may not have been the best preparation.

They must consider the Freedom Charter anew, for it embodies – again in my opinion – two incompatible aims.

One aim is the guarantee of what are called human rights, such as are found in the American Bill of Rights; the other is the nationalisation of the banks and the mines and State control of all other industry and trade, such as obtains in the USSR.

No country in the world has yet succeeded in reconciling them.

This procedure is more likely to bring results. It saves Mandela from what was virtually a "Yes or No" situation.

When Mandela and his friends are ready, they may or may not invite PW Botha and his friends to talk with them. If they do, then may divine wisdom be given to them all.

Sunday Times – *March 3, 1985*

~~~~~~~~~~~~

A Letter to the Prime Minister

DEAR MR PRIME MINISTER,

It is clear that the release of Mr Nelson Mandela from Robben Island is becoming a political issue of the first magnitude. It is going to have a profound influence on the constitutional talks which you are hoping to have with Black leaders.

In fact, I would predict that we are approaching the stage when recognised Black leaders will take part only if Mr Mandela is released and takes part also. Those who are willing to take part without making such conditions will lose all credibility and their careers as leaders will be finished.

This puts you in a very difficult position. Your predecessor, Mr BJ Vorster, was adamantly opposed to the release of Mr Mandela. It did not appear to disturb him at all that a man could spend the rest of his life in prison for opposing by unlawful means the Government of the day and for contemplating subversive acts that were strikingly similar to those contemplated by the Ossewabrandwag of the Second World War. Mr Vorster in his career as Minister and Prime Minister repeatedly announced his determination to uphold law and order, but he was prepared to overthrow a law and order in whose fashioning he had had no part.

This is the same stance as has been adopted by some of the opponents of your Government.

Those Nationalist opponents who were found guilty of committing unlawful acts during the years of the war were released from prison as soon as the National Party came to power in 1948. If a Black Government were to come to power in South Africa, it would release Mr Mandela and all political prisoners immediately. Is that what you are waiting for?

Those Nationalist opponents of General Smuts served but a mere fraction of their sentences. Mr Mandela has already served 16 years. Isn't that enough?

I earnestly hope that you will never contemplate releasing Mr Mandela and others from prison and then immediately imposing banning orders upon them. Such a step would not only be futile, it would also be dangerous. Mr Eddie Daniels, once a member of the Liberal Party, adopted unlawful means of opposition and was sentenced to 15 years. He spent that time in study and reflection, he was a law-abiding prisoner, he emerged from his bitter experience and was immediately given a banning order for five years. Can one never expiate an offence under a Nationalist Government?

I urge you to release Mr Mandela from prison and to invite him to your office to talk about the future of your common country. This act of release must be regarded as a prelude to a new era in South African history. The underlying assumptions will be that the progress towards the removal of all discrimination will be steady and sustained and that the use of violence will be totally proscribed.

Nelson Mandela is a man of the calibre of his predecessors, Chief Albert Luthuli and Professor ZK Matthews, and I have no reason to believe that 16 years of Robben Island have decreased his stature. Quite apart from that, if you do not talk to him, whom else are you going to talk to and who else is going to talk to you?

I realise fully the political and psychological difficulties that you will have to surmount before you can take a step of this nature. But if you cannot surmount them the consequences for our country will be grave indeed.

You have taken on a hard job, the hardest that's ever confronted a Prime Minister of South Africa. May you be given the courage and the wisdom to perform it. This is the wish and prayer of millions of your fellow countrymen.

ELECTIONS AND REFERENDUM

The Government should stop speaking with so many voices.

Why I Could Not Celebrate

I REMEMBER CELEBRATING THE coming into being of the Union of South Africa on May 31, 1910. We celebrated in Alexandra Park, Maritzburg, and were given buns and ginger beer. I did not know that the British Government had allowed the four South African colonies to form a Union with a Colour bar, but I can be excused for that because I was only seven years old. I am sure I did not even know the meaning of the words "Colour bar".

On May 31, 1961, the Republic of South Africa replaced the Union. I did not celebrate this event because I had voted against the Republic.

Nor did I celebrate on May 31, 1971.

But I was invited by letter in the most courteous terms to celebrate the 20th birthday of the Republic on May 31, 1981.

I was assured that the celebrations would have no Colour bar. I knew at once that I could not, and I replied, also in the most courteous terms, that I could not.

I think it very probable that I wrote that I "regretted" being unable to do so.

Why did I refuse?

My refusal had nothing whatever to do with the fact that I had voted against the Republic in 1961. Nor did it have anything to do with any prejudice against the republican form of government.

I did not refuse to celebrate because I do not like republics, but because I did not like the kind of republic I had.

I could not possibly celebrate a republic which claims to be a democracy and yet has shown such a contempt for the Rule of Law. Nor a republic that allows detention without charge, trial, or access, just like all the most disreputable republics in the world.

It is almost unbelievable that the authorities believed that the Coloured people would join in the celebrations. It is almost unbelievable that the authorities had the nerve to ask them.

In March 1961, the Government decided that Coloured voters would be excluded from the Republican referendum. What self-respecting Coloured person could celebrate in 1981?

It is equally unbelievable that it should have been believed that Indian South Africans would take part in celebrations. They, and the Coloured people, have not only borne the brunt of the Group Areas Act, but have paid for it, too.

They have paid to be kicked out of their own houses.

Dr Monty Naicker, who was silenced for more than 10 years, lost his beautiful house in Innes Road in Durban.

The loss of his home, and the years of silence, changed him into a grave, stoical man – in happier days he had been one of the jolliest of men and one of the most jovial hosts. But the Republic took away his parties and a great deal of his jolliness.

Chief Gatsha Buthelezi has already decided that the schools of KwaZulu will not celebrate.

It would be strange if they had celebrated. If KwaZulu children visit a White school, what can they do but compare it with their own?

Did I write that I "regretted" not being able to celebrate the Republic? Well, I do regret it. I regret that there isn't something better to celebrate.

But when I remember the death of Steve Biko, the death of Imam Haron who "fell down the stairs and died", the banning of decent, honourable men and women, the remorseless resettlements, the pitiful education, all in the interests of a rigid and heartless system that is falling to pieces about our ears, I realise that to celebrate would not only be impossible, it would also be a blow in the face for those who have stood for the same values as myself – some of which were despised and rejected by the Republic.

And, if the Republic of South Africa continues to despise and reject these values, there will come a time, not of celebration, but of utter desolation. The year 1981 has one bitter irony: the Afrikaner Nationalist, having hurt and alienated so many of us, now wants to bring us all together in a great celebration.

But many of us won't come. I have it in my heart to pity those gentlemen who invited me to join in.

Sunday Times – *February 15, 1981*

The 1983 Election

WE MAY DRAW one certain conclusion from the by-election results ... A bitter struggle inside Afrikanerdom lies ahead and that means a bitter struggle for White South Africa.

It is 10 years since Prime Minister BJ Vorster promised the world a "surprise" at the way we would dismantle racial discrimination. It is four years since Minister Piet Koornhof made the same promise in America.

Neither promise was fulfilled and neither promise will be fulfilled for a long time – except for the at-present unlikely scenario of revolution, external intervention and the collapse of White supremacy.

We may draw another conclusion. The National Party is now the middle-of-the-road White party. It will attract the support of all White voters who want to go faster but not too fast.

This now confirmed status of the National Party will not make things easy for the Progressive Federal Party. The initial successes of the PFP were gained because it offered change in a time of almost no change.

That time has gone.

All White voters with decent instincts and apprehensive natures will prefer change to no change, but they will prefer slower change to faster change.

That is what PW Botha is offering them.

I do not find it easy to draw conclusions about the Conservative Party. Professor Willem Kleynhans, for whose judgment I have much respect, says that it has emerged as a "most powerful force" both in the cities and on the platteland.

The Waterkloof result does not point to such a conclusion. But that the CP will become more powerful is certain. It would become even more powerful if it could come to terms with the HNP.

In Waterberg, CP and HNP polled 8,345 against the NP's 3,812. In Soutpansberg the HNP withdrew, leaving the CP to poll 5,479 against the NP's 6,100.

They are ominous figures for us all.

The CP can be expected to show great strength in the Transvaal platteland. Ironically, it will be aided by the electoral overloading of urban constituencies by 15 percent and the underloading of rural constituencies by 15 percent.

In 1947, Smuts was urged to abolish this, but refused, probably because he supported it in 1910. It would now be advantageous for PW Botha to abolish the differentiation, but perhaps he will refuse on sentimental grounds also, because it brought his party to power in 1948.

If he does not, the CP will probably oust the PFP from its role as the official Opposition.

The CP will capitalise on undiluted White fear, prejudice, even hatred. It will produce no political philosophy because it is totally irrational. It is led by a man of great intelligence and no sense whatsoever. Nor, I believe, is he a leader of the same class as PW Botha. For years he dithered and vacillated, unable to make up his mind.

PW is not a vacillator. He has a resolute face, even though he is resolute about many things I don't care for. He has no feeling for the Rule of Law, just like his predecessor. The rule of the party is all and soon, of course, the rule of the President may be all too.

I have described PW as a man who was born in the prison of Afrikaner Nationalism, but who doesn't want to die there, neither himself nor his people. And it's a hard prison to get out of.

When you at last open the gates, you don't emerge immediately into the fresh air. You emerge into a second prison, that of Separate Development. The air is certainly fresher, but it is still a prison.

We have been given these historic promises that we are moving away from racial discrimination. But separate development in its essence is racial discrimination.

Separate development has two irredeemable features:

- It offers 70 percent of the people 13 percent of the land;
- In the second place it shuts off Black people from the overwhelming bulk of South Africa's wealth and resources.

PW can create 50 chambers of parliament, he can have 50 president's councils, he can suck the brains of 50 Worralls and 50 De Crespignys, but if he can't remove these two weaknesses, he won't get anywhere.

There is a much used and abused expression that we are at the crossroads, the country even civilisation itself. But we in South Africa are truly at the crossroads, now in 1983.

PW is at the crossroads, too. I'll be quite honest – I want him to take the reform road. Only I want him to walk a bit faster.

Sunday Tribune – May 15, 1983

&xxxxxxxxxxx&

I Will Vote No

I SHALL VOTE NO in the referendum with no feeling of self-righteousness. I shall vote no with a feeling of deep regret that the Prime Minister broke his party in two to so little purpose. I guess, however, his party would not let him go any further.

I shall vote no for the most obvious reason of all, that the African people are excluded from the governing process. I can vote no and still look the Prime Minister in the face. But if I voted yes, I would not be able to look the Chief Minister of KwaZulu in the face.

I think it is possible the Prime Minister could lose all three referendums.

If he loses the White referendum, what will he do? He should resign of course. The alternative is that the party will depose him and that Mr FW de Klerk will become our Prime Minister.

White South Africa will move to the Right and nearer to some kind of disaster. The nations of the West will give up the policy of "constructive involvement" and the Afrikaner conscience will be more troubled that ever.

It is, I fear, a tragedy we are watching.

Sunday Tribune – *August 28, 1983*

❧❧❧❧❧❧❧❧❧

The Referendum

THE WHITE VOTERS of South Africa have handsomely endorsed the Prime Minister's new constitution. The much-feared shift of Afrikanerdom to the Right has not taken place. The results of the referendum must be regarded as a personal triumph of the first order for Mr Botha. I thought his speech of acknowledgment commendably modest. There was no sign of a tantrum. I would guess that the word boerehaat has been dropped from his vocabulary.

There can be little doubt as to what happened on Wednesday. White South Africa said to the Prime Minister, go ahead with change. Some of the Yes voters would have added, but go slowly. Others would have added, but go a bit faster.

I myself voted No, but I do not think the world has come to an end. I regard the referendum as a step in that process of painful evolution of which I have so many times written. I regard Dr Van Zyl Slabbert's statement that the official Opposition should support any real reform as morally and pragmatically sound.

The Progressive Federal Party is in no easy position. Many of its supporters voted Yes in spite of the decision of the party to say No. One cannot deduce from that any intention for such supporters to swing to the NP or the NRP. PFP supporters should not do that. The Prime Minister has moved to a central position, and should be opposed from the Left.

The Government itself should stop speaking with so many voices. The Prime Minister seems to think there is some finality in the new constitution. Mr Schlebusch says it is the beginning of a process, while Mr FW der Klerk has assured Nationalist women that there's not so much change after all. How can the Prime Minister speak as though there is some kind of finality? He has started a process that cannot be stopped.

There is talk of amending or modifying or abolishing the Immorality Act and the Mixed Marriages Act. But the two fundamental laws of racial separation are the Group Areas Act and the Population Registration Act. If the new Parliaments are to be worth anything, they must start with these two Acts.

I do not agree with those who dismiss the new constitution as merely tokenistic and cosmetic and as a blatant attempt to deceive the West. It is the best constitution that you could get from an Afrikaner Nationalist. It is therefore adulterated, because when you mix nationalism with things like religion, literature, justice, truth, the product must inevitably be adulterated. The more fierce the nationalism, the greater the adulteration. I hope that the nationalism of the National Party will now somewhat abate.

Is this new deal a slap in the face for the Black man? Yes it is. Chief Buthelezi has reacted very strongly and has made a proposal of a "marriage of convenience" between Inkatha and the ANC and PAC. It is a proposal made in desperation and frustration, but it won't work.

The exclusion of the Black man is, of course, the fundamental flaw in the constitution. It is justified by the argument that the Black man has his own homelands where he can achieve freedom, independence and presumably happiness. When will our Prime Minister and his party realise the bitter truth that there is no future for the homelands? They have no access to the resources and wealth of South Africa, without which they will never achieve freedom and independence, and certainly not happiness.

It was Dr. Verwoerd who created the myth of the homelands. It offered Afrikaner Nationalists an escape from the brutality and immorality of raw apartheid. It is now going to offer an escape from looking really hard into the future. But some of them are already looking.

Did I say that the referendum was a step in the process of painful evolution? Yes I did. It is a step on a long, long road, and in the words of Christina Rossetti, it winds up hill all the way. But that's the way our country is, and if you are going to stay in it, you might as well try to like it. A grim affection, that's what it is.

Sunday Tribune – *November 6, 1983*

THE CHURCH

The religious arguments of apartheid can only be described as fatuous.

A Great Test for the NGK

THE SUSPENSION OF THE Nederduitse Gereformeerde Kerk (NGK) and the Nederduitsch Hervormde Kerk (NHK) by the World Alliance of Reformed Churches at Ottawa in August was inevitable and completely justified.

The alliance has for years shown great patience in the hope that our White reformed churches would renounce apartheid, but their hopes were vain.

This suspension has a claim to be regarded as one of the great events in the history of Nationalist Afrikanerdom.

Our White reformed churches got what they deserved. Since 1948 they have stood foursquare behind the racial policies of apartheid and racial separation.

What is more, they have claimed scriptural and theological justification for these policies. That was the way God wanted things to be.

The religious, philosophical and moral arguments of apartheid and separation can only be described as fatuous. It was claimed that God had created the separate races and that therefore He would approve of policies to keep them separate.

At one time the story of the Tower of Babel was used to justify racial separation, but the argument has taken such a terrible world beating that it now lives on only in the most reactionary circles.

It has been replaced by what is thought to be a more intellectually respectable argument, namely that God's great gift to men and women was not their humanity but their membership of the nation.

It is time that Christ taught that we are all one, but this teaching must not be taken in a liberal or literal or sentimental sense, but in a spiritual and figurative sense.

This intellectual nonsense was preached by the three National Afrikaner prophets, the late Dr Nico Diederichs, Dr Piet Meyer of ex-SABC fame and by Professor G Cronje of the University of Pretoria.

It was propounded in the political arena by the late Dr HF Verwoerd. It deceived the overwhelming majority of the Afrikaner nation, but worse still, a considerable majority of Afrikaner churchmen.

One must not conceal the truth, they were looking for security.

In my younger days I was frustrated and exasperated beyond measure by seeing four of the best intellects in White South Africa committing the greatest of all intellectual offences, that of making their intellects the tools of their passions.

Sensible people try to harmonize the often conflicting claims of reason and passion. But these prophets used their intellectual powers to prove what they wanted to believe, to themselves and others.

They did not foresee that economic forces would make racial separation impossible. They were not interested in economics, only in Afrikaner and White supremacy and survival.

They had political power and were able to waste 20, 30 years, trying to force South Africa and its people into a mould into which they would never fit.

They committed another offence for which I find it more difficult to forgive them. They were willing to inflict injury and suffering on their powerless fellow-countrymen, on the grounds that the ideal was so lofty, the goal so ineffable, that any means were justifiable.

Now my Christian belief, and the belief of many others who are not totally obsessed with survival, is that one may never inflict injury or suffering.

I shall not here deal with the problem of the just war. I have never been challenged to be so brave in my belief as those young men who today will not do military service.

How does one reconcile the claims of God and of man? Peter said, obey God rather than man, but he was only a fisherman and was not learned in philosophy or theology.

The Nationalist Afrikaner philosophers found the perfect solution. Man had two first duties – one to obey God and the other to love and defend his nation.

Now luckily these two could be reconciled in that intellectual and moral monstrosity known as Christian-Nationalism, which was never taught in the Gospels.

Indeed the Gospels taught something quite different. They taught that whosoever would save his life would lose it.

One should not expect a political party to follow such teaching. But one can only be contemptuous of the attempt to identify Nationalist policy with the teaching of the Gospels.

My own judgment is that these three philosopher kings and their chief political ally inflicted a great wound on the soul of Afrikanerdom.

It was to be expected defiantly to the decision taken at Ottawa.

The NHK performed the intellectual and moral miracle of identifying its race exclusivity with its religion.

Apparently the Lord of the Church wants them to exclude all Black people, and this enables them to defy the Christian world. To the Christian world this identification is grotesque.

The NGK is not so defiant, even though one of its dominees (ministers) tried to prove to Ottawa that his church is open to all. He did not tell Ottawa that Black people have been asked to leave White funeral services and that some dominees have refused to continue the service while Black people remained.

I was at the historic Cottesloe Conference with both the NHK and the NGK. I found the NHK delegation unloving and arrogant and determined not to yield one jot or tittle of their racial dogmas.

I found the NGK deeply troubled. A leading NGK dominee named Dr CF Beyers Naudé called me into his room and urged me not to give up trying or hoping.

He indicated that important changes were pending in the NGK. That was 22 years ago. The important changes never came. Beyers Naudé was rejected by his own Church and in 1977 was banned for five years.

The one-time moderator had become an outcast. But he saved his soul.

Change is now coming to the NGK. A growing number of White dominees have decided that they can no longer accept apartheid.

The "Coloured" daughter church of the NGK has demanded that the mother church should confess its guilt and reject apartheid, otherwise the daughter church will reject her.

The "Coloured" church has gone further, it has joined the South African Council of Churches, hated by all "true" Afrikaners.

Will change convert the NGK? Or will it tear it in two, as it has already torn the Nationalist Party and as it threatens to tear the Broederbond?

The NGK has held a position of great influence in the lives of our rulers, an influence, I might say, that has hardly ever been used. Is the NGK going to use it now?

If the NGK – as a Church – came to its senses and renounced apartheid, I would see great hope for our country. But if the NGK breaks in two, I would not.

The NGK will then go down in history as the great Church that failed in its duty, not only towards Afrikanerdom, but towards South Africa and all its people.

Will the NGK meet this great test successfully? One cherishes that hope, but hope deferred makes the heart sick.

I hope, but fear also.

Sunday Times – *October 8, 1982*

FEDERATION

The road towards ultimate federation will not be easy, but at least it is a road, not a cul-de-sac.

Government Without War

SO THE PROGS AND the Bassonites have come together. That's good news in a country where all the news lately has been bad. I should like to look at this new party from the viewpoint of a veteran who now sits in the Retired Persons Enclosure. If one looks at him closely one will see that he is watching the game with what might be called ferocious detachment.

The Prime Minister has just told the cheering crowds in Bloemfontein that the political opposition is in a shambles.

For those of us who have no faith in the ability of the Prime Minister or his party to satisfy the just aspirations of Black people, the coming together of three of the opposition groups must be a matter for moderate satisfaction.

It must be moderate in view of the depth of our crisis. But it can also be a matter for satisfaction that the basis of opposition has become much firmer.

It is clear that between the determination to make South Africa a country of nine or 10 politically independent States, and the demand for a unitary State with a universal franchise, there can be no compromise whatever. One is total political separation; the other is total political integration.

If these two views are to be held unyieldingly, the only outcome is war, revolution and external intervention. And the inevitable outcome of that would be the end of Afrikanerdom, the end of any White tenancy and the destruction of the economy, its cities, railways, ports, medicine and agriculture.

Some Black people, in fact, desire this. In their view any price is worth paying to achieve the end of White domination and its oppressive laws.

But the price they would pay would be the exclusion of South Africa from the modern world for at least a generation.

Is any other form of constitution possible? The new Progressive Federal Party lays down that any new constitution must be drawn up, negotiated and agreed upon by representatives of all sections of the people.

That is essential. The days are gone when new constitutions can be decided by White party congresses meeting behind closed doors.

The PFP would not, however, go to such a national convention without proposals of its own. These proposals would be:

1. Separation of legislative, executive and judicial powers.
2. Decentralisation of power on a geographic basis – in other words, federation (or confederation).
3. A Bill of Rights.
4. A strong independent judiciary, empowered to maintain the constitution.

I am convinced that the federal constitution is the only one that could be achieved without war.

The powers and constitution of the federal Government would be decided at the convention, and should in the beginning be limited as far as possible.

The existing laws would be repealed, amended, or confirmed, with the avoidance of compulsory separation or compulsory integration always in mind.

The new party stands unreservedly for the reinstatement of the Rule of Law, so grievously eroded by our present Government. This does not mean the end of the Security Police, but it would mean the end of their monstrous powers, including those of indefinite detention without trial.

The total sovereignty of parliaments would disappear, and also the powers of parliaments to great sovereignty to their ministers. All parliaments would be subject to the constitution, and the constitution would be interpreted by the Supreme Court, as in the United States.

The PFP has come out in favour of a system of free enterprise, which must be such as to guarantee an equal opportunity to all to share in its benefits.

In other words, it would oppose unlimited capitalism and it would oppose unlimited socialism. The days of unlimited capitalism are gone, but unlimited socialism is still with us and leads always to the destruction of human liberty, and to the creation of totalitarian bureaucracies.

The policy is utopian, of course, as to a certain extent a party policy must be. But it avoids the danger of utopian ideology, which also inevitably leads to the destruction of human liberty.

In fact, human liberty is its chief concern, and that is how it should be. It is a relief to get away from the relentless Nationalist pursuit of racial identity.

Will the PFP ever be the Government? The question is unanswerable. Indeed one deduces from the policy that if the PFP ever becomes the Government it would of its own choice not be the Government for long.

At the moment the important thing is that it should be a united and principled Opposition.

Mr Colin Eglin ended his speech to the new party by saying: "I am excited. I am confident. I am full of hope."

I can't go as far as that, but it is my hope that his hope should be realised.

Sunday Tribune – *November 11, 1971*

〰〰〰〰〰

Focus on Federation

IN 1910 SOUTH AFRICA was a unitary State though without equality for all. Dr Verwoerd was the first of our Prime Ministers to realise that we couldn't go on like that. It was he who put apartheid into a new dress and called it separate development.

How much was fraud and how much was idealism makes an interesting discussion, but that is not our aim here. The important thing is that the recognition of the homelands, the creation of new instruments of power, however weak, the progress towards a measure of political independence, is an irreversible process.

Any White party that promises to reverse it is foolish. And what is more, the full consequences of the process can at that moment only dimly be foreseen.

One of Dr Verwoerd's main motives was naturally the fear of the unitary State. But I firmly believe – and this makes some radicals impatient with me – that he, although I do not think it mattered deeply to him, restored a measure of respect to Black people, that he made it possible for Black leaders in 1973 and 1974 to speak to White South Africa in a way that had not been heard since the days of Luthuli and Mandela, that he made it possible for these Black leaders to speak openly without the danger of being silenced, that he opened doors to a new kind of constitutional development.

In other words, he was opening the doors to a new kind of common society, though that was not his intention. The doors were not opened wide, but up till then they had not been opened at all.

That is why I think Mr Vorster's notion of a "power bloc" of say 10 completely independent States is an attempt to evade the conclusion that we might be moving towards a new kind of common society.

Power blocs are formed by nations that have a strong common interest. And the only way to create common interests is to give the homeland States a greater share in the wealth and resources of the whole Republic, and that includes a greater share of the taxes to which they, directly and indirectly, contribute so much. That is much more like a common society than it is like a power bloc.

Our 10 nations cannot be completely independent. They will certainly be completely interdependent. Inexorably our constitutional development points to the ultimate emergence of a federal society.

The homelands are economically dependent on "White" South Africa, as "White" South Africa is on them. But the relationship is grotesquely lopsided. It is a rich-poor relationship, where the rich are rich because of the poor, and the poor are poor because of the rich.

One cannot have a true federation while this disparity exists. Nor can Mr Vorster have his power bloc. It is a small ray of hope in a dark world that many influential White South Africans are growing ashamed of their inordinate share of wealth and power.

The road towards ultimate federation will not be easy, but at least it is a road not a cul-de-sac. Even the road towards partial or complete federation of the Black States will not be easy. It seems inevitable that the smaller States will be nervous of the larger. Personal animosities and jealousies may hinder the process.

And the biggest question of all is always sidestepped. What will be the political constitution of "White" South Africa, where there will be 4 million White people, 2 million Coloured people, 750,000 Asians and at least 6 million Black people?

Any supporter of the federal idea should be considering this, the most important political problem of all. Will White South Africans be any less afraid in "White" South Africa than they were in the Republic?

Because I have espoused federalism openly, and because I believe that the possibilities of separate development should be fully exploited, some people have "lost respect" for me.

I am sorry about that, but I was not writing to earn their respect. I write – and my pen and voice are all I have left – to try to make White South Africa aware of the facts of life, to make her realise that the days of her overlordship are at an end.

I use what brains I have to find if there is any way forward except that of revolution with external intervention. That seems to me to be an honourable occupation.

I am glad I have done with White party politics. The infighting fills me with distress. What we White people ought to be doing is sitting down together to discuss what contribution we can make, separately and together with our fellow South Africans, towards fashioning a society in which there will be a future and a purpose for all our children. I think that the first decision must be to move towards federation.

Rand Daily Mail – *April 6, 1974*

RHODESIA

Do the haves ever agree to have less so that the have-nots can have more?

Absolute Peace Unattainable

IT IS natural that many of the people of Southern Africa should rejoice in Mr Smith's announcement of a ceasefire, an amnesty and a constitutional conference.

One of our leading dailies announces PEACE AT LAST. It should rather have announced that a truce had been arranged.

Peace is an absolute. Rare individuals and rare families attain it. Countries are lucky if they achieve a relative peace. The poor old world has never had it.

Absolute peace is not only unattainable, it is not a thing in itself. It cannot be talked about as though it existed in itself. There are certain prerequisites to peace.

In a family they are primarily love and affection. In a human society the primary prerequisite is justice. If there is no justice there can be no peace.

Therefore, while we may rejoice that there is a truce, it is not because it brings peace but because it gives time here in South Africa to create a more just order of society. And that is going to be as hard a task as ever confronted a ruling class in all history.

I wrote that many people would rejoice in Mr Smith's announcement. There are two groups that will not, the extreme Right and the radical Left. The extreme Right is opposed to fundamental change, now and any other time. The radical Left wants fundamental change, not tomorrow, but now.

The extreme Right deserves only condemnation. It is White, yet if it had the power it would destroy the White people of Southern Africa. It is Christian, but has no understanding of the teaching of the gospel.

The radical Left is morally right; the only time for justice is now. But it is pragmatically wrong in supposing that one can have it now. The real political task is to *strive now* for the just re-ordering of society. This is the task that confronts the rulers of our own country.

The radical Left is also highly sceptical about the possibility of a just re-ordering of our society, and I don't blame it.

Do the haves ever agree to have less so that the have-nots can have more? The cynic replies: "Only when they feel the guns in their backs." I myself continue to cherish the hope that our rulers have intelligence enough not to wait till they feel the guns in their backs.

Yet, although I cherish the hope, I am troubled by doubt. My doubt is not whether or Prime Minister is politically able to bring about fundamental change. My doubt is whether he is psychologically able.

For if he is not, the destruction of Afrikanerdom – and of much else – seems inevitable.

The Prime Minister more or less promised significant change within six months, though he – regrettably – allowed himself to be irritated beyond endurance by a pertinacious, but polite, BBC interviewer who wanted to know exactly what that meant.

What kind of change could be significant? Must it not be a change in the fundamental assumption of Afrikaner Nationalism that the races should be kept apart in every conceivable place and on every conceivable occasion? Is that not really the fundamental assumption of Afrikaner Nationalism?

Is it not fundamental that no White man should ever take orders from a Black man? And how can one reward Black intelligence and Black skill while that is so?

Are the Nationalists psychologically able to repeal or amend the Immorality Act and the Mixed Marriages Act? That will mean amending the Group Areas Act and the Population Registration

Act, both of which were thought in 1950 to be fundamental to the grand design.

Is a Nationalist Government *psychologically able* to make it legal for a White man and a Black woman, or harder still, a Black man and a White woman, to have a sexual relationship?

To put it in a nutshell, can a Nationalist, or anyone else for that matter, make a significant change in a fundamental law? Can he change what he regards as his traditional and somehow sacred way of life?

Or will he be condemned to make those trivial changes which have made us a laughing stock? Can you, for example, remove the Colour bar in our international teams and continue to maintain it in all others?

Mr Vorster cannot give us justice tomorrow. If you have been determinedly building an edifice for 26 years, according to a master plan, you cannot radically reconstruct it in six months.

But you can begin. And you can be seen to begin.

Last year, Mrs Mapumulo of Nyuswa paid R59,50 for books and school fees and bus fares for her granddaughter Eunice. If Eunice had been my granddaughter I would have had to pay nothing.

Let Mr Vorster, for one thing, announce that African education will be free from January 1, 1975.

Let him, for another, raise all statutory minimum wages to what researchers think to be a decent living wage.

Let him provide for the registration of African trade unions.

Let him revise the scandalous pensions paid to all African, Indian and Coloured pensioners.

Let him revise the whole machinery of banning, detaining and silencing and sentencing of political opponents.

And let him through his Minister of Justice, as an earnest of his intentions, pardon and release from prison Mr Braam Fischer, gravely ill in Pretoria. That can be done NOW.

Then one might revise one's doubts of his ability, and the ability of his party, to make significant changes in the heavy burden of laws that they have laid on the backs of their countrymen.

For without such changes all ceasefires are meaningless.

Sunday Tribune – *December 15, 1974*

Braam Fischer was sentenced as leader of the banned South African Communist Party to life imprisonment in 1966, but was released shortly before dying of cancer in 1975.

THE UNITED STATES

Let no-one comfort himself that America has
no great investment in South Africa.

The US and South Africa

WHY SHOULD THE WEST show any consideration for the Afrikaner?
What consideration has the Afrikaner shown for Black people?
Under the Group Areas Act he took away much of their property.
Under the policy of resettlement he moved thousands of people
away from cherished homes.

This is true. But something else is equally true, that if he is
driven into a corner, he will destroy much more. I choose to use
what influence I have to prevent this.

I should like to place on record that I think the laager is the
place we must at all costs get out of. It is the cage, the prison, the
grave, the Edifice.

But universal suffrage and a unitary State imposed from without is not – for me – compatible with a liberal ideal.

I should also like to say that I believe that the just and eventual
outcome will be a unitary State. But if it is achieved at the cost of
the destruction of Afrikanerdom, the unity will not last long.

Some critics think that my estimate of Afrikaner resolution is
quite wrong. They argue that when the Afrikaner sees that continued resistance will mean his destruction, he will undergo a
personality change and be sweet and affable.

I don't believe it. But even if I did, I would ask myself the further question, and who then would care if he was affable or not?

I have already written about the danger from the north, if no meaningful changes were made and, of course, the danger of unrest from within.

Yet this danger would be doubled if the nations of the West used their economic weapons against us. It is my belief that they do not want to do this, because it would play yet further into the hands of those nations, who would be ready to destroy us militarily.

Yet if we do nothing they dare not refrain from doing it.

They want us to make significant changes, not just because President Carter is a moralist, but because it is not in the interests to see Southern Africa plunged into war.

If Afrikanerdom compelled the West to use economic sanctions, its doom would be finally sealed.

Its only hope of survival is to begin the dismantling of apartheid, to begin removing the gross disparities of wealth and possessions, to abolish Bantu education and improve Black education and to consider the whole question of our constitutional future, not unilaterally, but in whole consultation with the representatives of all our peoples.

Can the National Party do this?

I do not know the answer to that question.

Reality – *September 1977*
Reproduced in The Star – *September 2, 1977*

≈≈≈≈≈≈≈≈≈≈≈

A Visit to the United States

AMERICA IS ON the up and up and all because of the smile of a President. That is an exaggeration, but it is an exaggeration of the truth. I have had the luck to visit the United States four times in this decade, but the mood of 1977 is quite different. In 1971, 1973 and 1974, the burden of Vietnam – and later of Watergate

– weighed heavily on the American spirit. People not only doubted the American role in the world, they even doubted the role of the presidency.

Today the mood of confidence is returning. It is extraordinary that such a mighty country can turn from doubt to confidence in such a short time. It may be good, it may be bad, but it is a fact of life. And it cannot be doubted that the change is in large measure due to the fact that the new President has an infectious kind of smile. There hasn't been much presidential smiling since the days of Kennedy, but of course there hasn't been much to smile about.

That is not to say the new President has no critics. He has been given the traditional 100 days of freedom from criticism, but now he must take it.

Even his smile is a boon to the cartoonists and some of them convey the insinuation that one may smile and smile and be . . . not quite a villain, but far from divine. Some say he speaks too soon, for example on ways to meet the energy crisis. Some say he is ultra-moralistic and too idealistic for the cruel world. Some say he has no right to be moralistic at all while crime and poverty stalk the streets of his cities.

It would be presumptuous of me to pass any judgment on the President, whom I know only from the Press and television, and his own pronouncements. Judging from visual impressions alone, I should say that he is an upright man and above material corruption. When he shook ex-President Ford's hand at the inaugural and said (in effect): "We owe you thanks for healing this land," one sensed some potential of greatness. He is self-confessedly a religious man and one senses some grasp of what I would call the greater moralities.

The new President came to office with the help of the Black American vote, which went overwhelmingly to him. He was, and is, a champion of civil rights. He appointed a Black American as his Ambassador to the United Nations. He believes that America should exercise its great influence, both moral and material, in favour of the oppressed and voiceless of the world.

There he is bound to play an important part in the future of Southern Africa and, especially, in the future of our own country. What is more, it seems possible that he will be the leader of the Western world for the next seven years.

America has tried, not with conspicuous success, to improve the uneasy and dangerous Russian-American relationship, which has overshadowed all world politics for the past 30 years. I would say her resolve to contain Russia has changed drastically in character. Some Americans doubt this and think that once their country has recovered from the disaster of Vietnam it will become as aggressive as before. I cannot believe this. Among the younger generation, of whom I met many, there was a tremendous distrust of war as a means of bringing about any beneficial results whatsoever.

In fact, the present attitude of America towards Russia is deeply enigmatic. The President has given assurances to the Nato allies, but the coming to power of a Communist government, say in Italy, might affect the whole future of the alliance. This enigmatic attitude could possibly have grave consequences for South Africa.

It seems clear that the failure, or even the slowness, of the South African Government to implement meaningful social, political and economic change could elicit calamitous responses from both America and Russia.

Let us consider the Russian response first. It would not be overt. It would encourage interference from without and revolution from within. Whether Cuba would be involved or not would depend very largely on the future relationship between herself and America. If military attacks were launched against South Africa as a result of a failure to implement significant change, it seems clear – if words mean anything – that America would not intervene. We would, in fact, have encountered the event "too ghastly to contemplate".

This view of the future is dark indeed but the possibility of it is not discounted in those circles in America that study world politics. But America has her own reasons for trying to avoid such an outcome. These are partly moral – a real desire for significant change and a real desire for the peace of the world – and partly political, a fear of the future extension of Russian influence in Africa.

Therefore, America herself would respond drastically to any attempt on the part of our Government to delay or deny significant change.

Just how would or should such pressure be exerted? I declined to answer such questions in America if they were concerned with the overthrow of our Government. One reason was that I could make myself liable to the death penalty, or to a minimum sentence of five years. The other reason was that while I believe in a change of government, and the end of apartheid, I do not believe that the overthrow of the Government could be achieved except at a cost, in lives and suffering and happiness, in grief and desolation, that to me would be unendurable. It may be argued – and it is argued – that one should be prepared to pay such a price for justice. But I do not believe that justice would be the end result.

The new Administration in America is determined that significant change must come. The pressure would be economic, not military. Let no-one comfort himself that America has no great investment in South Africa. She is the leader of the Western world and has been acknowledged as such by our own Prime Minister. She has already acted in concert with leading European nations to change our minds about South West Africa. Her power to cripple us cannot be questioned.

Informed American opinion is not impressed by our moves away from racial discrimination as promised by Mr Pik Botha in 1974. It is astounded by the powers given by Parliament to the Minister of Justice to detain and confine citizens without recourse to any court of law. Some members of my audiences were shocked into unbelieving silence. The extent of the expenditure on Black education also shocked them. They were less shocked by the disparities of wealth and possessions, for they can be seen in America too.

It might be thought that I had gone to "blacken the name of my country abroad". I shall therefore record that with the help of Mr Walter Cronkite, renowned commentator of the Columbia Broadcasting System, I was given an interview with Mr Cyrus Vance, Secretary of State. He knew me already, having heard me speak at Kent School, Connecticut, 21 years ago. If I were the President of any country, I should like to have a man like Mr Vance as my Secretary of State.

I went to see him for one reason and one only. I said I knew that the President earnestly desired the peace of the world. But if he faced the South African Government – and the Afrikaner Nationalists – with a demand for immediate majority rule in a unitary State they would rather destroy themselves than accede. I urged him not to cease the pressure for change, but to exert it with the greatest skill and wisdom.

If the Afrikaner Nationalists were forced into a cul-de-sac with no hope of exit, they would die, and lots of us would die too; the whole country would enter a period of desolation far worse than anything previously known in Africa, because of the sophistication of our economy. Agriculture, for one, would collapse and the world would have to come and feed us, those who were left.

I have been heavily criticised for taking this stand, one of these criticisms being that the Liberal Party accepted majority rule many years ago. But the task of the Liberal Party was to persuade the White electorate and in this it did not succeed. If the White electorate is compelled, many will choose to die rather than yield. I believe that a unitary State is right and inevitable, but I do not choose to see it brought about by grief and desolation. I do not choose to end my life in desolation.

This distrust of White liberals is not new to me. Critics say that we want to creep into the laager. I went to see Mr Vance to ask him not to drive Afrikanerdom into the laager, for to me the laager is synonymous with the final destruction. And if it is of the kind that I fear, many of the critics will be destroyed too.

One thing is clear to me. America is determined that we shall change our ways, for her sake as well as for our own. The politically conscious Black people of America are determined too and they form President Carter's most solid block of support. One wonders how successful our enigmatic Prime Minister has been in persuading his party that the only hope of the survival of Afrikanerdom lies not in the retreat into the laager, but by the acceptance of the need for drastic social change.

So one leaves that beautiful and powerful country, with its riches and its poverty, its idealism that flares up overnight, its own tremendous problems, its immense power to affect our future, and returns – with love and fear – to the sweet and bitter land.

Sunday Tribune – *June 19, 1979*

STUDENTS

I am against the stupid kind of activism that demands everything NOW.

Where They Are Wrong

I'VE DECIDED that I could be doing wrong if I resigned my office as honorary vice-president of the National Union of South African Students. Whether my resignation would or would not do harm to the union in this crisis is not the main consideration. My big trouble is that I cannot get out of my mind those young men and women sitting among the ruins in Grahamstown trying to build something out of the dirt and rubble that is left.

A day or two ago I wrote 800 bitter words intended for this column about Nusas and about its departing president, Mr Karel Tip, the one who left them the dirt and the rubble.

Then I heard that Mr Charles Nupen was coming to see me urgently. This was ironic news, because he had left me almost entirely alone during his presidency, in spite of efforts on my part to have discussions with him.

I read him the 800 bitter words, some of which were written about himself. He listened to them with pain but no anger. He pleaded with me not to publish them. He asked me to remember the young men and women in Grahamstown.

Therefore I am writing a new 800 words, and if any thanks are needed they can be given to Mr Nupen.

It is quite clear that some of the leading members of Nusas have no conception of what it means to be a member, and especially a high official, of an organisation.

They have embarked on courses of action which are not known to their fellow-members, sometimes not even to their fellow-executives. In a president it is unpardonable.

I have sympathy with Miss Curtis's view that such actions are a consequence of identification with those who suffer under unjust laws. In a different context I would argue the same way.

But the argument cannot be applied to those who take high office in an important organisation. They cannot plead diminished responsibility. They have assumed another duty which in its way is as important as the identification with those who suffer.

It is my view that leadership of Nusas had set as its goal the radicalisation of the union. Mr Nupen says I am wrong, but in my view he has tried as hard as anyone.

There is nothing morally reprehensible in this, but it is intellectually stupid.

You cannot radicalise a national organisation with numerous branches, with five main constituencies differing widely in character, and with members drawn from many kinds of life. All you succeed in doing is to distance the leaders further from the members. That is exactly what has happened.

The union has not been radicalised but it has nearly been destroyed. Mr Tip is the typical end-product of this process of radicalisation.

The process of radicalisation has had another disastrous consequence. It has led to a glib opposition of radical to liberal, the good to the bad, the brave to the cowardly, the with-it to the effete.

The intensification of this radical-liberal dichotomy has done much to tear Nusas down the middle. The leadership didn't radicalise Nusas, it dichotomised it.

At this moment of writing, it is my opinion that to be an honorary vice-president of Nusas is a farce.

One does not expect to be consulted on every occasion, but I have not been consulted on any issue for years, and this is a time of great change.

My address to Nusas (I haven't been asked to make one for years) always encouraged activism. I know nothing more moving than the sight of a young person devoted to the service and the frank appraisal of, and the concern for, his or her society.

But I am against the stupid kind of activism that demands everything NOW and that throws away years of life to achieve – in my
view – exactly nothing.

South African politics is hard. It demands not desperation, but
courage and persistence. There is only one alternative, and that
is blood. I don't want to see our students, White or Black, led to
such a destination.

> Let the present leaders of Nusas pledge themselves again to
> the just society.
> Let them realise the limitations of legal action.
> Let them condemn violence, both of the State and of
> desperation.
> Let them be prepared to work and to pay – as many of my
> friends had to pay – the cost of a pledge to justice.

And let them drop this destructive liberal-radical dichotomy.

And for my sake, let them establish SOME kind of communication with their honorary officers.

The Star – *December 2, 1975*

Karel Tip (1945–) and Charles Nupen (1950–), both leaders of the National Union of
South African Students, were arrested on charges under the Suppression of Communism
Act and Unlawful Organisations Act in Durban in 1975, but fled South Africa the following
year.
    Jeanette Curtis (1951–), a former leading figure of Nusas, is the wife of Marius Schoon,
who was sentenced to 12 years in prison in 1964 on charges of sabotage. She was deported
with her husband to Botswana in 1977.

≈≈≈≈≈≈≈≈≈≈≈≈≈

A Microcosm of National Life

THE SNYMAN REPORT, the one-man commission on the disturbances
at the University of the North, is an important social document.
It is far more important than a report on a university. It is a report
on the state of the nation, on a country as divided as any other
on the earth. Many countries of the world are now in bitter travail.
So are we and most of us don't know it, or won't know it.

I am going to summarise and interpret the report, and draw one important conclusion from it.

The commission recommends equal pay for all university teachers of the same rank. This is a matter of absolute priority. One concludes that the commission sees no hope of future peace unless this is done.

It recommends that the university council should contain a majority of Blacks, and that the university administration and teaching should be a joint Black-White responsibility.

Black teachers should not forfeit promotion because they might thus be placed over Whites, and White teachers must accept such a situation.

All these moves would be away from racial discrimination and would give effect to the (so far) more or less totally unfulfilled promise which Mr Pik Botha gave to the United Nations.

Mr MC Botha, Minister of Bantu Administration and Development, said in effect that the recommendations were already Government policy. That is not the question. The question is, why not implement the policy at once?

The commission recommends that the university be given autonomy. That means, in effect, that the council would control the finances, that it would appoint whom it wishes, including the rector, who, at the moment, is appointed by the minister. But the university would not thus be empowered to admit whom it wished.

Admission is controlled by the law of the country. This law forbids the "White" universities to admit "Black students", unless by special permit from the minister. It also, of course, forbids "Black" universities to admit White students. But either the law or some regulation goes still further and forbids, for example, a Zulu student wishing to take pharmacy from going to the University of the North, where pharmacy is offered.

The commission now recommends that at undergraduate level all Black universities should be open to all Black students and what is more that all post-graduate students should be able to study at any university of their choice. This would, if accepted, be another move away from racial discrimination, and it would also be a move away from Black ethnic separation.

It is not clear from Press reports whether the Government would yield its cherished principle of Black ethnic separation. But the minister has already said that it "cannot accept all the commission's recommendations regarding post-graduate studies".

It is my belief that most, if not all, White universities, both English and Afrikaans-language, would be willing to accept post-graduate students of any colour. But it is clear that the Government would prevent it.

The commission reports that the majority of students reject ethnic grouping. This would be true throughout South Africa. Students pour ridicule on the notion, and this is in part due to the fact that it has been forced upon them. It is one of those products of the White inventive genius.

It was not necessary to ask the Black man whether he approved of it. It was enough to know that there was divine approval.

The commission goes further than to report that students reject ethnic grouping. It forecasts that the homelands when they become independent will reject it also.

Before one leaves this topic, there is one important thing to be noted. It is not for purely educational and moral reasons that the commission recommends this free movement of Black post-graduates within South Africa, but also because they might go to universities outside the country and come under "adverse influences".

Our Black students would be just as scathing about that as they are of ethnic grouping. It is to them a manifestation of White paternalism, White fearfulness and White bossiness.

According to the commission, the White staff thought Black-White staff relationships to be "excellent and satisfactory". The Black staff thought them "bad in some cases and unsatisfactory in others".

The university provided separate toilets, but when it provided a communal tearoom, the Whites did not use it. Members of Black staff resented the White swimming bath, the floodlit tennis court and the clubhouse. They asserted that the White staff "does practically nothing to show its objection to the system".

It is clear that the staff relationships are lamentable and that the equalisation of salaries cannot by itself bring the desired improvement. The University of the North exhibits all the flaws that so disfigure our national life.

The members of its White staff show all the complacency and obtuseness of White South Africans. One does not expect them to be perfect, but at least to be much better than that.

White staff think that White staff-Black student relationships are "on the whole satisfactory". The Black staff think they are "bad". It emerges clearly that there is a great gulf between White staff and Black students.

The commission's remarks on anti-White feeling are sombre. Black consciousness has made the Black man claim to be the White man's equal, yet the only practicable field of opposition is politics. "He sought to escape from his situation of inequality by obtaining political power on the strength of numerical superiority."

These feelings are aggravated by White treatment of him. The rector and Black staff members told the commission of numerous examples on campus of "senseless and deplorable behaviour by Whites". Here we encounter the deep underlying problem that underlies all the problems of the university.

The commission says that the university itself is ensnared in a much broader and deeper problem than just a university situation – that of the situation between White and Black outside the university.

Mr D Mji, president of Black Saso, says the ills recognised by the commission are in fact "anchored in the whole apartheid structure".

The commission and Mr Mji are saying the same thing, but Mr Mji is saying it in a more unequivocal way. He is, in effect, saying that it is much more than a question of "deplorable behaviour" by Whites, it is much more than a question of White fear, prejudice and hostility, it is the fact that all this has been enshrined and codified in a framework of rigid law.

The inquiry is not into the disturbances at the university, it is not even into the question of separate toilets and unequal salaries. It is into the whole system of law under which Black people live.

It would have been too much to expect a Government commission to say this. No such commission would ever question the fundamental philosophy of apartheid and separate development.

It will recommend better behaviour and better salaries. But it is the fundamental philosophy that is the basic cause of the disturbances. And so long as this fundamental philosophy rules us, just so long will anti-White feeling fester and grow.

Mr Pik Botha did not tell the UN that we were going to behave better and pay better salaries. He said that we were going to move away from racial discrimination.

There is one last observation to make. What attention will the Government pay to the report of the commission? I fear not much.

They might improve the salaries, but that is not the prime cause of the disturbances. They are much more likely to come down hard on Saso. The Government's idea of curing a disease is to punish the patient.

The Government was warned long ago that separate universities would increase racial conflict, that they would engender, not tribal loyalties, but an all-embracing Black nationalism that would be bitterly anti-White.

Mr MC Botha, Minister of Bantu Administration and Development, now finds this state of affairs alarming. But who did more to create it than he and his fellow-rulers? And who has the greater responsibility for changing it? Or are we waiting for Castro?

The Star – *February 18, 1976*

The Snyman Commission of Inquiry (named after Justice JH Snyman) studied, inter alia, the riotous events which took place on September 25, 1974 at the University of the North, near Pietersburg. It found that the students deliberately proceeded with an unlawful gathering and that the police did not use undue force.

The South African Students' Organisation (Saso) was established in 1969 as a Black Consciousness movement and played an important role in the Soweto riots of 1976. It was banned in October 1977.

SPEECHES

Questions that lie heavily on one's mind and
soul, day after day, year after year.

Can There Be a South Africa?

SOUTH AFRICANS hold little in common except the physical land
that they inhabit; and it is even doubtful whether they do that,
because one of the newest developments of political policy and
theory is that there are many separate nations and that each has
its homeland, and each can achieve a separate and independent
destiny, so that ultimately there will be no country that can properly be called South Africa at all.

For example, just over 1,000,000 White South Africans are English speaking. They have no national identity, though the Afrikaner Nationalists would like them to have, so that they could be
a living proof of the multinational theory.

I am not a good example of English-speaking South Africanism
at all, because to me it would be the height and depth of absurdity
to be proud of being an English-speaking South African.

There is one thing I should like to be proud of, and that is of
being a South African, but that is a dream at the moment, because
it involves belief in one common society, which is in a way a belief
in something that does not exist.

What is more, it is a belief in something in which it can be dangerous to believe, because the racial policies of the country are based on the premise that a common society cannot exist in South Africa.

A corollary of this is that if a person does not believe in it, he is a traitor, which means, as you no doubt guess, that he is a Communist, or that he is furthering the aims of Communism.

Politically the English-speaking South Africans are in bondage to the Afrikaner, but most of them don't mind, because economically they are better off than anybody.

Most of them keep their mouths shut, or keep their criticism moderate, but the English-speaking people cannot be given a group personality, because they also produce some of the most courageous people in South Africa, churchmen, public-spirited women, newspaper men and women, university teachers, and so on.

They are not unique in this, because every other group produces such people.

Extracts from a lecture at Edinburgh University – July 16, 1971
As published in The Star *– August 2, 1971*

⸙⸙⸙⸙⸙⸙⸙⸙⸙⸙

How Can We Prevent Terror?

IN OUR COUNTRY it is common for those in authority to assert that the causes of strikes, unrest and resentment are not the social conditions but the agitators who exaggerate and sometimes invent the grievances.

These agitators are Communists or, if not, they are the tool of Communists.

This tendency to deny the existence of social injustices and to extol the virtues of government is a distinguishing mark of the authoritarian personality and it leads its possessor to the disastrous belief that peace can be maintained by force, that law is the equivalent of justice, and that order is to be preferred above freedom.

What are the social conditions which, if not amended, can lead us into an era of blood and terror?

They are not primarily racial, though race is a factor of the utmost importance and has been made still more important by the laws, especially the laws of the last 25 years under the Nationalist Government.

Our State was founded on the assumption of White superiority and White superiority is explicit or implicit in almost every law. But when to White superiority is added the inevitable element of Black poverty, the mixture is explosive in the extreme.

It was estimated in 1968, by the research officer in economics at the Institute of Commonwealth Studies at Oxford, when the population figures were all lower, that 68 percent of our population – the African people – received 20 percent of all income and that 19 percent of the population – the White people – received 74 percent of all income.

Therefore each White person received four units of income and each Black person two-sevenths of a unit of income, and therefore White income per capita was 14 times Black income per capita. Allowing for error, it would be safe to say that White income per capita is 12 times Black income per capita.

This is the social condition which if it goes unamended will lead us into terror and blood. For no police action, however restrained and skilful can control the anger and the desperation of the people who feel that they are denied a just share of the wealth they produce and who know they are denied it because they are politically powerless and who know that they are politically powerless because they are Black.

I suppose that one must be thankful for every sign that White South Africa is beginning to feel guilty about Black poverty.

The recent raising of wages – following the Natal strikes – though far from spectacular, was such a sign. But there are more difficult lessons to learn.

South Africa must learn that there is no hope for her own survival unless Black poverty is totally eliminated.

Her only hope of survival is to create a common loyalty to South Africa and it is quite impossible to do that if White South Africans continue to earn 12 times as much as Black South Africans.

What Black man can be expected to feel any loyalty towards such a society?

But there is still a harsher lesson to be learned and that is that White wealth comes from Black poverty, that the riches of the gold mines and many industries come not from gold and manufacture but from Black wages.

We are a parasitic society, where Blacks live off Whites and Whites live off Blacks. Is it possible to change such a society?

There are many people who will tell you that it is not possible, that no-one ever gives up what he has until he is facing a gun, that if White South Africa is given a breathing space she will go off to sleep again and will not waken till death is knocking on the door.

I must admit to you that this is not a totally unfounded view of human nature. Yet it makes no allowance for intelligence or foresight and certainly no allowance for moral behaviour or the operation of that strange organ known as conscience.

Till now White survival in South Africa has in the last resort depended not only on intelligence or foresight or moral behaviour, but on the gun.

But it cannot depend on the gun anymore.

This truth may not have percolated through to the lower echelons but it is certainly known at the top. That gives me a small ground for hope.

It is ground for hope that there is a growing realisation on the part of the White South African that the wage gap, which has been rightly called the gap of shame, must be narrowed for reasons both of justice and her own survival.

What we need, and urgently, is minimum wage legislation. We already have wage determination, but some of the determinations are well below the poverty datum line.

There is another important truth about poverty. A man who earns a quarter or an eighth or a twelfth of what you earn, is not just a poor man, he is another kind of man – you cannot cherish any common goal with him, you cannot share a common love of country, unless under the influence of some transcendent love.

He is alien to you.

Although he is poor, you fear him, even hate him. You form the habit of referring to him and those like him as "they".

There are many nasty words in the English language, but none is nastier than "they". Therefore the removal of his poverty is the first urgent indispensable step towards the avoidance of that holocaust of which we all, in our hearts of hearts, are afraid.

It is government not industry that must take the lead. It is only when this step is taken, or when this step is being taken, that the terrible otherness of "them" begins to abate.

It is then, too, that White South Africa could begin to dismantle the gaunt machinery of apartheid, whose monstrous pylons stride across the land from one end to the other, disfiguring not only land and sky but casting their shadows on every man, woman and child, both ruler and ruled.

We know it is all wrong. The world has been telling us for 25 years. At first our rulers were outraged by this interference in their domestic affairs. But now they know it isn't domestic anymore.

Does this knowledge help? Must one do more than know before one acts? Must terror fly screaming around the house before one knows that one must act? Or does one wait till death itself knocks on the door?

These are the questions that lie heavily on one's mind and soul, day after day, year after year. If it had not been for that strange thing called hope, one would long ago have turned one's face to the wall and died.

Our rulers at last realised that apartheid was not a domestic concern. So it was given some new content and a new name. It is now known as separate development.

Separate development, like apartheid, is fundamentally the child of fear. It's a dream, have no doubt about that.

Is it a fraud? I am not prepared to say that on a university platform, though in the past I would have said it on a political platform. Into the ethics of that I will not go.

But I am prepared to say that the theory of separate development has both fraudulent and idealistic elements.

The fraudulent element is that political independence, without a healthy economic interdependence, is worthless; and there is at the moment no prospect whatsoever of healthy economic interdependence.

The homelands depend for their money on the wages earned by their people in what is called White South Africa in the cities of Johannesburg, Durban, Port Elizabeth and Cape Town. The grand theory is that as they develop industrially, they will be able to support their own people.

Here the fraudulency and the idealism come into sharp conflict, for White South Africa could not continue without the labour that comes from the homelands.

And, let us face it, the homelands could not continue without the wages that come from White South Africa, inadequate though these wages often are. It looks as though only death will us part.

The exponents of Black Power in South Africa condemn the homelands programme root and branch. They condemn it for its fraudulence and scoff at its idealism.

They condemn the leaders who have undertaken to govern the homelands, such as Buthelezi of KwaZulu, Matanzima of the Transkei, and Mangope of Bophuthatswana.

They regard these leaders as co-operating with the Government, as giving respectability to the Government's racial doctrines, as giving tacit approval to the hundred cruel laws of apartheid, and finally as giving "authenticity to the White man's lie".

I understand these arguments but I do not agree with them. For the fraudulence and the idealism of the theory of separate development are not to me the most important things about it.

The most important thing about it is that it has given official status and an official platform to Black leaders, and they have been using this status and this platform to talk to White South Africa in a language that has not been heard since the days of Luthuli and Mandela.

The point I wish to make is that the implementation of separate development, however much it may give respectability to White South Africa – which possibility I very much doubt – has generated new ideas and created new possibilities.

And this has given another ground for hope.

The Republic of South Africa is a unitary State with an all-White franchise. Any proposal for a different kind of franchise, a non-racial franchise or a qualified franchise has never received any support from the White electorate, because of the deep-seated White fear of being overwhelmed.

But White South Africa might feel less fear of entering a federation or confederation where she might keep some of the things she fears most to lose where, above all, the Afrikaner could keep his language and culture.

It is my earnest hope that the emergence of these new legislative assemblies, and these new administrators who speak with such dignity and authority, may be the first light of dawn after dark unending night.

Condensed version of a lecture at Yale University
As published in the Sunday Tribune *– March 11, 1973*

Lucas Mangope (1923–) became Chief of the Motswedi-Barutshe-Boo-Manyane tribe in 1959 and President of Bophuthatswana when it was granted independence in 1977.

❧❧❧❧❧❧❧❧❧❧

A New Nationalism Wanted

IN 1938 I GREW a commemorative beard for the Voortrekker celebrations and drove from Johannesburg to Pretoria under the Vierkleur. When we arrived at the site of the Monument, I made for the showers and another bearded man asked me: "Het jy al die skare gesien?"

And when I said: "Ja," he said to me with unspeakable comradeliness: "Nou gaan ons die Engelse opdonder."

British nationalists should always listen to such remarks when they are under the shower.

At one of these centenary meetings, the voice of Mr EN Douglass, KC, one of the descendants of the 1820 Settlers who had given Jacobus Uys a Bible when he set out on the Trek, and who was bringing a message of goodwill in English, was drowned by the singing of "Die Stem".

After the singing, a man in Voortrekker costume took over the microphone and began to recite a patriotic verse. There was tumultuous applause, and above it, the chairman, Advocate EG Jansen, then Speaker of the House of Assembly, could be heard saying in tones of great distress: "Ek is bedroef . . . ek is diep bedroef . . . vriende, ek is diep bedroef!"

His words were then drowned by the singing of another patriotic song, "Afrikaners, Landgenote". By this time it was clear that the crowd was in no mood to listen to any English, and Jansen announced that Douglass would say a few words in Afrikaans.

This gesture was acclaimed, and Douglass said his few words, which were loudly applauded.

When I got home I said to my wife, "I'm taking off this beard, and for the rest of my life I'll never grow another."

It is an ironic reflection that it was Afrikaner Nationalism which opened the door for me to escape from the house of British Nationalism and closed the door on me when I tried to enter its own.

Do not think I complain. It was a blessing in disguise. It sent me on my pursuit of a new nationalism, a South African nationalism, which exists as yet only in the hearts of some.

You must not get the impression that I am anti-Afrikaner. But I am totally opposed to the Africaner Nationalism that has ruled us till today.

I understand the historical necessity of it, but today, so immense are the challenges that confront all of us in South Africa, that it is becoming an anachronism.

The only hope for us, when we aim at a non-racial or multiracial or unitary or federal or confederal society, is that we should find a nationalism that transcends even if it includes the lesser nationalism that is based on history and language and race.

I will here give thanks to Afrikaner Nationalism.

Extracts from a lecture at the Lutheran Theological College, Mapumulo
Condensed by The Star *– September 16, 1974*

Vierkleur – Four Colours, i.e., the flag of the Zuid-Afrikansche Republiek (South African Republic) of Paul Kruger in the 19th Century. It has lately been used as a revived symbol by the far Right movements in South Africa.

"Het jy al die skare gesien?" "Ja." "Nou gaan ons die Engelse opdonder." – "Have you seen the crowd?" "Yes." "Now we are going to f . . . up the English."

"Ek is bedroef . . . ek is diep bedroef . . . vriende, ek is diep bedroef?!" – "I am sad . . . I am very sad . . . friends, I am very sad!"

"Afrikaners, Landgenote." – "Afrikaners, Countrymen."

The Value of Truth

YOU ARE GRADUATING into a world that is not simple at all. You do not know if the long and strange relationship between Russia and your own country will erupt into a violence that will destroy what we call civilisation. You do not know if man can reverse the process of his own destruction of the earth. You do not know if the system known as Capitalism – which many of you are going to serve – is capable of adapting itself to the new challenges of the coming century. You are entering a world in which everything is shifting, in which every value, every custom, every institution is being questioned, so much so that many people believe that there is nothing safe and certain any more.

Is there anything in this shifting world that can give some kind of integrity to our lives? I believe there is, and that is when, of our own will and choice, we decide that our lives are to be spent in the service of our society; when we decide that we shall devote them to the pursuit of a just order of society. It is a goal that has never been reached, and never will be reached. But we remember people like Abraham Lincoln, William Wilberforce, Florence Nightingale, Mahatma Gandhi, not so much for their learning as for their single-minded direction of their lives.

If one is to devote one's life to the pursuit of a more just order of society, one of one's highest moral values will be justice. One of the noblest concepts of sinful man is the Rule of Law. By consenting to the rule of law he ensured that the baser instincts and impulses of his own nature would be contually held in check by the higher. He yielded the tasks of trial and judgment, and if necessary, punishment, into the hands of an authority which was to be higher than himself. That authority was the court of law, and in the civilised society it is only the court of law that has the right to touch the person or the freedom or the property of the citizen of the State.

In the pursuit of the just order of society, there is another high moral value that must be cherished, and it is a value cherished by every true university. It is the value of Truth. It is the assertion of the primacy of reason in any discussion of human affairs. This is not to suggest for one moment that emotion is going to be distrusted. Emotion may determine what we are going to reason about, but it must not try to control or distort or colour reason. The two are inseparable, and the balanced man or woman is the one in whom emotion and reason have achieved an alliance in which emotion does not dictate what reason must say, and in which reason respects the validity of emotion, but will expose all prejudice, and all sham which is masquerading as high-mindedness. There is nothing more vulgar than the attempts of reason to justify the actions of unworthy emotions.

If you set out to be a servant of society, one of the first things you will learn is that the world is a hard place, and that while individual man may become a saint, collective man is a tough proposition. You will – I trust – never come to believe that man is wholly good or wholly evil, but in fact that he is noble enough

237

to consent to the control of his evil nature by the Rule of Law. You will learn that any good course is to be followed, not for reward or success, but because it is the expression of some goodness in yourself – in other words, because it has to be done, not just for the sake of society but for your own – for if you don't do it, you are doing harm to your moral self.

In the pursuit of justice and truth, you will find many temptations. There is a cynical saying that justice is the interest of the strongest. Be on your guard against identifying justice and truth with self-interest, even enlightened self-interest.

University of Michigan, Flint Honors Convocation – May 12, 1977

~~~~~~~~~~~~~

Liberty and Order

HOWEVER ONE CATEGORISES THEM, Order and Liberty are inseparable. Order without Liberty becomes Tyranny, Liberty without Order becomes Chaos. No institution in the world reconciles Order and Liberty as does the university, though even there the reconciliation is sometimes difficult to achieve.

I have no doubt that some of our rulers regard this university as an institution where there is sometimes too much liberty and too little order. They think the same of certain writers and publications.

The authoritarian personality is very uneasy with the whole idea of liberty. If you talk to an authoritarian about liberty, he will soon remind you of the need for order.

If you talk to him about rights, he will soon remind you of the existence of responsibilities.

Almost inevitably the one who talks to you about responsibilities is the one who has the rights already.

There can be no true liberty without order. But there can be order without liberty, as Hitler and Stalin have taught us.

It is that terrible kind of order which has a total distrust of individuality, of personal and intimate responses to things which have nothing to do with the State; of responses to art and music and beauty, and flights of imagination, of painting and writing and poetry, of any belief that art and music and poetry exist in some kind of absolute right of their own.

Therefore, the authoritarian ruler is never a patron of the arts, except for the purpose of controlling them. He will never offer prizes for writing, unless it is patriotic writing.

As for imagination, it is to be distrusted most of all and is usually found in those who wittingly or unwittingly are furthering the aims of Communism, and in Russia, presumably the aims of capitalism.

I am often asked by people abroad if South Africa is a Nazi country. And I am able to tell them the story of how I lost my passport in 1960 for saying it was not a Nazi country, but unfortunately I added the rider that it was only a good imitation.

But in fact this country is not an imitation of anything. It is a regime sui generis. If this were a Nazi country, this address on Order and Liberty could never have been delivered. Helen Suzman would be dead. Helen Joseph would be dead, Nelson Mandela would be dead, Gatsha Buthelezi would be dead.

Anyone who announced an address on Liberty would have died too. It is the most bitter of ironies that the vocabulary of freedom did not die out in Nazi Germany. Over the gate of Dachau concentration camp are the words "Arbeit macht frei" ("Work makes one free").

As the prisoners entered the camp, these were the words that greeted them, in the place where more than 30,000 of them were going to die.

One reads of the advent of neo-Nazism in Germany, but I was conscious only of being in the presence of a kind of miracle. In the lobby of the University of Munich is the memorial to those members of the White Rose who gave their lives for freedom. Streets and squares near the university are named after them.

But Germany and the world had to pay a heavy price for this miracle.

This is not a Nazi country, but we also have a grievous sickness, an obsession with racial identity, an exaltation of Order over Liberty, an idolatrous worship of the State. I pray that we do not have to pay such a price for our own liberation.

I must make one qualification of my statement that this is not a Nazi country, by which I mean that it is not a totalitarian country. It is a White South African who is giving this verdict.

239

If a Black South African were addressing you, the verdict would almost certainly be different. If the Black South African addressing you had with his wife and children been bulldozed out of his humble home and possessions, where he had been trying to earn an honest wage and to keep his family together, then his verdict would certainly be much harsher than mine. And he would be right too, because the act of bulldozing men and women and children out of their homes is one which is incompatible with what we call civilisation.

Our rulers are not totalitarians, but they are certainly authoritarians. In our country Order is put above Liberty. Order which is only a means has been made into an end. The great pronouncements of the last few years have been about Order, not about Liberty.

Order has, in fact, been separated from Liberty, whereas in the good society they are inseparable; they have been fused, synthesised, reconciled. If I may use and change the famous words of Karl Kraus for my own purpose – in the good society Order and Liberty are not like body and clothes, they are like body and soul.

It is inevitable that when Order has been separated from Liberty, something will go wrong with the Order too. One of the irreplaceable bulwarks of the Order of a good society is the Rule of Law.

There is no Liberty without the Rule of Law. It is one of the noblest achievements of sinful man. When it is set aside, it is not only the liberty of the wrongdoer that is lost, but the liberty of us all.

We in this country took a disastrous course when in 1950 the Suppression of Communism Act set the Minister of Justice above the Courts of Justice. The next step was to give the Minister the power to detain without charge, but the most grievous step of all was to give him power to detain without access.

For the result of that, not just in this country but in any country in the world, will be torture and death. That is what happens when Order is exalted above Liberty.

But Liberty and Justice are not the only casualties in the extreme authoritarian society. The great virtue of Compassion suffers also. Is our authoritarian society noted for its compassion? I would answer No. There is no compassion in the Group Areas Act or the Population Registration Act or in the administrative process known as "resettlement".

It is true that our liberty has been abridged, but it is not lost. We lose liberty only when we cease to desire it.

I am reminded of the words of William the Silent:

It is not necessary to hope in order to undertake, and it is not necessary to succeed in order to preserve.

You fight for liberty because it has to be done, whether you are going to succeed or not. And if you do not fight for it, you will lose it forever. Even if it is restored to you, you will not know what it is.

I trust that the day is drawing near when the lost liberty will be restored to the University of the Witwatersrand.

Extracts from a speech at the University of the Witwatersrand
Published in The Star *– October 6, 1978*

Helen BM Joseph (1905–) is one of the most active critics of South Africa's apartheid system. In 1957 she received her first banning order under the Suppression of Communism Act and after that was banned on numerous occasions until 1982. She was elected a patron of the United Democratic Front in 1983.

≈≈≈≈≈≈≈≈≈≈

Commemoration Day

IT IS A GREAT HONOUR to me to be invited to give the first Commemoration lecture of the University of the Witwatersrand. It could rightly be said that there are others who have been more intimately concerned with the life of this university, but I also have some credentials. In 1975 I received the honour of the Doctorate of Laws from this university. My elder son David is an MB BCh, and MMed of Wits, and my younger son Jonathan teaches here in the Department of English. But I shall always feel that my closest link is that I wrote the life of Jan Hendrik Hofmeyr, the first principal of the University of the Witwatersrand.

In 1916 the South African School of Mines created nine new professorships, one being in the classics. Hofmeyr, then teaching in Cape Town, and aged 22, applied for it, and the Senate sent for him so that they could see what he looked like. One of his friends urged him to buy a new suit for the occasion, for he was wearing the jacket of one and the trousers of another. His response was to buy a black Homburg hat, and with this, the jacket, and the trousers, he set out on his venture to the interior, and returned a professor-to-be.

The School of Mines was determined to become a university. The South African College had just become the University of Cape Town, and the Victoria College had become the University Stellenbosch. The Government had just allowed the Beit bequest of £200,000, which had been left for the future University of Johannesburg, to be diverted to the new University of Cape Town. The Johannesburg public was stung into action, and at a big meeting in the City Hall on March 17, 1916, set up the Witwatersrand University Committee.

This university owes much to the Council of the School of Mines. Names such as Samuel Evans, RN Kotze, William Dalrymple, and HJ Hofmeyr come to mind. It was these men and their fellow-councillors who decided to establish the nine new professorships.

It was a bold step, for there were only 171 students, many of them only half-time. A grand new medical school was planned for 31 students. Thirty full time arts and science students were showered with professors. Great expansion was planned in the engineering courses, where there were only 44 full time students. In 1919 the School of Mines became a university college and moved to Milner Park. In that year the Principal, Dr Corstorphine died, and the Council did an extraordinary thing. They appointed the young Hofmeyr, who was 24 years of age. This was remarkable, but the new Principal was a remarkable young man. He went through school from bottom to top in five years. He matriculated at 12, graduated BA Arts First Class at 15, and was awarded the Rhodes scholarship while still in short trousers. At 16 he graduated BA Science and took the mathematics prize away from a young lady who had reigned supreme till her final year. At 24 he became Principal of the university college, which, three years later in 1922, became the University of the Witwatersrand.

One of his prodigious gifts was memory. He had an unfair advantage over his fellow-students for when he entered the examination room he in effect took all his books with him, and could open them at the required pages. He could deliver important speeches without a note. The story is told that on one occasion he thought one of his speeches exceptionally important, and wrote notes on, say, a dozen small sheets of paper. These he held behind his back, and as he came to the bottom of a sheet, he would peel it off and put it under the others. His memory once earned him a rebuke from Mr van der Brugge, his registrar. Seeing Van der Brugge open the telephone book, Hofmeyr said: "Can't you remember the number?" to which Van der Brugge replied with some heat: "I use my brain for better things."

Hofmeyr was just the man for the planning of a university's expansion, for he had another prodigious gift – that of administration. But his precocious career, his extreme youth, and his dominating mother, did not fit him to cope with the human problems of the university. The young principal warned one of his professors to discontinue what he considered to be improper behaviour, and when the professor denied the principal's right to interfere in his private affairs, a not very full meeting of the Council dismissed him. A fuller meeting of the Council would have liked to rescind the decision, but Hofmeyr made it clear that the Council must choose between himself and the professor. The Council then adopted an ancient strategem, and persuaded the professor to resign rather than be dismissed. It then took the extraordinary step of deciding to destroy the minutes which recorded the dismissal.

This led to two of the most unhappy years of crisis in Hofmeyr's life and in the life of the university. The crisis was to alienate almost every member of the Senate from their Principal. It was to estrange Council and Senate. It was to cost the Hofmeyrs the friendship of the leading liberals of the time, Alfred and Winifred Hoernlé, JD and Edith Rheinallt-Jones, and Margaret Ballinger. It almost certainly played a great part in the Council's decision not to appoint Hoernlé as the next principal of the university. He had said that Hofmeyr had used the gallows to punish a peccadillo. It also had the consequence that Hofmeyr would not accept an honorary degree from this university. Its happy outcome was that the relations of Council, Principal and Senate were to be more clearly and satisfactorily defined.

It is not surprising that the Council refused more than once to allow me access to the minute books of the university. They had no desire to see this lamentable history set out in black and white. This was a serious setback for me, for it meant that I would have been compelled to write the history of this episode from evidence collected nearly 40 years after the event. I would have been compelled to say that I could not vouch for the complete truthfulness of the account.

But I was fortunate. A member of Council let me know that a further request would probably be granted, as indeed it was. One could not help asking oneself how it was that a man of Hofmeyr's integrity could have first consented to the dismissal, then to the writing of a letter to the professor informing him of it, then to the destruction of the record of the dismissal, then to the persuading of the professor to resign to avoid dismissal, without telling him that although his dismissal had not been rescinded, the Council meeting at which the dismissal had been decided, had in fact never taken place at all.

One must suppose that a man of integrity could only consent to such a step when he feels threatened in his very self and being. It would be a person of rare quality who would put that integrity above any feelings of ambition or pride or self-esteem. It is a very human story, is it not? I am glad that the university Council finally decided that the truth ought to be written. In any event, that chapter is for me one of the most fascinating in the book.

Hofmeyr was now living in a state of deadlock with his Senate. He was rescued from this intolerable situation by General Smuts, who in 1924 appointed the 29-year-old Hofmeyr to the administratorship of the Transvaal. In 1929 Hofmeyr entered politics, and won the seat of Johannesburg North. In 1933 he became the Minister of Education, Interior and Public Health in the Hertzog-Smuts coalition, which in 1934 became a fusion. Hofmeyr allowed himself a prediction, namely that there was not one chance in a hundred that Hertzog and Smuts would be antagonists again. In 1935 the meaning of Hitler was not fully seen.

Hofmeyr was one of 11 MPs who voted against the Representation of Natives Bill of 1936, which removed African voters to a separate roll. The tension between him and General Hertzog increased and in 1938 Hofmeyr resigned from the Cabinet over the appointment of APJ Fourie as a senator with a "thorough acquaintance with the reasonable wants and wishes of the coloured races". His reputation as a defender of liberty was at its highest, and in 1939 the University of the Witwatersrand asked him to become its Chancellor. The breach was healed.

On the occasion of his installation, Hofmeyr delivered a great address, as he always did when he avoided the props of memory. It was, in fact, an address on 'Order and Liberty'. He said: "Undoubtedly the greatest conflict in the world today is the conflict between the spirit of democracy and the spirit of authoritarianism. In that conflict no university worthy of its great tradition can fail to range itself on the side of democracy." Hofmeyr acknowledged as he had done before, the weaknesses of democracy, but he told his hearers: "The great advances of humanity have not come from discipline – they have come from the operation of the free human spirit."

Hofmeyr reserved his final words for the students themselves.

"To you ... I am speaking today for the first time as your Chancellor. I have spoken to you of freedom and the modern world's menace to it. It needs, as never before, defenders, stern and resolute, but withal lavish of the best that is in them. I want to enrol you for that fight. There is no fairer cause to fight for than the cause of freedom. Six hundred years ago the nobles and commons of Scotland at Arbroath made that historic declaration:

> We fight not for glory, nor for wealth, nor for honour, but for that freedom which no good man will surrender but with his life.

"That freedom which no good man will surrender but with his life. That is the good fight I ask you to fight. And may you quit you like men, men at once conscript and consecrated of your own free will, in the warfare that lies ahead."

The day after Hofmeyr spoke in Johannesburg, Hitler marched into Czechoslovakia. Six months earlier he had assured Chamberlain that once the Czechs were out of the Sudetenland, he would have no further territorial claims to make in Europe. Some of you will know the letter written by a farm boy from the Sudetenland to his parents. It is one of the noblest letters of the 20th Century and one of the least known.

> Dear Parents: I must give you bad news – I have been condemned to death, I and Gustave G. We did not sign up for the SS, and so they condemned us to death. You wrote me, indeed, that I should not join the SS; my comrade Gustave G, did not sign up either. Both of us would rather die than strain our consciences with such deeds of horror. I know what the SS has to do. Oh, my dear parents, difficult as it is for me and for you, forgive me everything; if I have offended you please forgive me and pray for me. If I were to be killed in the war while my conscience was bad, that too

would be sad for you. Many more parents will lose their children. Many SS men will get killed too. I thank you for everything you have done for my good since my childhood. Forgive me, pray for me . . .

I see the farm boy from the Sudetenland as a young lad of 19 or 20, red of cheek and simple of nature. But he knew as much about the meaning of freedom as the nobles and commons of Scotland 600 years before him, for he was prepared to pay his young life for freedom.

But he was not alone in Germany. In 1942 Christoph Probst, Alexander Schmorell, Hans and Sophie Scholl, Wilhelm Graf, all young students of the University of Munich, guided and encouraged by Professor Huber, wrote the Pamphlet of the White Rose, calling on the German people to throw off the yoke of Hitler. Hans and Sophie dropped their leaflets from a gallery into the main lobby of the university. Four days later they were dead. By the end of the year all of them were dead. They too were prepared to pay their young lives for freedom.

Christoph Probst wrote to his sister: "I never knew that dying is so easy . . . I die without any feeling of hatred . . . Never forget that life is nothing but a growing in love and a preparation for eternity."

I should like to say a word about this title, Order and Liberty. It is terrifying to be telephoned at 9 am by a representative of a great university and to be told: "We haven't yet received the title of your address, and everything has to go to the printers at 11 am so could you do us the inestimable favour of letting us know your title before that time?" One has to humble oneself and become a supplicant and beg for more time, say till 1 pm. The representative of the great university says: "No-one is ever here at 1 pm, so let us make it 3 pm", and one humbly and thankfully agrees.

Why is it such an ordeal to decide on the title of an address to be delivered on an occasion such as this? You sit down in a kind of panic, having only six hours to decide upon it. Because once you have let the title go, not all your piety or wit can lure it back to cancel half a line, nor all your tears wash out a word of it, for once a thing has gone to the printers, it costs a fortune to get it back again. And in your panic all the great words go through your mind, Justice, Liberty, Freedom, Order, Authority, Truth, and each one seems more impossible than the last. You begin to regret bitterly that you studied physics and mathematics and not philosophy. You are filled with envy of the philosophers, of those whose whole lives are devoted to sustained and orderly thought and your envy grows all the greater when you realise that some of them actually get paid for it. At least you have the comfort that Hoernlé and Macmurray won't be there to hear you. Hoernlé of the clear mind and generous heart, who concerned himself unceasingly with the problems of the poor and voiceless of this great city, Macmurray who after he had left this university set the Thames on fire with his radio talks on "Freedom in the Modern World". Both these men had the greatest of all teaching gifts, that of expounding the deepest things in the simplest words.

The time was now nearly 1 pm and my panic was growing insupportable, when I suddenly remembered Hofmeyr's first speech as Chancellor of the university. I read it again, and decided on Order and Liberty. I was full of joy, but there was no point in ringing the university, because no-one would be there at 1 pm and apparently no-one would be there till 3 pm.

You will remember that Hofmeyr said: "The great advances of humanity have not come from discipline – they have come from the operation of the free human spirit." One must not deduce for a moment that Hofmeyr was decrying the need for discipline. His own self-discipline terrified ordinary beings. He disciplined himself in all things except work, and too much work shortened his life. Work for him was an anodyne for what hidden pain one could but guess. But one thing seems clear – he did not put discipline in the same category as freedom. Order was the means to liberty. One must remember that Hofmeyr was speaking on the day before Hitler marched into Czechoslovakia. Hitler's new order was threatening the peace of the world and the liberty of all men and women. It was natural at such a time for a man like Hofmeyr to have only one theme for the Chancellor's address, and that was the theme of liberty.

I should like to conclude this address with a few words about the university's policy in respect of race and colour. Before 1959 the university was an open university, but in that year was enacted the Extensions of University Education Act. No person who is not classified as White may be admitted to this university without the written consent of the Minister. In other words, the liberty of this university to admit has been circumscribed.

In April 1961 a plaque was unveiled at the university which declared:

> We affirm in the name of the University of Witwatersrand that it is our duty to uphold the principle that a university is a place where men and women, without regard to race and colour, are welcome to join in the acquisition and advancement of knowledge; and to continue faithfully to defend this ideal against all those who have sought by legislative enactment to curtail the autonomy of this University. Now therefore we dedicate ourselves to the maintenance of this ideal and to the restoration of the autonomy of our University.

This declaration is not merely an affirmation of the autonomy of the university. It claims also an autonomy for principles and ideals, in fact it claims an autonomy for conscience. It refuses to allow order to be exalted above liberty.

It is true that our liberty has been abridged, but it is not lost. We lose liberty only when we cease to desire it. Therefore this declaration is annually reaffirmed.

If I calculate correctly, this declaration has now been reaffirmed 18 times. Some people argue that it is a waste of time, a labour of Sisyphus. This argument can be applied to the labours of WP Schreiner and John Dube and JT Jabavu and Dr Abdurahman and Walter Rubusana who went to London almost 70 years ago to try to prevent the incorporation of the Colour bar in the Constitution of the Union of South Africa, of Alfred and Winifred Hoernlé, the Rhenallt-Joneses, Margaret Ballinger and Hofmeyr in the Thirties and Forties, of ZK Matthews and Albert Luthuli whose noble lives received no recognition in their own country, but to them at least it came at last, to ZK Matthews who was made Ambassador to Washington by the Government of Botswana, and to Luthuli who received the Nobel Peace Prize in 1961. One should note I think that the Government of South Africa lifted his ban temporarily to enable him to go to Oslo.

To make a list of names would be invidious. There are so many who have affirmed their liberty under an inimical order. What would have become of our history if they had thought the affirmation of their liberty to be a waste of time? They are as much the heroes of our history as any of those who have exercised the temporal power. But I should like to mention one more name, that of a graduate and an honorary graduate of this university,

248

Helen Suzman, who is at present in America, fighting a tough battle against the advocates of disinvestment. Her life exemplifies the ideals of this university. A devotion to the rule of law, a determination to search for and to speak the truth without fear, an unswerving allegiance to the cause of liberty, an abiding concern and compassion for the voiceless and the dispossessed. I have no doubt that her devotion, her courage, and her compassion were strengthened by her years at this university.

University of the Witwatersrand Gazette – December 1978

Reinhold F Alfred Hoernlé (1880–1943) was one of the first White liberal philosophers of South Africa, a pioneer of race relations in the country. He taught at various universities, inter alia Cape Town, Harvard and the University of the Witwatersrand.

Agnes Winifred Hoernlé (1890–1960) was a leading South African anthropologist, ethnologist and social worker who actively campaigned against apartheid.

JD Rheinallt-Jones was first elected to the Senate in 1931 and later played an important role in the struggle against apartheid in the Institute for Race Relations.

Margaret Ballinger represented the African voters of the Cape Eastern Circle in terms of the Representation of Natives Act from 1937–60 and became the first parliamentary leader of the Liberal Party in May 1953.

✖✖✖✖✖✖✖✖✖✖✖

Is SA Worth Fighting For?

IS SOUTH AFRICA worth fighting for? Can young White men go in good conscience to the border, to fight against men who almost without exception are Black, and who believe that they have a duty to liberate this country from its present rules, and in particular from the oppression of its racial laws?

When we go to the Border, what do we, in fact, fight for? Our present Foreign Minister once said in a public speech: "I'll fight to the death for the right to exist, but not for an apartheid sign in a lift."

That's a very nice epigram, but it doesn't answer the question.

We don't want to know about the sign in the lift. We want to know whether we can, in good conscience, go to the Border to fight for the Separate Amenities Act, and the Population Registration Act, and the Mixed Marriages Act, and Security Acts that give the Minister of Justice powers of life and death over the citizens of our country.

Has the Afrikaner Nationalist indeed built for himself a fortress so mighty, so impregnable that he will never get out of it, that it will, in fact, cease to be a fortress and become a prison, so impregnable that there can be no liberation but by death?

And if a young man goes to the Border to fight is he, in fact, going there to defend a fortress that is indefensible?

There is for a person like myself, and for any young person who thinks as I do, only one decent reason for going to the border, and that is to fight for the chance to make this a more just society.

I would go there because I do not want to be liberated by the Cubans and the Russians.

I would go there because I would want the chance for the White people of this country to liberate their country themselves.

That is the reason that many of our young people give themselves . . . They hope for the change of heart. That is what they are fighting for – with the weapons of war – a change of heart.

Extracts from Dr Paton's Alfred & Winifred Hoernlé Memorial Lecture
Published by The Citizen *– July 5, 1979*

Only Federation Can Save Us

WE HAVE LIVED in this country for 333 years. It sounds like a mystic number – 333. Perhaps it is, and perhaps good will come out of the sorrows of this year 1985.

This is my 83rd year and it has been one of the most sorrowful of my life. What have we done? How have we got ourselves into this sorrowful condition, of hatred, stonings, shootings and deep anxiety.

Can we get ourselves out of it?

It is possible that I shall offend some of you and disappoint others, that some will think I am naive, and some that I have deserted the ideals of my youngers days . . . I am interested in only one thing, that is to speak the truth.

I am not a member of any party, I am not a believer in Utopia. I just have a perverse patriotism, a deep love of a country that can be cruel and harsh and beautiful, and frightening too.

These days I have to brace myself to look at the morning paper. It is bad enough to read about Northern Ireland and Lebanon, but it is almost unbearable to read about Uitenhage. And the small fabled town of Cradock, where Olive Schreiner lies on Buffelskop, where Guy Butler spent his boyhood . . . but now one reads about stoning and burning and killing in that once quiet town.

In Kwanobuhle 17 Black civilians were murdered in the month of April. Even children were not spared. In these last few months 43 schools were damaged or destroyed by fire. Seventy-eight private houses were destroyed. Churches, libraries and shops were damaged or destroyed. Seventy-three buses were destroyed by fire.

I know you find it painful to listen to it. But unless we look at our country as it is, we shall never be able to make it what we want it to be.

After Sharpeville in 1960 many of our friends left South Africa. After the events of this year more will leave. As far as they can see the problems of our complex society are insoluble.

Some leave because they have growing sons, and they do not wish them to go into the Army, where, if they fight, they will be fighting Black people . . . Some of them decide that under no circumstances will they bear arms – they are in other words pacifists.

Is there any solution to our problems except that of violence and destruction, if this is indeed a solution?

We are a country born of conquest . . .

The only (conquest in our history) that was not achieved by force of arms was in 1948, when the Afrikaner Nationalist conquered us all and embarked on the great programme of Apartheid and Separate Development, and on the building of a new Utopia.

In 1985, the majority of South Africans realise the Verwoerdian Utopia has fallen to pieces. The long age of conquest has come to an end.

He (the Afrikaner Nationalist) no longer has the will or power to rule as a conqueror. Therefore, he devised a new constitution. He did it all by himself. When you have been doing things all by yourself for 37 years it is hard to give up the habit. His constitution, like the one it replaced, was fatally flawed.

In an attempt to atone or compensate for the deep flaws in the new constitution, all sorts of new bodies are being created to bring

Black people into the governing process. The trouble is that you cannot compensate for a deep flaw. The only thing you can do is get rid of it.

I titled this lecture "Federation or Desolation". That is what I have come to believe . . . that federation is the only possible form of constitution that holds any hope for this country.

The time is short, I know, and the times are grave, but we either make up our minds and our wills to travel the hard road ahead, or we relapse into despair, and if we relapse into despair we ought to get out of South Africa as soon as possible.

There is one thing our State President could do to give people more confidence in him, and that would be to issue a "declaration of intent". Whether his declaration would be called "rhetoric" or "cosmetic" and therefore disbelieved I do not know, but I do know that such a declaration would help some people to emerge from the melancholy that afflicts them.

I have no doubt that if South Africa became a federation with a Federal Government given as limited power as it is possible for a Federal Government to have, there would be an immediate abatement of the fear and anxiety and mistrust that so characterises our present society. I believe there would be a great increase in confidence.

I would expect certain early results of a federation. I would expect a return (although not complete) to the Rule of Law. I would expect the wounds of conquest to stay healing. I would expect a greater measure of what is called happiness in our lives. I would expect a change in the attitude towards South Africa on the part of the people who now have little for it but condemnation.

Dr Paton's second Alfred & Winifred Hoernlé Memorial Lecture
Condensed by The Star – *May 24, 1985*

Olive Schreiner was a well-known South African authoress who wrote *The Story of An African Farm*. She was the sister of William Schreiner, Prime Minister of the Cape.

Rule of Law Damage

WHEN I RECEIVED the invitation of P.E.N. of the Federal Republic of Germany to come here to Hamburg as your guest of honour, I knew at once that I would come. My first reason for coming is that it is a great honour and, what is more, it is the kind of honour that is rarely given to White South Africans any more. The second was that I wanted to come here to pay tribute to what the Federal Republic has done for the peace of the world since 1945.

Now while I was writing these words, I realised that I had a third and very considerable reason, and that is that I wanted the rulers of my country to realise that the ideals and values cherished by International P.E.N. which are the ideal and values to which I have tried to devote my life and strength – and my writing too – are the same that are cherished by the democratic countries of the world. My rulers are as you know almost without exception Afrikaners and the main contributors to this new race of human beings were the Germans, the Dutch and the French. So you will see then that this new race – although its members called themselves the Afrikaners, the people of Africa – had its beginnings in the West. But because of their long period of isolation from the continent of Europe from which their forebears had come, they gave up many of the ideals and values of what we call democracy, the Rule of Law, the equality of all before the law, and their claim to certain rights which the Americans in 1776 called inalienable. That is a strong word and it means that these rights cannot be taken away by any power on earth. One of these rights is that of any person who is alleged to have committed an offence to have a fair trial, in what is called a Court of Law. But in my country this right has been denied to any persons who are detained under the security laws. They can be detained for long periods of time and possibly may not be charged with any offence; but worst of all, they can be denied access to any person whatsoever except those representing the very power that has detained them. In democratic countries it is only a Court of Law that can touch a person's liberty, but in my country that right has been given to the Minister of Justice, and in certain circumstances to senior officers of the police.

I do not need to tell this audience – many of whom like myself are readers of that superb magazine *Index on Censorship* – that once a State allows detention with access, then the torture of those detained becomes inevitable.

However, this is not the time or place to tell you all about our country and its present sad and dangerous condition. But I would like to make one thing clear. It was by no means only the Afrikaner (or the Boer as he was then called) who was responsible for the conquest of the Black people of South Africa, and for the rape of their land, and the denial to them of the inalienable rights of man. My own forebears, the British, were equally responsible. They destroyed the Zulu kingdom in 1879 and in 1905 allowed the White colonists of Natal to tear Zululand into pieces, the best of which they took for themselves. It was the British who, in 1910, gave to the Union of South Africa a constitution with a Colour bar. In 1986 it is the British – with other nations – who are now trying to get us to renounce the Colour bar that she gave us in 1910. And good luck to them.

Before I leave the topic of my own country, I must in honesty say one thing more. The political power in the Union of South Africa was captured by the Afrikaner Nationalist in 1948. It was then that the grave erosion of the Rule of Law began. If the Minister of Justice deemed you to be furthering the aims of Communism, he – without reference to any Court of Law– could ban you from all public life, forever if he wished. In the political sense he could silence you completely, and you could attend no gathering. I must tell you one more thing about this business of "banning". You could – in the jargon of those times, that is, the Fifties and Sixties – be furthering the aims of Communism "wittingly" or "unwittingly". If you did it wittingly, you were a traitor; if you did it unwittingly, you were a fool. But whether you were a traitor or a fool, the punishment was just the same.

I must remark here that many Afrikaners today acknowledge that their Government did great damage to the Rule of Law, and they would want to see it restored.

The theme of our conference is "Contemporary History as Reflected in Contemporary Literature". In South Africa we hardly write about anything else but our contemporary history. Thomas Mann wrote about *Death in Venice,* but if we write about death, it is in Soweto or Mamelodi or Cape Town. Our novelists could not write a novel about any bridge of San Luis Rey or about our man in Havana. The conflict in the writer between his history and his writing, or one could say between Politics and Art, is intense and often the art must suffer. However, I must not go on any longer. I was given between eight and ten minutes, and you will all agree that to bring greetings to one's hosts, and to say a word about one's own country, and to pay tribute to this Federal Republic of Germany, and to say a word about history and literature, in the space of ten minutes is quite impossible. I apologise for going on longer.

Hamburg – June 1986

P.E.N. – Poets, Playwrights, Essayists, Editors and Novelists organisation.

❧❧❧❧❧❧❧❧❧

What Liberalism Means to Me

"LIBERALISM" is a label word and means many things to many people. It does not possess a firm clearcut meaning like "Totalitarianism" or "Anarchism", though I suppose there are brands of these too. For the enemies of the old Liberal Party, the word "liberal" had also many meanings. For some of the students of the University of Pretoria, for example, it means a White person who wanted his or her daughter to marry a Black man; at least that was what I concluded after addressing a hair-raising party meeting in our capital city.

To the people who write letters to the *Natal Mercury,* the word "liberal" has some extraordinary meanings and I have been able to get a pretty good idea as to what a liberal is. He is, in the first place, extremely naive; he imagines that if he is good, everyone else will be good too. He imagines that in his liberal society everyone will have no fears, that no-one hurts or destroys. He is easily duped, especially by Commies. He abhors violence, and therefore leads you into ambush so that the Commies can kill you. If he is White, he thinks that everything White is ugly and that everything Black is beautiful.

255

Sometimes, however, he is full of guile. He calls himself a liberal, but in fact he is a capitalist. He therefore believes in the sanctity of property and if he is White he uses Black people to protect his property. If he is White and he employs Black servants, he will certainly underpay them. In fact, he is quite one of the most loathsome specimens of humanity that one can possibly imagine and when his party was outlawed in 1968, the Nationalist Government was wholly justified. It is extraordinary to think that we have gathered here in Grahamstown to pay some kind of homage to this ancient body of dupes, disguised racialists and capitalists, fellow-travellers, exploiters and intellectual ninnies.

After these words of introduction I am almost afraid to say what liberalism means for me. Perhaps I have gone too far and will not be able to find my way back again. But I must try. What did I believe in 1953? Why did I think of myself as a liberal? Why was I attracted by people who called themselves liberals? Why did I think that we ought to make a stand for the things that we believe in, for make no mistake, the things that we believed in were being attacked and derided and destroyed by the Afrikaner Nationalist Party? I believe that this party is now called the National Party and I shall call it that from now on, but for this once I call it the Afrikaner Nationalist Party, for that is what it was. It came to power in 1948, and its triumph was the reparation of history for the defeat of the Anglo-Boer War, and the wrongs done to Afrikanerdom by the British. I shall mention only one of these wrongs, for in a way it tells everything – one of the great wrongs was that Black people were allowed under British rule to buy land, and that was the origin of the "black spots", settlements of Black landholders surrounded by White farms, or, as in the case of Sophiatown, a large Black township later developed by the growing White city of Johannesburg. A great deal of the energy of the Nationalist Party Government was devoted to the eradication of the "black spots", and one of the reasons for the formation of the Liberal Party was to protest against and to resist these unjust and cruel expropriations.

What did liberalism mean to me in 1953? I set out what it meant in a lecture given at Yale 20 years later. I quote the paragraph.

By liberalism I don't mean the creed of any party or any century. I mean a generosity of spirit, a tolerance of others, an attempt to comprehend otherness, a commitment to the rule of law, a high ideal of the worth and dignity of man, a repugnance for authoritarianism and a love of freedom.

I do not claim that this is the world's greatest definition of liberalism, but it so impressed our host, Dr Homer Babbidge, the Master of Timothy Dwight College, that he asked me to write it out and he put it up in his office.

Let me return to the question, what does − and what did − liberalism mean to me? One of the most powerful motives that impelled people to join the party was a moral one, and this was certainly so in my case. Of course there were other motives, as there always are for any human action. I joined the party because I wanted to lead the kind of life that was implied in the *Principles and Objects*, first published I think in 1954. I shall state the principles very briefly:

1. The essential dignity of all human beings and the maintenance of their fundamental rights.
2. The right of each human being to self-development.
3. The Rule of Law.
4. Full participation in the democratic process.

And the objects:

1. Equal political rights on a common franchise roll.
2. Freedom of worship, expression, movement, assembly, association.
3. The right to acquire and use skills and use them freely.
4. Access to an independent judiciary.
5. Compulsory State-sponsored education.
6. Right to own and acquire property.
7. Right to organise trade unions.

This statement concluded with two undertakings:

1. The employment of democratic and constitutional means.
2. Opposition to totalitarianism, such as Communism and Fascism.

We fought over these last two statements for probably our whole existence, and as you know they are still contentious issues today. I make one last remark about our formulations. You will note that we agreed on a common franchise, but never considered the constitutional issues of the unitary and the federal State. You will also note that the words "capitalism" and "socialism" are not mentioned. Although we were a political party, our preoccupation was with moral rather than constitutional matters. Donald Molteno made a famous remark to me at a meeting of a national congress or committee. He said: "The trouble with you, Paton, is that you think the Liberal Party is a Church."

Those were 13 of the fullest and toughest and happiest years of my life. As most of you know, I am a member of a church, but I must place on record that the deepest fellowship of my life I found in the Liberal Party. Now that I have done that, let me tell you some of the things I would have talked about if I had had more time.

1. I would have talked about banning, the effect that banning has on men and women and on their personalities, the success of banning in shutting off people from all public and much private life, the failure of banning to change the beliefs and loyalties of those banned, the view – that I strongly hold – that banning is the extreme example of the abrogation of the rule of law and that banning and detention without trial are two of the greatest barriers to our return to the company of free nations.
2. The effects of exile on men and women, on their personalities and on their views and beliefs, and on their relationships with those who did not go into exile.
3. The work, training, methods of the Security Police, and the evil to which they – the great majority of them – must give consent.
4. I would like to have told you of some of the extraordinary characters we had in the Liberal Party and the genius displayed by at least two of our national chairmen in holding together a party that contained such diverse elements as Donald Molteno, Margaret Ballinger, Marion Friedman, Jock Isacowitz and Hans Meidner.

However, there is one last thing I must talk about. I must say a few words on the subject of "wasting one's life". Interviewers, some sympathetic and some not, like to put the question: "Don't you think you wasted those 13 years of your life?" Or more considerably: "Do you think you wasted those 13 years of your life?" The first question comes very close to being an insult. The implication is that you acted foolishly, over-quixotically perhaps, but certainly foolishly and wastefully, by devoting 13 years of your life to a cause that could never win, to a party that would never come to power, to a country that wasn't worthy of any devotion. What did William the Silent say? He said that it is not necessary to hope in order to undertake, and it is not necessary to succeed in order to persevere. Of course, those 13 years were not wasted. How can you waste 13 years by standing up for the Rule of Law and the rights and dignity of men and women? How can you waste 13 years by standing up when you ought not to sit down? It is a stupid question.

I shall close with a story of myself and the Security Police. Two of them came to search the house on the morning of the day on which the Defence and Aid Fund was banned. They asked me to show them where I kept my Defence and Aid papers and so I took them into the library. One looked at the other and said: "God, man, die boeke!" There were two explanations for this, one was that they had never seen so many books, the other was that they were appalled at the prospect of opening every one of them to find incriminating papers. But it must have been the first, for when I told them there was nothing in the place where they were searching, they took my word for it. In fact, the senior one of them phoned his superior officer in Durban and spoke words that are engraved upon my heart. He said: "Kolonel, die ou-baas koopereer baie goed." At our final meeting in Caxton Hall in April 1968, at which there were eight security men present, I told the story of the books and four laughed and four didn't. I assumed that the four that didn't laugh didn't read books either.

Grahamstown – July 1986

"God, man, die boeke!" – "God, man, the books!"
"Kolonel, die ou-baas koopereer baie goed." – "Colonel, the old boss co-operates very well."

FEARS AND HOPES

You can't buy a White future with a Black lunch.

These Irritating Laws

LAST WEEK'S *Sunday Tribune* reported that a Cabinet committee of six is investigating racial discrimination. It says that "it can be accepted" that four basic measures are not negotiable:

- No sharing of political power.
- The Population Registration Act.
- The Mixed Marriages Act.
- The Immorality Act.

And surely one must include the Group Areas Act, which Dr Malan regarded as the "cornerstone of apartheid".

The purpose of these basic measures is unmistakable. It is to define each racial group, to allocate all persons to a racial group, to prevent any racial mixture and to keep all races physically apart as far as is possible.

The purpose of the first measure, no sharing of political power, is to ensure that in White South Africa – that is, after the homelands have all become independent – this legislative control will remain in the hands of the White group. The homeland Governments can presumably do what they like about race classification and race mixing.

Now is it really possible to remove "irritating" laws while one keeps these basic measures? These basic measures define what a man is, how he may move, where he may live, whom he may love, whom he may marry, and what is more, how his children must move, live, love and marry.

It is not only his life, but the life of his descendants, which is in these respects to be determined for ever. I have friends who not only detest, but also fear, living in KwaMashu and would like to live in a village like Botha's Hill and to bring up their children there but they are compelled by law to live where they do.

What are the "irritating" laws that could be removed? They are without exception trivial – the removal of the Colour bar in lifts and offices, at counters and concerts.

I am astounded by the possibility that the Colour bar may be lifted in hotels and bars. This is going much deeper, beyond the realm of the casual into that of the intimate.

The lifting of the Colour bar in international sport is relatively easy. One is not entitled to feel hope until it is abolished at the lowest level, until any sports club can invite whom it likes to join it. In fact, any other way of doing it would be dangerous. I cannot think of anything more likely to cause riots than games of White versus Black.

One must face the fact that this august committee will be in the gravest danger of snipping out here and patching up there the grand design of apartheid, that has taken 27 years and almost as many draconian laws to construct.

If they confine themselves to that, the future of Afrikaner-dom, of which they are presumably the custodians, will be no future at all.

And is it really the "irritating" laws that so urgently require the attention of this august committee? One would have thought that it was the humiliating laws that needed attention, the fact for example that a person passing for White should have to face investigation if someone informs, the fact that an old Black woman is forced to urinate in the gutter in a public street because she can find no place to go.

The humiliating laws can be – or could be – seen at their worst in a place like Knysna where the dark "White" children at the White school go – or went – during the play break and sat against the lavatory wall because they were not welcome on the playground.

And how we have humiliated the Coloured people during the past 27 years and more years – but especially the past 27 – by showing them, our own offspring, how deep is our contempt for them.

Members of the Cabinet committee, you have no easy task. But if you are able to comprehend it, your task goes far beyond the removal of irritations.

Mr MC Botha has just told the Transvaal National Party congress that a Black man ought to have a place in the city where he can hang up his jacket and eat his lunch. This does him credit, but he seems not to be able to express it very tastefully.

He says that "the Bantu must go and eat somewhere". He is not wholly to blame. You can't really go much faster with a Transvaal Nationalist.

Let us say – at the risk of being repetitious – that you can't buy a White future with a Black lunch.

And let not the UP and the Prog-Reformists be too holy. This rooting out of the irritating and the humiliating – which is the inheritance of most White South Africans – is not going to be easy for them either. It is much easier to be noble in opposition than in government – though, of course, rulers would not accept such a statement.

But so far very few White opposition voters really understand what the consequences of the removal of discrimination will be. Opposition leaders should be telling them.

Good Luck, Mr Vorster. But now you are back from the bridge you must build some bridges here at home.

I won't say, too little and too late, but I'll certainly say, too little, and too slow. And think hard about those "basic measures".

Sunday Tribune – *August 31, 1975*

❧❧❧❧❧❧❧❧

Fear of Justice Is Worst of All

EVEN THOUGH we do not speak much about it, Angola is the prevailing thought in our minds. Those two words "the Border" have suddenly acquired a new and sometimes painful meaning.

One of my close friends has decided that if he is called up for duty, he will refuse to go. He has spent the best years of his life fighting against apartheid and he does not see how he can now take up arms to defend it.

I respect his decision and I would in fact have expected it. But I find this a most difficult question. The alternatives are obscure.

Would the defeat of our armies mean freedom for all, or would it mean living under a Russian-dominated or Communist Government? Would the refusal to bear arms mean that we are denying our rulers the chance to come to their senses?

This question troubles many honest people.

My associates of the past and I believe in a common unitary society.

I still believe in it. However, a moral ideal, though it may inspire a political programme, is not in itself a programme. It is my belief that a unitary society could only be achieved now by bloodshed and violence and that this era of grief and desolation might last for many years.

And who knows what sort of unitary society would be found at the end of it?

Yet we must ask ourselves what alternative is there? Can our Government offer us an alternative which should be and must be a visible and determined move away from apartheid?

I come to the last question that troubles so many.

Should we see it out? This is not a matter on which one can give advice. For at the moment it is not possible to see far into the future.

One can only say that fear and gloom are not the best advisers. Nor is a facile opinion any better. So one goes forward – assuming that one decides to go forward – if not exactly with certain hope, then with resolution.

I presume to end with a few words to Whites. It is the statement of a moral ideal which I have practised imperfectly.

Fear of numbers, fear of revenge, fear of otherness, all these are understandable.

But fear of justice is the worst of all.

If we White South Africans could conquer our fear of being just, if we could choose to make justice the yardstick of our actions, we could have a future. This is very difficult advice, but who dreams that there is any easy way out?

The Star – *January 12, 1976*

Fighting Can Be Made Easier

NO-ONE DOUBTS the urgency of the crisis that confronts White South Africa today. It is not, however, this crisis that I wish to write about. I want to write about the foolish use that is being made of it by the more intemperate Nationalists.

Patriotism is the big word today. If you are not bursting with zeal to get to the borders – or beyond, of course – you are not a patriot. You are not keen to fight for South Africa.

What does fighting for South Africa mean? It means two distinct things. For the Nationalist these two are one and the same. For the rest of us they are not.

When I talk of fighting for South Africa, I mean fighting for the physical land, the land where all my life has been lived, the country which holds the deepest meanings for me.

I mean also fighting for the right of all its people to live a good life there, with a future that is secure. I mean also fighting for the chance to build a better and more just society.

The Afrikaner Nationalist would fight for more than this. He would fight for his language, his culture, his identity. Well and good.

But he would also fight for the impossible and often cruel in-struments that he has created for the maintenance of his identity.

When he speaks of fighting for South Africa he means fighting for apartheid and separate development, for the Group Areas Act, the Immorality, Mixed Marriages, Racial Classification,

Suppression of Communism, Sabotage and Terrorism Acts.

But he has no right whatever to expect that we non-Nationalists should want to rush to the borders to fight for apartheid.

Apartheid certainly existed before 1948, but it was the Nationalists who gave it its present codified and unyielding form.

They complain that the West is leaving them in the lurch, but when they embarked on their draconian laws they totally ignored the protests of the West. It is overwhelmingly their doing that White South Africa is so alone in the world.

The call to fight for South Africa causes the most anxious soul-searching among many White non-Nationalists. The argument is heard that we must fight on the borders, so that our rulers can change things at home.

Many argue so.

They do not like being ruled by the Nationalists, but they would like still less to be ruled by a Russia-controlled Government, imposed by war and terror. They say, better the devil you know than the devil you don't.

But if people are Black they could well say: Better the devil you don't know than the one you do.

I myself am by nature inclined to trust rather than distrust someone who gives an undertaking. When Mr Pik Botha with the consent of the Prime Minister promised that we would move away from discrimination, I was not prepared to say it was a fraud.

But I doubted strongly if Mr Botha and his Prime Minister knew what they were promising. I doubt it still more today. I do not think Mr Botha meant to defraud. I merely think he did not understand what he was saying.

How does one undo – to any significant extent – the laws that were supposed to be fundamental for the survival of the Afrikaner?

How does one bring about a more just distribution of wealth and possessions?

Do the powerful ever re-distribute wealth?

If there is a way to do these two miraculous things, there is no sign that our rulers know what it is.

If these doubts and reservations trouble White non-Nationalists, one may be sure that they trouble Black people much more.

In last week's *Sunday Tribune*, Dr Treurnicht was asked if he thought that the "homelands Black people will feel patriotism towards the general South African cause in the likely event of escalating conflict on our borders". Dr Treurnicht answered: "Decidedly yes." And he also said: "There is a sense of belonging to the South among these people."

This is pure mush. Dr Treurnicht's knowledge of what Black people think cannot be much above zero.

What is this occult nonsense about "belonging to the South"? What about the homelands people who work in our White cities? Does this give them some deep sense of "belonging to the South"?

And when one refers to one's Black fellow South Africans as "these people", does that increase their sense of belonging?

One can perhaps console oneself that at least it is better than referring to them as "those people".

I have written about my deep doubts of the promise to move away from race discrimination. The appointment of Dr Treurnicht strengthened the doubt. There is no doubt that he is a firm believer in race discrimination.

Does this mean the end of detente?

Has the Prime Minister come to the conclusion that the power of Kaunda is fading away?

That the fate of Rhodesia may be settled by Machel and Nyerere, not Smith and Nkomo, not Kaunda and himself?

Had the Prime Minister already given up detente when he appointed Dr Treurnicht?

These are the grave questions that beset the minds of White non-Nationalists in these grave days. Many of them who go to the Border will go there with courage but little joy.

And unless our rulers can give them better reasons to believe in what they are fighting for, and unless they can make visible or substantial moves away from race discrimination, there can only be a grim future for us all, for us Whites the grimmest of all.

Some White non-Nationalists will refuse to fight. They will say that they always fought against apartheid and they are not going to fight for it now. All respect to them.

Others – some with heavy hearts – will "do their duty".

Buthelezi once said: "We'll fight if you give us something to fight for."

Forty-three years ago Dr JS Moroka said to Mr JH Hofmeyr: "In your speech you say that we must love our land. We love it and we shall always do so. We only hope that it will be made possible by the rulers of this country that we have some land to love."

May all our new purveyors of patriotism ponder these patriotic words.

Sunday Tribune – *February 15, 1976*

Julius Nyerere (1922–) was the first President of Tanzania and one of the leading proponents of Pan Africanism. He retired in 1985.
Dr Kenneth Kaunda (1924–) was elected first President of Zambia in 1964. He held discussions with South Africa's Prime Minister John Vorster at Victoria Falls in 1975 and later with PW Botha on various matters regarding the sub-continent.
Dr James S Moroka was elected President-General of the African National Congress in 1949 and instituted the Programme of Action of the ANC's Youth League during the Defiance Campaigns of the early Fifties. In 1952 he was replaced by Albert Luthuli.

>✕✕✕✕✕✕✕✕✕✕✕<

1976—The Four Years Ahead

WHAT WILL SOUTH AFRICA be like in 1980? The answer is, I don't know. All that I can do is to give the possibilities, and I have chosen to give five. I have tried not to be influenced by what I hope and by what I fear, in so far as such an attempt is possible.

Possibility one: A White retreat into the laager in the face of actual military action.

It is my belief that Mr Vorster is trying to emerge from the laager. He is not doing it very spectacularly. That is because politically he is still not sure of his strength and psychologically he is not really used to being out in the fresh air.

If he had to face military action in which Russia, Cuba, Frelimo, the MPLA and Swapo launched sophisticated attacks on our country, and if the United States and the countries of the West did not intervene, Mr Vorster would be compelled to retreat to the laager. All internal reforms, i.e. all moves away from racial discrimination, would come to an end. White South Africa would face not only external enemies, but also enemies at home.

If this catastrophic situation were to arise, the ultimate defeat and destruction of White South Africa would be unavoidable.

Possibility two: A White retreat into the laager in the face of the threat of military action.

So far the Government has shown restraint in the face of such threats. After all, they have been made for many years. It is true that some years ago Mr Vorster said he could eat Zambia before breakfast (or eat Zambia for breakfast, I never remember which). But he has shown greater wisdom in later years.

Therefore I guess that such a White retreat would not be led by Mr Vorster. It would have to be led by Dr Hertzog, and if you take one look at his face and one at Mr Vorster's, you will see where most people will put their money.

Possibility Two is unlikely.

Possibility three: Intervention (not necessarily armed) on the part of the United States and the West.

Strong diplomatic intervention might lead to the diminution of the threat of war.

If it failed, that would be bad for us. If it succeeded that would be good for us. If it led to nuclear war, there won't be anything much in 1980 anyway.

What do I mean by good for us? I mean a chance to make those moves away from racial discrimination which so far exist largely in the imagination of Mr Pik Botha, the South African Ambassador to the United Nations. The West would demand this.

But we must note the disturbing fact that, so far, the threat of war has delayed such moves. We spend so much money on defending our country that we haven't any left to make it worth defending. At the moment many of our Black people don't think it worth defending.

Possibility four: A cautious White advance for four years (i.e. till 1980) in the face of the possibility that is "too ghastly to contemplate". This would be useless. Trivial relaxations in hotels, buses, concerts, libraries, would achieve nothing. Caution in sport would send us back to the wilderness. I would say to Dr Craven, for instance, what's the good of keeping your badge and losing your country? It may be your last test, Mr Rugby.

Outside intervention would certainly follow halfhearted advance.

Possibility five: A substantial and sustained advance for four years in the face of the "ghastly possibility".

This would mean that we had made genuine moves away from racial discrimination. A new approach would have been made to the whole problem of governing 25 million people inhabiting the same country.

The federal solution, so far rejected by Mr Vorster, would have been re-examined. The scandalous situation of African education would have been greatly improved. The conditions of labour, in regard to wages and to the right to organise, would have been vastly changed. The release of political prisoners would have been earnestly reconsidered, not just by Mr Kruger, but by the Prime Minister himself (and General Hendrik van den Bergh, of course).

The consequences of this could be to give patriotism a new meaning.

Such a programme would have increased hope and decreased resentment. Nineteen-eighty would see South Africa a happier and less anxious country than it is today.

Outside intervention would be less of a possibility, but still possible. And it would stay possible until the majority of South Africans no longer wanted it.

My fear for 1980 – Possibility One.

My hope for 1980 – Possibility Five.

But I must add that I fear Possibility Four as well, and in view of Mr Vorster's recent speeches it looks as though that's the one we're going to get. Apartheid is going to stay and racial discrimination is going to go. It's a case of political power shackled by psychological impotence, and it's tragic for us all.

The Star – *May 4, 1976*

∞∞∞∞∞∞∞∞

This Is a Collision Course

IT SHOULD NOW BE CLEAR that Afrikaner Nationalism and Black Power are embarked on a collision course. It is because Sir de Villiers Graaff recognises this that he has called for a new Opposition and has announced that he does not seek to be the leader of it.

I have no doubt that men like Jan Marais, Anton Rupert and Harry Oppenheimer recognise it too. Certainly the leaders of the homelands do. All non-Nationalist Whites and all non-Black-Power Blacks are like passengers on two great ships of war that are bearing down remorselessly upon each other.

Outwardly the Nationalists are magnificently victorious. All their opponents are under lock and key. Chief Buthelezi calls it a terrible mistake. And so it is. Every kragdadige step taken by the Minister of Justice – presumably with the approval of the Prime Minister, though how is one to know? – makes the chance of consultation and co-operation and evolutionary advance more and more remote.

It is a horrible thing to contemplate, this putting under lock and key by the Nationalists of their own creations. And by doing it, they create yet more, and these too will have to be up under lock and key, as long as the going lasts. It is a nightmare of non-compromising power creating a non-compromising opposition.

Who gains any comfort from this spectacle of non-compromising kragdadigheid? Two groups of people, I should say, both extreme. One is the HNP and the Right-wing of the National Party, the other is the radical wing of Black Power, who now regard internal peace not only as a fantasy, but as a veritable hindrance to the cause of emancipation.

I should like to address a few words to those Afrikaner Nationalists who watch with apprehension the collision course on which their chosen Government has embarked.

It seems to me that Afrikaner Nationalism has two main strands: one is the love of land, language, culture, people. I take it that this is the kind of nationalism professed by men like Professor Dreyer Kruger of Grahamstown, who recently predicted the doom of Afrikanerdom.

The other main strand is the ideology of apartheid, discrimination, differentiation, separate development, that many Africaners regard as totally inseparable from their nationalism.

It is an ideology that has blended two irreconcilables, the beauty of identity with the destruction of happiness. How else does one explain the hatred on children's faces? Apartheid (call it what you will) has destroyed Black happiness, and now slowly and surely it is destroying White happiness too.

It is my view that any earnest Afrikaner Nationalist who wishes to do what he can to alter the collision course, must yield the ideology that has so corrupted Afrikanerdom. I just cannot understand how, after the tragic events of these last two months, anyone can still believe that the goal of racial separation must still be pursued. The goal of development of the homelands is desirable and good, but the belief that it holds some golden key to the future is no longer tenable.

Let me make a final observation: it is not just ideological Afrikaner Nationalism and Black Power that are on a collision course. It is also two political concepts, that of a South African commonwealth of nine or ten totally autonomous States, and that of a unitary society with one loyalty and one franchise.

I believe it is our certain destiny to become a unitary State, and I was a member of a political party now outlawed whose goal was a common society. I chose to yield the goal for one reason and one reason only, namely that I realised that the Afrikaner Nationalists would rather destroy us all than consent to the unitary society. And I did not choose to see us all destroyed.

But the Afrikaner Nationalist, with his determination to rule himself and his obsession with a White Parliament which destroyed his 300-year-old relationship with the Coloured people, refuses to consider any compromise between the commonwealth and the unitary ideals. He refuses to consider any kind of federal structure.

The fierce maintenance of Afrikaner identity makes the unitary society unacceptable. But Black Power will hear of nothing else.

If, therefore, anything comes of the call of Sir de Villiers Graaff, and if there is to be a new and unified opposition, it must give earnest and urgent attention to the formulation of federal proposals that are clearer and more uncompromising than any we have had yet.

Is there time? Well who knows? No-one can answer the question and there is therefore no point in asking it. The great thing is to get moving.

The Star – *August 25, 1976*

Sir De Villiers Graaff (1913–) was elected to Parliament in 1948 and became Leader of the United Party and official Opposition in 1956. He retired from politics in 1977.

Dr Jan Marais (1919–) changed the concept of banking in South Africa when he established Trust Bank in 1954–55. After being ousted as chairman in 1976, he was elected to Parliament as an enlightened National Party member for Princetown. He left politics in 1981.

Dr Anthony (Anton) Rupert (1916–) established the Voorbrand Tobacco Co in 1939 and from that built the giant Rembrandt Group. Dr Rupert is well known for his protection of the arts and has been Chancellor of the University of Pretoria since 1987.

Harry Oppenheimer (1908–) succeeded his father, Sir Ernest Oppenheimer, as head of the financial mining giants, De Beers and the Anglo American Corporation.

Kragdadigheid – potent, strong-armed tactics

Professor Dreyer Kruger was one of the group of Afrikaner academics who resigned from the ruling National Party in the Seventies because they felt that the party could not be reformed from the inside.

Hoping Against Hope

LAST WEEK I READ the interview given by Professor Lawrence Schlemmer to the *Sunday Tribune* and it compels me to return to the subject of hope. Professor Schlemmer is obviously in that strange state which is described by strange words. He is hoping against hope. And so are hundreds of thousands of South Africans at this time. I am one of them.

People like the Prime Minister and Mr PW Botha, our Minister of Defence, are very scathing about those White South Africans who do not face the future with absolute confidence. I am one of them too. I have no intention of prostituting my intelligence for the sake of a false security, especially a security whose only guarantee is the kragdadigheid of the National Party.

Professor Schlemmer was born in South Africa in 1936, the year in which Hertzog and Smuts, opposed by Hofmeyr, removed the Cape African vote to a separate roll. He took his degree in Sociology, through the medium of Afrikaans at the University of Pretoria. He is as keen a student of our country as there is, and what is more he loves it. His heart is warm and his head is cold, essential qualifications for a student of society.

I want to quote a few phrases from his interview: ". . . action before it is too late".

". . . White and Black attitudes were polarising fast".

"If the no-change Whites become a clear majority" then confrontation will be inevitable.

". . . the reservoir of goodwill has already dried up among young Blacks in Soweto".

". . . I am becoming increasingly pessimistic" about the possibility of negotiations.

Now although Professor Schlemmer is becoming increasingly pessimistic about the possibility of negotiations, he said that there was a tremendous amount that strong and courageous leadership could do to change White attitudes rapidly. This is hoping against hope. This is the lover of his country asserting himself against the sociologist, the warm heart resisting the cold head. And that is the case with many of us.

The cold head asserts itself again when he says he does not foresee a split in the National Party. Nor does he foresee a victorious Opposition. If change is to come – the right kind of change – it must come from the Nationalists.

At this point the professor comes out somewhat more hopefully. He thinks it is too soon to say what the true response of the Government has been to the riots and the international pressure. He says: "That will only emerge in the future and one must hold judgment until then."

Well well, I can only say that I hope he is right.

Has something really big been cooking up behind the barrier that shuts off the PM from the rest of us? Is Mr Pik Botha really something bigger than a very superior kind of party hack? Is Dr Treurnicht really prepared to face substantial social change?

How we hope against hope!

It is clear to me that Professor Schlemmer just cannot bring himself to become a prophet of doom. This is not the scientist acting, it is the lover of his country. He's thinking of himself too. He doesn't want to see no future for himself and his kind. He doesn't want to see his years of service to his society brought to nothing. Neither do I.

Both he and I have been compelled by events of recent history to speak and write as White persons. This is not wholly because non-racialism has taken a knock. It is also because our message has been primarily to our fellow-Whites. For God's sake come to your senses, "before it is too late". Not just for God's sake. For your own sake and for ours too.

I say to my fellow South Africans: if you have no hope, you should get out as soon as possible. If you have unbounded hope you should go and see a psychiatrist. If you can't give up hope, if you insist on hoping against hope, then persist with all the things you have been doing to make this a better country.

That's all for now. More later, when we know "what the true response of the Government has been to the riots and the international pressure". It had better be good.

Sunday Tribune – March 6, 1977

Professor Lawrence Schlemmer has been Director of the Centre for Applied Social Sciences at the University of Natal since 1972.

⊱⊱⊱⊱⊱⊱⊱⊱

Advice to Verligtes

SO MR VORSTER is going to stick to separate development whatever anyone says or thinks. But according to him, implementing separate development implies moving away from race discrimination.

What exactly does that mean? Ex-Judge Kowie Marais says it means nothing. He says the policy of separate development collapsed.

BECAUSE some homelands would not accept inependence.

BECAUSE it was clear that millions of Blacks (six? seven? eight?) would be permanent residents of the Republic.

BECAUSE a Black generation has arisen which demands a hand in making the laws it would have to obey.

So ex-Judge Marais left the National Party.

Professor Dreyer Kruger also left the party, because he believes separate development is racist in essence. But he also was driven to conclude that the party could not be changed from inside. What is more, it was leading the Afrikaner to destruction. He thinks that the Wimpie de Klerks and the Erika Therons are conducting a futile exercise.

Dr Johan Prins says forthrightly that such "inside-workers" should realise that the National Party is part of the problem, not of the solution.

So I ask myself the question, where does the Afrikaner verligte go from here?

It's the rational mind crippled by the irrational fetter, the dogmatic belief, that in one piece of land inhabited by a dozen races each can have a separate destiny.

It's enough to make one weep to see a clear and generous mind condemned to juggle with minor truth because it can't face the major truth.

And the major truth is that race is *not* the measure of all things and that a common country forces on its inhabitants some kind of common destiny, however painful the journey is going to be.

Until the Afrikaner verligte can face the major truth, he had better stay where he is. For it is mighty uncomfortable – at first – to escape from the irrational context, to lose the warm company of your fellow non-thinkers, to miss the encouragement of being told that your utterances are wonderful when you know in your heart (which means in your head in this case) that there's a worm in the bud.

But if the verligte wants to take part in the salvation of the Afrikaner, he has to open his unwilling eyes and look at the harsh light of the truth. He must emulate such characters as Beyers Naudé, Dreyer Kruger, Kowie Marais, EG Malherbe and the hard-headed, generous-hearted Afrikaner of earlier days, Leo Marquard.

Now Mr Vorster has given notice that the irrational context will remain, that the rational minds of the National minds of the National Party will go on thinking in the irrational context. Or should I say – they will go on twisting and turning in the irrational context?

How does Mr Pik Botha fit into this irrational scene? Consider his statement that he would fight for the right to exist but not for an apartheid sign in a lift. That sounds very good, but Mr Botha left out a lot of things that lie between the two extremes.

Would he die for the Group Areas Act? For racial classification? For separate universities? The removal of apartheid signs in lifts and post offices is good, but as a move away from discrimination it is trivial.

What does Mr Botha mean by discrimination? And what does the PM mean? Neither of them spells it out. I suspect that Mr Botha has bigger ideas than the PM on the subject. And I suspect that the PM put Mr Botha there to do a job that he finds politically and psychologically impossible.

The PM's statement on the respect due to human dignity is a typical example of the way language loses its meaning in the irrational context. He challenged anybody to give an example of injury done to human dignity by his Government. Here is one.

At the beginning of the century Mr Joseph Mngadi bought a half-acre plot at Roosboom, near Ladysmith. His son Elliott increased the family holding to four half-acre plots and owned two four-room houses.

In 1976 he was ordered to move to Ezakheni, to a plot 15 metres by 20 metres, to a Flatcraft hut erected on bare earth, an ice-box in winter, an oven in summer.

He had to abandon his nine head of cattle, which gave him milk for his family and manure for his garden. He suffered "a wound to my spirit" from which he may never recover.

He is one of many, moved from humble and cherished homes to tents and huts in the open veld.

According to Mr Mngadi, he was wounded in his spirit. According to the PM no injury was done. The two men are speaking different languages, one the language of bitter experience, the other the arrogant language of an irrational ideology.

There is only one thing for an Afrikaner verligte to do and that is to repudiate the doctrines of apartheid and separate racial destinies.

The alternative is to try to live rationally and humanely in an irrational and cruel context. And according to the pitiless logic of Marais and Kruger, it can't be done.

Sunday Tribune – *May 1, 1977*

Professor Erika Theron, a sociologist from the University of Stellenbosch, headed the Theron Commission relating to matters in the Coloured community, which brought out its report in 1976. Recommendations – many of them refused at the time – included direct representation of Coloureds in Parliament and adjustments to the Group Areas and Immorality Acts.

Joseph Mngadi was one of thousands of victims of the policy of resettlement vigorously practised by the administration of Minister MC Botha during the Seventies. Blacks were removed, often forcibly, from what the Government regarded as White areas.

Dr Johan Prins resigned from the National Party in the early Seventies to join the Democractic Party and later the New Republic Party, of which he became the Transvaal chairman in 1977.

I See Some Hope Now

IS THE PRIME MINISTER going to save South Africa from doom? Is he going to save Afrikanerdom from self-destruction and the English from taking the chicken run? Is he going to save us all from that future of violence and revolution so often predicted for us?

Of course I don't know the answers to these questions, nor does anybody else. But I am prepared to believe that Mr PW Botha wants to save us all. I used to despair of him when he thundered about boerehaat, but lately I've had a feeling that he won't do it anymore. He says there's no room for hate in our national life.

He said, at Upington I think, he wanted to build a country that would offer security to every child, White, Black and Brown. This is a new style for prime ministers. I do not remember Dr Verwoerd and Mr Vorster ever speaking like that. On the contrary, I came to the conclusion that neither of them was temperamentally capable of speaking like that. If either had warmth, he kept it for his own.

The Prime Minister has said other extraordinary things – extraordinary by Nationalist standards, I mean. He has said if White people can accept their coffee from Black people, and let them look after their children, then they can stand next to them in post offices. He has said baasskap is out, that apartheid "as our enemies know it" is dead.

Of course it is not only our enemies who knew it like that; some of us knew it like that, too. And you mustn't shoot the pianist when he's doing his best.

Mr Botha told his party's Cape congress that South Africans should realise their country had entered a new era. If I were asked to fix a date for it, I would say we entered this new era on April 25, 1974, when President Caetano of Portugal fell from power. Then followed the "liberation" of Angola and Mozambique and, on June 16, 1976, the serious unrest which began in Soweto and spread to the Coloured people of Cape Town. After that South Africa could never be the same again.

Mr Pik Botha knew it. Mr Vorster knew it too, but he ended up by doing nothing. He accepted that change was necessary but could never summon the will to do anything.

Will Mr PW Botha be able to bring it off? He faces great obstacles and not only from intransigent Nationalists and a new breed of seemingly intransigent Black radicals.

He faces the Coloured people whom his party humiliated so deeply in 1956 when the Coloured vote was segregated and later abolished altogether.

His party also humiliated tens of thousands of African people by evicting them from established homes and gardens and giving them tin huts on the bare veld.

The party's treatment of its fellow South Africans has too often been characterised by callousness and indifference. The bulldozer was its main instrument in building the new society in which every man, woman and child would at last come into a heritage uniquely their own. Never was such noble cant uttered about such ignoble deeds.

Will Mr PW Botha be able to heal these deep and ugly wounds? I am prepared to believe he wants to do it. I am prepared to put my head on the block and say I feel more hopeful of the future than I have felt for 30 years. But I cannot forbear to say it is easy to feel hopeful when one has been without hope for so long.

The Prime Minister has one defect of personality that could bring his brave plans to nothing. He has an authoritarian personality and is too quick to take offence. This is clearly seen in his attitude to the Press, an attitude unfortunately shared by Mr Schlebusch, his Minister of Justice. They believe in the freedom of the Press so long as it behaves itself in ways they approve.

Of course the Press will make mistakes. Yet it is the persistence of the Press that has finally helped the National Party Government to see that many of its enactments are intolerable, destructive of morality and damaging to race relations. That in itself should make Mr Botha and Mr Schlebusch think again before regarding the Press as an enemy to be curbed and punished.

In the year 1978/79, 118 complaints against newspapers were presented to the Press Council and of those only four were found to be justified. This seems to prove the Press can be trusted to respect its own freedom.

I hope the commission on security legislation will restore the rule of law and abolish detention without charge or access. Many public-spirited South Africans have suffered severe penalties because they advocated the same changes the Prime Minister is now advocating. He should make some kind of amends to them, even if only to say he regrets the extreme authoritarianism of the past.

The Prime Minister must be on his guard against his authoritarian tendency to take offence too easily. There is a considerable feeling of goodwill towards him because of his recent statesmanlike pronouncements. I am by no means the only one who feels more hopeful about the future than at any other time in the past 30 years.

Sunday Tribune – *September 30, 1979*

Baasskap – master-servant relationship

What Must Be Done

UNDOUBTEDLY ONE of the most important developments of the Seventies was the awakening of Afrikanerdom to the realities of the world in which it is placed.

To what realities was it an awakening? To put it dramatically it was an awakening to the fact that the great fortress of Afrikanerdom was becoming its prison and that if it became a prison there would be no way out.

It was an awakening to the fact that the Great Verwoerdian Plan wasn't going to work, that there would be no turning of the tide back towards the homelands, that the Natives Land Act of 1913 was an error, that the altering of the Cape franchise was an even greater error.

It was an awakening to the fact that Black Power, Black Consciousness, was becoming a political force, and White South Africa could no longer prevent the interference of the outside world in her so-called "domestic policies".

There was a belated recognition of the harshness and injustices of the Great Plan and the inhumanity of many of the so-called "resettlements". In a different category altogether was the realisation that exclusion from world sport was a much more painful thing than it was thought it would be.

I should like to say that I believe there has been, and there is continuing to be, an Afrikaner awakening. It may be too late and too slow, but I do not believe it is cosmetic, tokenistic, intended to deceive. In any case you can't deceive anyone any more. I shall cite only one proof of these contentions and that is the report of the Cillié Commission.

I must also say that I regard Mr PW Botha as a convert to this enlightenment. If there is to be an evolutionary "way out" he will play a great part in it.

That Mr PW Botha wants to find a way out I have no doubt. He said last year at Upington that he wanted to create a society that would offer security and a future for every child, White, Black and Brown.

No other Prime Minister has ever spoken in such a way before.

Will he find a way out? No-one can answer that question. All we can do is to discuss his chances.

What are the factors that could prevent our finding a way out? I shall mention four:

1. A retreat on the part of Mr Botha. I don't think it likely. But he has two grave personal weaknesses and one grave weakness in his political philosophy. I wish that he had a more even temper and I wish that he would learn to take criticism.

I wish that he had a different attitude to our security legislation, especially to the banning of people without recourse to the courts and to detention without trial and detention without access.

In other words, I wish that he understood the importance of the Rule of Law to a society that claims to be civilised. Dr Nico Diederichs, the philosopher-prophet of Afrikanerdom, wrote more than 30 years ago: "Love of nation is not in the first place love of people, territories, or states, but rather love of the ever-prevailing values on which the nation is based." Neither he nor Mr PW Botha understood that the Rule of Law was one of these values. But Mr Botha still has time to learn. However, I do not think he will or can retreat from the position he has taken on the need for social and political change.

2. The defeat of Mr Botha by the Right wing of Afrikanerdom. If this happened that would mean the end of Afrikanerdom and the end of our White tenancy in Africa. Then factors three and four would come into operation. I myself do not foresee the defeat of Mr Botha, but I earnestly wish that he would dismiss Dr Treurnicht as soon as possible. For one thing I do not think that the Broederbond would allow Mr Botha's defeat.

3. The political triumph of Black radicalism, leading to internal revolution. We can expect a continuance of terrorism and of the general Black attitude towards it, the revelation of which has shocked many White South Africans. We can expect a continuance of Black demands for greater participation and of the growth of Black consciousness. But I do not expect an outbreak of anything that could be called revolution, unless factor four comes into operation.

4. External intervention. If this happened, Russia and Cuba would spearhead it, with the aid no doubt of Nigeria, Libya and East Germany, but not Egypt or Ethiopia, who have enough problems of their own. At the moment, Angola, Mozambique and Zimbabwe would not participate.

A milder though not pleasant form of intervention would be international sanctions, from which the Western nations could only with difficulty abstain.

If there were military external intervention then there would be internal revolution. I think Mr Botha and his generals know this well and I think they know well that only internal political and social change can lessen the chances of internal revolution.

And I hope with all my heart that White leaders will be able to convince Black leaders of their sincerity and their determination.

I repeat – because it is of the utmost importance – that Mr Botha will not be able to make effective political and social changes so long as he keeps Dr Treurnicht in his Cabinet. He faces the intensely difficult challenge of putting the country before the party.

The Star – *April 16, 1980*

The Cillié Commission (named after its only member, Mr Justice Petrus Celliers) researched the causes of the Soweto riots of 1976 and found that an immediate cause for the unrest was the Government's decision to introduce Afrikaans as a medium of teaching in Black schools.

Homelands Policy Won't Work

LIFE IN SOUTH AFRICA in 1981 is uncertain and the future is unpredictable. The alienation between White and Black is greater than at any time in our history. I admire those women who work for peaceful change, but the prospects for peaceful change are darker than they have ever been.

Be patient, reader, I am not writing a tale of woe. I am writing the tale of Dr Hendrick Frensch Verwoerd. For our certainty, our alienation, our dark prospects are due more to him than to any other actor in our long and tumultuous history. I never met him, but in one important sense, he influenced my life more than any other person.

Although born in Holland, he became totally an Afrikaner. The maintenance and survival of Afrikanerdom became his supreme passion. He was in no sense a man of the world, and only in the narrowest of senses was he a South African.

He was a man of commanding intellect, but he was ruled by his supreme passion. His intellect, like some magnificent and powerful steed, ran between the shafts, but passion drove the chariot. It was a passion created by the arrogance of the British and the menace of the Blacks, and no doubt by other secret forces not yet revealed to us.

How could Afrikanerdom survive? He knew the answer. Apartheid was already part of his inheritance, but he knew that by itself it was not enough. He knew that the White supremacy, the baasskap of his predecessor, Mr JG Strijdom, was not enough either.

Although he was proud, he knew that apartheid and baasskap by themselves would invite the hostility of the entire world. So he enunciated the new doctrine that was to save Afrikanerdom, the doctrine of Separate Development.

Dr Verwoerd must be given the credit for turning Nationalist Afrikanerdom away from apartheid and naked baasskap. He must be given the credit for giving the churchmen and the academics something to still their troubled consciences. But this must not prevent us from recognising that the child Separate Development had the blood of its parents running strongly in its veins.

What was the Great Plan? It was based on highly moral considerations. White South Africa had achieved total political independence. But now every other racial group in South Africa (except two) was to have its own territory and its own institutions, was to be enabled to preserve its own language and its own culture, was to control its own education and was to be able, finally and irrevocably, to achieve total political independence.

Dr Verwoerd did not envisage the total political independence of the Black homelands until he became Prime Minister in 1958. In fact, as late as March 1959 his eminent co-architect, Dr WM Eiselen, stated that political independence was never intended. However, later in the year Dr Verwoerd repudiated this statement and Dr Eiselen prudently retracted.

Dr Verwoerd's hold on his Cabinet and his party was absolute, and has never been equalled in our political history. Even co-architects knew their place.

It would appear that Dr Verwoerd's confidence in himself and his Great Plan was also absolute. He was once asked by an interviewer how he slept at night, with all the problems and the challenges that confronted him every day. He replied that he slept like a child because he knew that what he was doing was right.

He was convinced that the homelands would not only become politically independent, but that they, with White South Africa, would become members of "What I call a commonwealth", enjoying a healthy economic interdependence.

In this commonwealth there would "be no danger of hostile Bantu States". It was nothing less than Utopia that he was planning, a commonwealth of peace, where racial friction and racial hatred and racial fear would die away.

So compelling was he in Parliament, so lucid in debate, so confident of himself, that even some of his political opponents fell under the spell and wondered if he could possibly be right. The sight of grand passion driving great intellect presumably overawed them. I am sure that Margaret Ballinger and Helen Suzman were not among these opponents.

Dr Verwoerd's confidence in the Great Plan was such that he risked a tremendous prophecy. He predicted that in 20 years' time the Black tide to the cities would turn and that it would begin to flow back to the homelands. It is commonly accepted that the predicted date was 1978. By that time, life in the state of the future commonwealth would have become so attractive, the chances for employment so many, the air of independence so heady, that Black people would be leaving the delights of Johannesburg and Cape Town and Durban for the deeper satisfactions of their ancestral homes.

But it hasn't happened. The Great Plan never will work. Black people won't stream back to the homelands. There is nothing to stream back to. The wealth and the work of South Africa is to be found in the "White" cities.

Therefore, those of us who are not Afrikaner Nationalists, observe with a mixture of frustration and fascination that the great brains of the party, Dr Gerrit Viljoen and Dr Piet Koornhof, regard that warriors, Mr PW Botha and Mr Pik Botha, still believe in the doctrine of Separate Development.

They believe, or seem to believe, that the Black people of Ciskei and Transkei go to Cape Town, not because they are hungry and workless, but because they are wicked, or at least because they do not respect law and order, those two gods whom Mr BJ Vorster used to shout about over the loudspeakers.

And Dr Piet Koornhof, who was reputedly so brilliant at Oxford, is forced to blame the Black Sash and the Council of Churches and the Women for Peace, who are just as loyal South Africans as he is, and a good deal more compassionate.

Dr Koornhof is a Christian and so am I, and I would not dream of debating which of us is the better one. But in no circumstances could I give an order for public servants to smash down the pitiful shelters that desperate people have erected to protect themselves from the cold and the rain.

Dr Koornhof might well say to me, it is easy for you to talk like that, you are not a Minister of State, you have no responsibility. And I would say to him, I thank God that I am not a Minister of State, that I have never been caught in the web of the Party and the Broederbond and the Cabinet, the web from which it appears that you are powerless to escape.

And I would say to him, when I go to the Church of the Holy Spirit in the Valley of a Thousand Hills, or the Church of St Wendolin, the 100-year-old settlement which your Government proposes to demolish in the name of Separate Development, then I marvel that Black people still go humbly into a Christian church, and I can only suppose that they find something in their faith that is hidden from the high and the mighty, something which is called compassion or love or justice, words which are to be found in the Gospels but not in any of the statutes of Separate Development.

Why is Dr Verwoerd's Great Plan falling to pieces about our ears? Mr Henry Kenney, in his splendid book, *Architect of Apartheid*, says one of the reasons was that Dr Verwoerd was an economic illiterate. In other words he had no conception of the limitations of ideology or of rigid systematism. He tried to force one of the most complex of human societies, with a most complex history of conquest, great migrations, the discovery of fabulous wealth, the confinement of a Black majority to small pieces of land so that they could never become agriculturalists and finally the growth of White industrial cities that are now two-thirds Black – he tried to force this complex society into a mastermould conceived in his own mind. And when the society and its peoples proved recalcitrant, he cherished the foolish notion – this highly intelligent man – that the powers of the State and the law and the police and the bulldozers could bring them to heel.

This is the heritage that he bequeathed to us. It was intended to safeguard the future of Arikanerdom, but unless Afrikanerdom gets rid of it, the White tenancy in this rich and beautiful country will come to an end. So long as Mr PW Botha and Mr Pik Botha and Dr Viljoen and Dr Koornhof regard themselves first and foremost as Afrikaners, we, and they, have no future at all.

There is another part of this heritage that must be got rid of. Dr Verwoerd did great damage to the Rule of Law. Detention without charge or trial or access must go too.

In this work of destruction he had as his righthand man Mr BJ Vorster, the Minister of Justice. These two men imperilled the future of Afrikanerdom more than any others. But it is Dr Verwoerd who bears the main responsibility.

Good luck to the Women for Peaceful Change. But there won't be any peaceful change until our rulers discard for ever the notion that the magical year is coming when the homelands are going to work.

Sunday Tribune – *September 6, 1981*

Four Top Priorities

BEING LOYAL to the country is to love it, serve it and want to make it more just to all its people. But to be blind to the faults of society is a false kind of loyalty.

It is easy to believe the way to show love of country is by taking up a gun and being prepared to die on the Border, but this is not true.

There are young men today who say: "No, I cannot fight. I can't lift up a gun. It is against all I believe." And they're prepared to go to prison for it. I am not proud to belong to a society that will send a young man to prison because he really believes in something, something good, with his whole heart and soul.

There is no doubt that we White South Africans are too ready to boast about what we can do with our guns, especially this beautiful new gun that we have got, but you can't make a good society with a terrible and powerful gun. To build a good society is a much harder task than that.

Being loyal to your country does not mean you must not see its faults; it means to see the faults and want to correct them. It is very dangerous not to see the defects of society because it means you will do nothing to remove them.

There are foolish men and women who like to say this is the most beautiful, the most happy, the most just society in the world. They say that because they do not want to look at the truth. I am prepared to believe this is one of the most beautiful countries in the world, but I cannot believe this is the most happy and the most just. But we must also remember there is no country that is perfect and perfectly just and you must never believe any man who says if you give him power he will make such a society for you. For what he really wants is the power and when he gets it there will be more death and more sorrow and more pain.

I would like to suggest four things that have to be done before a just society that would be reasonably happy could be achieved.

The first thing is the state of Black education and Black schools. I live on the edge of the Valley of a Thousand Hills and when I go down into the valley, I see the schools. I see boys and girls playing on a desert piece of wasteland. I go into the library, which is about one quarter the size of my own and seldom does it have a quarter of the books. Then I go back up the hill and I see beautiful schools with beautiful buildings with wonderful grounds and magnificent libraries and I am ashamed.

The education of a Black child costs about one tenth of the education of a White child and this is something that can't go on. This country is not going to be able to run its industries and its factories and its enterprises without a much higher standard of education for Black people.

The second thing that has to be done before this country can claim to be a just society is to restore the Rule of Law. The Rule of Law means that if you are accused of committing some offence against the law, no-one can touch you, no-one can punish you, no-one can touch your possessions or your life except a court of law.

Under the security laws, the Rule of Law has suffered tremendous erosion. Under those laws, the State, that is the Minister of Justice, has the right to detain a man or woman without trial and, worse still, without access to any person except the ones who are detaining him or her. Let us face the fact that if people are detained without access, more of them are going to die in detention than will die in a country that allows access. It is inevitable that one or two people will always die of natural causes in prisons, but the number that have died in South African prisons while being detained is too great to occur naturally in a just society.

The Rule of Law is the greatest political achievement of humankind. The Rule of Law is a miracle; it is nothing less than man protecting himself against his own cruelty and selfishness.

The third thing is that we must stop destroying families. We must stop this terrible practice of taking a man's labour and then taking no responsibility for his wife and his children.

It happens that a wife and children long to be with the husband and father of the family and they move from the homeland and go to the city, where they find some sacks and some cardboard and they put up a shack. It is pitiful, but it is their home where they can be together. Then it is discovered that the wife and children are there against the law and so come those terrible, powerful, yellow machines. And, you know, if you want to make a just society, you cannot do it with yellow machines, however terrible, however powerful. That's another thing that must be done; we must stop putting law and order above human beings and their natural desires and needs.

That last thing that would concern us is the great disparity in wealth and possessions between White people and Black people. It cannot go on because that is what creates a revolutionary situation. But, again many people don't do anything about a revolutionary situation until they are frightened out of their wits.

From a speech at King's School, Nottingham Road, Natal Midlands –
December 4, 1982
Published in the Sunday Tribune *– December 5, 1982*

END-OF-YEAR REVIEWS

Is our world in any danger of becoming like Oceania?

And Now It Is 1984

THIS YEAR WILL SEE an event unique in the history of literature, not just English literature but all literature. A large part of the intelligent world will be reading and re-reading a novel that was published nearly 35 years ago.

It will be re-reviewed and rediscussed. Its name is *Nineteen Eighty-Four* and it was written by George Orwell, who in 1903 was born Eric Arthur Blair, at Motihari in Bengal.

So far as I know no writer of distinction ever called a novel by the name of a year.

Sellars and Yeatman wrote a humorous book called *1066 And All That*. Solzhenitsyn called a book by the name of a month, *August 1914*. Tschaikowsky called an overture by the name of a year, *1812*.

But the tremendous interest in Orwell's novel is not only because the fateful year has arrived; it is primarily because it was one of the most extraordinary novels of this century.

Indeed it could be said that of its kind, it was one of the two most extraordinary novels of the century, the other being Arthur Koestler's *Darkness At Noon*. The third place I would give to Aldous Huxley's *Brave New World*.

Nineteen Eighty-Four can well be called a prophetic book, but not in the sense that it attempted to predict what the world would look like in that year.

It is a book of warning – this is what your society will become if you are not vigilant to protect and maintain what is called human freedom. And human freedom means the liberty to do what you like, provided you do not hurt or harm others.

The limits of this freedom are laid down in what we call the law, and you may be as free as you like so long as you obey the law. If you are accused of having disobeyed the law, then your innocence of guilt will be decided by what is called a court of law, and no authority in the land will have any power to limit your freedom, or to touch your person or your property, except a court of law.

The majestic conception is known as the Rule of Law and it is the supreme moral and political achievement of man. It is, in fact, man's safeguard against his own cruelty and rapacity.

In *Nineteen Eighty-Four* the Rule of Law has gone. But not only the Rule of Law – law itself has gone too. Thoughts and actions, which when detected mean death, are not forbidden by any law. They are not even forbidden by Big Brother and the Party and the dreaded Thought Police.

But everyone knows what thoughts and actions mean death. They are any thought or action which has the slightest smell of freedom about it. Therefore even pleasure is forbidden.

The pleasures of sex are forbidden; sex is practised solely for the purpose of procreation and no true citizen of the State should find any pleasure in it. The only pleasure a citizen should ever show is the pleasure of hating the enemy.

All day long the citizen is watched by the millions of telescreens situated at every vantage point. Therefore, he must never be caught showing pleasure at the wrong time or at the wrong thing. This grave offence is known as facecrime and it means death, because it too has the smell of freedom.

Another grave offence is ownlife; it means individualism, eccentricity, even a taste for solitude. It is slightly dangerous to go for a walk by yourself because that too has the smell of freedom.

This is the terrible society that Orwell describes for us. It exists in the superstate known as Oceania, there being two other superstates, Eurasia and Eastasia.

Oceania is a vast territory of what we might call a super-USA and includes Britian, Canada, Australia and New Zealand. The whole of Europe, excluding Britain, is part of super-USSR. China, Japan, the Philippines are part of Eastasia.

All three superstates are freedomless. In all three, the individual counts for nothing. In all three, practises long abandoned have been brought back; imprisonment without trial, public executions, torture to extract confessions and the deportation of whole populations.

In all three, television has brought private life to an end. The citizen is watched 24 hours a day. It is an offence punishable by death to endeavour to hide in your own home from Big Brother's telescreen.

I must relate one more thing about life in *1984*. All three superstates are continuously at war, one of them against the other two.

Why is there continuous war? It is to keep the wheels of industry turning without increasing real wealth, because increase of wealth means increase of leisure and increase of literacy, both of which are dangerous to the Party.

War also satisfies the lowest cravings of people and keeps them from dangerous and subversive thoughts.

Some high members of the Party know that these wars are spurious, but at the same time they must know that these wars are real. Therefore, they employ the technique of doublethink, which enables a person to hold simultaneously two totally contradictory and incompatible thoughts.

Orwell died in 1950, five years after Hiroshima and Nagasaki. But his main obsession was not the bomb, it was the danger of the loss of human freedom.

In his novel the three superstates, although continuously at war, had decided never to use the bomb and for a thoroughly good reason, namely that the destruction of the human race would destroy the very material upon which they could impose their total and terrible power.

The novel makes it clear that the Party was not interested in power for the sake of the nation or for happiness or for any cause whatsoever. It was interested in power for power's sake.

Lenin and Hitler were hypocrites and pretended that they had seized power for some noble end.

Nor did Orwell deal with another threat to human society, the increasing pressure of population, which threatens to change certain reassuring characteristics of human behaviour, such as charitableness and generosity.

It is also no doubt a contributory cause of the increase in violence, on the streets and the playing fields and in the homes of little old ladies.

Nor did he deal with the soul-destroying effect of chronic unemployment, nor the deterioration of our human environment and the threat to wild life and forests and the very air we breathe.

But these remarks are not intended to be criticisms of *Nineteen Eighty-Four*. Orwell's theme is the danger of totalitarian power and no writer has ever surpassed him.

Do novels, and what one might call literature, affect human thought and action? Orwell's distinguished biographer, Bernard Crick, wrote "Orwell's life and his writings should both guide and cheer us." A writer can't do much better than that. Orwell himself wrote:

"What I have most wanted to do through the past 10 years is to make political writing into an art. My starting point is always a feeling of partisanship, a sense of injustice. When I sit down to write a book, I do not say to myself, 'I am going to produce a work of art.' I write it because there is some lie that I want to expose, some fact to which I want to draw attention, and my initial concern is to get a hearing. But I could not do the work of writing a book, or even a long magazine article, if it were not also an aesthetic experience."

I would like to pay my own tribute to Orwell. I first read *Nineteen Eighty-Four* 30 years ago and it made a powerful impression on me. I read it again 20 years ago and again it made the same impression. I read it again this week, in preparation for this article, and found it as powerful as ever.

I am, of course, more critical now than I was then, but these criticisms I shall deal with later. I cannot say that I owe my love of freedom and my hatred of totalitarianism to Orwell, but I can say that his writings certainly cheered me.

Is our world, and particularly our Western world, in any danger of becoming like Oceania?

I do not think so. I regard the transformation of West Germany as the political (and moral) miracle of the 20th Century.

Will such a miracle happen in the USSR? I have no doubt that the grip of Russia on the other Communist countries is weaker than it used to be. It is almost an article of faith with me that man will never give up the love of freedom.

I also believe that man is sometimes terrified of freedom. But that's not doublethink. It is simply a recognition of the truth of a very old saying, that man is fearfully and wonderfully made.

Is our own country in any danger of going totalitarian? I would say No. It is altogether too difficult and complex a country for that.

We have had many authoritarians in power, the strongest of whom was Verwoerd. I would say without hesitation that the people of South Africa are more vocal and less afraid than they were 30 years ago.

I would say that people like myself have more confidence in the judiciary than they had 30 years ago. I would conclude by saying – with deference, mark you – that our judiciary has more confidence in itself than it had 30 years ago.

But this, of course, is the opinion of a White South African. There are Black people who believe that they are at this very time living under totalitarian rule.

Their movements are restricted, they are sent to prison for offences that are offences for Black people only, they can still in this year 1984 be evicted from land that their fathers and grandfathers bought legally in the early years of the century, their houses can be bulldozed down and they can be sent to the desolation of tents and tin huts on the bare and barren veld.

Therefore, one must not judge too harshly a Black man who says that he lives under totalitarian rule. One can only tell him gently that the very good and expensive periodical that interviewed the Prime Minister recently has still more recently interviewed Bishop Tutu.

But although we are not a totalitarian country, we are still pretty good at doublethink.

We invented Christian Nationalism, which enables us to worship God and the nation simultaneously.

We invented Separate Development, which enabled us to jettison that nasty word apartheid and allows us today to believe in the myth of the happy homelands.

We bought a magnificent and deadly submarine and called it Emily Hobhouse.

The latest achievement goes to the credit of our Defence Force, which last year awarded four Swords of Peace.

These things could have come straight from *Nineteen Eighty-Four*.

Now what about the novel itself? Orwell thought he had "ballsed it up". He told Anthony Powell that it was "a good idea ruined". His biographer Crick said it was "a flawed masterpiece", which I regard as an extreme statement. Crick should have said it was a "masterpiece with flaws".

The great flaw, of course, is the 20-odd pages of close print devoted to the writings of Emmanuel Goldstein, the arch-enemy of the Party.

This was Orwell's attempt to explain the phenomena of Oceania, the telescreens, the Ministry of War whose official name was the Ministry of Peace, the Ministry of Law and Order and Thought Police and Torture whose official name was the Ministry of Love, the necessity to wage incessant war and the infallibility and omnipotence of Big Brother, whom no-one has ever seen.

Orwell was urged to take these 20-odd pages out, or at least to abridge them, but he would not. It is doubtful whether they added much to the novel. They bring the book temporarily to a stop.

Ironically enough, these pages were not written by Goldstein at all, but by the Thought Police. They were used to trap those suspected of thoughtcrime, of whom Orwell's "hero", the pitiable Winston Smith, was one.

But he saved his life by repenting fully of his crime and by learning – after many prevarications – truly to love Big Brother.

Orwell made one other error. He called the whole vicious system Ingsoc and so gave some critics the impression that he had turned anti-Socialist. These were the only criticisms that troubled him. Yet there can be no doubt that he realised the danger that extreme socialism could lead to Stalinism. But that was not his theme.

Orwell was born a few months after myself, but we never met. As I entered the company of writers, he was leaving it. The story of the last brave days of his life is related very movingly by Crick. I am sorry that I never knew him, because he was a man after my own heart.

Crick ended his "life" with these words:

"He hated the power-hungry, exercised intelligence and independence and taught us again to use our language with beauty and clarity, sought for and practised fraternity and had faith in the decency, tolerance and humanity of the common man. And what is even more heartening, he was all that and yet as odd in himself and as varied in his friends as a man can be."

There are two statements of Orwell that I shall certainly remember. He had a "sort of aesthetic distaste" for Gandhi and did not regard him as a saint, "but regarded simply as a politician, and compared with the other leading political figures of our time, how clean a smell he has managed to leave behind!"

The other is about Sartre. Orwell wrote to Fred Warburg: "I have just had Sartre's book on anti-semitism, which you published, to review. I think Sartre is a bag of wind and I am going to give him a good boot . . ."

How can one not help liking a man who can write things like that?

Sunday Times – *January 1, 1984*

※※※※※※※※※

1985–Unhappiest of Our Lives?

THE YEAR 1985 is nearly over, and no-one will be sorry to see it go, except those who believe that it brought freedom nearer. It has earned a special distinction among my 82 years. It was the unhappiest of them all. I did not want to use that word, thinking it was too strong, but Helen Suzman said I ought to use it, so I do.

When I write that it was the unhappiest year of my life, I am referring to my life as a South African, not to my personal relations. It is, in fact, only one's family and one's friends that make life endurable so long as one lives in this present state of violence and hate and death.

There are two reasons or causes for this year's unhappiness. One is impersonal, the thing that we call History.

In 1850 my mother's grandfather left the security of Bristol to come to Natal with the Byrne settlers. In 1900 my father left the beauty of Scotland to come to Johannesburg. In 1903 my father and mother had their first child, and that was me.

That is when my personal history began.

However, one of the troubles with history is that most of it is written before one is born. But my pre-natal and my post-natal history have more or less the same pattern. It is a history of conquest, of Black by White, of Black by Black, of Zulus and Boers by the British, and finally the conquest by the Afrikaner of us all, on that fateful day of May, 1948.

The trouble is that the British and the Boers conquered too many people. The bigger trouble is that the conquered people won't lie down any more. That is the outstanding mark of 1985.

What do the conquerors do about that? That is what our present-day politics are about. That is what the year 1986 is going to be about.

There is a second great cause of the unhappiness of the year. That cause is the National Party. It is true and quite irrelevant to say that apartheid existed before 1948. It was the National Party that gave apartheid its cruel teeth.

The Christian-Nationalist thinkers of the year before 1948 produced an un-Christian philosophy of race. It was something given by God. It was more important than individuality. Therefore, 1948 was an act of God, and it put a duty on the National Party to separate every race from all other races, in every conceivable place and on every conceivable occasion.

The success of this Great Plan depended on one indispensable factor, the creation of the "homelands", a haven for Blacks and a guarantee of Afrikaner security.

It is not necessary for me to point out these tragic errors of the past. It was done in May 1985 by a Nationalist, Dr Stoffel van der Merwe MP, in a party booklet which admitted the myth of the "homelands" and thus took away what was thought to be the very foundation stone of Afrikaner security.

But a Nationalist cannot take a cherry in one bite. Dr Van der Merwe had to reassure the National Party, and perhaps even the Conservative Party, that separate schools and residential areas were "non-negotiable".

Dr Van der Merwe represents a constituency with the interesting name of Helderkruin (clear view). Well yes, but not so helder as all that.

A few months later Mr Pik Botha also made a recantation. He told some Italian interviewer that the National Party had come to see that there were many things that different groups had in common after all. Well. Well!

Pik Botha was born on April 27, 1932, so it has taken him a long time to realise this truth. However, he was born in the rural Transvaal and that may account for the delay.

Why doesn't he, or better still the State President, apologise to all those whom the party made to suffer because they realised that truth 30 years ago? And why does the party not apologise to those who had to suffer under their inhuman separation laws?

The dominant figure of the year was President Botha. The new tricameral Parliament met on January 27. It had some good results, among them the moratorium on forced removals, which was another half-bite at the cherry.

The Mixed Marriages Act was scrapped, but the authorities still penalise those who contract them. Section 18 of the Immorality Act was scrapped, so now fewer White men will have to commit suicide.

The Political Interference Act was scrapped and this repeal faces the Progressive Federal Party with new problems. On August 15, President Botha made a disastrous "Rubicon" speech in Durban in front of half of the Press of the world. Six days later the rand plunged to 34,80 American cents.

Worse still, Chase Manhattan Bank pulled out of the country. Just when we need money for "reforms", we haven't got any.

What is one to think of President Botha? I have given much thought to this question, having been reproached by some of my friends for saying that he was the most courageous of all our eight Prime Ministers and was the first to recognise that the destruction of the unity of the National Party might be necessary for the sake of the country – a distinction up till then thought impossible.

Do I still think he is sincere? Yes, I do. Do I think he can save the country? I don't know. I begin to think that he does not realise the magnitude of the task he has set himself. He still looks the picture of confidence. Is he as confident as he looks, or is he just a master of emphatic vagueness?

He speaks of a common citizenship, universal suffrage in a

country that is a single geographic entity and rejects White domination, partition and one-man-one-vote in a unitary society.

What can that mean but the construction of a federal society? Why doesn't he say so? Why doesn't he admit that the new construction isn't going to work and that he will instruct the industrious and well-intentioned and sometimes evasive Chris Heunis to plan a federal constitution?

This paragraph that I write now is pure gossip. It is said that PW is on his way out. Some say health and some say indecision. Some names are tipped for the succession, B, V, H and D.

There is another much more sinister rumour and that is that the military will take over, a rumour encouraged by our incursions into Cabinda and Botswana.

I have two comments on this. The first is that it is not my reading of the psyche of the Afrikaners that they will tolerate a military dictatorship. The second is that if such a thing happened, that would be the end of Afrikanerdom and the end of any evolutionary process.

The result could only be increasing unrest, economic chaos, a deepening of Black hatred and White melancholy.

I have one more thing to say about our State President's performance in 1985. It is time he learned some South African history.

He said in October in Delareyville that if anyone was to blame for the delay in Black constitutional development it was the former colonial powers and not the South African Government.

Is the State President trying to tell us that the republics of the Transvaal and the Orange Free State were on the brink of such development? Has he never heard of the Great Trek?

Has anything good happened in 1985? Luckily yes.

In August, Mr Paddy Kearney of Durban was detained because Colonel Coetzee of the Security Police had "reason to believe" that Mr Kearney had committed a subversive offence. It has for too long been assumed that if a colonel has "reason to believe", no court can challenge him.

Mr Justice Leon ruled that "reason to believe" is subject to objective review and ordered the release of Mr Kearney. The inviolability of the Security Police had been, not shattered, but shaken.

In September, Mr Justice Eksteen granted an order restraining police from assaulting detainees in Port Elizabeth. Dr Wendy Orr and 44 others applied for the order. Dr Orr, district surgeon, gave evidence that in 153 cases injuries were such that they could not have been inflicted lawfully.

All this is encouraging but what kind of country is this where police have to be ordered to stop assaulting those in their custody? Or where a judge must be commended for his courage? And hats off to 24-year-old Dr Orr, who is not only a brave girl, but has done something to restore the tarnished reputation of the district surgeon.

Is the Rule of Law creeping back? It seems to be, but its restoration cannot be left to judges and district surgeons. Its restoration can only come through the Government, through the same ruling party that inflicted such wounds upon it.

Dr Orr has testified in court to something that we knew already. And how did we know it? Because we know that detention without access can lead only to torture.

A responsible citizen in a democratic society does not easily turn to criticism of the police. He knows that in the last resort he depends on their protection.

I know this too. I know that it is the police who have had to carry out the laws of apartheid, and therefore have incurred the hatred of many Coloured and Black people. I know that they often face danger and some are very brave and that some carry out their duties with great brutality.

In any country the police find most of their recruits among the tougher and more aggressive members of the population. So do we. It is a problem every society must face, but in Africa it is especially difficult.

It is also a problem that all our senior police officers must face, that some of their younger men are insensitive and irresponsible and think they are still fighting the Border wars.

If I had anything to do with police training, I would try to make every young recruit realise that brutality in the townships endangers the whole future, not only of the Afrikaner volk, but of us all.

If I decided that a young recruit had not realised it, I would not accept him into the force.

In a few days we enter the year 1986. It is not my duty to write about it, but I want to say – what everybody knows – that it is going to be very tough.

I hope that the State President will earnestly consider the possibility of federation. Let him start in Natal-Zululand, where we might give hope to a desparing country.

What about the Western Province as another member of the Federal Republic of South Africa? It might stop the rioting of schoolchildren. I don't know what else will.

In 1986 a new actor will join the Big Four – Botha, Buthelezi. Mandela and Slabbert. His name is Elijah Barayi, the leader of the new Congress of South African Trade Unions, Cosatu. He sounds as though he is going to be tough too, but I hope he does not turn out to be an irreconcilable. He has called on President Botha to resign, which is not very useful.

We won't move fast in 1986. We certainly won't move at the pace some people are demanding of us. As John Kane-Berman wrote wittily in the *Sunday Times* of December 8, South Africa makes progress only by marching up all the dead-ends first.

We will move at the pace of the National Party and we will hope that it will be faster than it was in 1985. I wish a faster New Year to you all.

Sunday Times – *December 22, 1985*

Dr CJ (Stoffel) van der Merwe is a former professor in political science at Rand Afrikaans University and entered politics in 1981, when he was elected to Parliament for Helderkruin. At present he is Deputy Minister for Information and Constitutional Development and Planning in the Office of the State President.

1986–Violence Lives On

IT IS A YEAR AGO since I wrote a piece called "1985" for the *Sunday Times*. I wrote that it was the unhappiest year of my life. What were the reasons for that? They were the violence, the hate and the death. It was the hate that was worst of all.

We don't need to look at the pictures of hate any more. They are forbidden under the State of Emergency, which is now nearly 200 days old. We don't need to read about the hate any more. That is forbidden too.

300

While all my friends condemn the continuance of the emergency, some of them have confessed to me that it is a relief not to see and read about hate every day.

Just as bad as the hate itself is the fear lest the hate should now be incurable, that the desire of the haters is not reform, but the total destruction of authority and of the economy, and the reduction of our society to a giant heap of rubble.

The fear is of course greatest in White people, for this would mean their destruction too. That is why so many of them have left and are planning to leave South Africa. This is particularly true of the parents of young children. They do not want their children to grow up in a land of hate.

I wrote a year ago that we wouldn't move fast in 1986. We would move at the pace of the National Party and we would hope that the pace would be faster than it was in 1985.

Has the pace been faster? Does the Government give the impression of wanting to go faster? Is there any sign that Black people acknowledge the good intentions of the State President and the National Party? I think the answer to all these questions must be No.

For me the most important event – it could also be called a non-event – of 1985 has been what appears to be the paralysis of the Government and the National Party. This is not only important, it is puzzling in the extreme. When one watches President Botha on the TV screen, he does not look like a man who is paralysed or who thinks he may be paralysed. He looks always determined and confident.

An outsider like myself is not allowed into the sanctum of the Nationalist psyche. He, and all other outsiders, can only guess at what goes on there. All we can say is that what goes on is extremely complex, and at times totally baffling.

That is not to say that Afrikaner Nationalists are beings totally alien to us. They share with us certain great ideals and principles that are in large measure derived from a common Judaeo-Christian culture. But the interpretation of these ideals and principles allows them to do things that we would regard as incompatible with the ideals themselves.

For example, their interpretation has allowed them in this very month of December to impose curbs on individual and institutional freedom, and particularly in the Press, which are quite irreconcilable with democracy.

Their Deputy Minister of Information, Dr Stoffel van der Merwe, has declared that these steps are "necessary to preserve the future of democracy in South Africa". He conceded, however, that democracy could not be maintained "without freedom of the Press". He said further: "It is an abnormal situation which we will get rid of as soon as possible." No-one expects that to be very soon.

I can remember that as far back as 1924 the freedom of the Press was threatened by an angry General Hertzog, who was then our Prime Minister. It has been threatened many times since. Now, 62 years later, the freedom of the Press in regard to all those matters that concern us most deeply of all has been taken away.

Why does the Government not want us to know what is happening in our own country? Is it because it does not want us to know how bad things are? Or is it because it fears a further lowering of White morale? And therefore perhaps an increase in the number of White emigrants? Or is it because it does not want us to know the extent to which army and police are involved, nor to know the costs – in life and destruction – of this involvement?

How far is the National Party's paralysis due to its fear of losing more ground to the Conservative party of Dr Treurnicht, to Jaap Marais, to Eugene Terre'Blanche?

Terre'Blanche represents the 15 or 20 percent of radical Afrikaners who captured the Voortrekker celebrations of the centenary in 1938. It is not my reading of the Afrikaner psyche – insofar as one can read it – that he would ever entrust his future to any ranting demagogue.

He has certainly done some ranting in his time, but I would not describe any of his Prime Ministers as a demagogue. Nevertheless, I believe that the pace of "reform" has been very much slowed down by the party's fear of the Afrikaner Right.

I do not see much chance that this pace will quicken in 1987. It is ironical that those who oppose "reform" should dictate the pace of it. They have certainly postponed further discussion of the Group Areas Act.

There is yet another reason for this paralysis. The Afrikaner Nationalist does not easily adopt the role of reformer. It is a role he has never played before.

He is used to being a ruler and had ruled all the peoples of South Africa for nearly 40 years. During this period he has got his country into an unholy mess, largely because he never really understood what a ruler can and what he cannot do.

Now that he has realised it, he has become a reformer, but he has found that it is harder to reform than it is to rule. This makes him irritable and he adopts the firm and confident PW look. If you scratch the reformer deep enough you will find that the ruler is alive and well, but when things go badly he is as foolish as ever.

I will say one kind word about him. His history must take a great share of the blame for making him what he is. The hard life of the trekker, the harsh Karoo, the bloody frontier wars, the coming of the British, the Great Trek to freedom, the defeat of the Anglo-Boer War of 1899–1902, the desertion of Botha and Smuts and – praise be to God – the miraculous victory of 1948.

Now at last we would put right everything that had gone wrong under the British. Especially would he make laws, first to guarantee the security and the purity of his own people and secondly to make clear to all the other people of South Africa just what their place was.

It didn't work. The other people of South Africa didn't accept the places that the National Party allotted to them. Many of them turned to the stone, the bomb, the necklace of fire.

The age of violence and hate and death had begun. The year 1986 was characterised by a growth of that kind of turbulence that makes decent life impossible.

Before I close this short discussion of the powerful influence of one's racial history, let me give the names of six Afrikaners who recovered completely from the corruption of history.

They are Leo and Nell Marquard, Ernst and Janie Malherbe, Beyers and Isle Naudé. These are given as examples, there are many more such. But they showed that it could be done, and not one of them lost anything by doing so. In fact, their emancipation led to an increased richness of life.

It was in 1986 that the outside world really turned on us. The United Nations and the Organisation of African Unity have always been against us. If they could have had their way, we would have been destroyed militarily a long time ago.

It was the nations of the West who always resisted any proposal to intervene actively in our internal affairs. But in 1986 it was the leading nations of the West which imposed certain sanctions upon us.

There can be no doubt that these sanctions will do harm to our economy and it seems clear that unless our Government speeds up its programme of reform, other nations – so far reluctant –

will join in and that the range of sanctions will be increased.

The sanctions debate has raged furiously throughout 1986. I shall quote only one of the anti-sanctions arguments, because after all it is the most weighty.

I, among many South Africans, do not believe that sanctions will have the effect that their supporters hope for – some with absolute certainty – namely, the total abolition of apartheid. The whole fearsome apparatus of apartheid has taken nearly 40 years to construct and it is so unbelievably complex that the demand that it should be abolished by some date in April 1987 cannot be treated seriously.

I have no doubt that the imposition of sanctions will further delay the policy of reform.

We won't have the money to proceed with it. A great deal of human energy that would have been directed into reform pro-grammes will now be diverted into attempts to minimise the effect of sanctions.

The effect of sanctions on thousands of South Africans who think more or less as I do has been to make us determined to resist them. It is impossible for us to support them or to be neutral about them. We don't think they will work, but they will certainly do harm.

The idea that the wrecking of the economy will bring about a more just society and an era of peace is to us quite preposterous. Most of us are admirers of the United States, but we regard this action as an instance of extreme self-righteousness.

Has the year 1986 been one of unrelieved gloom? If one listened only to the gloom-merchants, one might think so. According to them nothing good has happened, and all attempts to do anything good are doomed to failure. The Afrikaner Nationalist is not just an enigma, he is a wicked man; he is also a fool, because he thinks he can defy the world.

I get my fits of gloom but I never cease to find encouragement when I look at the efforts of so many people to improve the quality of human life in our society, to help those in need and to uphold and reaffirm those moral ideals and principles on which all de-mocracy is based.

I cannot give a list of all these efforts here and I hope I shall be forgiven if I give only a few examples – the Urban Foundation, the school feeding schemes, the work of the Black Sash and Women for Peace, the opening of the once exclusive private schools, the decision of BP to create a fund of R50,000,000 for the reconstruction of District Six.

Of all these efforts "to do the best things in the worst times, and to hope for them in the most calamitous", I shall give the place of honour to the Natal-KwaZulu Indaba.

For the last eight months a responsible cross-section of the citizens of this area have met together to hammer out a constitution for a self-governing region which will remain part of the Republic of South Africa. The Indaba is proof that the hatred and the alienation that so characterised the year 1986 are not universal.

If we do not seize this opportunity, I think it possible that we will never get another.

This year has been just as tough as 1985. Next year is going to be tough too. It is not possible to give any easy words of cheer. We shall hope, of course, but we shall wish that we had firmer grounds for hoping. Those of us who love our country must become stoics, because we are going to be buffeted, both from within and without and we musn't fall down.

I shall not wish my readers a happy New Year, but I hope for them – and myself – that in 1987 we shall see some more decisive movement towards that society of peace and justice to the pursuit of which so many of us have devoted our lives.

Sunday Times – *December 28, 1986*

The Indaba was an effort by the Natal Provincial Executive and the KwaZulu Government to devise a concept of non-racial regional government in Natal. Its recommendations were rejected by the Government in 1986 because it made no provision for the protection of group rights.

TWO SLANTED VIEWS

Afrikaner Nationalism had to be lived through (and I hope lived out).

Rich Book, Poor Book

HAD I READ *White Power and the Liberal Conscience* by Paul Rich 30 years ago, it would have saved me from wasting my life. I have learned from it something that I had never realised, that White liberals belong to one or more of the following categories – crooks, fools, opportunists, tools of capitalism and manipulators.

Mr Rich writes about the "Liberal Conscience" and it is obvious that he doesn't think much of it. There is never any suggestion in his 136 pages that courage and hatred of injustice were striking characteristics of these White liberals.

They were on the whole a group of manipulators, some sadder than others because things just didn't come right for them.

They were always coming up with "new strategies". Changes in Black attitudes, changes in world pressures, changes in South African politics, were continually demanding new strategies.

But one by one their strategies failed. One can at least admire their persistence, for when one strategy failed, they came up with another. But their motives remained constant. They wanted to mould and control Black politics and not let it get too radical.

They wanted to prevent revolution, for – alas, let us face it – they had great possessions.

Mr Rich has chosen a dramatic title. But that is the only dramatic thing in this book. Rheinallt-Jones, Alfred and Winifred Hoernlé, Brookes, DDT Jabuvu, Self Mampuru, the Ballingers, Yusuf Dadoo and many others – they all pass through the pages of this book and not one of them comes to life.

It is clear that Mr Rich is a great student of documents and that he found a veritable treasure trove of papers about Rheinallt-Jones.

Therefore, he gave to this diligent and not extraordinary man an extraordinary role in this story of liberalism.

Mr Rich's opinion of Rheinallt-Jones is very low and therefore it follows that his opinion of the South African Institute of Race Relations is also low.

He gives no recognition to the work of the institute in providing a storehouse of invaluable information in its annual surveys.

But, basically, Mr Rich is not interested in a hypothetical subject like "race relations". For him the real subject is class conflict. For him the institute was primarily an instrument of "accommodationism".

His preface and introduction differ in one most important respect. The preface says that this book is a study of the years 1921 to 1960, but the introduction says it is a study up to the establishment of the Liberal Party in 1953.

I would guess that Mr Rich originally intended to stop at 1953, but later decided to continue till 1960. However, he was in a hurry to finish. This would account – though only partly – for the fact that the Liberal Party years 1953 to 1960 are given six and a half pages of the book.

As a record of the Liberal Party from 1953 to 1960 it is quite shocking. The Liberal Party, whatever its merits, or demerits, was the most concrete and articulate expression of the liberal conscience in this century, and amongst its members were some of the best human beings that I have encountered in my long life.

The author does not, however, stop at 1960. He jumps to 1968 when the Liberal Party disbanded, he sneers at the university protest lectures, he gives a friendly nod to Beyers Naudé, and a not so friendly nod to the PFP, he jumps to 1976 and the Soweto riots, to 1977 and the death of Steve Biko, all this in the same six and a half pages.

Mr Rich, you can't write history like that.

Let me close by saying that no Liberal strategy could ever have brought political successes in these years. Afrikaner Nationalism had to be lived through (and I hope lived out).

The Liberal Party of 1953 was a party of men and women who felt that they were obliged to make a stand against apartheid and a stand for the Rule of law.

I think it was weak on economics, but it certainly was not a tool of the capitalists. In fact, we had to battle to get money and most of it came from ourselves.

My opinion of Ravan has taken a bad knock. It is quite one of the dullest political theses that I have read. The author has, by great industry I am sure, collected thousands of pieces of information, but he has no idea of how to give them shape or coherence and, as I have said, his dramatic sense is non-existent.

The book is written by what is – for me – an entirely alien mind. He chooses to write about "conscience", but he shows no awareness of the possibility that people do certain things because they think that the doing of them is right.

Am I writing out of hostility? Of course I am. I am doubly hostile because I am sure that the self-satisfied writer of this book has never paid a fraction of the price so many others have paid for their beliefs.

That is, of course, if he has any belief except that the end justifies the means.

Mr Rich writes at the end of his book:

"The degree to which South African liberalism was able to mould this nationalism (African) into an effective ideological off-shoot of itself has been a question outside the main focus of this study and demands considerable further research."

May heaven save us all.

Sunday Times – *June 24, 1984*

Dr Edgar Brookes was a well known educationalist who was elected to the Senate in 1931, for years representing the African voters in Parliament.
Dr Yusuf Dadoo was elected President of the Transvaal Indian Congress in 1945. He was a member of the Central Committee of the South African Communist Party and partly responsible for the Joint Declaration of Co-operation, which was signed between Blacks and Indians in March 1947.

Move Your Shadow

IT IS TO BE EXPECTED that a book by Joseph Lelyveld about South Africa should be out of the ordinary. He served two terms as the correspondent of the *New York Times* and travelled the whole country. He met innumerable people and was, and is, no doubt possessed of great energy, a ceaselessly inquiring mind and a splendid memory.

The percipient reader would no doubt judge from this opening paragraph that I shall later have criticism to offer, and he or she would be right. I shall also later have some high praise to give.

This book claims to be a book about South Africa. Well it is and it isn't. It is primarily a book with two themes that run side by side throughout and these are White wickedness and Black suffering. Athol Fugard says it is one of the most profound and compassionate books he has ever read about his own country. If by comparison Mr Fugard means that Mr Lelyveld has a deep concern for injustice and especially injustice meted out by the White conqueror to the Black conquered, he is right. Otherwise, I do not find compassion to be the dominating element in this book. Its dominating element is excoriation.

Let me say at once that White wickedness and Black suffering are ever-present features of our life. Our best writers have been writing about them for the last 30 or 40 years. Our lonely forerunner, Oliver Schreiner, wrote about them nearly a century ago in her novel *Trooper Peter Halket of Mashonaland*. But the constant repetition of these two themes for 377 pages is too much. Mr Lelyveld plays on a two-stringed lyre, an instrument that cannot do justice to the terrible and tragic music of our times.

Mr Lelyveld is 100 percent anti-Afrikaner Nationalist, and so am I. But he is almost 100 percent anti-Afrikaans as well. There are notable exceptions of which I shall tell later. But if I read his book correctly – and I have spent four days on it – he sees no hope that the Afrikaner will repent. Mr Lelyveld pours contempt on the erudite outpourings of the Afrikaner philosophers of the past who produced highly plausible irrationalities that give moral justification of apartheid. He also has nothing but contempt for the possibility that State President PW Botha will produce anything more than complex constitutional changes that will have one purpose, and one only, and that is to prolong the life of White domination.

I earlier intended to write that Mr Lelyveld simply had no idea of the drama of history and of its corruption of peoples and nations, and particularly of its corruption of the Afrikaner, and that he saw everything in terms – in burning terms – of wickedness and justice. But I had to change my mind after reading his story of Cornelius Hoffman – a farmer at Enkeldoorn, Zimbabwe. Mr Lelyveld writes: "The father (of Cornelius Hoffman) had escaped the Boer War, the son its sour heritage, and that gave the White tribal feeling he expressed in its fixed, primordial quality, a seeming innocence – not without sweetness . . ." I stopped there. I thought, the man is human after all.

Although Mr Lelyveld is extremely sceptical of the Afrikaner's ability, and willingness, to abandon apartheid, he has a good word for men like Beyers Naudé and Frikkie Conradie. He does not always twang away on his two-stringed lyre. He has another instrument, which I shall call his biographica, from which he evokes some very good music. His sketches of Joe Seremane, of Dominiee Eerlik (not his real name), of Beyers Naudé are superb.

He is less enthusiastic about White non-Afrikaners. Helen Suzman gets a nod, two nods in fact; so does Helen Joseph. He has a good word for the "small fraternity of South African lawyers that have continued the battle for civil liberties, most of whom are White non-Afrikaners." Indeed White people don't earn much distinction except for their wickedness.

My biggest criticism is not of what is in the book, but what has been left out. In my opinion there are at least four important political figures in South Africa today. One is PW Botha, our State President, or whoever succeeds him as leader of the National Party. The second is Chief Mangosuthu Buthelezi, Chief Minister of the Government of KwaZulu. The third is a Mr Nelson Mandela, who has been in prison for 21 years; he is a powerful legendary figure, and what he would be like if he came out of prison no-one knows. The fourth is Dr Van Zyl Slabbert, the leader of the Progressive Federal Party. Mr Lelyveld mentions neither Buthelezi nor Slabbert and I find this omission unforgiveable. One can only suppose that Mr Lelyveld doesn't like them, or thinks they are irrelevant, or finds they do not fit into his twofold theme of wickedness and suffering. He writes on Page

237 that on one particular day "instantly carried away, I was seized by the hope that maybe somehow, it would all work out."

I have that hope too and I do not know if it will be realised. But I can tell Mr Lelyveld that it will never be realised unless Buthelezi and Slabbert take part in the search for it. It is a great flaw in the book that they are not mentioned.

I find it in my heart to envy Mr Lelyveld, who is now back in America with the security of the Constitution and the Bill of Rights and the United States Supreme Court. We have had to work and fight for a just order of society these many years without the aid of these majestic instruments. But of our fight there is scant recognition.

I am certain of one thing after reading this book. I do not like the music of the two-stringed lyre.

Sunday Times – *October 27, 1985*

Athol Fugard is one of South Africa's best known playwrights and actors. His plays have been staged in London and on Broadway.

A LAMENT

Inside this church there is nothing but love,
but outside there is hate.

Lament for a Young Soldier

Alan Paton attended the funeral in Pietermaritzburg of a young National Serviceman killed on
the Border. It moved him to write this . . .

THE CHURCH IS already full when I get there although I am not
late. The atmosphere of love and grief is palpable. I have to sit
near the front, in fact very near the family. Therefore I have to
watch – I cannot help watching – the grief of a young boy weeping
for his soldier brother. It makes me weep also.

The usual unanswerable questions are asked. Why so young?
Why does God demand the life of one who has hardly begun?
Has he been called away to some other service?

We are counselled not to blame God, or the Government, or
the Army, or the ones who killed him. This is life and one must
accept it.

Man that is born of woman has but a short time to live. He
comes up and is cut down like a flower. He flees as it were a
shadow, and never continues in one stay.

There is one question that is not asked aloud here, and that is for what did he die? But it is in the minds of many of those who have come to mourn for a young soldier, and for those whom he has left behind. For what did he die?

Did he die for the maintenance of our way of life? I mean, for the White way of life, for it is the White people of South Africa who say what the way of life must be.

Did he die for the continuance of the Group Areas Act? Did he die for detention without charge or access?

Did he die for a system of justice, one of whose chief officers found that no-one could be held responsible for the death of Steve Biko?

Did he die for a system of education that has sent thousands of children into the streets, burning, stoning, cursing?

Or did he die in the hope that the Group Areas Act might be repealed? That detention without charge or access might be abolished? Or the hope that any person who sent a sick prisoner naked to Pretoria might be brought to what is called justice? Did he believe that he was gaining time for such things to happen?

Or did he go to fight because his friends were going to fight? Or because he felt no call to be a conscientious objector? Or because he loved his country, and didn't want to leave it?

One is not supposed to ask these questions. The asking of them is supposed, in some queer way, to show that one does not love one's country. The asking of them is supposed to undermine morale, and to sap the confidence that the cause is just.

The reasons for fighting are quite simple for some. You fight to resist the attack of Communism on your Christian world. You fight for the right to go on living your just and free life. You fight to repel those who want your gold and your platinum and your coal. Your society may not be perfect, but you are trying to make it better.

Inside this church there is nothing but love, but outside, even in the streets of this quiet city, there is hate. You don't just weep for the young soldier who is dead, and the younger brother who grieves. You weep also for your country.

It's the Comrades Marathon today, one of the greatest sporting spectacles in the world. Everyone has come to watch, everyone is happy, everyone is gay. There are more Black runners than ever before. As each one appears, a young Black woman with great bobbing breasts joins the race and runs with him, laughing and ululating, an exhibition of pure and innocent joy. I suppose she is interfering with the race, but the other runners do not seem to mind.

In front of me are four older Black women. They also clap and call out to the Black runners, but they also have a soft spot for the White running madams, and call out encouragement to them.

They have another soft spot for the White khehlas, most of whom acknowledge this applause. A Black man on the bank banters the khehlas in Zulu, and those that understand him acknowledge his witticisms.

A White runner, say in his forties, still full of energy after five hours' running, claps his hands vigorously at the four women, and calls out to them in Zulu: "Clap for me, clap for me," which they do enthusiastically.

Is it all real? It seems real enough. People could not simulate this gaiety and joy. There are no stones here, no curses, only encouragements.

Two faces of South Africa, the one full of hate, the other full of joy. Or should we say three faces, for there is one that is full of grief. Not just because a young soldier is dead, but because of this vision of what our country might be, and is not.

The Natal Witness – *June 6, 1980*

Khehlas – old people

CURRICULUM VITAE OF ALAN PATON

Born: January 11, 1903, Pietermaritzburg, Natal.

Educated: Maritzburg College and University of Natal.

1922:   Graduated B Sc.

1923:   Higher Diploma of Education.

1924–35:   Schoolmaster.

1928:   Married Doris Olive Lusted.

1930:   Son, David, born.

1935:   Principal Diepkloof Reformatory.

1936:   Son, Jonathan, born.

1948:   *Cry, The Beloved Country* published. Resigned as Principal of Diepkloof Reformatory.

1949:   Received London *Sunday Times* Book Award.

1951–55:   President Convocation University of Natal.

1953:   *Too Late the Phalarope* published.

1954:   Honorary L H D Yale University

1954–68:   Chairman, later President, Liberal Party of South Africa until the party, being multiracial, was outlawed.

1955:   *South Africa and Her People* published. Received Benjamin Franklin Award.

1956:   *South Africa in Transition* published.

1957–59:   President Convocation University of Natal.